I0549616

THE ENEMY WITHIN
THE AFFLICTION: BOOK 2

M.J.PETRIN

THE ENEMY WITHIN

ISBN: 978-1-73346443-7

ACKNOWLEDGMENTS

I cannot express enough gratitude for the love and support from my wonderful wife, Misae. Without her amazing attitude, I would have been so lost.

My son Dylan offered his expertise and time to help me create the covers for my books. I could not have done it without his help. I am forever grateful.

CONTENTS

CONTENTS

CONTENTS

CONTENTS

PROLOGUE

"Sheriff Jackson?"

"Bill, ma'am, please call me Bill."

The Asian reporter smiled. "Bill, thank you for seeing me today. I know you're a busy man. I'm Miyake Aeko from the New York Times."

Bill smiled in return and gestured for her to take a seat. "What can I do for you, ma'am?"

"Please, call me Miyake," the reporter said. "I came to Bends Creek to see if I could get some background for a story I am writing for the Times."

"What can I help you with?"

"Can you tell me how you met the alien?"

Bill laughed, "You mean Pete?"

"Yes."

"He just showed up in one of our alleys. He didn't know who he was, where he was from, or how he got into the alley."

"Please go on." The reporter was writing in her pad and never looked up at Bill.

"Well," he continued, "Around the time Pete showed up, the Affliction hit our town. Pete was instrumental in helping us deal with the Affliction. I don't know how he could concentrate on helping us with everything he was going through."

"What was he going through?"

"He didn't know his real name. He didn't know where he was from and wasn't sure if he was human."

"So he confided in you, and that's how you became friends?"

"Yeah, Pete shared everything with me, Maggie, and Jessica. We were the first to learn about Pete's connection with the Wen. But Jessica helped Pete figure out things on a personal level."

"That would be Jessica Morales from the Center for Disease Control in Atlanta?"

"Yes."

"How so?"

"One of the findings that resulted from Jessica helping Pete was that the Wen experimented on Pete without his knowledge. When he was their guinea pig, he lost all his memories. The experiments took away his ability to experience emotions and feelings, too. The Wen didn't want Pete to be distracted while he was on his mission."

"Experiments?"

"Yeah, the Wen experimented on Pete to make him their herald in the fight against the Xanoclax. Their experiments helped Pete gain

2

special skills, but at a cost. When he first came to Bends Creek, it was so bad he wasn't sure if he was human."

"Was he able to gain any of these abilities back?"

"Eventually, with time, Pete regained some of his memories. His feelings and emotions aren't 100%, but he's working at it."

"And Jessica Morales is responsible for Pete regaining his emotions and feelings?"

"He's a lot better off than he was, thanks to Jessica."

"Did Jessica have any help?"

"Maggie Carter, my girlfriend, spent a lot of time with the two of them and did her best to help."

"Do you know the blue alien? I believe her name is Oz? Who is she to Pete?"

"Oz is Pete's Wen guide. Oz is a Vailen from the planet Wen'q'rixsh, where they exist on logic without emotions. She is an organic being, but enhanced technically. She was assigned to Pete after the experiments on him were successful. She can shapeshift—wait a minute, I believe she called it…hell, I don't remember what she called what she does. It's some type of shifting. She can melt into walls and take on different forms, but she doesn't call it shapeshifting. Oz said that was a human term."

"Can you explain her abilities and role in all of this?"

"She helped Pete stay focused on their mission. She said that when she is inside Pete's head, she plugs into him and can enhance his abilities. For example, she can protect him by producing a force field when threatened by an enemy and other stuff above my pay grade."

"I have seen Oz on the news; she has a sense of humor. How is that possible for a logic being?"

Bill scratched his head. He knew Pete had explained this to him and Maggie at one point. He thought that Maggie would be great to have by his side. She had a better memory than he did.

"I think it involves exposure to the Earth's atmosphere. The gases in the atmosphere affect Oz's logic somehow, and she acts a little human sometimes."

"Can you talk about the mission Pete was performing for the Wen?"

"You don't know about the mission? I'm sure you would have got all the details in your research."

"I have a lot of pieces, Bill. I want your answers to help corroborate my research."

Bill shrugged his shoulders. He thought he had given this answer to so many reporters and government officials that one more time wouldn't hurt.

Bill answered, "The Xanoclax, as you know, form a barbaric alien tribe that feeds on civilizations that are destroying themselves. The Wen see the earth on a path of self-destruction due to our acts of racism and hate toward each other. This path of self-destruction somehow showed up on the Xanoclax radar. The Wen wanted to stop the Xanoclax from invading our planet, so they devised the affliction, which allows people with prejudices to see other people as their own race. They concluded that if people who judged others by outward appearances saw others as their own race, everyone would get along. If everyone stopped the hate, the Xanoclax would change their mind about invading Earth."

Miyake wasn't writing; she only listened while Bill explained the mission.

She interrupted, "You are right, Bill, I know this part. Can you tell me Pete's specific role in the Wen mission?"

"I guess you could say he was a liaison for the Wen. He contacted all the world leaders and had them gather for the arrival of the Wen Council. The Wen Council explained the affliction and why they were doing what they were doing to the planet. Pete was to stay on earth and make sure that the Xanoclax did not interfere with the progress of the plan."

"Has Pete relayed any information to you concerning the mission's progress? Is the mission proceeding as the Wen predicted?"

"Pete has told us, Maggie and I, that everything is going well."

"Do you get to see or talk to Pete?"

"Yeah, he pops in every once in a while. But now that Jessica has moved back to Atlanta, I'm unsure how often we will see him."

Miyake leaned forward, "While conducting my research, I heard that Pete and Jessica might be romantically involved."

"That's too personal for me to discuss. It would be difficult for Pete to be romantically involved with anyone without 100% of his emotional capabilities. I know Jessica cares about him, and I believe, in his way, he cares a lot for her. But I can't honestly say they are romantically involved."

"Sheriff, thank you so much for your time." Miyaki stood up and shook Bill's hand.

Bill smiled as the reporter walked out of his office.

***

The clicking of Miyake's high heels against the metal floor echoed throughout the ship's hallway. She walked up to a tall, blue-robed figure. The hood of the robe concealed the tall figure's face. When she reached it, she smiled and morphed, donning a robe similar to the one she faced.

"I don't know how these humans wear these accursed high heels," she grunted and tossed them down the hallway.

"Did you procure any intel vital to our cause?" The robed figure asked in almost a whisper.

Miyake nodded slightly and answered, "I have found the herald's weakness."

1 SAME AS IT EVER WAS

Pete, he's coming back. Watch out!

The Xan warrior floated through the air on an invisible force field under his feet. Pete noticed a circular heat haze under the Xan's boots. The Xan had struck Pete from behind, knocking him down to the ground on the Lawn, and sped off flying. The Xan circled a building and headed back towards Pete.

Oz, I see him. Pete stood up, brushing the dirt and grass off his coat while staring intently at the flying Xan.

I didn't know they could fly. Oz, did you know?

Technologically, they are incredibly advanced. I'm not surprised.

So, no. The answer is no. You didn't know.

If you need to be picky, then you are correct. I didn't know.

We need to discuss this when we are through here.

Yes, sir.

Smartass.

The Xan warrior was approximately 50 yards away, heading towards Pete. His dark green armor did not shimmer, appearing matte black in the sunlight. The warrior raised his hand and began firing laser energy balls in Pete's direction. Each projectile was the size of a softball, the color of the sun, and equally as bright. They descended toward Pete, no smoke emanating from them.

Struggling to dodge the shots' intense brightness, Pete immediately had Oz activate the lens reflectors in his eyes. Like sunglasses, the reflectors toned down the light of the projectiles and made them more accessible to dodge. The projectiles exploded on the ground, creating holes ten times their size. The grass around each hole burned, and smoke filled the air. When Pete dodged the last shot, he stood up and looked around, watching the smoke rise from the fires on the ground. The area resembled a battlefield that had just received massive tank fire. By Pete's count, the Xan shot over a dozen times.

As the Xan flew over Pete's head, he let out a loud, low, tonal, raspy laugh. Pete watched the Xan fly away.

He threw his arms up in the air and yelled, "A gun? Where the hell did he get that gun? Xans have guns? What the hell, Oz? You didn't know about their guns either?"

Come on, man. All aliens have weapons! Oz shouted from inside Pete's head.

But you need to tell me about them before they shoot at me, Pete continued.

Yeah, you're right. My bad.

I'm waiting.

Oz was confused. *What?*

Oz, tell me about it now.

Ok. The Xanoclax can manipulate matter and forge whatever weapon they need to eliminate the threat they are confronting.

Manipulate matter?

Yes, Xans utilize a biotech process to link a warrior's armor to thought. The biotech process enables a Xan to construct a weapon immediately upon request.

Good to know. Thanks.

Pete shook his head and readied himself for the Xan's next pass. He squinted slightly to see through the smoke that surrounded him. He knew if the fight went on much longer, the bystanders who were watching might be hurt and even killed. He stood still, waiting for the Xan to appear through the smoke.

The TV cameras on the National Lawn were trying to capture all the action. Reporters brave enough to stay on their truck roofs called the action sounding more like a play—by—play announcement for a sporting event than anything else.

"Here is our second sighting of a Xanoclax warrior." The reporter made no effort to hide the excitement in her voice. "The first sighting, as you recall, was just a few weeks ago at the White House, where many of the world's leaders gathered to hear the Wen speak for the first time. It appears this Xan warrior is making another pass and heading back."

The Xan circled and came back towards Pete. Pete knew he had to do something on this pass. He didn't know how much longer he could avoid the energy blasts. The Xan came closer and fired. Pete dodged the first blast and leaped toward him.

Pete grabbed the Xan from behind and wrapped his arms around his waist, fighting to get a grip on the slick metallic armor. The Xan kept laughing, looking straight ahead and ignoring Pete. Pete's legs were flailing in the air, and, from a distance, he looked like a banner waving in the wind behind the black-armored Xan. There was nowhere to place his feet, so he just held on.

I didn't think this through at all, he thought.

The Xan increased his speed as he headed up towards the clouds.

Pete's body continued to fly in the air behind the Xan as he fought to keep his grip around the Xan's waist. The moisture from the clouds made the Xan's armor slippery. The Xan's laughter grew louder and more sinister. Then Pete heard the laugh a lot more clearly, and Pete knew that clarity wasn't a good sign.

The warrior never changed direction or speed as his laughter grew. His armor blocked the wind from Pete's face, allowing him to look up. Without slowing his speed, the Xan's head made a 180-degree turn while his body remained forward, looking down at Pete as he was holding on.

"How did he do that?" Pete screamed at Oz.

I don't know. It must be their...

Pete cut Oz off; *yeah, I know their advanced technology.*

Pete looked down. The Xan had taken them up above the clouds. The Xan looked down at Pete. His laughter stopped, and he spoke in a deep, low, grizzled voice, "I need proof of your death, herald."

The Xan raised his right arm, and a slightly curved, green sword was instantly in his right hand. The Xan brought his sword-bearing hand to the opposite side of his face and made a slicing motion down towards Pete's head. Pete instinctively reacted, releasing his grip on the Xan and sailing backward through the clouds. He raised both his hands and presented two middle fingers to the Xan. The Xan looked shocked that his sword had missed its mark. Then he laughed again, switched his head back to the front of his body, and started flying in a semicircle through the clouds. When the Xan hovered below them, he didn't see Pete. He immediately maneuvered himself in a straight line to where he estimated Pete's trajectory would end, waiting directly above the Lawn. He saw the Wen spaceship below, but no falling Pete. His tech did a complete and thorough scan of the area and found no sign of Pete's falling body.

The Xan warrior yelled out an angry, raspy scream. "Where are you, herald?" He looked dumbfounded.

The Xan kept looking down and didn't notice Pete above him.

"Hey, ugly!" Pete yelled, falling through the clouds feet first towards the Xan.

The Xan looked up and yelled in his gravelly voice, "How is this possible, human?"

As Pete's feet hit the Xan in the face, he yelled at the Xan, "I'm a Wen herald; I'm full of all kinds of surprises!"

The blow to the Xan's face sent the Xan spiraling downward. As he tried to redirect his force field from his feet, an alarm went off in his tech. The Xan redirected his attention to it.

"There is an alien explosive attached to your facial armor. Remove it immediately. Warning. Warning. There is an alien explosive attached to your facial armor." And the warning repeated itself in the Xan's language.

Pete watched the Xan grab the device. Still falling backward, the Xan looked up at Pete, raised the device towards Pete, and laughed.

Pete raised his right hand. The Xan looked confused as he saw a switch in Pete's raised hand. Pete shrugged his shoulders and tilted his head as he looked at the Xan. The Xan looked at Pete, tilted his head as if mirroring him, and gazed at the device he held. He tried to toss the device, but it stuck to his hand like glue. Pete waved the fingers of his left hand without moving his wrist, a goodbye gesture to the Xan, and pressed the switch. The device immediately exploded, increasing the Xan's velocity as he flew towards the ground. Pete levitated downward, following the Xan as he plummeted to the earth. The Xan was descending so rapidly that he looked like a falling meteor.

After the Wen meeting in the White House with the world leaders, the president's office ordered the immediate construction of a ten-foot fence along the horizontal perimeter of both sides of the National Lawn. The wall continued from the north end of the fence horizontally across the lawn to the other side, connecting both sides. The process was repeated at the southern end of the wall connecting both sides of the Lawn. The structure resembled a large rectangular box, like a football field, with the spaceship lying directly in the center. The fenced-in area was patrolled 24/7 by the U.S. Army.

In a further effort to control the masses, the military was instructed by the White House to set up a fenced pedestrian walkway that passed directly in front of the spaceship. Military contractors constructed a high fence on both sides of the walkway. The pedestrian walkway stretched across the Lawn from the west side of the perimeter fence to the east side. Pedestrians could use the walkway to take pictures of themselves and their families directly in front of the spaceship.

Each visitor had three minutes to take pictures before they were hurried off by the Park Police. The visitors who finished taking photos of the spaceship continued walking across the pathway to the other side of the Lawn. They were allowed to continue taking pictures as long as they kept moving.

Everyone in the crowd around the spaceship waiting in line focused on the action above the clouds, even though the clouds were thick and blocked most of it from the sightseers. Loud oohs and ahs rang out in unison every time the figures became visible. People kept their cell phones pointed toward the sky, hoping to capture all the activity they could.

The following family—a man, a woman, and a small child—was next in line and hurried onto the walkway to see the spaceship. The man lifted his four-year-old son onto his shoulders and stepped away from the fence. His wife backed up to get the best possible shot. As she was clicking her camera, people started shouting.

"Oh my God, look!"

Everyone instinctively looked to the sky to see a large object falling from the clouds. People were filming and taking pictures of the event with their phones. The man with his son on his shoulders turned around and faced the spaceship. Everyone watched in shock as the Xan fell faster and faster until he landed on the top of the spacecraft. The clunk of metal on metal resounded across the Lawn on impact, and the crowd gasped in unison. He bounced straight back up, over 100 feet into the air.

The people in the crowd of onlookers continued to film as the Xan descended towards the ground. Everyone yelled when he hit the earth, making a terribly loud thudding sound. The fall created a 20-foot diameter hole in the ground. The four-year-old pointed and laughed. The crowd stood and gawked through the fence at the newly formed crater. Some smoke was rising from the hole. The crowd's grumbling turned to cheers when they saw Pete slowly descending from the clouds. The closer he got to the Lawn, the louder the cheers became.

Pete stopped on the ground next to the hole. He ignored the crowd, his gaze fixated on the hole.

Pete knelt on one knee and looked down into the hole. *What do you think? Did he survive?* He asked Oz.

It's possible. But if the Xan did survive, it would be logical to assume he is unconscious.

Why is that logical?

There is a high percentage that the explosion knocked him unconscious. Therefore, he could not make the proper adjustments to his force field. The fact that he bounced extremely high off the ship substantiates my conclusions. The bounce height indicates that he did not adjust his force field appropriately.

Man, you're a high-tech data analyst all of a sudden?

Just doing my job, man. Just doing my job.

Pete looked down into the hole. It was difficult to see how deep the abyss was through the gusts of smoke lingering inside, so he jumped feet first into the pit through the smoke. He levitated back up through the hole slowly, holding the Xan warrior by the neck of his armor. When Pete emerged, the crowd of bystanders began cheering again. Pete headed toward the ship. He floated just high enough to not drag the Xan on the ground.

When Pete came to the front of the ship, Oz opened the door. Pete descended and entered the vessel, dragging the Xan warrior behind him. Oz closed the door.

2 MUCH ADO ABOUT NOTHING

Pete tossed the Xan against the metal wall. The sound echoed in the ship. Pete noticed his coat was burned in some areas and extremely dirty in others. He took it off and tossed it across the room, kicking the mud and grass off his boots

He walked towards the control center and said, "Oz, run a scan. See if he's still alive."

Oz materialized and headed for the control center. She sat down and immediately started a scan of the Xan's body.

"Not good."

"What is it?"

"All my readings say he's still alive."

Pete looked down at the Xan warrior. One of his hands was missing, and green blood trickled from his arm where it used to be. The Xan must have squeezed the bomb tightly to minimize the damage. The armor around the warrior's hand prevented the explosion from taking his whole arm.

Pete looked away from the unconscious warrior. "So what are we going to do with him? If he's alive, eventually, he's going to wake up. My guess is he won't be happy when he does."

"You have to terminate him immediately. That's the only logical next step." Oz answered.

"Terminate him? That's logical? How the hell is that logical?"

"When he awakens, he will attempt to terminate us. His mission is his priority, Pete. And our death is his mission."

"Killing another being while he is unconscious is not logical, Oz. It's murder."

"Pete, he wants to kill you."

"Not while he's unconscious, he doesn't. Let's figure out alternatives, please."

"I can't think of any logical alternative."

"Can't or won't?"

"Both."

"That doesn't seem like a Wen answer. I thought logic dictated zero emotional response? Maybe you need to do a reboot again. The Earth's atmosphere could still be affecting you."

"Maybe it is," Oz responded.

"What's this about Oz?"

Oz walked over to Pete and looked up at him. She increased her height to look Pete in his eyes when she spoke.

"Pete, there is no reasoning with the Xanoclax. Any being outside of their species is considered inferior and serves only one purpose: to be a supply for what humans call 'souls.'"

"So we just murder him?"

"If you want to call it murder, then yes."

Pete stared at Oz for what seemed an eternity. He couldn't believe what he was hearing. *Was this the development of logic? No, this wasn't logic; this response was personal,* he thought.

"Oz, you are not telling me something. What is it?"

Oz turned away from Pete and stared at the control screen on the wall. She lifted her hand and passed it from left to right in front of the screen. Pete walked up next to her to watch. There, on the screen, was a Vailen. Pete was confused. "Oz, who is this? Is it you?"

Oz spoke softly, "No, this was a fellow Vailen on an assignment similar to mine. Her name was Cass."

Pete looked back at the screen. The landscape was a rough terrain of mostly sand and boulders. There was a mountain range in the background, bare rock with no sign of trees or vegetation. The wind was blowing the sand in various directions, making it difficult to focus on any one place on the screen for too long. A light-red hue covered the sand and rocks.

He saw Cass kneeling over a body, but he couldn't make out any physical features on the body because it was lying face down. The sand was blowing around the figures. Pete assumed the body belonged to a Wen herald.

Pete pointed at the body on the screen, "Is that her assignment lying on the ground?"

"Yes."

"What happened to him?"

"Watch."

Pete watched the screen. Cass had her head lowered, looking at the body on the ground. She began to speak.

"Oz, I can't understand her. Can you put on the translator, please?"

Oz complied.

Cass continued, "It is not logical to kill me; you achieved your mission. My herald is dead."

A rough, harsh voice came from the left side of the screen. "What does logic have to do with killing?"

Cass stood up. "What is the point in killing me? I am no threat to you. I am just standing here in a peaceful manner."

The Xan stepped into the frame from the left side and walked up to Cass. The sand swirled around their bodies, and the Xan's armor was barely visible in small flashes. The warrior ambled towards the unarmed Cass.

"You are interfering with our livelihood. Your purpose is to disrupt our logic belief."

"My purpose is to help save lives."

The Xan put his face up to Cass's face. "You, my little Vailen, should have been trying to save your own life."

A sword took the place of the Xan's arm. Without taking his gaze off Cass's eyes, he plunged the blade into the center of her body, just below her chest. The warrior gripped the back of Cass's head tightly, and she let out a horrific scream. Fluorescent, blue-colored blood started flowing freely from the wound. The Xan slowly pulled the sword up through Cass's body as she continued to scream. When the sword reached her throat, she stopped crying. The Xan continued in a slow, deliberate manner, cutting through her head and splitting her in half.

When the Xan finished cutting Cass's lower body, he held the halves of her body up, one in each hand. He raised his arms over his head, offering the body parts to his invisible God. Within a few moments, both arms holding his precious cargo began to glow bright yellow. The Xan started laughing as the light from the glowing body parts grew more colorful.

Then, as quickly as the glow appeared, it disappeared into the Xan's body. When the glow had disappeared completely, the Xan looked at his hands. The Vailen was gone, and in her place was a mound of dust in each fist. The Xan lowered his hands and turned his palms upside down. The dust, all that remained of the Vailen, Cass, blew away and swirled in the air, mixing with the red sand. The Xan's laughter became uncontrollable.

That's when Oz turned off the screen.

There was dead silence in the spaceship. Pete looked at Oz, sitting in the control chair, still looking at the screen.

"Oz, I am so sorry about what happened to Cass."

"I know, Pete."

"Oz, we are not machines, and neither are they. We can all make choices. We should at least allow this Xan that opportunity."

"So what happens when he awakens, Pete? We kill him then?"

"Look, there has to be a way of containing the Xan, so we are safe when he wakes up."

"The only way to be sure we are safe is to remove his tech. "

"How do we do that?"

"How am I supposed to know? It's not like we had special training on stripping a Xan."

"Ok, I get it. Do a scan of the Xan armor and see what you can find. Look for any creases in the armor or hidden switches."

The Xan was lying on his back. Oz slowly walked up to his body and knelt beside him. She began to pass her hand over the armor. Blue light from her hand beamed down onto the armor. She stopped just under the right armpit.

"Here. There is a switch."

"Is it safe to open?"

"My scans do not detect a self-destruct logarithm."

Oz reached inside the armor plate under the arm and touched the switch. The sudden burst of air mimicked the release of air brakes on a bus. The sound was just as loud. It startled Oz and Pete, and they took a few steps back. Green smoke billowed from the armor. Oz immediately turned on the ship's emergency sensor, and it detected the green smoke, immediately sucking it up through vents in the ceiling of the vessel. The vapor it left behind made Pete cover his nose and mouth.

Pete looked at Oz. She seemed lifeless, standing over the Xan. She was still, and her eyes remained locked onto the Xan.

Pete spoke up. "Oz, you okay?"

Oz didn't answer; she kept staring down at the Xan.

Pete walked over to her and touched her shoulder. "Oz, are you alright?" Pete asked again.

Oz looked at Pete. "Please let me kill him."

"No. It would be murder. That makes us no better than the Xanoclax."

Oz shook her head slowly in agreement. "I know."

"Come on, let's get this tech off him."

Oz moved closer to the Xan and passed her hand over the armor. The armor separated into several pieces around the Xan. Oz levitated the pieces above the Xan and moved the pieces in front of his body. Oz then waved her hand across them, and they fused to form the empty Xan's suit.

Oz looked at Pete. "I'll lock this away in our armory."

Pete watched Oz slowly walk down the hallway. The Xan's suit was hovering over the floor in front of Oz at the height of her waist, so she could easily place one hand on the armor and guide it forward.

Pete slowly walked over to the armorless Xan. There was a dark film wrapped around his body, resembling a bodysuit, a lining the Xan wore underneath their armor to protect their skin. Pete couldn't make out the Xan's features under the black film. What sparked his curiosity were the many wires running through the suit. The bodysuit resembled a large circuit board.

"The circuitry integrates with their skin to enable the armor to move as if it were their skin." Oz had come back from the armory.

"So the armor becomes their body? No wonder they move and react so quickly."

"The Xanoclax are constantly upgrading their tech to stay at the top."

"The top of what?"

"The food chain."

"Sounds a bit dramatic, Oz."

"They will never stop advancing their tech for fear that another race may be stronger."

"Can we remove his bodysuit? Or is it fused into his skin?"

"I can remove it, but I can't promise it won't kill him."

"Can you attempt it slowly? Don't just rip it off him. You'll have time to stop if your scans pick up a problem."

"I'll try."

Oz knelt beside the Xan and held her hands close to the body, palms down. Blue light emanated from her palms as she slowly lifted her hands, starting at the feet of the warrior. The bodysuit began to pull away from his skin. Pete could hear small popping sounds as each wire separated from the Xan's skin. Green blood oozed out of the tiny holes left behind by the separation. The skin, now riddled with little holes, had a light green hue.

Pete watched from the opposite side of the warrior as Oz continued at a slow pace. She had the freed parts of the suit levitate above the warrior's body. "Are your scans seeing any problems?"

"His blood pressure is rising, but he can handle it."

"Oz, please don't kill him."

"I won't. Not on purpose."

Oz began to stand slowly, keeping her hands steady over the Xan's body. The bodysuit pulled off the body as she stood and rose to the programmed height. Pete looked down at the suit but could not see the body underneath. The end of the bodysuit connected to the head would not separate from the Xan.

Pete looked at Oz. "What's happening?"

"The connections from the bodysuit to the head are a lot deeper. I'm trying to disconnect them."

"Let's lay the rest of the suit off to the side and leave it connected to his head."

"We can't. If any part of this tech remains connected to the Xan, we won't be able to contain him. I almost got it."

Pete watched on, feeling helpless. There wasn't anything for him to do but watch and wait.

After several agonizing minutes, Oz spoke up. "I think I got it." She pulled her hands up quickly, and the connections separated from the Xan's head with a horrible tearing sound.

The Xan let out a loud, ear-piercing scream and sat up, sending the bodysuit flying across the room. Oz immediately shot an energy blast from her hand and knocked the Xan unconscious.

Pete yelled at Oz, "What the hell was that? You tried to kill him!"

"No, if I tried to kill him, he wouldn't have screamed."

Oz and Pete were facing each other when they heard a moan. They both turned to the Xan, sitting up, rubbing his head. Oz and Pete looked on, surprised at what they were seeing.

"Pete, do you see what I see?"

Pete kept staring at the naked Xan. Without looking away, he said, "Yeah, Oz, I see, but I don't understand it."

3 MOVING ON

"I don't understand why you have to do this right now. Shouldn't you put more time into such a big decision?"

Bill was pacing back and forth in his living room while talking to Maggie. She was on his couch, watching him walk around the sofa.

"Bill, I have to try to make a difference."

"You're making a difference right here in Bends Creek. Why do you need to go to D.C.?"

"The affliction has bought us some time, Bill, but it hasn't stopped the racists from continuing to commit atrocities against people of color."

"It's gotten a lot better. Those racist assholes only see the same color now. They can't commit acts of hate towards anyone because they don't know who is white or nonwhite."

"For the most part, you are right. But people who aren't afflicted are being scrutinized and even paid to point out nonwhites to various racist groups. There have been several reports that some police officials are harassing non-afflicted officers to point out persons of color. So the opportunity is there for them to commit more hate crimes."

"But what are you going to do to stop that?"

"I can't stop it. But I can be part of a group that works to fight these factions. Oz was right, Bill. We have to act. Social media is not the answer. I want to organize a concerned group of all races to fight racism. We need to be able to take racists out of positions of power so they can't harm anyone under the guise of justice."

"How are you going to do that?"

"I don't know. I have some ideas that I would like to discuss with other like-minded individuals. As you said, everyone has to be part of the fight, or we will never achieve peaceful coexistence."

"I think you say it much better than I do," Bill smiled.

"Bill, I have to try to do something. If I can get others to see that they need to take action against racism, then it's a win."

Bill could see how determined Maggie was to accomplish this goal. He always respected her for following through with everything she started. Bill knew that if Maggie had started this cause in D.C., she wouldn't stop until she had succeeded.

"So, you're moving to D.C.? How long will you be gone?"

"I'm not sure. You can come with me, you know."

"I can't leave here, Maggie. You know that."

"You've always wanted to leave. Why not now? Maybe you can take some time off and see whether this is worth doing."

"I don't know, Maggie."

"Look at it as a vacation. You can take a few weeks and help me get this going."

"I suppose that makes sense. I'll come with you to make sure you settle in okay. I don't know how long I'll be able to stay."

"Maggie got up and hugged Bill. She loved how he always supported her and cared about her. Maggie pulled away and met his eyes. "This is why I love you, Bill Jackson."

"Why do I feel like I'm getting over my head?"

"You're not. If anything, you can help me with organizing a special interest group. Your knowledge of the law will be a big help."

"Yeah, it still makes me feel uneasy."

"Jessica will be in D.C. for a few weeks for a work-related visit. It will be great for all of us to get together."

"When will she be in D.C.?"

"She's leaving Atlanta next week. I have already called Pete, and he's set up a meeting for me to talk with a few congressmen to explain my ideas and goals. Pete thinks these men and women will be interested in supporting my cause."

"You're going to meet congressmen?"

"Yes, that's why it's important to do this now. Pete can get me an audience with them, and maybe this could start some conversation."

"I guess knowing a space alien on a personal level will get you into some important doors in D.C."

Maggie laughed. "Yeah, better use that connection while I can. I have a lot of ideas that I hope will get some support from legislators. I wouldn't have been able to do this without our friendly space alien."

Bill grinned in return. "Yeah, I guess he came in pretty handy after all."

Maggie shook her head. "He's done enough for all of us already. Inviting me to meet these politicians is just icing on the cake."

"Okay, what have I got to lose except my mind?"

Maggie laughed again, and Bill smiled back at her. Bill loved seeing her laugh.

I can't believe I'm doing this, he thought.

4 RECKLESS RALLY

Bronson Pike was thrilled to be in D.C. He loved riding around the city with all the members of his bike club. He felt confident that the white nationalist party White for Right would have a strong showing in D.C. over the next few days. All the members were told by word of mouth to meet on the Lawn. Bronson would never call his meetings rallies or protests. He didn't want to prepare the law by filing for a permit. He liked just showing up and taking advantage of the ensuing chaos. So when all the bikes began rumbling into D.C., law enforcement went on high alert.

The bikers parked their bikes and headed for an open area on the Lawn. Pockets of visiting tourists rushed off the Lawn as they approached. Some bikers laughed and called out to the scared tourists as they hurried away.

"Run, you little pukes!" A biker yelled at the tourists.

"Go home to your suck-ass lives, haha!" Another yelled out.

The roar of their laughter grew louder as the mass of bikers increased. Hundreds of bikers were on the Lawn, cussing and laughing. Most bikers held a beer can; many had six packs straddling their shoulders. It didn't take more than 30 minutes before they started chanting, "Pike! Pike! Pike!" The chant kept going for 15 minutes without letting up. The chant broke off a little when cheers from one end of the crowd grew louder. Bronson Pike had arrived.

Pike was walking with both hands over his head. He had a bullhorn in one hand and made a fist with the other. He was screaming at the top of his lungs while walking through the crowd. "Yeah! Hell yeah! That's right!" As he walked by, bikers showed their support with a pat on his back. He made his way to the center of the crowd.

A couple of bikers followed behind Pike. They carried a six-foot ladder stolen from a nearby construction site. When they stopped in the center, they opened the ladder. One biker held the left while the other had the right. Pike smiled at them and climbed up.

When he got to the first step from the top, he stopped. He turned around and leaned his legs against the ladder. Pike looked around the crowd.

Awesome turnout, Pike thought.

Pike raised the bullhorn to his mouth and began shouting.

"Welcome, all my brothers!"

The crowd cheered and screamed.

The local police started maneuvering around the Lawn, positioning themselves strategically. They planned to have the bikers exit the Lawn through several lines of law enforcement officers. All the officers were at attention, awaiting orders.

Pike noticed the human barricades established by the police. He laughed and began pointing them out to the crowd of bikers.

"Okay, brothers, here we go! We came to D.C. to meet and party peacefully, and The Man has already shown up to crash our party."

The crowd started screaming at the police officers.

Pike watched the crowd get riled up and started talking to them again.

"Brothers, don't worry about the police right now! We have more important matters to discuss."

"Like what?" one biker yelled from the crowd.

"I'll tell you what. We have to expose the bullshit lies that the government has been feeding us. The shit we've been seeing isn't true. The government is telling us to believe that everything is okay when all it is bullshit!"

The crowd was screaming louder, raising their fists in the air.

Pike continued with his speech. "Just because you see everything as white don't mean it's true. The government of liberals is poisoning us to control us. They think we're too stupid to see what the freak they are doing. But we ain't stupid! Are we brothers?"

The crowd screamed, "Hell, no!"

"We ain't weak either, are we?"

"Hell no!"

"We need to expose this lie for what it is and get this country back on track!"

Everyone in the crowd was screaming, "White for right! White for right!"

Bronson Pike had both arms raised high in the air. With every chant, he punched the sky with his fist. Everyone followed suit. The chanting and screaming disturbed the police. The officers standing in formation began to get nervous — the police chief onsite had called the National Guard earlier, and they were there for backup support. The sun was setting, and the chief didn't want this to continue in the dark.

Pike was feeling more excited by the moment. The energy from the crowd made him feel invincible. He continued with his speech.

"What we're seeing isn't real. The government is hiding all non-whites with this poison to keep us quiet. But we will cleanse this country of all these lies! Are you with me?"

"Hell yeah!" the crowd screamed. Many bikers went into frenzy mode and started heading towards the police lines.

The chief ordered his men to hold their ground. The National Guard moved in behind the police lines. A large group of bikers swarmed one of the TV trucks, on top of which a reporter and cameraman were perched. The bikers gathered on one side of the truck and turned it over. The reporter and the cameraman jumped off the truck and rolled out of the way of the falling camera equipment.

The order was given for the police and the Guard to put on their gas masks and proceed. The chief raised his bullhorn. "You are ordered to disassemble immediately and move away from the immediate area."

The reaction from the crowd came as expected.

"Freak you!"

"We ain't moving!"

"Kiss my ass!"

The police shot several canisters of tear gas into the crowd. As soon as the gas appeared, the police attempted to escort the bikers off the Lawn. Some bikers went without resisting, but the majority insisted on not cooperating. Many of those who refused to leave began attacking the police officers. The Guard entered the melee and fought off the bikers. They dragged individuals to the side of the Lawn and set up a holding area for the most violent of the group.

Pike loved every minute of the action. The more chaos and confusion he could spread, the more justified he felt. The thick smoke from the gas made it hard for him to make out all of the action. But the volume of the screams narrated the violence of the unfolding scene. As Pike walked through the smoke, he saw a shadowed figure approaching him. Thinking it was a police officer, Pike shouted and swung his fist towards the figure. His fist hit it, and a horrible crunching noise resounded. He felt the bones of his fist shatter. He let out a horrifying scream.

The smoke cleared around the silhouette. It was a Xan warrior. Pike had struck the Xan's armor with his fist, shattering the bones in his hand.

Pike was in extreme pain. He held his injured wrist with his other hand. Looking up at the Xan, he said, "What the freak do you want?"

The Xan reached out with one hand and grabbed Pike's injured wrist. Pike felt his wrist become hot.

"What the hell are you doing to me?"

The Xan didn't speak. After a moment, he let go of Pike's hand. Pike held up his hand and moved it as if nothing had happened to it.

Pike laughed, "Pretty good trick, man."

The Xan spoke in a deep, rough voice, "It's no trick, human."

"Why are you here? What do you want?"

"We need to talk."

5 DISCOVERY

Pete couldn't take his eyes off the Xan sitting on the floor, leaning against the wall. He looked at Oz, who was still staring at the Xan. Pete had imagined what a Xan would look like under their armor in many different ways. But what was now sitting before him didn't come close to anything he had envisioned.

"What are you gawking at?" the Xan warrior responded to their stares.

Pete stumbled to find his words. "You're a female? And you look like a human female?"

Pete suddenly found it difficult to look at the Xan when she glanced up at Pete from the floor. He felt her stare cut right through him. She had short red hair, and her face was young. She was maybe in her late twenties or early thirties, Pete thought. The Xan's facial features were human. Her eyes were round and wide, her irises a haunting, emerald green. Her nose seemed almost perfect, sitting in flawless symmetry with the rest of her face. Her cheekbones were unusually high, and her lips were dark green. Her mouth seemed smaller than Pete thought it should be.

Maybe she can enlarge her mouth when needed to expose her three rows of teeth, he thought.

The Xan's skin looked human from where Pete was standing. Pete didn't see any markings on her body, and he was surprised at how smooth her light-green skin looked. The Xan sat against the wall, naked, her long legs bent at the knees with the heels of her feet pulled up close to her body. Her bent legs blocked Pete and Oz's view of her naked upper body.

"Just because our physical appearance may be similar doesn't make us human, you Earth pig."

"How do you explain the striking similarity?"

"I won't explain anything to you. I don't answer to you or your Vailen slave."

Oz had been staring at the Xan the whole time, oblivious to Pete's conversation, but when she heard the Xan say Vailen slave, she snapped out of her trance. Oz took a few steps towards the Xan.

"For a higher intellect, you don't seem so bright."

"I will speak my mind freely because I am not afraid to die."

"Keep speaking your mind freely, you Xan dog, and I'll put your lack of fear to the test."

Pete stepped between Oz and the Xan.

"Oz, that's enough. Don't let her rile you up. That's what she's trying to do, and you're playing right into it."

"Listen to your master, Vailen pet."

Oz took another step towards the seated Xan. Pete grabbed her arm and walked her to the opposite wall. She walked backward to the wall, never taking her eyes off the Xan. The Xan smiled and waved goodbye to Oz with her one good hand.

Pete whispered to Oz, "Listen to me, please. We have an opportunity to observe and possibly get answers from this Xan.

Don't ruin this one important advantage by going human on me, okay?"

Oz was still glaring at the Xan.

"Oz!" Pete raised his whisper. Oz looked at Pete with a cold, hard stare. "I know this is hard for you, but please think logically. Do not waste this opportunity."

Oz's expression went blank. She knew Pete was right. They had to take any chance to gather intel on the Xanoclax. She just couldn't take her eyes off the Xan. The shift in her blood pressure was confusing her. Her internal sensors were acting strangely. Her body temperature was rising.

Her mind began racing. *What is going on? Am I experiencing anger?*

"Okay, I'll back off. But we need to put that psycho bitch in lock up. There's no way I trust her."

"Agreed, we'll lock her ass in a secured cell right away."

Pete left Oz and walked over to the Xan. She was still sitting on the floor. He looked down at her and noticed her wounded hand was healing.

"Your hand is healing. So you can replace missing limbs?"

"We are advanced beings. We have many abilities that an underdeveloped mind like yours would never comprehend."

"Try me."

"Our technology is incorporated within our physiology. As our species advanced, we evolved not only to a higher mental level but a physical one as well."

Pete smiled at the Xan warrior. "See? That wasn't so hard, was it?"

The Xan warrior was apoplectic when she realized Pete had tricked her into answering his question. She screamed, "Kill me already!"

"I am not a Xanoclax warrior; I do not kill for the sake of killing. I get no joy from taking the life of another being."

"You know nothing of the Xanoclax. Do you think you will get answers about our mission because you captured me? Maybe make a friend, human? The green blood of the Xanoclax runs through my veins, and we are warriors, not diplomats. I would rather die a thousand deaths than become friends with a pathetic race like yours."

Pete leaned down and came face-to-face with the Xan.

"I admire your loyalty and tenacity, but as of now, you are my prisoner, and unlike your race, my race knows patience. I have all the time in the world to get answers from you, whereas you will be sitting in a cell alone, thinking about how you let a pathetic human capture you."

The Xan let out another angry scream right into Pete's face.

Pete turned away from the Xan. "Oz, can you please find something for our prisoner to wear?"

When Pete turned around, the Xan was standing, wearing old pants and a shirt. The clothes were brown and made from burlap sacks. The Xan stood up and immediately started scratching her backside.

Oz laughed, "Look familiar, Pete?"

Pete laughed.

Still scratching with her good hand, the Xan cried, "What is this?"

Pete responded, "You are our prisoner and will not receive special treatment. Only diplomats receive special treatment. Once you cooperate with us, we will make your stay more comfortable. But until then, we will make your stay miserable."

"Human pig!"

"Oz, shackle her legs. We don't want our Xan princess running off."

Oz smiled. "Absolutely."

Shackles appeared suddenly around the Xan's legs, and she almost fell from the surprise. She looked down and screamed again.

"You like that?" Oz smiled at the Xan. "I've got more from where that came from."

Pete walked up to the Xan. Without her boots on, she was shorter than Pete.

"Once you have regenerated your hand, we will shackle them together. Oz, please take our princess to her new home."

The Xan raised her hand to hit Pete. Pete caught her arm. They stared at each other for a moment. "You seem to be at a loss without your tech. Maybe you didn't evolve as intelligently as you should have."

Oz waved her hand over the Xan's face as Pete continued holding the Xan's arm. The warrior was still staring at Pete when she fell asleep and dropped. Her body made a loud noise when it made contact with the floor.

"You could have let her land a little easier, Oz."

"Yes, you're right, I could have."

Oz levitated the sleeping Xan and flopped the bodysuit onto the Xan's stomach so she wouldn't have to carry it. Oz started for the Xan's cell, the warrior's levitating body following close behind.

Pete watched Oz walk away. He knew he would have to proceed with extreme caution from this point forward. The only thing he was sure of right now was that Xan hated him.

Maybe I can use that to my advantage, he thought.

Pete went to the control board and turned on the screen. He was shocked to see the haze of teargas lingering over the Lawn. Police lights rotated, lighting the area in blue and red. Several spotlights exposed the Lawn. The local police and National Guard soldiers were chasing and apprehending bikers. Some bikers were in handcuffs, while others either ran away or physically confronted the police and the Guard. The authorities appeared to have the situation under control, so Pete did not intervene.

"What the hell happened here?"

Oz walked in behind him. "Looks like they had a party."

"Not a fun party."

Oz looked at Pete. "The Xan bitch is locked up, and her armor is secure. Even if she were to get out of her room, there's no way she can get to her armor."

"Thanks, Oz. I know this isn't easy. I appreciate you handling this the right way."

"We'll see if it's right. Okay, I need to contact Krix'x and discuss our new discovery."

"Why? What are you hoping to accomplish by calling him?"

"Pete, we have to report in. You know that."

"Yes, I know. But if Krix'x learns of our captured Xan, he'll want to take her back to your planet and experiment on her."

"What is so wrong with that? You said you wanted answers, Pete. Krix'x will get answers out of her."

"He'll kill her, Oz. You know that."

"I don't see a problem with that."

"I wish you did."

"I'm confused. Why do you care so much for this Xan?"

"It's not about caring so much as curiosity."

"Your curiosity is not logical. This Xan warrior is a dangerous being that no one understands. Her sole mission is to kill and steal other beings' life forces. And you want to keep her around because you're curious? It's not logical."

"Oz, I want to know more about the Xans, and I believe we can find out more if she stays with us." Pete was losing his patience, trying to explain what he felt should be evident to Oz.

"I do not concur. I will have to report to Krix'x with progress updates. And a live captured Xan is an update." Oz refused to back down.

"Just give me a few weeks to see what I can get from her."

"Not logical, Pete. Can't do it."

"I promise that if you don't do me this one solid, I will request a new guide."

Oz took a few steps backward. She looked shocked. Pete realized what he had done and quickly apologized.

"Oz, I didn't mean it. I wouldn't do that, I promise."

Oz hung her head low, looking at her feet as she spoke. "Pete, you are more important to me than that Xan back there."

"I know. I'm sorry. I would never ask for anyone else. I was an ass."

Oz was still looking down. She spoke in a soft voice, "But you said it."

Before Pete could answer her, Oz vanished.

"Oz! Oz, come on, talk to me! Come back and talk this out."

No answer. Pete sat in the control chair, turning it towards the screen.

Great job, Pete. Great job, he thought.

***

Pete walked down the corridor back to where the Xan was locked up. As he walked into the Xan's room, the wall on his left side grew shorter in equal increments, and as it tapered off, it revealed a more extensive room behind it. Turning to his left slightly, he could see the Xan's cell. On his left were three steel columns approximately two feet apart, lined up with the end of the short wall and stopping just before the Xan's cell. Like all the other rooms on the ship, there were no decorations or furnishings.

He could see the warrior through the glass barrier that imprisoned her. She was sitting on the floor in the corner of the room, away from the light. In the center of the back wall of her cell was a small cot with a single blanket and pillow on a thin mattress. A toilet was in the opposite corner.

"Why don't you want to send me to the Wen'q'rixshi?" The Xan's voice came from the dark. Pete heard her but could not make out her face. Her head and body were in the shadows, and only her long legs were in the light.

"What makes you ask?"

"I heard your conversation with your pet."

"She's not my pet. She's an intelligent being to whom I owe my life."

"She wants me gone. Why don't you do as your friend wishes?" The warrior emphasized the word friend as if to mock Pete.

"I'm trying to understand that myself."

"So you have no reason? So typically human of you. You are too weak and fail to make the right choices."

"The right choice is to send you to your death among the Wens?"

"As your pet said, it is the logical decision."

"It's the right decision because you're a part of a cold-hearted, murdering race?"

The Xan warrior rose to her feet and walked to the glass. "You know nothing about my race. The Wen spread many rumors and lies to gather support to defeat us."

"Support from whom?"

"Other species from around the galaxy."

Pete laughed. "Seriously? You're going with that?"

The Xan looked confused. "I don't understand."

"You are trying to tell me that your race is the victim in all of this?"

"The Xanoclax are no victims. We do not need sympathy from anyone, especially Earth pigs." The warrior's breath steamed up the glass in front of her.

"There it is. There's the Xan I know and love," Pete responded sarcastically. "You need to work on your attitude if you want anyone to fall for your bullshit."

"This is not bullshit!" The Xan raised her voice and punched the glass with her good hand.

"You're trying to tell me you're the victim in this story while at the same time giving me this attitude? I'm not buying it." Pete started walking away, waving his hand in the air from side to side slightly. The Xan stared at Pete's back and yelled out to him.

"I'm not selling anything." She turned away from the glass and sat on the bed. She looked out past the glass to where Pete was walking. He disappeared from her sight.

She yelled louder, "And what is 'bullshit'?"

6 FRIENDLY VISIT

It had been two weeks since Jessica had last seen Pete. She had been keeping up with his activity in the news and on the internet. She was thrilled when her boss asked her to go to D.C. and report to Congress on the CDC's findings concerning the affliction. She was excited to see Pete. She felt like she was back in high school, going on her first date.

She kept reminding herself, *Keep it together, girl. You've come this far, so don't blow it now.*

She had called Pete the day before her arrival, and he had promised to meet her at the airport. She flew into Reagan and hurried to the baggage claim. She pulled her bags off the baggage carousel, headed through the departure doors, and into the outside arrivals area.

Jessica looked around and didn't see Pete. She sighed and shrugged her shoulders.

Probably too busy, she thought.

She walked down the sidewalk towards the taxi waiting area and waited in line for the next driver. Jessica was looking in her purse for her phone when she heard a voice.

"Get your bags, ma'am?"

Without looking away from her purse, she answered, "Yes, please."

"Where to, ma'am?"

"The Marriott, please."

"Nice, but wouldn't a spaceship be better?"

Jessica looked up. She almost screamed when she saw Pete standing there. He was in his trench coat and wore a Washington Nationals baseball cap and sunglasses.

Face to face with him, she threw her arms around his neck.

"I didn't think you were coming."

Pete looked at her and smiled. He leaned his head down and kissed her, squeezing her tightly.

"Wow!" Jessica smiled at Pete. "I missed you, too."

Jessica hugged Pete again. When she let go of him, they were standing inside the ship.

"Holy shit!" she shouted. "Are we on your ship?"

Pete smiled. "Yes."

Pete was having a hard time not staring at Jessica. He didn't realize how much he had missed seeing her.

"You want to look around?" Pete asked.

"Hell yeah, I do. Hey, where's Oz?"

Pete looked down at the floor. He appeared too embarrassed to answer.

"What's up, Pete. Did something happen to Oz?"

"No. I said something I didn't mean, and it hurt her feelings. I was an asshole."

Jessica walked up to Pete. "I'm sure it will all work out. You two care so much about each other. There's no way this will go on for too long."

"I don't know, I was pretty mean. And I think—"

Oz interrupted Pete, "Hey, Jessica."

Jessica ran over to Oz, who was standing behind Pete. "Oh my God, Oz, how are you?"

"I'm great, except for putting up with this human male."

Jessica laughed. "Yeah, they can be a lot of work sometimes. But it can be worth it if you find the right one."

Pete walked over to Oz. "Oz, I'm really sorry."

Oz smiled, "Don't sweat it; it's all good."

Pete looked surprised. "Really?"

"Yeah, I overheard what you said to the Xan princess. How you defended me. We're good."

"I meant every word, you know?"

Jessica chimed in, "Xan princess? What am I missing?"

Oz looked at Jessica. "Well, we captured a Xan. And fearless leader here wants to keep her for observation."

"Whoa, girlfriend. You captured a Xan? Are we talking about a living, breathing Xan? Shut the freak up!"

"Yeah, she's in the back."

"She? The Xan is a female? No shit?"

Pete laughed, "Yeah, no shit."

"Wow, I assumed all their warriors were male."

"I think we all did."

Oz looked at Pete, then turned to Jessica. "Pete wants to keep her around to get more information from her. I think it's a bad idea."

"Why do you think it's a bad idea?"

"I think it's best to let our Council have her and get some answers."

Jessica turned to Pete, "Why don't you want to send her to the Council?"

Pete shrugged his shoulders. "Because they'll dissect her and eventually kill her. If we try a different way, we can get her to talk."

"I figured it was a sign when the CDC wanted me to come here. You guys need me to help arbitrate this dilemma, right?"

Pete looked at Oz, and Oz looked at Pete. They simultaneously turned to Jessica and answered together.

"Yes!"

Jessica laughed. "Can we go sit down somewhere to discuss this?"

Pete nodded and walked Jessica into one of the rooms in the spaceship. It was open and had no furniture in it.

"Oz, can you make the proper adjustments for this room?" Pete asked.

Oz walked over to the wall. A keypad materialized. Oz hit some numbers, and a meeting room table with chairs appeared.

Jessica smiled, "Cool. How about some wine and glasses?"

Oz laughed, "Right away."

The three of them sat at the table. A large wine bottle with three glasses was in the middle of the table. Jessica immediately began to pour three glasses of wine.

"So why can't you two agree on this? Be honest with me, please," Jessica asked as she poured the wine.

Oz spoke first. "It's very personal for me. A Xan killed my sister."

Pete was surprised. "Oz, you didn't mention that Cass was your sister."

"It's hard to talk about."

"Oz, I am so sorry."

Jessica looked at Oz. "I'm sorry, Oz. I bet she was wonderful."

Oz smiled wistfully, "She was. She was always trying to help, always volunteering. I miss her so much."

"Are you being logical in your opinion about the Xan, then?"

"No. Not at all."

"Pete, what's happening in your head about the Xan?"

Pete looked at Oz. "My reason isn't as tragic as yours, Oz. But I know what the Wen can do to you on a table. They will try to get her to talk; we all know that won't happen. Then, they will kill her. Then, they'll open her up and dissect her to see what makes her tick. It's just a disgusting thought to me."

Jessica reached across the table and held Pete's hand. "It's good to know that you're gaining your emotions back."

Jessica turned to Oz. "What about a compromise?"

Oz looked at Jessica. "You mean give Pete a little time to see what he can get out of her, don't you?"

"How did you know?"

"You humans think alike."

"What do you think would be a fair waiting period?"

"One day!"

"Come on, Oz. You can do better than that."

"Alright, how about a week?"

"Pete, how's that sound?"

Pete shook his head. "I wanted two weeks."

"Okay, so we compromise. Let's say ten days."

Oz looked at Pete. "Agreed."

Pete looked at Oz. "Agreed."

They all raised their glasses and clinked them together. They sat in silence, drinking their wine for several minutes.

Jessica spoke first after they finished their wine.

"So, can I see this Xan princess?"

Oz said, "You mean the Xan bitch?"

Pete looked at both of them, laughing. He spoke up.

"We won't go see her just to call her names. Is that clear?"

Oz saluted Pete, and Jessica nodded.

They all got up and headed to the Xan's cell. When they got there, Oz didn't enter the room. She stayed back, out of sight. As Jessica approached the glass, Pete stopped at the end of the short wall. The Xan got up from the cot and walked over to the glass to stand before Jessica.

"So now I am a caged animal in your zoo for everyone's entertainment?"

Jessica turned to Pete. "She speaks English?"

Pete nodded as he stepped from behind the wall. But it was the Xan who spoke.

"I'm right here. You can ask me."

Jessica looked at the Xan. "I'm sorry, I didn't mean any disrespect."

The Xan looked at Pete and then at Jessica. "Some of you have manners? That's a surprise."

Jessica asked, "What's your name? I'm Jessica."

The Xan took a step back from the glass. She hesitated for a moment before stepping back forward. She focused on Jessica and looked her over, inspecting every inch of her that she could see. All her instincts told her to turn her back and ignore the human. But when her eyes caught Jessica staring at her, she froze momentarily. The eyes of the human in front of her, on the other side of the glass, were not the eyes of a warrior. They were not eyes brimming with anger or hate. The eyes she was looking into were warm and friendly. The Xan warrior had never experienced such warmth before. Her curiosity became unbearable. She had to know more about this human.

"Are you the human female species?"

"Yes, I am a female."

49

The warrior stood tall, looking directly into Jessica's eyes. "Why do you want to know my name?"

"It would be nice to get to know you. That's all."

The Xan tilted her head slightly, never shifting her gaze. "Aren't you afraid of me?"

"Not while you're behind the glass, I'm not."

The Xan looked at Pete. "I like this human. Is she your mate?"

Jessica's laughter confused the Xan.

"Is that humorous?"

Jessica wiped the tears from her eyes. "It's not you. I had a little too much to drink tonight."

The warrior looked at Jessica while she laughed. In her hand was a glass containing a red liquid. She pointed at the glass. "What is this drink that causes laughter?"

"It's wine, a girl's best friend. Want to try some?"

"Yes."

Jessica turned to Pete. She walked closer to him and whispered, "This could loosen her up."

Pete turned to Oz, who was standing outside the door. "Oz, please get the Xan a glass of wine."

Jessica yelled, "Me too, please."

Pete looked at Jessica. "I hope you know what you're doing."

"Chill, I got this."

Jessica returned to the cell, and a glass of wine was on the floor. The Xan looked like a WWII prisoner of war in her burlap outfit, an image directly opposed by the glass now in her hand. The Xan held the glass up to her nose.

"This has a nice aroma."

"Yes, it does," Jessica responded, holding her glass and sipping.

The Xan repeated what she saw. She pulled the glass away from her mouth and looked at Jessica. Her eyes widened, and her face looked surprised, like a child tasting chocolate for the first time. Jessica raised her glass, and they both drank, emptying their glasses.

Oz had placed a bottle of wine next to the Xan's bed. The Xan walked over to the bottle. She picked it up and rotated the bottle around, causing the wine to swirl in a circle inside the bottle.

Jessica smiled at the Xan through the glass. "It would be better to pour the wine into your glass."

The Xan warrior nodded at Jessica as she poured herself a glass of wine. She walked to the glass window of her cell and sat down, facing Jessica. The Xan placed the bottle on her right side and held the wine glass with both hands. She raised the glass to her mouth and began drinking.

"Slow down, sister!" Jessica yelled at the Xan. The Xan stopped drinking and looked startled. "You need to drink it slowly and enjoy it. Don't just gulp it down. You're not an alcoholic, are you?"

"What is an alcoholic?"

"An alcoholic is someone who can't live without the buzz."

"The buzz?"

"Yeah, after you finish this glass, you'll know what a buzz is."

"Are you trying to poison me?"

"Relax, we're both just chilling together, having a drink. That's all this is; don't read into it more than that."

Pete walked out of the room, leaving Jessica alone with the Xan. It was apparent she was more adept at interrogating than he was. He met Oz in the control room.

"Jessica still in there?"

"Yeah, she is."

"What's she doing?"

"She's getting to know the Xan."

"Why?"

"If she can gain the Xan's trust, maybe we can get some answers. Can you turn on the screen so we can monitor their conversation?"

"Yes."

The screen turned on, and they could see Jessica and the Xan sitting on the floor on opposite sides of the glass, facing each other, sipping at their wine.

A thought came to Pete when he saw the Xan and Jessica in the room. "Oz, could our atmosphere affect the Xan the same way it affected you?"

"Are you referring to my reaction to the neon gases in your atmosphere?"

"Yes. Do you think that could happen to the Xan?"

"I am not sure. Maybe. I could run some tests."

"Please do."

Oz looked at the screen and was confused. "I don't understand. It looks like they're best friends having a conversation."

Pete looked away from the screen and faced Oz, who was still watching. "This is the human way of treating someone you met for

52

the first time. Jessica is the type of human who likes someone until they give her a reason not to like them. It's called giving someone the benefit of the doubt."

"What if the being you are talking to turns out to be an ass?"

"Then you have a choice. You can be friends with them or disassociate yourself from them."

"Why would you be friends with an ass?"

"Oz, being friends with someone means liking them and accepting them for who they are."

Oz looked at Pete, confused and then angry. "Pete, you humans are so screwed up. No wonder this planet is in so much trouble."

"We're not in trouble because we accept people for who they are, Oz."

Oz looked at the screen and then back at Pete. She said in a softer voice, "I think I understand."

Pete smiled and turned back to the screen. "Can you turn the volume up a little? I can barely hear what they're saying."

Oz raised the volume, and they sat there, watching and listening to two beings from different worlds get to know each other.

7 GIRL TALK

"So, are you going to tell me your name, or are you going to keep being a bitch?" The wine had been well absorbed into Jessica's bloodstream, giving her the bravado to speak her mind.

The Xan looked at Jessica. "'Bitch'? What does this bitch mean?"

"It's when one person thinks they are better than everyone else, like they're doing you a favor by talking to you."

The Xan lowered her head and stared at the wine glass she was holding. She was trying to understand how the liquid in the glass was relaxing her. Her mood was pensive. "You think I am this bitch?"

Jessica noticed the Xan's voice had taken on a disappointed tone. "No. I wasn't saying you really are a bitch. I was saying you were acting like a bitch."

"Is it not the same?"

"Not to us. If I call you a bitch, then I am accusing you of being a bitch. If I say you sound like a bitch, it means you're acting like one."

"So you are saying I am acting like this bitch because you do not think I am a bitch?"

"Yes!" Jessica squealed. "You got it. I don't think you're a bitch, but by not telling me your name, you are acting like a bitch."

The Xan looked up from her wine glass. "I am Rialla."

Jessica smiled. "Rialla? That's a beautiful name. It's a pleasure to meet you, Rialla."

Rialla smiled for the first time since being held in captivity. Jessica continued. "What does it mean?"

"In Xanoclax stories of old, Rialla was the warrior who helped free our people from the Quls. The Quls imprisoned our race and kept us as slaves. But Rialla rallied our people to fight for our freedom."

Jessica watched Rialla take another sip of wine. "A strong female, I like her. What happened to Rialla?"

"She was killed in the last great battle that ended all battles. She stepped in front of a sword meant for another. She died, saving many Xans. She was our first hero."

"She sounds fearless."

"There are none braver."

"Why do you look like us?"

Rialla looked at Jessica as she poured another glass of wine. She tilted her head and asked, "Are you trying to get me to talk by making me drink this wine?"

"Hell yes, I am!" Jessica laughed and rolled over onto the floor.

Rialla looked confused. She watched Jessica lie on the floor, laughing. Then, for reasons Rialla could not explain, she laughed. She laughed so hard that she also rolled onto the floor.

Pete and Oz were still watching the screen, observing the conversation between Jessica and Rialla. Oz looked at Pete. "What the hell are they doing?"

Pete smiled. "They're bonding."

"By rolling around on the floor?"

"Well, apparently, the Xan can feel emotions after all. Bet you didn't know that?"

Oz looked at the screen. "No. No, I didn't. I don't believe we ever knew that."

"See, you already learned something new about them."

"How does knowing that they have feelings help us?"

"Oz, if they have feelings, we can reason with them."

Oz turned away from the screen and began working on her computer. She turned the audio from the screen off in her head.

Crazy human behavior, she thought.

Jessica sat up first. She was still laughing. She slowly calmed down and started wiping the tears from her eyes and face. When Rialla sat up, she noticed Jessica wiping away her tears.

"Are you sad?"

"No. I'm very happy. You are a lot of fun to talk to."

"Then why do you have tears running down your face?"

"When we laugh too hard, we tear up. We don't just have tears for sadness. We also have tears for joy."

"You think I'm fun?" Rialla was shocked to hear the words come from her mouth. She would have never mentioned the word fun in a conversation with other Xans.

"Right now, I do."

"You are fun as well."

Jessica looked at Rialla. Rialla's face had an aura of innocence that Jessica had not seen earlier. Jessica wanted to know more about her.

"Why do you look so much like us?"

Rialla laughed, "Why do *you* look so much like *us?*"

Again, the room filled with laughter. When the laughter died down, Jessica tried again.

"Okay, smartass, tell me. Why do you have human features?"

Rialla took another sip of wine. "Why do *you* have Xan features?" Rialla started to laugh again, causing Jessica to begin laughing. They continued to laugh for a few minutes. Jessica held up her hand, palm out.

"Stop it. I can't laugh anymore. My stomach hurts."

Rialla stopped laughing and continued to sip her wine. She wasn't sure what was going to come of this situation. But she enjoyed Jessica's company. She felt like Jessica could be trusted.

Jessica lay straight on her back and looked up at the ceiling. "I can't do this anymore. If you make me laugh again, I may vomit all over this room. It's cool if you don't want to answer any more questions. I'm just glad I got to meet you."

"Are you leaving?"

"Yeah, I have to go to work tomorrow." Jessica rolled up onto her hands and knees. Jessica's new posture made Rialla laugh again. Jessica yelled, "Stop it! It's not funny. You're going to make me laugh again."

Hearing Jessica's response made Rialla laugh harder. Jessica began laughing, too, and fell flat on her face.

Rialla stood up, concerned, "Are you okay, Jessica?"

Jessica was making noises on the floor. Rialla couldn't tell if Jessica was laughing or crying. Finally, Jessica had the strength to roll over and clearly laughed.

"Please, no more. I can't do this anymore." Jessica kept trying to stop laughing.

Rialla watched Jessica sit up. "Do you have to go now?"

"Yeah, I need to get some sleep. You want me to check in on you tomorrow?"

"That would be good," Rialla responded.

Jessica found a column to grab and used it to pull herself up. Rialla did her best not to laugh at Jessica as she attempted to stand up. While staring at the column, Jessica spoke to Rialla, "I know you're watching me, bitch. I know you want to laugh at my ass right now, but I'm begging you, please don't."

Rialla smiled and covered her mouth to hold back her laugh. She couldn't comprehend what was happening and why she responded to Jessica this way. Nothing in her Xanoclax training prepared her for this. All Rialla had known her whole life was war. This warmth, although new and strange to her, was a welcoming change from the brutal warrior ways of Xanstar.

Jessica finally stood up. She held on to the column as if her life depended on it. She slowly made it to the next column. After she got about 20 feet from Rialla's cell, she turned around to look at her one last time.

"Thank you," Jessica said.

"For what?"

"For being nice and talking to me. I enjoyed your company."

"I enjoyed yours too."

Jessica turned away and headed towards the door. She raised her hand without looking back. "See you tomorrow."

Rialla yelled back, "See you tomorrow, bitch!"

Rialla couldn't see Jessica when she yelled one last time. "Stop it!"

Rialla smiled, went to her cot, and finished her glass of wine.

8 MEETINGS AND SUCH

The next day, Jessica had several meetings with different congressmen and women. These were introductory meetings with other committee panel members. The discussions aimed to gain more insight into the agendas for each committee briefing scheduled for the next day and for Jessica to better understand what was expected from her.

The day trudged on as she went from one meeting to the next. The wine headache she was dealing with made it more challenging to get through the meetings than it should have been. She did her best to be polite and patient. She excused herself several times to go to the restroom. The cold water she splashed on her face and neck made her feel better with each visit.

The hangover she was experiencing wasn't the only cause of her tension. She was anxious to return to the ship and speak with Rialla again. She liked Rialla and was curious to get to know more about her.

It's not every day you make friends with a bitch from another planet, she thought.

This thought caused Jessica to let out a small laugh, to the bewilderment of the senators talking to her.

"Did I say something funny, Ms. Morales?"

"No, Senator, I apologize. I drifted off and thought of something else. Please forgive my rudeness, sir."

"I hope we don't bore you in tomorrow's committee meeting." Jessica's outburst had visibly perturbed the senator.

"Sir, I assure you the committee will have my 100% attention. Again, I sincerely apologize for my sudden outburst. I meant no disrespect."

"Very well, Ms. Morales. I hope you are right. Goodnight." The senators stood up, shaking their heads and going their separate ways. Jessica sighed and started for the exit. She walked down the hall to the restroom again. When it was empty, she pressed the dial of the watch Oz gave her. The device signaled Oz, who promptly tightbeamed Jessica back to the ship.

"How did it go?" Oz asked.

Jessica stepped sideways to her left and then back to her right. She paused and took a breath. "Teleportation is dope."

Oz shrugged her shoulders, "This isn't Star Trek; it's called tightbeaming."

Jessica smiled at Oz, "You say tomato."

Oz looked puzzled as Jessica walked by her out of the tightbeam room.

Jessica dropped her bookbag containing her research and notes to the floor. She rubbed her shoulder and slowly turned her neck in a circle to stretch it.

"I am so glad that today is over."

"That bad, huh?"

"It's boring crap, to begin with, but when you add a hangover to it, it's like hell."

"Your head still hurts?"

"Yeah. I just want to lie down and sleep this off."

Oz opened her hand and showed Jessica two small, white capsules. "This will get rid of that headache."

"I am very tempted, but I have a thing against putting drugs into my body."

"Isn't alcohol a drug?"

"Come on, Oz, do we have to have a debate on alcohol versus drugs right now? I'm so tired."

"I was just wondering what the difference was."

Jessica looked at Oz and smiled, "I'm sorry, I shouldn't have barked at you. I have a thing against drugs because my sister died of an overdose. The drugs were given to her by a doctor. She became depressed and eventually decided to swallow as many pills as she could."

"I apologize for asking. I didn't mean to pry."

"It's all good," Jessica said quietly and hugged Oz.

Oz nodded, "No problem, I can wake you up later if you want?"

"That would be great, thanks." Jessica headed to her room but stopped and turned to face Oz again.

"Is Pete here?"

"No, he's meeting Maggie and Bill at the Capitol Building."

"Are they coming here afterward?"

"I believe so."

"Cool, it would be nice to see them. Don't forget to wake me in a few hours, okay?"

"No problem."

"Thank you, Oz."

Jessica headed to her room. She wanted to stop and say hello to Rialla, but she knew she wouldn't sleep if she did. Jessica got to her bed and didn't bother to undress. She fell onto the bed with a large sigh and promptly fell asleep.

***

"Pete!" Maggie yelled and ran to greet him on the steps of the Cannon House Office Building. Bill walked after her.

Maggie got to Pete and threw her arms around him. She kissed him on the cheek and stepped back. "Look at you, dressed like a movie star trying to avoid the paparazzi."

Pete wore his trenchcoat, the same hat, and sunglasses when he met Jessica at the airport.

"Yeah, being the most popular kid in class is tough." They both laughed. Pete turned to Bill and shook his hand. "It's good to see you, sheriff," Pete smiled.

Bill smiled back, "You too, Pete."

They started walking up the building steps, side by side, with Pete in the middle. Pete looked at Maggie. "How was the trip?"

"Not bad, except for the old worrywart over there. All he did was complain about how he wouldn't fit into the D.C. landscape."

Bill spoke up. "Not the whole way."

"No, that's true. You did sleep for some of the trip."

The three laughed as they made their way through the front door.

When they reached the security guard, Pete asked for Congresswoman Crandall. The security guard made a call and told them the Congresswoman would be right down. The guard kept staring at Pete, trying to figure out if he had seen him before, as he asked them to sign the attendance sheet. Once they finished, they were given a visitor's pass and asked to sit in the waiting area.

Crandall walked up to them with a big smile on her face. She greeted Bill and Maggie and then addressed Pete. "I like the outfit." She smiled at him.

"Thanks," Pete said.

"Come on upstairs. I have a few other congressmen interested in what you have to say. Follow me."

They all headed toward the elevators. Once inside, Pete noticed Crandall's perfume. The scent was subtle, with a clean spring odor and a touch of flowers. The perfume made Pete smile. He liked the fact that he had a response to the aroma. Crandall looked over at Pete a few times during the ride, smiling. Pete couldn't help but notice how beautiful she was. Her blonde hair fell neatly below her shoulders, and her black-framed glasses accented her facial features perfectly. Her figure made the boring gray suit look more like a fashion statement than office attire. *It's nice to have some of my feelings back*, he thought.

Crandall stepped out of the elevator first. "Right this way, please."

Everyone followed her down the hallway to a conference room. She held the door open as Pete, Bill, and Maggie stepped in. Inside the conference room was a long, thick, wooden table with at least two dozen chairs swarming around it. Three other people were already sitting at the table, all dressed in suits.

Crandall started introductions as the three senators stood up to greet the group. "Okay, I believe you all know Representative Higgins from Mississippi."

Bill perked up. "Yes, sir, it is a pleasure to meet you. I'm a big supporter of yours."

Maggie chimed in, "I am as well, sir. Thank you for your work with our innercity youth."

Pete shook the senator's hand. "Pleasure to meet you, sir."

Higgins smiled at the three of them. "The pleasure is all mine."

Higgins stood about six feet tall and had a grey mustache. He was African-American and very popular as a hands-on government official in his home state. No one ran against him because he was so well-liked.

Crandall continued with the introductions. "Over here, we have Congresswoman Frazier from New York and Representative Johnson from Alabama."

Frazier was the shortest of the four representatives. She was a heavy-set African-American woman in her 60s. Like Higgins, she had a reputation as a hands-on official back home in New York. Pete noticed that Frazier had a serious look on her face during the introductions. It was apparent to Pete that someone, or something, was bothering her.

Johnson was an older white man and the opposite of Frazier in terms of attitude. He was medium height and wore a black suit with a red tie. He talked with a heavy southern drawl. "It's a pleasure to meet ya'll," he grinned. Pete noticed that as they were all taking their seats, Frazier made a point to sit on the opposite side of the table from Johnson.

Crandall was the first to speak. "Great. Now that all the introductions are handled, let's get down to business."

Maggie started to shake her leg under the table. Bill looked at her and put his hand on her leg to calm her down, but he failed to slow Maggie's shaking. He laughed internally, thinking about how easy it was for Maggie to stop him when he did the same thing. Maggie smiled, realizing she was taking a page from Bill's how-to-act-nervous book. She put her briefcase on the table and waited for her opportunity to speak.

Crandall continued, "First, on behalf of the senate, may I personally thank Pete for saving all the dignitaries at the meeting two weeks ago. We are all in your debt, sir."

The four representatives clapped, and each expressed their gratitude. Pete took his hat off and brushed his hair back with his hand. Then he took off the sunglasses and smiled. "No need for that. I'm glad everything turned out okay."

"Well, sir, it would have been a lot worse if you didn't do what you did," Johnson spoke in his southern drawl.

Frazier agreed, "Yes, thank you very much."

Pete nodded and anxiously waited for Crandall to change the subject back to the purpose of the meeting. Crandall smiled, noticing Pete's shyness made him uncomfortable, and moved on.

"The four of us have decided to discuss a few ideas Ms. Carter presented. If these ideas have merit and benefit the people of this country, we will arrange a hearing to get discussions started with other legislators. But first, Ms. Carter will need a sponsor to get her before the appropriate House committee."

Pete and Bill looked at each other. They were confused about the whole process. They looked at Maggie sitting at the table quietly, still shaking her legs.

Johnson spoke up first. "Ms. Carter, I'm having a little difficulty understanding how this new anti-racism task force you propose will work."

Maggie stood up, pushed her chair back slightly, and looked at Bill. Bill smiled and nodded his support.

Maggie began, "Well, sir, I believe the affliction has afforded us a unique opportunity to start a program that will enable us to, if you will, police the police."

"Yes, ma'am," Johnson smiled. "I understand your intentions, but I question if it is ethical to single out people just because they are afflicted."

Frazier spoke up. "I don't see a problem with using the affliction to help us identify potential candidates for rehabilitation."

Johnson responded, "With all due respect, I would think you, of all people, would be offended by any attempt to single out individuals based on hearsay instead of fact."

Frazier refused to back down. Sarcastically, she said, "With all due respect to you, sir, the affliction is now a fact, not hearsay."

Everyone could feel the tension building between the two senators sitting across from each other. The atmosphere in the room was becoming increasingly uncomfortable. Crandall stood up from her seat and looked at Pete.

"Pete, you asked us for this meeting with Ms. Carter. What is your take on whether we should use the affliction as a tool to help identify individuals as possible future threats?"

Maggie and Bill turned to Pete. Pete knew they depended on him for support.

"Ms. Crandall, I don't think Ms. Carter's proposal suggests that whoever is afflicted is a potential threat. It is identifying individuals in positions of power with the affliction to get them the support they need. More importantly, I believe the Wen gave this planet an incredible opportunity."

"In what way?"

"This country and the rest of the world have a chance for a do-over. Maybe by looking at this as an opportunity instead of a burden, everyone would understand that."

"So you're saying Ms. Carter's proposal is the best way to start our do-over?"

Pete looked at Maggie and smiled. He looked back at the four senators sitting and listening intently.

"I'm saying everyone in this room can make something good out of all this. Ms. Carter's proposal is a plan that can be expanded and improved when more representatives become involved. If the house can commit its support for Ms. Carter's proposal, I believe this country will achieve great progress in eliminating opportunities for racist acts."

Crandall and Higgins both clapped. Frazier stood up and clapped as well. Johnson, not to be left out, stood slowly and clapped. Bill and Maggie stood and clapped along with the congressmen.

Crandall said, "You should think about going into politics, sir. "You are an effective speaker."

Pete looked at everyone. "I just answered your question, that's all."

Everyone laughed, even Frazier. Crandall addressed the senators.

"I believe the proposal to start a department to 'police the police,' as Ms. Carter stated, is worth serious consideration."

Frazier spoke next. "People of color will never trust the police unless we make a serious effort to change the arrogance of law enforcement. There are too many examples of police officers going out of their way to disrespect people of color."

Johnson interrupted Frazier, "If you look at it on a case-by-case basis, you will often see the officers are following protocols."

Frazier raised her voice, "Is it protocol to drag a 65-year-old woman out of her car because she's too frightened of the police to get out? Is it protocol to shoot and kill an unarmed teenage boy? Sir, we have a serious problem with the 'protocol' against people of color. And only a fool would try to defend the actions of these officers."

"I am not defending these actions. But these men and women are risking their lives to protect our communities. We have to allow them the benefit of the doubt. Mr. Jackson, you are a law enforcement officer, sir, are you not?"

Bill looked surprised. "Yes, sir. I am the sheriff of Bends Creek, Mississippi."

"Sir, what do you say about all this? Do you believe you should be singled out and rehabilitated as an officer of the law?"

Bill stood up even though he was unprepared to participate in the meeting. He was concerned about messing up Maggie's opportunity. "Sir, I am a third-generation law officer. It's all I ever wanted to be. I was fortunate enough to be raised by a Southern father who would not allow racists around his children. He was punished both physically and mentally for his beliefs. My father always told me that if the people of the town you protect don't believe you're a good person, they will never trust you."

Johnson looked confused. "I don't understand your answer."

"Sir, if the people of this country believe that the officers sworn to protect them are not good people, then they will never trust them. I support this proposal because, under this action plan, all officers can show that they are good people."

Frazier looked at Johnson and smiled. Johnson glared at Frazier and shifted his body in his chair. She turned to Maggie, "You got a good one there."

Maggie smiled back at her and then looked at Bill. "I know."

Higgins spoke, "I am so very proud of both of you. It is an honor for me to serve as your congressman. Thank you both for representing the good people of Mississippi."

Maggie and Bill responded at the same time, "Thank you, sir."

Crandall agreed to sponsor Maggie's proposal and asked if other senators would join her. The other three decided to support Maggie's proposal.

"There it is then." Crandall said, "We will present Ms. Carter's proposal to the floor this week."

Everyone looked at Maggie. She was sitting at the table with a huge smile on her face. Tears were running down her face.

Crandall asked, "Ms. Carter, are you okay?"

Maggie began laughing. "I've never been better."

9 ROUND TWO

Jessica woke up before Oz came into her room. She rolled out of bed and headed to the shower. She removed her clothes and left them on the floor, where they fell. Jessica entered the shower and let the water run down her head and face. At the same time, she stood there, paralyzed by the water's gratifying sensation. She slowly turned around, never letting the water miss any part of her body. After a few moments, which seemed longer, she washed up, rinsed off, and exited the shower.

Stepping out of the shower, she realized she had forgotten a towel. She looked around the room and saw a towel hanging on the wall.

"Thanks, Oz," she called out. She wrapped the towel around her body and headed out of the bathroom. Oz had picked up her clothes off the floor, and her suitcase was on her bed. Jessica smiled and found some clothes to wear.

Jessica headed to the control room, looking for Oz. She found her sitting at the control panel.

"What's up, girlfriend? Thanks for the towel and for setting me up."

Oz was staring at the screen on the wall. Without turning, she answered, "No problem."

Jessica felt like there was something wrong with the way Oz had answered. "Is everything okay?"

Oz turned away from the screen to face Jessica. "I know you're trying to help by making friends with the Xan. But you need to know more about who you're dealing with."

"What are you talking about?"

"I want to show you something." Oz played the same video of Cass that she showed Pete.

Jessica gasped, "That was horrible!"

"That's what you're dealing with, Jessica. These beings are heartless and cruel."

"Oz, I understand what you're saying. And I know how hurt you are by this, but maybe not all the Xanoclax are like this."

"I don't understand how you and Pete can be so illogical regarding these creatures. All they want to do is kill and become the superior universal race. Why can't you see that?"

"Oz, maybe you're right. Maybe they want to rule over the universe. But what if there are some Xans that don't want to be a part of universal domination? What if some Xans want to live in peace? Do we turn our backs on them as well?"

"I see why Pete has strong feelings for you, Jessica. You have a very optimistic way of looking at the world. But I have seen the Xan in action. I have seen the results of their savagery against weaker beings. It is difficult to see the Xan locked in a cell on my spaceship as anything but a threat."

"Oz, you have every right to feel the way you do. I am not defending the Xan in any way. All I am saying is that Rialla seems different to me. She doesn't come across as a barbarian who lusts for killing."

"Just be careful. I wouldn't want to lose you, too."

Jessica smiled and walked over to Oz. She pulled her up from her chair and hugged her.

"I know you can't feel what this is emotionally, but humans hug to make someone feel better. It's the human way of telling somebody they care. That they love them." Jessica pulled away from Oz and looked her in the eyes.

"Oz, I love you. You are my sister, and that will never change."

Oz wanted to tell Jessica how she felt and that the earth's atmosphere stimulated her emotional senses. But Oz was unsure about her feelings and didn't want to jump to conclusions. Her logical side cried out to run more tests. Oz just smiled softly and said, "Thank you."

***

Before Jessica walked through the opening to Rialla's room, she heard Rialla.

"Glad you decided to show up, bitch."

Jessica strolled around the corner of the short wall and saw Rialla's face light up. Rialla was standing at the glass.

"Bitch, don't get me started." Jessica laughed, and Rialla joined her.

"I'm glad you decided to come back."

"Me too."

"Did you bring the wine?"

"Hell no, I didn't bring any wine! I'm still hurting from last night."

"Why do you hurt? Was it not pleasant for you?"

"It was really great. It was so great, I had a wicked hangover today."

"Hangover?"

"How did you feel when you woke up this morning?"

"Like I usually do. Why?"

"You don't know how lucky you are. When we drink too much, our body punishes us the next day by giving us a headache and making us feel like we want to puke all day."

"That doesn't sound pleasant."

"It wasn't. So, how was your day?"

"Great. I got to sit in this hellhole all day by myself, wondering if that Vailen dog was going to terminate me somehow."

"Oz isn't a dog. She won't terminate you or hurt you."

"Because her master told her not to."

"It's not just that. Oz agreed to leave you alone. She isn't leaving you alone because she has to; she chooses to."

"I suppose there's a first for everything."

"Yes, there is. Look at us. We're a first, aren't we?"

"I suppose."

"Really? You suppose? How many other human girlfriends do you have?"

"None."

"So this is a first! Lighten up a little."

"How do I do that?"

"By trusting me. I'm not going to hurt you, and I'm not going to ever lie to you. You can trust me. Can I say the same about you?"

"I am not sure."

"Well, if you can't feel the same way about me as I feel about you, then maybe we can't be girlfriends."

Jessica turned around and began walking towards the door.

"Don't go!" Rialla shouted. "You can trust me. I won't lie to you either."

Jessica turned around and walked back to Rialla's cell. Oz had provided a chair in front of the glass for Jessica. She sat down and opened her arms toward Rialla.

"Was that so hard?"

"No. But it was easier with the wine."

Jessica laughed so hard that her head hurt. "Ow."

"What's wrong?"

"I guess I'm still feeling the after-effects of my hangover. You made me laugh too hard."

Rialla started to laugh. "I can't remember the last time I was able to laugh. Laughter feels pleasant."

"We say laughter is the best medicine."

"I can understand that."

Jessica wanted to find out more about Rialla and the Xans. She didn't want to be pushy but knew Rialla had only ten days. Ten days to communicate with Pete and Oz and give them a reason not to hand her over to the Wen Council.

"Rialla, I want to ask you some personal questions, but I don't want to pressure you."

Rialla looked at Jessica for a long moment. "This is where the trust part comes in, right?"

"Yeah, exactly."

"Okay, but if I don't like the question, I will be honest and not answer. I cannot answer any questions concerning the details of my mission."

"Good, I don't want to know about your mission. I want to know about you."

"Really?"

"Yeah. We're friends, right?"

"Yes."

"So, let's get to know each other. Listen, this works both ways. If you want to ask me anything, please ask, okay?"

"Okay."

"Let's start where we left off last night. Why do humans and Xans look so much alike?"

"Not sure. Humans got lucky, I guess."

Jessica laughed. "Come on, be serious."

"Our planet, Xanstar, has many similar characteristics to your planet, Earth. We have an atmosphere close to yours, and we, too, revolve around one star."

"So your species evolved in similar circumstances as we did. There are no extreme elements that you need to adjust to."

"It's the only reason I can think of."

"It's a pretty damn good reason. What about the three rows of teeth? How do you fit all those teeth inside your pretty little mouth?"

"How do you know about that?"

"I saw it."

Rialla looked disappointed. "You saw a dead Xan, didn't you?"

"I'm sorry. Yes, I did." Jessica regretted asking about the dead Xan so nonchalantly.

"Killed by your mate, no doubt?"

Jessica saw that Rialla was getting upset. "Rialla, Pete was defending himself. He doesn't like killing."

Rialla looked down at her feet. She became silent, deep in thought. Jessica decided to wait and see where this contemplation was heading before speaking.

Rialla slowly lifted her head. "This is very difficult to talk about," she said softly.

"I know, I'm sorry I brought it up." Before Jessica could finish her apology, Rialla spoke up.

"We have different classes of warriors. Each class comes from a different region of Xanstar. That particular warrior class hails from the southern region of our planet. They are called Xankrids. During the Quls' rule, the Quls conducted terrible experiments on the Xankrids. The Xankrids evolved with horrible mutations that they have adapted to."

"Thank you," Jessica said. "Your turn, ask me anything."

Rialla looked at Jessica with a puzzled look on her face. "Why is there so much hate on your planet?"

Jessica was startled by the question. She wasn't expecting this type of question from an alien warrior. "Wow, where did that come from?"

"Did I offend you?"

"No, I just wasn't expecting that at all."

"Is it too personal to answer?"

"No, it's not too personal to answer. I can try to answer that, but I can't promise that it will come from an objective point of view. I have been the victim of many hateful attacks simply because I am Hispanic. My skin is a little darker, and I have an accent. That's the reason I get the hate. As far as why people on this planet hate others, I can't give you a logical answer to that."

"It doesn't make sense to me."

"Yeah, well, welcome to my world because it doesn't make sense to me either. Some people on this planet don't need a reason to hate. Hate is justified in their minds with excuses that are logical to them. People hate others over differences like skin color, religious beliefs, and political beliefs. The list of reasons can go on and on. It's easier on our planet to hate someone than to love someone. It's sad, really."

"Maybe if you figure out why you hate each other, you can find solutions to stop."

Jessica looked at Rialla. A few tears rolled down her cheeks.

"I did not mean to upset you."

"You didn't. It just sucks that it takes a being from another planet to state the obvious, and we can't see it for ourselves."

There was silence for a few moments. Jessica wiped her tears and smiled. "You keep surprising me, Rialla from Xanstar."

"And you, me, Jessica of Earth."

Oz was listening in on the conversation. She decided to check the information she had in her database for Xanstar. As Rialla said, their planet was similar to Earth. Oz was surprised when no historical data was on file for the planet Xanstar. It seemed odd to her that there was nothing. Usually, her database had at least a few historical documents on other planets. But Xanstar's file was empty. She decided to look deeper to see if any information existed about Xanstar.

***

Pete tightbeamed Maggie and Bill back to the ship. Oz was at the control panel when they arrived.

Maggie was the first to call out to Oz. "Hey, girlfriend."

Oz turned around from the control panel and approached Maggie's open arms. "How are you, Maggie?"

"I'm wonderful. Our meeting with the congressmen went very well. I'm excited to see what happens next."

"That's great, Maggie. I am glad it went well." Oz turned to Bill, "Hey, sheriff."

Bill walked up to Oz and hugged her. "How are you doing, Oz?"

"Oh, you know. Same shit, different day."

Bill laughed. "I think you've been on this planet too long."

Pete spoke up, "That's what I keep telling her." Pete looked at Oz. "Where's Jessica?"

"She's with the Xan."

Maggie and Bill looked confused. Maggie asked Pete, "Jessica's here, and she's with a Xan?"

Pete gestured to Maggie and Bill on the monitor. They all looked at the screen as Oz turned the volume up. Maggie and Bill watched and listened closely.

"Maybe if you figure out why you hate each other, you can find solutions to stop."

Jessica looked at Rialla. A few tears rolled down her cheeks.

"I did not mean to upset you."

"You didn't. It just sucks that it takes a being from another planet to state the obvious that we can't see for ourselves."

There was silence for a few moments. Jessica wiped her tears and smiled. "You keep surprising me, Rialla from Xanstar."

"And you, me, Jessica of Earth."

Bill looked shocked. "That's a Xan? Is she a visitor?"

Pete replied, "She's a Xan warrior, minus the armor."

Maggie shouted, "No way! I thought the Xan warriors were male!"

Oz looked at Maggie. "Yeah, there's a lot of that going around."

"Wow, a female warrior? It's like a sci-fi fantasy."

Maggie furrowed her eyebrows. "Say what? Females are only warriors in fantasies?"

Bill scrambled for the words to reply. "Oh, shit, I didn't mean it that way."

"Well, it sounded that way. We can kick ass too."

"Oh, I know! Believe me, I know," Bill answered.

Maggie cast Bill a 'we'll talk about this later' look before turning to Pete.

"Pete, what's Jessica doing talking to a Xan warrior?"

"She's trying to find out more about the Xanoclax. Frankly, she's gotten a lot farther than I could have. I don't think the Xan wants to talk to the guy that tried to blow her up."

"You think?" Bill laughed.

"She's built trust with her, and the talks are going well. Would you two like to meet the Xan?"

Bill and Maggie both shook their heads. Pete walked Maggie and Bill to Rialla's room. When they got to the opening of her room, Pete told them to walk in. He was going back to the control panel.

"Knock, knock," Maggie called out from behind the short wall.

Jessica jumped up. "Maggie?"

Maggie turned the corner, and Jessica ran into her arms. "It's so good to see you, Jessica! How have you been?"

"I've been great. Is Bill here too?"

Bill walked around the corner. "I'm here."

Jessica ran up to Bill and hugged him. "It's so good to see you guys. Come in! I want you to meet my new friend."

Bill and Maggie ambled towards the glass. They looked confused. Jessica spoke up, "I know. She looks human, right?"

They nodded.

"Bill, Maggie, this is Rialla from the planet Xanstar. Rialla, these are two good friends of mine, Bill and Maggie."

The couple smiled. "It's nice to meet you, Rialla," Maggie said.

"It's an honor, ma'am," Bill agreed.

Rialla looked at the pair. She tilted her head slightly as though she was trying to figure something out. Jessica looked at the Xan's puzzled face. "What's up, Rialla?"

Rialla looked at Jessica. "These are your friends?"

"Yes. Maggie and Bill are wonderful."

"Why did the male call me 'ma'am'?"

Maggie laughed. "It's a polite, respectful way to address someone you just met for the first time."

Rialla smiled. "Nice to meet you, too, ma'am."

Jessica laughed, "We'll talk more about greetings later. Right now, we can all get to know each other."

Rialla responded, "All of us?"

"Yes. Right now, I have three wonderful friends in the same room. I would love it if everyone got to know each other."

"They can be trusted?"

"With my life."

Bill was standing in awe of Rialla. He continued to stare with his mouth open.

"Why is the male just staring at me? Does he fear me?"

Maggie elbowed Bill in the side to wake him from his trance-like state.

"No, ma'am, I have never seen a warrior from another planet before."

"Do I repulse you?"

"Not all. If you permit me to say this, I think you are quite lovely."

Maggie smacked Bill on the back of the head. "Snap out of it, man."

"I like her," Rialla told Jessica, pointing at Maggie. "Did she just hit her mate?"

Jessica laughed. "Yeah, she did."

"Is she his master?"

Bill answered, "She likes to think so."

Maggie laughed, "I have him trained; that's all I will say."

Bill just nodded.

"You two are mates, but you look different from one another."

"Yes, I'm African-American, and he's, well…he's Bill."

The humans all laughed, and Rialla smiled at the sound of their laughter.

10 SIGHTSEEING

The following day, everyone got up and went about their business. Jessica went to her meetings while Bill and Maggie set out to meet members of the new organization Maggie was spearheading. All three were anxious to get through the day and get back to Rialla. Jessica's meetings ended before lunch, which was earlier than she thought they would, so she was back on the ship first.

"No, no way," Pete said to Jessica.

"Why not? I talked to Oz about it already. She can set a non-removable device around her neck so she can't run off anywhere."

"Jessica, you're asking me to release a Xan warrior into the public."

"She doesn't look like a Xan warrior. I can put some light makeup on her face, and she looks like one of us. Nobody will know who she is."

"What purpose will this serve?"

"If Rialla can see us the way we see us, maybe, just maybe, we can enlist her aid as an ally. Besides, Rialla is running out of time before you send her to the Wen."

"Jessica, what you are trying to do is admirable, but it's also dangerous."

Oz chimed in, "Pete, I will have full control over the Xan at all times."

"I thought you hated her? Why the sudden change of heart?"

"Oh, no. I still hate this Xan bitch. I might get the chance to blow her psycho ass up if she runs."

Pete's eyes widened in response to Oz's comment. He turned to Jessica. "Jessica, do you see how wrong this is on so many levels?"

Jessica looked at Oz and then at Pete. "She's not going to blow anyone up. Oz said the necklace could put out an electrical charge to stun Rialla if she ran. If that happens, which it won't, you can come to pick her up."

"Let's review. You want me to send a Xan warrior out into public with you."

Jessica nodded. "Si."

"The Xan will wear a necklace that she cannot remove."

"Yes."

"Oz will have control over the necklace."

"Yes."

"Oz will monitor everything, and if she deems it necessary, she will press a button and blow the Xan's head off."

"Yes. Wait, no! Oz will stun her, not kill her."

Oz said, "Me like this plan."

"Jessica, Oz hates the Xan."

Jessica walked over to Oz. She looked at Oz, but she was still talking to Pete. "But Oz values our friendship too much to make that kind of mistake, Pete."

Oz shrugged and just nodded slowly in agreement.

Jessica smiled and turned to Pete. "Well?"

"I know I'm going to regret this, but okay."

Jessica screamed, "Thank you so much!"

"But you have to stay away from government buildings," Pete warned her. "You can walk on the Lawn to the museums, but not government facilities."

Jessica was nodding and smiling from ear to ear as though her father had just allowed her to go to a friend's party.

"You have to promise to call me when there's a problem."

"Yes, Papi."

Jessica ran back to Rialla's room. Rialla came to the glass with a worried look on her face.

"Is everything okay, Jessica?"

The glass began rising, and Rialla stepped back. She looked at Jessica, who was jumping up and down excitedly like a little girl.

Rialla looked confused. "I don't understand." The glass had fully retracted. There was only open space now between her and Jessica.

Jessica walked up to Rialla. "I trust you."

Rialla looked at Jessica and smiled. She heard a click come from her neck. She felt the necklace that Oz put on her. She looked up at Jessica. "But you're the only one who does, I see."

Jessica sighed. "You have to earn their trust, Rialla. I'm sure that won't be a problem."

"So, what's this all about?"

"Well, I convinced my mate to let you come outside with me for a walk around the area."

Rialla smiled. "And the necklace is insurance?"

"When you negotiate, you have to give a little. By the way, how do you like your new threads?"

"Threads?"

"Yeah, I picked them out myself."

Rialla looked at her arms and realized she was wearing different clothes. Something felt strange on her feet. When she looked down, she noticed she was wearing pink sneakers.

"What are these?"

"Sneakers. We'll be doing a lot of walking. You need to be comfortable. You also have jeans, a black T-shirt, and a light blue hoodie. You're ready, girl!"

Rialla didn't move. Something still didn't feel right to her. She didn't understand why this Earthling was so kind to her. Was this a trick or a trap?

Jessica noticed Rialla's hesitation. "What's wrong?"

In a soft, quiet voice, Rialla said, "I don't understand any of this."

"What's to understand? It's only two girls going for a walk, enjoying the day and each other's company, that's all."

Rialla slowly walked away from her cell. She hesitated and turned her gaze back for one more look. She then turned her head back towards Jessica and smiled.

Jessica was in front, and Rialla was close behind when they entered the control room.

Pete walked up to Rialla. "I want you to know I was against this."

Rialla said, "I assumed as much."

"Make no mistake, Xan warrior, if any harm befalls this woman, I will hold you accountable."

Jessica had never heard Pete talk this way. He was confident and commanding.

Rialla nodded. She looked over at Oz. "I assume you are the one who has control of this device around my neck?"

Oz just waved goodbye to Rialla and said nothing.

Jessica was still excited. "Okay, I have my tracking device on, check. I have a quarter to make a phone call; if I need anything, check."

Everyone looked at her in confusion.

"Sike! Lighten up already," Jessica laughed.

Pete tightbeamed Jessica and Rialla just outside the fenced area on the Lawn.

Jessica tilted her head towards the clear blue sky and closed her eyes. She loved how the heat from the afternoon sun felt on her face. She opened her eyes and looked over at Rialla. She was looking upwards towards the sun with her eyes wide open.

"Your sun's heat reminds me of home. It feels good on my face."

"I love the way it feels on my face, too. Doesn't that hurt your eyes, staring at the direct sunlight?"

"No, we have auto sensors that filter out the harmful rays. Much like your sunglasses."

Jessica smiled. "Cool. Come on, let's go."

"Where?"

"Who cares? Let's walk and see where we end up."

They walked across the Lawn among the crowds of people. Rialla observed a few children running by them, chased by their parents. They walked past an older couple strolling across the lawn, laughing and holding hands.

Jessica and Rialla ended up in front of a food vendor on a side street. The vendor inside the food truck spoke to Rialla, "What will it be?"

Rialla looked at Jessica and then back at the vendor. "Wine."

The vendor laughed and looked at Jessica, "Your friend is a comedienne?"

Jessica smiled back, "She's not from around here. Why don't you get us two dogs loaded and two sodas, please?"

"Coming right up."

Rialla looked at Jessica and smiled. "This place smells good."

"Yeah, it's hard to resist a good loaded dog and soda."

Jessica paid the vendor, and he thanked both of them. Rialla nodded to the vendor. Jessica went to the side of the truck where the condiments were. She picked up a few ketchup packets and told Rialla to do the same. The packets were side by side on the condiment stand. Rialla watched Jessica open a ketchup packet and squeeze it onto the top of her hot dog. Rialla took a ketchup packet and opened it, quickly squeezing the packet. The contents squirted out abruptly. A small amount of ketchup went onto her hot dog, while the remainder flew over the hot dog and onto the grass.

Rialla looked at Jessica. "I don't understand. Why did mine explode?"

Jessica laughed. "You have to squeeze it slowly, like this." Jessica opened a packet and squeezed it onto Rialla's hot dog.

Jessica took a bite of her hot dog and motioned to Rialla to do likewise. Rialla was hesitant. She took a small bite, and her eyes widened with surprise. Jessica nodded and smiled at her. Rialla looked at Jessica, smiled, and put the hot dog in her mouth. She extended her mouth more than normal for a human, so broad that it frightened Jessica.

"Holy crap, Rialla!" Jessica shouted.

"What?" Rialla chewed three times, and she was finished.

Jessica approached Rialla and whispered, "You can't do that publicly. You'll freak everyone out."

"I just consumed the hot dog as you did."

"No, not quite like I did. I didn't stretch my mouth out wider than my body to fit it in my mouth."

"Oh, sorry," Rialla apologized.

"No need to be sorry, just be careful, okay? Did you even taste it?"

"Yes, it was delicious. Can we have another?"

"Just one more. You have to be careful when eating these things. Too many will make you sick."

Rialla took another hot dog from the vendor. As Jessica paid the vendor, she watched Rialla go to the condiment island and take a ketchup packet. She noticed how careful Rialla was as she squeezed the packet gently over the hot dog. She felt like a proud teacher watching her student repeat her lesson

Rialla turned around to Jessica and held up her hot dog, which she had successfully coated with her ketchup. She slowly opened her mouth and took a human-sized bite. She gestured to Jessica, imploring approval. Jessica smiled and gave Rialla a celebratory thumbs-up.

Jessica walked over to Rialla and smiled. They stared at each other for what seemed to be the longest time. Rialla gazed at Jessica as she slowly reached up to Rialla's face and wiped some ketchup off the side of her mouth with a napkin. Jessica pulled her hand back slowly, and they smiled at each other.

Jessica was excited to show the museums to Rialla. She started with the Smithsonian National Museum of Natural History. It had become her favorite after her mother and father had taken her there when she was seven years old.

Rialla walked into the museum and immediately stared at the giant mastodon. Her head was constantly looking up at the animal. Jessica smiled and took her hand to guide her from walking into other people. Rialla just gawked at the giant elephant in amazement.

She finally looked at Jessica. "What is this beast?"

"This is a mastodon. It lived over a million years ago. Mastodons are a part of our past that this museum shares with the public."

"It's an amazing beast."

"Yes, it was. Do you want to see more?"

"Yes."

They walked around the museum, stopping at every exhibit. The exhibits that were larger than life seemed to appeal to Rialla the most. At each, Jessica answered Rialla's questions. It was the longest time Jessica had ever spent in her favorite museum. They could have spent even more time there, but Jessica wanted Rialla to see a few other museums.

"Rialla, let's go to another museum, okay?"

"Do we have to go?"

Jessica looked at Rialla. Her face was that of an innocent child wanting more, bringing back memories of her childhood visit to the museum with her parents.

"Yes. I promise you'll like the next museum."

Rialla reluctantly followed Jessica through the crowd of visitors towards the exit. As they walked down the stairs, Rialla looked at all the people. She stopped just a few steps down, observing the surrounding area. It was as though she noticed all the people for the first time.

"They all come and visit these museums?"

"Yes," Jessica answered, standing next to Rialla.

"For pleasure?"

"Yes, and for educational reasons."

Rialla sauntered down the stairs, noticing how different everyone looked. "You have a variety of human species, don't you?"

Jessica laughed. "This isn't half of it. Come on, let's go to the next one."

Jessica took Rialla's hand and led her out the door. At the top of the stairs, Rialla stopped and looked around curiously at all the people.

"I don't understand."

Jessica guided Rialla down the stairs and out of the way of all the people scurrying around the museum.

"What don't you understand?" Jessica asked, looking at Rialla.

"All these different species of humans are getting along."

"Why does that confuse you?"

"If everyone appears to get along with each other, where does the hate originate? I see different species laughing and being friendly with each other everywhere in this area."

Jessica smiled at Rialla. "Unfortunately, in our world, we publicize hateful acts instead of concentrating on all the good people."

"I don't understand," Rialla said, looking at Jessica.

Jessica sighed. "Hateful and violent acts sell newspapers and get more hits on the internet than acts of kindness."

"That is not logical."

"Welcome to Earth, Rialla. The most illogical planet in the galaxy."

They both laughed and began walking towards the Space Museum. Rialla was observing all the people and seemed to be enjoying herself. When they entered the Space Museum, she became excited. She looked up and around, and Jessica had difficulty keeping up with her. Rialla blended into the crowd, and Jessica lost sight of her. She began to panic.

Jessica looked around nervously. Then she began thinking terrible thoughts.

Was Rialla playing me?

Did I set her up for a perfect moment to escape?

Jessica reached into her pocket and pulled out her communication device. She hesitated for a moment before placing her thumb on the call button.

"What's up?" Rialla stood behind Jessica, smiling. "I turned around and couldn't see you."

Jessica slid the device into her pocket.

"Please stay close to me. You worried me. I thought you were lost."

"Sorry, I guess I got a little too excited."

"No problem," Jessica smiled.

"This is all interesting, but it's primitive technology. I don't think I have ever seen technology like this."

"Yeah, we've come a long way, tech-wise."

"From this, you have, but you still have a long way to go."

Jessica smiled as the two friends walked out of the museum. "It's best we pace ourselves. We don't want to have people who are less caring of others have more power in their hands. We already have a problem controlling all the guns. I can't imagine the destruction a laser gun would cause in the wrong hands."

"That is a wise statement, Jessica." Rialla smiled.

The orange and red glow of the setting sun reminded Jessica to look at her watch.

"It's getting late. We need to head back."

Rialla looked disappointed, but she understood. "Will we be able to do this again?"

"As long as I don't piss off Papi, we will. He wants us back before nightfall, so we must start back."

Jessica picked up her device and called Pete.

"Is everything all right? Are you okay?" Pete answered the phone.

Jessica laughed. "Hello to you, too."

Pete calmed down. "Sorry. I think I was anxious."

"It's all good. It shows you're feeling something."

Pete continued, "Did you find an isolated area from which I can beam you back?"

"Yup, we're ready."

Pete transported Jessica and Rialla back. Jessica walked Rialla back to her cell. Rialla stopped in front of the entrance and turned to Jessica.

"I can't ever remember a time in my existence that I went a full day without physical pain. Whether it was pain from fighting or training, every day consisted of some level of pain inflicted upon my body."

Jessica's face saddened. "I'm sorry, Rialla."

Rialla smiled. "Please do not apologize. You have shown me experiences outside of my sensory perceptions. I am feeling confused but happy at the same time. Thank you, Jessica."

Jessica smiled and put her arms around Rialla's upper body. Rialla's body tensed, and her eyes widened. She didn't understand why Jessica was attacking her. But when Jessica squeezed her gently, Rialla smiled and returned the hug. Rialla didn't want to let her go.

Jessica laughed, "I take it that this is your first hug?"

Rialla was squeezing Jessica. "Yes."

"You have to let go now," Jessica laughed softly under her breath.

Rialla let Jessica go and apologized.

"No need to apologize, Rialla. A hug is how humans show they care about one another. We hug each other to let the person know we are there if they need anything and that they mean so much to us."

Rialla smiled softly at Jessica. "Thank you."

Jessica smiled back. "Thank you for trusting me."

Rialla nodded, turned away from Jessica, and went to her cot. The glass barrier slowly descended from the ceiling. Jessica looked at Rialla the entire time, and Rialla looked back, smiling. They nodded slightly to each other. Jessica turned and walked out of the room.

***

Jessica and Rialla spent afternoons and early evenings around the Lawn for the next three days. Jessica, keeping with protocol, would always call Pete when they were ready to return, and he would tightbeam them back to the ship.

When they were ready to return on the fourth day, Jessica called Pete. "We're all done, Papi, she laughed.

Pete laughed, saying, "Hold tight, I'll bring you back."

Jessica interrupted quickly, "Listen, I want to walk back instead of beaming in. Will that be ok?"

Pete hesitated, but he knew if Jessica wanted to walk back, he would have difficulty convincing her otherwise. "OK, just make sure you don't get sidetracked and take too long. Call me when you're ready."

"Thanks, Papi." Jessica laughed and turned off her device.

"We're good to walk home. Gives us a little more time outside in this beautiful weather."

Rialla looked at Jessica. "I still don't understand why you are doing all this."

Jessica smiled, "Rialla, you don't need a reason to be nice to someone."

"Very logical. You keep surprising me, Jessica of Earth."

"And you, I, Rialla of Xanstar."

The sunset disappeared behind the buildings, and the lights around the park came on. Jessica and Rialla walked down the sidewalk, turned right onto the Lawn, and started towards the spaceship. Neither saw the figure jump out from behind one of the trees until he came upon them.

Rialla turned around first, and Jessica followed. The man wore a biker's sleeveless denim vest and torn jeans. He was a muscular figure and taller than Rialla. The figure began moving slowly toward Jessica.

Jessica yelled, "Rialla, run!" She grabbed Rialla's hand and tugged her. Rialla began running and passed Jessica quickly. It was Rialla's turn to pull Jessica. The figure caught up to Jessica and tackled her from behind. They both hit the ground, and Jessica released Rialla's hand as she fell. Rialla took a few more steps and then turned back toward Jessica. The figure pulled Jessica up by her hood, and Jessica screamed.

Rialla moved towards the figure slowly; he was in the light now. It was Bronson Pike. He began laughing as he looked over Jessica while still clinging to her hood tightly.

"It seems you're worth some big money, bitch," Pike snarled.

Jessica looked at Pike, shocked. "What the hell are you talking about?"

"Some important people want you dead. I need to send a message to your alien boyfriend, spic."

Jessica tried swinging at Pike, then tried to kick him. He was too strong and tall. She couldn't reach him from the position he held her in. She yelled out, "Freak you, you racist pig."

Rialla hit Pike on the head with her fist. Pike stutter-stepped back in surprise. "You hit hard for a girl," he laughed. Jessica was able to shake free when Pike moved backward.

Rialla stood there defiantly. "You have attacked my friend. Now you deal with me."

Pike snarled and then laughed. He pulled a long-bladed knife from his knife holster. The light from the park lamps reflected off the metal blade. The reflection made the knife appear more threatening.

Rialla watched and waited for Pike to make his move. Pike darted forward and thrust the knife towards Rialla. Before she could counter, Jessica jumped in front of the knife. Pike's weapon penetrated her back, and she yelled out in pain. Rialla fell backward onto the ground with Jessica in her arms. The knife remained in Pike's hand as he laughed and ran away. A policeman who saw the incident rushed to Jessica.

"Miss, are you okay?" The policeman asked.

"I could be better," laughed Jessica as Rialla slowly turned her body onto the grass. Rialla sat on the ground, holding Jessica's head in her lap.

A pool of blood began to rush out from under Jessica's body, soaking the grass below her. "Hang on, miss," the policeman said. He called for an ambulance and assistance to pursue Pike.

Rialla took off her hooded sweatshirt and placed it under Jessica's back to try to stop the bleeding. Jessica looked up at Rialla and noticed the concerned look on Rialla's face.

"No worries, girlfriend," she spoke softly. "It will all be okay. Please tell Pete I'm sorry."

Rialla looked down at Jessica. "For what?"

"For not coming back sooner," she tried to laugh, but it came out as a cough. Blood started to trickle from the corner of her mouth.

Rialla watched as Jessica closed her eyes. Rialla lifted her left hand from under Jessica's body, covered in blood. Rialla looked up at the sky and let out a pained scream.

11 LETTING GO

Pete walked into Jessica's hospital room. He saw her lying on the bed with tubes in her arms and a mask over her nose and mouth. He slowly walked up to the bed and caressed her hair. He knew he should be crying, but he couldn't. The pain was there, tearing at his insides, but he was at a loss to express it. He wanted to hold Jessica and tell her that everything would be okay. But he knew it was far from all right. For the first time, he was second-guessing his assessment of a situation. For the first time, he felt panic. For the first time, he felt fear.

The doctor standing next to the bed spoke up. "The laceration was deep. We believe one of the kidneys was damaged, and we are attempting to control the internal bleeding."

Pete looked at the doctor. "How long will it take until she leaves the ICU?"

The doctor shrugged his shoulders. "That all depends on her system. The next few hours are critical."

The doctor walked out of the room. Pete turned from the bed and noticed Rialla sitting on a chair in a dark corner of the room. He walked up to her and glared at her angrily.

"What happened?" he asked in an angry, rough voice.

Rialla stood up and looked over at Jessica. She turned to Pete and quietly said, "She stepped before me and took the blade intended for me."

Pete walked up to Rialla and started yelling. "If I had let Oz kill you, none of this would have happened. By keeping you alive, I may have killed Jessica."

Rialla nodded. "I agree. It is my fault." She knelt on both knees in front of Pete. Her head was hanging down as she stared at the floor before her. In a voice that she didn't recognize, she apologized.

"I deeply regret causing harm to Jessica. Please end my life in honor of this great human being."

Pete raised his right hand as it began to energize. He looked down at Rialla as she knelt silently, awaiting her fate. Pete yelled out angrily as he fired an energy blast.

Rialla looked behind her and saw the hole in the wall made by Pete's blast. She looked up at Pete. "Please, end my life. I need to right this wrong."

Pete looked down at Rialla. "Stand up. Get off your knees, Xanoclax. Your death will not justify what has happened here. Jessica would not want you to end like this. Do you want to honor her? Find out why this happened and who was responsible."

Rialla sank back into the chair in the darkness of the room. She wanted to be invisible. She was not sure if it was out of sadness or shame. Perhaps it was both.

Pete, Krix'x is coming, as you requested. Oz reported telepathically.

Static appeared on the TV hanging on the wall in the hospital room. Then, as quickly as the static appeared, it was gone. A bright blue light radiated from the screen and filled the room. Rialla sank further into her dark corner. The blue light slowly faded, and Krix'x's face appeared on the screen. He looked around at his surroundings before moving tentatively through the screen. His face came out and stopped at the foot of Jessica's bed. A long, blue, tube-like trail extended from inside the TV, connecting to the back of his head and keeping him floating in the air.

Krix'x looked over the situation and then addressed Pete. "Why have I been summoned to this place?"

Pete looked at Krix'x and spoke. "I need your help."

"To do what?"

"I need you to save this woman's life."

"I cannot."

"Bullshit!" Pete yelled at Krix'x. "You can, and you will."

Krix'x looked at Pete. The look on his face was one of surprise. Pete later deduced that this was the first time anyone dared raise their voice to Krix'x. That explained the puzzled look and the momentary pause in his response.

Krix'x's face floated towards Pete and stopped in front of him. Krix'x looked Pete over as if he were analyzing him. "What has changed, J9-1-7? There is something different about you now. Vailen, report!" Krix'x called for Oz.

Oz appeared beside Pete with a tablet in her hand. She looked at Pete and then at Krix'x. "My report is as follows." Oz went on. "J9-1-7 has regained some of his emotional capabilities. He is not at a 100% level, but it is improving. His capability to express human feelings is also progressing."

Krix'x looked at Pete. "This explains your attachment to this human female. She is not of concern to us. I advise you to leave her to her fate."

Pete took a step closer to Krix'x. "I advise you to heal her immediately."

"And if I do nothing?"

"I will refuse to help you any further. I will not come to your planet and train other heralds."

"And Earth? What happens to Earth if you decline to help?"

"I'll help Earth because it is my home. But I will no longer assist you in any way whatsoever."

Krix'x looked at Jessica and then at Pete. "You do realize my help comes with a price."

"I'll pay your price; just help her."

"Oh, I know you will, J9-1-7. That is not what I am referring to."

"What then?"

"Your human female will lose all prior memories and feelings. She won't know who you are, J9-1-7. You will be a stranger to her."

Pete turned away from Krix'x and ambled over to Jessica. He leaned over and kissed her forehead, stroking her hair lightly. Pete replied to Krix'x. "Do whatever you have to do." He never took his eyes off Jessica.

Rialla had never witnessed unselfish behavior like this in the past. Sadness overcame Rialla as Pete stared at Jessica. Rialla was confused and didn't understand why her head and body were acting so strangely.

Krix'x responded, "Very well. Let's begin."

A sound came from Jessica. Pete could not distinguish it and removed the mask from her mouth.

In a soft, weak voice, Jessica moaned, "No, Pete, don't." Her eyes were barely open as she spoke.

Pete looked down at her and smiled, "Don't do what, Jessica?"

She squeezed his hand and forced a smile through the pain. "Pete, I don't want to lose my memories of us and how I feel about you."

Pete placed his free hand over her head and leaned closer to her. He felt tears begin to trickle slowly down his cheeks. He smiled gently, "Jessica, I can't lose you."

"If they fix this, you will lose me, Pete. And I will lose you."

"But you will live. You can go on living."

"Pete, I am living thanks to you. I will never be as happy as I am right now. Please understand."

Pete didn't know what to do. His mind began filling with random thoughts that had no meaning. His hand shook as he stroked her hair. He bent down closer and kissed her gently.

"Jessica, I don't want to lose you. I can't do this without you."

"Pete," Jessica replied softly, "You don't need me. You are the strongest and kindest person I know. Oz and Rialla will look after you."

Jessica's breathing began changing. She was taking deeper, shorter breaths.

"Hold me, Pete. Please hold me," Jessica spoke between breaths.

Pete took off his coat and let it drop to the floor. He carefully climbed onto the bed and pulled Jessica close to him. Her face was on his chest, and Pete lay his chin gently on her head. He smelled her hair. He wanted to capture the scent of her hair and keep it with him forever.

Jessica felt Pete's energy, and her body became lighter. Her pain disappeared, and she began breathing regularly. She smiled and slipped into the familiar euphoria of their connection.

"Pete?"

"Yes?"

"Don't let me go."

Pete squeezed her tighter. "Never, Jessica, never."

Rialla never cried in her life before this moment. Now, she felt what it was like to be human and suffer loss. She could not hold her tears back any longer. She sank further in her chair. She pulled her legs up onto the chair and hugged them tightly. Her chin rested on her knees, and she watched Pete and Jessica. She watched, and she cried.

Jessica smiled and whispered. Only Pete could hear her whispers, and he answered her with a nod. Then she spoke one last time.

"Pete, I love you."

Pete squeezed her tighter and replied through tears, "I will always love you, Jessica. Always."

Pete felt Jessica's grip loosen around him, and she let go. Jessica's monitors began beeping and flashing different colors.

***

Everyone in the room remained silent for several moments, which felt like several hours. Pete gently got up from the bed, still holding Jessica's hand. He looked away and glanced over at Rialla. She was sitting on the chair, crying. Krix'x was hovering above the floor directly in front of her. A blue light beam scanned her body as she sat there, her head buried in her knees.

Krix'x looked over Rialla. "And who is this?"

Pete wiped his nose on his shirt sleeve. He gently laid Jessica's hand down and walked over to Krix'x. Pete looked at Krix'x and spoke loudly. "Krix'x, your help is no longer needed. I apologize for the inconvenience."

Krix'x kept his gaze on Rialla, ignoring Pete. "You are not human. Who are you?"

Before Rialla could reply, Krix'x disappeared. Pete looked over at Oz.

"I turned off the switch," she shrugged her shoulders.

Pete nodded, "Thanks, Oz."

Rialla stepped out of the dark and came to the side of the bed. She looked over at Oz, "Thank you, Vailen."

"I did it for Jessica."

"I know."

Rialla leaned over Jessica and started reciting a prayer in her native tongue. When she finished, she touched Jessica's cheek with the back of her hand, "Sleep, sister, and dream of better things."

Pete approached the bed slowly. He placed his hand on Jessica's hand and smiled.

"She was the best person I knew." He looked up at Oz, standing next to Rialla.

Oz bowed her head slightly. "Pete, we were fortunate to meet her. Without her guidance, I don't know how things would have turned out."

"I don't understand why this had to happen. Who did this?" Pete was now looking directly at Rialla.

"We were attacked by a large human male. He said there was money to be made by killing Jessica."

"A bounty? On Jessica? The Xanoclax?"

Rialla spoke up quickly. "No, it was not Xanoclax."

Pete grew angrier, "How could you tell?"

"The human that attacked us was not dremarsked."

"What the hell is dremarsk?"

"Our ability to take on the appearance of another is called dremarsk."

"How could you tell he wasn't a Xan?"

"Because when I struck him, his blood was red, not green."

Pete was confused. He stared down at Jessica. Rialla and Oz stood silently, watching, not knowing what would happen next. The doctors and nurses rushed into the room, alerted by the EKG monitor. The nurses asked Pete, Rialla, and Oz to move so they could attend to Jessica. The three of them knew it was too late and silently stepped away.

12 HEAR ME OUT

Bill kept squirming in his new suit. Despite Bill's protests, Maggie bought the suit from the mall two days earlier. He hated clothes shopping and disliked suits even more. But here he was, squirming in his brand-new suit in a congressional meeting hall. He was sitting at one of the front tables next to Maggie. Maggie smacked Bill under the table for the third time and whispered, "Bill Jackson, sit still."

The third smack on his leg was much harder than the first two. The powerful third smack was a universal sign that Bill had to take her seriously. Although he itched and was uncomfortable, he remained still.

The proceedings began in their ordinary manner, with the introduction of the Senate panel. Once all the introductions were finished, the meeting started. Senator Crandall began by announcing her sponsorship of Maggie's proposal. Once all the formalities were concluded, the meeting officially began.

Maggie was both nervous and excited. Senator Higgins from Mississippi spoke first. "First, let me say how proud I am to represent such thoughtful and caring citizens of Mississippi. I believe the time is right to follow this example of unselfishness. I believe Americans are ready to put forth a combined effort in the fight against racism."

The gallery of citizens that were attending broke out in cheers of approval. The chairman of the Senate panel hammered his gavel and requested the room to be silent.

"Please, we will have no more outbursts. If these outbursts continue, we will have to close the doors to the public. Now, let's proceed. Ms. Carter, you have the floor."

Maggie stood up slowly and addressed the panel. "Ladies and gentlemen, I would like to propose a bill to help unite this country as one people. For too long, too many of us have been sitting around complaining about racial issues, but have not taken any action to improve them. We are all Americans, and we should all be proud of that. We are citizens of one of the strongest and richest countries on Earth. We shouldn't live in a country where we are afraid to go out at night. We shouldn't live in a country where we fear our law enforcement officials. Racism isn't a battle that should be fought by minorities alone. Everyone in this country is a part of this fight. We need to make an effort to bring all these fears to an end so that everyone in this country is treated fairly and with respect."

"Every free society on earth is dealing with one form of racism or another. For too many years, we have yelled and complained about racism. But we are no better off today than we were twenty years ago. Some statistics even prove we are worse off today. We have to look at the source of racist acts, not just the results. In a free society, people can believe however they want. No one wants that right taken away."

"I believe that the crux of the issue lies within positions of power. I propose that we start with the law enforcement branch of the government. We need to reach the point where people of color can trust law enforcement. If we can achieve this goal, our attempts to work together to rid this country of its racial issues will be fruitful. I am not saying that all law enforcement officers are bad. What I am saying is that we need to be aware of racism in positions of power. If we can identify and remove racists from positions of power, I believe we can move forward together as one people and make this country better for everyone."

"I have outlined what I believe would be a fair and just way to identify racists in positions of power and try to rehabilitate them or remove their titles. This new government department will consist of employees of different races and political beliefs. This department will investigate all violent, racist acts committed by law enforcement. It will take immediate action on reports of racist acts. It is time to stop relying on the media bickering about racism to resolve these horrendous acts."

Maggie smiled at the panel and said, "Thank you for your time." She sat down and prepared for the debate to start. She knew not everyone on the panel would agree with her recommendations.

Maggie kept telling herself, *Just stay calm. If you react emotionally, the panel will not hear your message.*

"Ms. Carter, I would like to begin by saying that this Senate agrees that racism needs serious attention," Senator Johnson began in his Alabama drawl. "My concern, however, is with your suggested approach of identifying potential racists. You recommend that we use the affliction as a starting point. If an officer of the law is afflicted, his guilt is automatically assumed. I find this to be a scary proposition. It seems like we are leaning towards the idea of a witch hunt."

"Hogwash, senator," Senator Frazier from New York responded. "The affliction shows us who is possibly racist and who isn't. If you asked the question 'Are you a racist?' on an entrance application, how many would honestly answer yes? None. Not one applicant would admit to such a question. But guess what? With the affliction, you cannot hide that there is that possibility."

Johnson fired back, "So everyone who is afflicted is presumed guilty of being a racist? What if the affliction isn't solely attached to racism? Our scientists cannot determine why certain people are affected, and others are not. Some people who are affected have never had a racist incident in their lives."

"The measures we use today do not identify potential racists. And when violent racist acts do occur, nine times out of ten, there is no record of previous racism. I believe the affliction is a starting point that will enable us to avert racial violence," Frazier responded.

Congressman Sherman from Minnesota broke in, "I am a little concerned that we may cause anxiety within a law enforcement community that is already dealing with high stress levels. Don't you think this will impede their ability to perform their duties?"

Congressman Raynes answered, "I don't think it will impede their ability to do their job. Having a watchdog may encourage them to become more aware of proper procedures."

The congressmen continued to take turns offering their opinions. Maggie leaned over to Bill and whispered, "What do you think? I'm trying to keep track of who is for my proposal."

Bill leaned in, "I think it's just about even right now."

One by one, each member joined in with their opinion. Maggie and Bill had a difficult time following all the conversations. While one senator spoke, a few others would carry on a conversation. The whole process was confusing and irritating to Maggie. She would have been satisfied if they all read her proposal and took a vote. The continuous banter was starting to give her a headache. She was happy when the chairman struck the gavel down and announced an hour break for lunch. Maggie and Bill went through the doorway and were greeted by Congressman Higgins.

"How are you two holding up?"

Bill looked at the senator, shaking his head. "Sir, no disrespect, but I don't see how anything gets done here."

The senator laughed and patted Bill on the back. "It takes a while, but sometimes it's worth the effort. And you, young lady, how are you doing?"

Maggie looked up at the senator, "I'm just happy we're having this conversation, sir. I hope we see more of this from our leaders."

"Well said, Ms. Carter. Well said." The senator smiled and walked away. Bill and Maggie headed for the cafeteria to get lunch.

***

After lunch, the room filled up again, and the chairman spoke. "It appears we all have firm opinions on this matter. From what I have gathered, the panel is at odds over the procedures with which this new department would identify racist behaviors. Perhaps Ms. Carter can enlighten us with a theoretical occurrence."

"It would be my pleasure, Mr. Chairman," Maggie smiled. "I envision a department that performs two duties. The first function is to identify afflicted law enforcement personnel. In the beginning, questionnaires will be sent out by the new department. A law enforcement official who is afflicted will not be treated as a racist. The new department will be available for counseling and guidance."

"The second function will have the department investigate claims of racist acts perpetrated by law enforcement officials. The investigation aims to act swiftly and thoroughly to accomplish justice for the victims. Swift action will also benefit law enforcement officers involved in bogus accusations. The new department protects everyone, offers rehabilitation as needed, and builds trust between communities and law enforcement. "

The chairman looked at Maggie. "Ms. Carter, please give us an example of the second function. I assume a claim would come into the new department, and that's when you would act upon it?"

Maggie took a breath, "Yes, sir. The complaint could come from the victim, the victim's family, or the police department."

"What is the next step following receipt of the complaint?"

"An investigative team would be sent to the city where the complaint originated. The team would begin their investigation and make a decision or suggestion based on all the evidence gathered. The decision could be to suspend the officer or have him arrested, depending on the severity of the crime in question. Again, other decisions could be made based on the severity of the crime in question, such as to have the officer seek counseling."

"Why do you feel that this is a better tactic than the procedures that are currently in place?"

"Sir, with all due respect, there are still many cases out there that are still open. The victims and their families have no closure. Too many times, we see the report of a racial incident, and ten days later, the case is old news and forgotten. We need an honest, non-biased conclusion to these horrific acts."

Okay, Maggie, keep calm. Focus on the point you are trying to convey, Maggie thought.

"I also believe an external investigation will build trust between all parties concerned. If the investigation is done by the police department within which the racist event occurred, the conclusion could be tainted or perceived as tainted. If the investigation is conducted by an outside department, it would add legitimacy and impartiality to the conclusion. Neutrality is how we start building trust between our law enforcement agencies and the communities they are sworn to protect."

There was silence in the room. Then, the senators began mumbling to each other, and the mumbling grew louder. The chairman banged his gavel several times, and the chamber became silent again.

The chairman spoke. "I believe we have much to discuss and consider, thanks to Ms. Carter. Our next step is to discuss these proposals and their repercussions and reconvene later. I would like the panel to communicate the appropriate day and week and have it on the calendar. Ms. Carter, thank you for your time and effort on this critical issue. My assistant will contact you within the next few days with the agreed-upon date for the next meeting."

The chairman pounded the gavel three times and dismissed everyone.

Maggie looked at Bill and hugged him tightly. "You will never know how much it meant to me that you were here by my side," she said while hugging Bill.

"This right here is worth every moment, Maggie. Thanks for wanting me to be here."

The chamber emptied, and they were the last to leave.

13 BEHIND DOOR NUMBER 1

Oz watched Rialla closely as she sat on her cot in her cell. Oz never lowered the glass door. Rialla still wore the necklace, so Oz didn't see the point.

Oz went back to the control room. She was still confused as to why there was so little information on the Xanoclax in their database. The Council proclaimed the Xanoclax the number one threat in the universe, yet there was so little information to be found. Oz went back to the screen and watched the recording of Cass again.

"What are you viewing?" Rialla's voice came from behind Oz.

"You should be in your cell," Oz answered, never turning around to face Rialla.

"Thank you for not closing the door."

"Don't make me change my mind."

"Please tell me what you are viewing."

Oz turned around and faced Rialla. Her demeanor was threatening, and it made Rialla take a step back. "I am viewing the reason why I hate you so much!" Oz raised her voice.

"I'm sorry, I didn't mean to upset you."

"Well, you did. Now buzz off!" Oz turned back to the screen. Rialla started to go back, but the recording started, and she stood there in silence, watching.

When it was over, she spoke softly, "Vailen, can I point something out to you about your visual?"

Oz turned around and screamed, "No! No, you can't!" And she pressed the control that set off Rialla's necklace. Rialla screamed in surprise, but it was a short sound. The electricity around her neck made her drop to the floor. She rapidly convulsed on the floor as Oz pressed the control in her hand.

"This is nothing compared to what Cass went through. There is no punishment fitting for what you did to her."

Rialla tried to speak, "Listen...please–"

"No! You have nothing to say to me. I would love to turn the power up and burn your head off your body, but I can't. I promised. But I didn't promise I wouldn't make you suffer a little."

"Please, lis...ten...to...me...the...I...I...eyes..."

Oz looked at the convulsing body and then at the screen. She took her finger off the control, and Rialla gasped for air. She rolled onto her side and coughed violently. She was choking while tugging on the collar to add space between it and her throat. She curled up into a ball and tried to regain her normal breathing.

Oz turned the recording back on. She slowed the motion of the recording. She could barely make out the face of the Xan on the screen through the sandstorm.

"There," Rialla rasped. "Look closer," Rialla was on the floor, pointing at the visual.

For a split second, Oz saw something she hadn't noticed before. She rewound the recording and stopped it. She did this several times and then screamed, "No! There's no way this is possible!"

Rialla rose to her feet slowly. "You see it, don't you?" she whispered hoarsely.

Oz was staring at the paused image on the screen. Under her breath, barely audible, she said, "I do."

Rialla whispered as loudly as she could without causing pain to her throat. "I am sorry for your loss, Vailen. But as you can see, your quarrel is not with me."

Oz kept staring at the image on the screen. She had never noticed before, but now she had seen it. The Xan's eyes were clear in this brief second. The second it was paused, she could clearly see his eyes. The Xan standing next to her had green eyes. Yet these eyes frozen on the visual were blue. Wen's eyes are blue.

"How is this possible?" Oz kept staring at the image. "How can his eyes be blue? Did he cover them to hide his identity?"

"A Xan is a proud warrior, Vailen. They do not hide who they are." Rialla responded as she rubbed her throat.

"Then how can this be explained? Didn't the Xan conduct your ritual?"

"He did, but our ritual is well known throughout the universe. The ritual can be easily imitated."

"I don't understand any of this."

Rialla looked down at the sulking blue Vailen. She wanted to say something to help, but hesitated, fearing to make Oz angrier.

"I am going back to my cell, Vailen. I am available to listen and discuss this if you are inclined to do so." Rialla walked away.

Oz continued to gaze at the screen. The sudden appearance of static on the screen broke her stare. She knew right away that Krix'x was coming. She straightened out the top of the control panel and hid any evidence of her research concerning Xanstar.

Krix'x appeared on the screen. "Vailen report."

"I am alone on the ship," Oz lied.

"Where is the herald?"

"He's out trying to clear his mind. Do you want me to summon him to the ship?"

"That is not necessary, Vailen. I need you to answer a few questions for me."

"Of course."

"Who was that being in the hospital room with the herald?"

"I don't know. The female just showed up. I assumed she was Jessica's relative or her friend."

"My scan revealed alien DNA. Is she alien?"

Oz responded quickly, "My scans did not pick up any evidence of alien composition."

"Very well, I want you to get me some information on her. And do it discreetly. I don't want the Herald to know what assignment I gave you. Are we clear?"

"We are."

Krix'x disappeared into the static, and the Xan warrior's image reappeared.

Oz continued to stare at the eyes of the Xan. It didn't make sense. She calmed herself down and headed back to Rialla's cell.

"You lied to your leader," Rialla said, sitting on her cot. "I thought that Vailens could not lie?"

Oz sat in the chair in front of the cell. Her head was heavy, and her eyes stared down at the floor. "He's not my leader. He's a representative of the High Council. I think the neon trace elements in this planet's atmosphere are affecting me. I am not only thinking irrationally, but it also appears that emotions and feelings are beginning to impact my decisions. I can only assume that these changes free my capacity to challenge logic-speak."

"Have you run tests on this trace element? Is it dangerous?"

"No, I haven't had the time or resources to analyze these elements properly," Oz said softly. She lifted her head and looked at Rialla. It was the first time Oz noticed Rialla's comforting green eyes.

Rialla noticed Oz was confused. "You need to try and look at this predicament with your Vailen logic. You may have done so already and do not like the answers you discovered."

"You are correct. I do not like the answers I discovered through my logical reasoning."

"What will you do now?"

"I'm lost right now. I'm not sure what happens next."

"You need to talk to someone whose opinion you trust."

"Yes, I need to talk to Pete immediately." Oz jumped up, kicking her chair back across the floor. She hurried to the control room and called Pete.

Pete was staring down at the water on a bridge overlooking the Potomac. An occasional boat passed under the bridge, causing waves to form and collide with the stone supports. Jessica's face appeared, floating in the water, smiling at him. He reached his hand out to touch her, and she disappeared as Oz's alert went off.

"Oz? What is it?"

"Pete, you need to come to the ship immediately," Oz sounded desperate.

Pete never heard such desperation in Oz's voice before. "Oz, are you okay?"

"No, Pete. I need you here, now."

Oz turned from the control panel and saw Pete standing there. "Thanks for coming so quickly, Pete."

Pete walked towards Oz. "Of course, what's up?"

"I need you to watch this closely," Oz turned on the visual.

"Oz, why do you keep watching this?"

"Pete, just look closely, please."

Oz paused the recording on the Xan. She waited for Pete to notice. He looked at the screen. After a few moments, he stepped back. "What the hell?"

"You see it too, don't you?"

"The Xan's eyes are blue. How is that possible?"

Oz walked away from the screen and walked back to it again. "Pete, this changes everything. Everything I hold dear to me is now in question."

Pete saw Oz was visibly troubled. "Could there be another species with blue eyes that would have done this?"

"To what end?" Rialla asked as she entered the room. "Why would any species do this to begin with?"

Pete looked at Rialla and nodded. She made sense. He looked at Oz, who looked like her whole world was crumbling. "Oz, what are you thinking? We need to discuss all the possibilities."

Oz looked at Pete with sad eyes. "Pete, I am confused for the first time in my existence. I cannot rationalize right now."

Pete approached Oz slowly. "It's okay. We don't have to come up with any answers right now. Let's take some time and think about what this could mean. We don't want to jump to conclusions without proof to back our assumptions."

Oz shook her head in agreement. Pete looked at Rialla. "Can you keep an eye on her, please?"

"Yes, I will."

"Thank you, Rialla. Oz, listen to me. We will figure this out, I promise. Take a break from all this and clear your head."

Oz looked at Pete. "Thanks, Pete."

Pete nodded at Rialla. She nodded back, and Pete was gone. Rialla pulled Oz up and walked her back to her room. She laid Oz on her cot. Oz sat up and looked at Rialla.

"Why are you doing this?"

"I told the Herald I would watch you."

"But why? I hated you. I wanted to kill you."

"True, but you were acting with bad information. I don't believe you would have done the same if you had seen the blue eyes earlier."

Oz bounced her backside up and down on the cot. "This cot sucks. Let's change that right now." Oz replaced the cot with a queen-size bed. She then added a few pillows and some warm sheets and blankets. She placed curtains over the glass doors to allow Rialla privacy.

"Thank you," Rialla said.

"It's the least I can do for you, especially after what I put you through."

"Can I ask a favor?"

A wine carafe appeared on the floor at their feet. Rialla laughed. "Am I that transparent?"

"Yeah, you are." They both laughed.

Rialla raised her glass, "To our dear sister, Jessica."

Oz looked at the Xan and touched her glass to Rialla's. "To Jessica."

"Do Vailens drink wine?"

Oz looked at Rialla, "We do now."

***

Pete was standing at Jessica's crime scene. The yellow crime scene tape was still present, and a policeman was guarding the area. Pete walked up to the policeman and shook his hand.

"Mind if I ask you a few questions?"

"Not at all," the policeman said.

"Were there any eyewitnesses?"

"Yes, there were two."

"Were they able to identify the attacker?"

"Sir, I can't tell you any details about an ongoing case." The officer apologized.

"The victim was very dear to me, and I would like some closure for her family."

"Sir, I understand. I'm not trying to be disrespectful, but I have my orders."

Pete knelt on the ground near the blackened grass. He closed his eyes tightly at the realization that he was looking at Jessica's blood. Still kneeling and not looking up at the officer, he said, "She died tonight."

The policeman looked down at Pete, staring at the grass. "Sir, I am so sorry." He looked around and determined they were alone. The officer squatted next to Pete and put his hand on his shoulder.

The officer whispered into Pete's ear, "The witnesses identified the leader of the White For Right nationalist group as the assailant. His name is Bronson Pike. We have an all-points bulletin out on him now."

Pete turned his head towards the officer. "Thank you, sir." Pete stood up. The officer stood up with him. Pete shook his hand and disappeared, leaving the officer's hand suspended in the air.

When Pete arrived on the ship, the control room was empty. He walked back towards Rialla's cell. He stopped before entering when he heard voices. Rialla and Oz were conversing as if they were best friends. He leaned against the doorway.

Jessica would have loved hearing them laugh together, he thought.

He waited for a pause in their conversation before entering the room. He was shocked to see Rialla's cell open and both sitting side by side on a new bed. He didn't want to interrupt, but he had to.

"Oz, I need your help, please."

Oz jumped up and came to Pete. "What is it?"

"I have the name of the creep who jumped Rialla and Jessica. I want to find him before the police get him."

Oz hurried to the control room, yelling, "I need everything you have on him."

Pete followed quickly behind her. When he reached the control room, Oz ran a search program. Parameters were popping up on the screen.

"What's his name?"

"Bronson Pike."

"What else do you have?"

"He's the leader of a racist group called White for Right. They're a biker club."

"My search is getting a lot of hits. He's all over the airwaves."

"There's an APB out on him now."

Oz jumped in her seat, "I've got something. The authorities have cornered him in a vacant warehouse near the Potomac River. They are awaiting backup before they go in after him."

"Address?"

"I put the coordinates in the system."

Pete looked at Oz. "Thanks, I'll be right back."

"I'm coming with you."

"Okay," Pete smiled. "Let's go."

They tightbeamed inside a dark building. There were pools of water all around the floor from rain entering the holes in the roof. Cast-iron columns supported the ceiling and walls. All the windows on the upper level were shattered and broken. There was a distinct odor of mold and mildew mixed with the low-tide smell from the river. Raindrops were slowly falling from the holes in the metal ceiling of the warehouse, making slight echoes as they hit the puddles on the floor.

Pete walked slowly over the damp floor, occasionally stepping in a puddle. He looked around. "Oz, run a heat signature scan."

"I'm on it. Pete, he's behind that column of barrels in the eastern corner of the building."

"Thanks."

Pete walked over to the 50-gallon drums and knocked them over. Pike leaped forward, lunging at Pete with a knife. Pete easily sidestepped him, and Pike flew by without touching him. Pete walked up to Pike and let Pike make the first move. Pike struck Pete's head with the knife. The knife stopped without making a sound when it hit Pete's forcefield. The intensity of the blow to the forcefield caused Pike to drop his knife.

Pete picked up the knife and held it in his hand, walking towards Pike. Pike screamed, "Come on, you alien faggot, finish it. I ain't going in peacefully. I ain't rotting away in no prison. Finish it!" Pike closed his eyes and awaited the final blow.

Pete walked up to Pike without saying a word and struck him in the jaw. The blow sent Pike flying back against the wall 15 feet away. The sound of his body smashing against the metal tin wall echoed throughout the warehouse. Pike lay still against the wall. Pete walked over to the unconscious Pike and kicked a few barrels out of his way.

Pete heard sirens outside the warehouse. Reinforcements had arrived, and he knew they would storm the building at any moment. He bent over Pike and lifted him. Pete tightbeamed him back to the ship.

Back on the ship, Rialla was drinking wine on her new bed. She looked down at the empty chair before her cell and began crying. She closed her eyes and heard Jessica's laughter. She smiled when she saw Jessica rolling around the floor, laughing. Rialla tried hard to understand the empty feeling inside her stomach. The little shocks that darted up through her body felt like pinpricks.

Is this fear? She thought. *I feel so empty right now, like I am nothing. Is this loneliness?*

She sat up suddenly when she heard a loud noise outside her room. She wiped her eyes and ran to the control room, and saw Pete standing over Jessica's murderer. Rialla screamed and jumped onto Pike. She began feverishly swinging her fists, each connecting with Pike's face. Pete pulled Rialla off and tossed her against the far wall.

Pete yelled at her. "Not now, Rialla! I need him alive."

With tears in her eyes, Rialla screamed, "Why?"

Pete walked up to her and extended his hand. "I need to find out who's behind this attack." Pete lifted Rialla to her feet, and she nodded in agreement. Pete walked away from her and back towards the bleeding Pike. He was barely conscious. Pete had Oz pour water on his face to revive him.

"What the hell?" Pike screamed.

Pete looked down at the bewildered Pike and began his interrogation. "I need to know who hired you to kill Jessica."

Pike spat out a mouthful of blood. "Freak you."

Pete moved his hand to the right, and Pike flew to the far right wall. His body made a horrifying, thudding noise when it hit the wall. Pike was moaning when Pete got to him. His moan turned to laughter when he looked up and saw Pete standing over him. Pike leaned over and wiped his face on Pete's boots.

Pete moved his hand up slowly and forced Pike to stand with his back against the wall.

"I can do this all day, Pike."

"Go on, then. I got nowhere I gotta be," Pike laughed, and Pete flung him back against the opposite wall. Pike's body crashed with an even louder thud than the first time. He lay on the floor, coughing up blood. Pete was getting impatient and tried to hold back his anger. Oz sensed Pete's vitals increasing rapidly.

Pete, you need him alive. Remember, alive, Oz said telepathically.

I know! Pete screamed back.

Before he reached the choking Pike, Rialla stepped in front of him. "I can do this. Let me do this. I can make him talk before he dies."

Pete moved toward Pike. Rialla placed her hand on Pete's chest to stop his forward progress. Pete looked into Rialla's sad, green eyes. "Herald, please let me try. Please."

Pete nodded and left the room. As he was walking, he called out to Oz, "Set up the room for recording. I don't want to miss anything he says."

Oz appeared in front of Rialla. She smiled at her and looked to see if Pete was out of her line of sight. When he was, she turned back. Still smiling, she tilted her head sideways and shrugged her shoulders. Rialla looked confused until Oz kicked Pike in the head. He let out a scream as blood poured out of his new head wound. Oz immediately looked back down the hallway. There was no sign of Pete.

Oz smiled. "Cool."

Rialla laughed at Oz. "You feel better?"

"You know it."

"Alright, levitate him into another room and strap him onto a table, please."

They flanked the floating unconscious Pike and headed to a vacant room. Oz had a table waiting, and they strapped him in. Oz ensured the recording equipment was active and asked Rialla what else she needed.

Rialla smiled deviously. "Larxsha."

Oz looked surprised. "How do you know about Larxsha?"

"I thought everyone knew of it. It never fails to get the job done."

Oz laughed. "I can't believe it! You are crazy, and I love it." Oz went to the wall and passed her hand over a small sensor. A tall door opened, exposing a large storehouse. Oz clapped twice, and the lights came on.

"I still love doing that."

Rialla tilted her head to the side, confused. Oz laughed. "I'll explain later."

The shelves, full of containers of all sizes, appeared to go on forever.

"How can you find it here? These shelves are full, and I do not see any labels."

Oz went to the wall and passed her hand over another sensor. A screen appeared, suspended in the air in front of her. She entered 'Larxsha' in her native language, and a blue spotlight beamed onto a small container. Oz walked down the walkway and retrieved the container.

Pike was lying on the table with two large metal bands straddling his body. One wide metal band straddled his chest, and the other, equally as wide, tightly bound his lower body. Oz had placed smaller metal bands around his wrists so he couldn't move them. Rialla came into the room first, followed by Oz.

Pike raised his head and spat blood at Rialla as she got closer. He noticed Oz as she stepped out from behind Rialla. "Two freaks coming to see me? How lucky can I be? I see we have a blue freak now. What is this, a circus?" Pike laughed hard and began choking on his own blood.

Rialla smiled at Pike. "Don't choke yet; we're not finished with you." Rialla tore Pike's shirt open and began unbuckling Pike's pants.

Pike looked at Rialla. "What are you two going to do to me? Screw me to death?" Pike continued laughing. Oz came up to Pike with the Larxsha container. She smiled at Pike and pulled the lid off.

She looked at Pike with a devilish grin. "You, sir, will become obsequious voluntarily. We won't have to say a word." Oz tilted the container, pointing the open end toward Pike's stomach.

"What the hell is that, you freak? What are you doing?"

As Oz promised, neither she nor Rialla would speak. The Larxsha, a tiny, metallic-looking bug resembling a spider, crawled slowly onto Pike's bare stomach. The Larxsha had five legs connected to its metal body. There was a sharp needle at the end of each leg in place of feet or toes. Each time the Larxsha moved, the needles penetrated Pike's skin. Before taking the next step, a tentacle branched out from the needle while the needle was inside his skin. The tentacle would take several bites from the inside, causing excruciating pain.

Pike screamed every time the Larxsha took a step. His eyes began to tear up. He was cursing profusely at Rialla and Oz. Oz pressed a button, and the Larxsha stopped. Pike was breathing heavily. Sweat and tears were rolling off his face.

"You two are crazy," he screamed.

Oz picked up the quieted Larxsha and placed it in the palm of her gloved hand. She turned to Pike and smiled. Then she slowly walked closer to his waist.

"Wait, what the hell are you doing?"

Rialla smiled along with Oz, but neither said a word. Pike's breathing became heavier and faster. He lifted his head and saw Oz's blue hand grab his penis while holding the Larxsha close to it with her other hand.

"Wait, wait, please! I'll tell you anything you want to know. Just put that thing away!"

Rialla finally spoke. "Here's the deal, you racist pig. My friend keeps her finger on the controller, and if we don't like your answer, she presses the button. The Larxsha will enter your human appendage and eat its way out."

Oz laughed at Rialla, "They call that human appendage a penis. It's a silly name for a silly appendage."

Rialla smiled and nodded.

Oz looked at Pike. "I beg you. Please lie to us. Please. It's been a long time since I saw a Larxsha destroy a penis." Oz raised her head as if she had an epiphany. "Wait," she addressed Rialla suddenly. "I don't think I have ever seen it, so this will be my first. Cool!"

Pike was screaming to the point of squealing. "Okay! Please, don't! What do you want to know?"

Rialla looked Pike in the eyes. "Who paid you to attack my friend?"

Pike swallowed deeply. He took a few more deep breaths and yelled out, "One of those freaking aliens!"

Rialla shouted back, "What did he look like?"

"Like the one on the news last week that attacked the White House."

Rialla became enraged. "You lie. Oz, drop the Larxsha."

"No! Please, I swear it's true. He came to me during our riot the other night."

Oz held up her hand and waved it across the air before them. A picture of a Xan warrior appeared on the floating screen.

"That's what he looked like," Pike screamed.

Rialla screamed back, "Xans do not hire bounty hunters!"

Oz looked at Pike and spoke softly with purpose. "Listen to me closely, Pike. I will ask this only once. What color were his eyes?"

"I couldn't see them with all the tear gas. I swear, I couldn't see any details!"

Oz shook her head slowly, left to right. "Well, Pike, I guess I will finally get to see a live penis explode from the inside out. Thank you for your time."

Oz moved back towards Pike's penis and held out the hand that contained the Larxsha. Pike screamed, "Wait! He was an alien. I know he was!"

"If he was difficult to see, how do you know what he was?" Rialla retorted.

Oz lowered her hand and let the Larxsha rest on Pike's abdomen. Pike was squealing uncontrollably. "He was an alien, I know it!"

The Larxsha began crawling across his abdomen, heading for his penis. Pike was squirming and screaming as the Larxsha tore at Pike's insides with every movement. It approached its destination, and Pike screamed, "He healed me! He freaking healed me!"

Oz stopped the Larxsha and placed it back into the container. Rialla looked at Oz, who was staring at Pike. Oz asked, "What do you mean, he healed you?"

Pike was crying like a little boy when he answered, "When I struck him in the fog, I shattered my wrist. He grabbed my hand and healed my wrist. My wrist became hot as hell, and in seconds, it was like nothing ever happened. You have to believe me; that's the truth. That's all I know."

Oz leaned over Pike. "What did the alien say to you?"

"He had a job for me. He'd pay me ten grand if I wasted the girl."

Oz began hitting Pike in the face, splattering his blood everywhere, along with his tears and sweat. Rialla pulled her away. "Oz, we have what the herald wanted to know. We are done with this pig."

Pike lay there on the table, terrified and crying. Oz walked out, and Rialla followed. Pete sat in the control room, staring at the blank screen. When they entered, he addressed them without turning around.

He spoke softly, his tone sad. "I saw it all on the visual. Jessica's life was only worth ten thousand dollars? Oz, if you don't tightbeam him to the police right now, I can't be responsible for what I do next."

"Okay, Pete. Right away."

"Wait a minute," Pete called out to Oz.

Oz walked back to him.

Pete handed Oz the knife that Pike used. When Oz grabbed the knife, Pete added, "Send a piece of the recording along with him. Make sure it shows him ratting out. That should go over big in prison."

Oz smiled and walked out of the room.

Pete continued staring at the screen. Rialla walked silently over to him. She placed her hand tenderly on his shoulder and stared along with him.

14 SAYING GOODBYE

The funeral for Jessica Morales was in a small cemetery in South Miami. Jessica's family, including her mother Maria and brother Luis, sat under the canopy surrounding the gravesite in the first row of chairs. The remaining acquaintances and relatives filled the remainder of the empty seats. The CDC representatives stood behind the chairs, and Bill and Maggie sat in the last row. Pete and Rialla sat next to Maggie.

Pete closed his eyes and felt the warm breeze that rustled the Miami palms. The aroma of beautiful flowers filled the air while the scent of fresh-cut grass wrapped the event like a comforting blanket. Pete felt the moment could not be any better to pay homage to such a wonderful human being. The priest spoke in both Spanish and English. When his sermon ended, he invited all those who wanted to say a few words. Jessica's brother, who was a few years younger than she, spoke first.

"Thank you, everyone, for being here. I know Jessica cared about you all very much. My sister had a wonderful heart. She loved everyone. She never faltered when it came to helping someone. There are so many stories about her love and unselfishness that choosing one would do her an injustice. I loved my sister, and I will miss my sister. But I will always keep her with me. She helped me become a better person, and I will honor her memory by continuing down the path she helped me find."

Luis said a few more things in Spanish, wiped his tears, and sat beside his mother. Having trouble keeping her eyes dry, Maggie walked up to the podium.

"I'm so sorry for coming in front of you bawling like a little girl, but it hurts so much. I didn't know Jessica as long as all of you. I am sure you have the most wonderful stories to remember her by. In the short time I got to know Jessica, I saw how amazing she was. With Jessica, you can tell right away what you're getting. Yes, she was beautiful and intelligent. But you could feel wonderful positive energy when you stood next to her. And when you spoke to her, you felt better. She had the power to make you feel good about who you are. She was always concerned about everyone else. She never put herself first. She was a loving and caring human being. She was one of the most amazing people I have ever known. This world has lost a great soul, one of the good people we need. I will always take her loving, caring smile wherever I go. I will miss her tremendously. I will always love her."

Maggie was crying heavily and couldn't move from the podium. Bill walked up and escorted her back to their seats. A few more speakers came up. A cousin, a girlfriend, and someone from the CDC. Pete walked up to the podium slowly. He hung his head, looking at his feet.

He looked up and began speaking in a soft, caring voice.

"What else can I add? Jessica was amazing. She helped me in so many ways. When I first arrived in Bends Creek, I had no idea who I was. With Jessica's help, we figured out what happened to me as time passed. She ignored her common sense and fear of aliens to help me. A stranger. A homeless stranger. She helped me figure out that my memories and emotions were stripped from me by aliens. Without knowing or caring how badly I was damaged, she encouraged me to never give up hope. Jessica never gave up on me, even when I thought she should have. She made me rediscover things I thought I lost, things I may have never known if not for her. I owe her everything, and it's still not enough. If I could be half the person she was, I would be happy." Pete paused. He stared out at the beautiful, sun-filled, blue sky.

He turned and looked directly at Maria, Jessica's mother.

"I believe we get the chance to occupy the same space with someone amazing once in our lifetime if we are lucky. I am thankful that Jessica made that possible for me. I am also thankful to her for helping me regain some of my emotions and feelings. However excruciating, the pain is right now. I will miss her with all my heart."

Pete turned back to the clear, blue sky. "I will always love you, Jessica. Always."

Pete held out his hand, and Oz appeared. She startled the attendees.

"Sorry, I didn't mean to scare anyone. On my planet, emotions are nonexistent. We practice logic over all else. I have been struggling since I came to Earth with my logic, and one of the reasons is the wonderful Jessica. She hugged me and explained that hugs are how you show someone you care about them. A simple gesture, I know, but when she hugged me, I felt something. I couldn't explain what I was feeling. I learned to accept Jessica's answer, which was 'love.' She'd tell me to relax and let it in. Love. I had never experienced love before I met Jessica, and I believe I loved her too."

Oz pointed to Jessica's tombstone, and a small blue hologram floated above the stone. Jessica's picture was on the screen, and she was smiling.

"This is how I shall remember Jessica Morales."

15 ALLIANCES

A week had passed since Jessica's funeral. Pete was away from the ship more than he was on it. Oz continued her research into the blue-eyed Xan. Rialla made herself available to help Oz, but she was never needed. Oz gave Rialla the files she had on Earth culture and recommended she start with her favorite, *The Wizard of Oz*. When Pete showed up in her room, Rialla was sipping her wine while lying on her bed, watching the film.

"Can we talk, Rialla?" Pete asked in a low, soft voice. He was standing next to the chair in front of her cell. Rialla looked at Pete and sat up, noticing he was standing awkwardly. He looked fatigued. His clothes were disheveled, and his knees were bent as if they couldn't bear his weight. She placed her wine glass down and walked towards him.

"Is everything okay?"

"No, I don't think so," Pete answered with a confused look.

"What can I do to help you?" Rialla asked with a concerned voice.

"I don't know, Rialla." Pete lowered his head and began to sway slightly.

Rialla grabbed Pete's arm and put it over her shoulder. She walked him to her bed and laid him down on it. She heard him mumble a few words but did not understand what he was saying. She removed his boots and placed them quietly on the floor. She sat him up gently and removed his coat. She put a pillow under his head and stood beside the bed. He raised his hand to her, and she took hold of it delicately. He opened his eyes slightly.

"She liked you a lot," Pete said in a low whisper.

"I know, and I liked her a lot as well," Rialla's eyes began to water.

"Rialla, we have to figure this mess out. We're like pawns on a chessboard. We have to figure this out," Pete whispered, closing his eyes.

Rialla placed her hand on his chest. Rialla covered Pete with a blanket and stood there, feeling sad. She stared at him, watching him sleep. She didn't hear Oz come up behind her.

"Good job," Oz smiled at Rialla.

"I suppose."

"Can we go into another room and talk?"

Rialla followed Oz out of her room. She looked back several times at Pete, concerned for his comfort. When they entered another room, Rialla asked, "What would you like to talk about?"

Oz had a table, and two chairs appeared in the room. She pulled one back from the table and sat down. She gestured for Rialla to do the same. Oz looked at her and spoke in a serious tone.

"Rialla, do you want to know why I have not asked for your help?"

Rialla looked slightly startled at the question, but it was on her mind. "Yes, I am curious."

"It's because you haven't offered to align with us."

"I don't understand."

"Out of respect to Jessica, Pete and I do not wish to pressure you into something you do not want."

Rialla looked confused. "I am not trying to be difficult, but I do not follow."

Oz sat up straight and looked Rialla in the eyes. She stared at her for what seemed to Rialla like an eternity. She simply sat and waited for Oz to continue.

Oz took a deep breath and began, "Rialla, you must choose a side. You cannot continue to stay with us if you don't believe the way we do."

It was Rialla's turn to sit up straight. She stared at Oz, took a deep breath, and responded, "I am here and support you and the herald. I want answers to all this chaos as much as you do."

"You haven't offered any information that makes us feel like you give a crap."

"What kind of information?"

"Your mission, Rialla. Somehow, you being here, the Xan with blue eyes, the healing Xan…it's all intertwined."

"How will I telling you about my mission aid this scenario?"

"For one, it will let us know we can trust you. And that you care about this as much as we do."

"I do care about this as much as you do. I want to know why Jessica had to die. I need to know." A few tears trailed from her eyes.

Oz spoke softly. "Listen to me, Rialla. A lot is happening here, bigger than anything I have ever encountered. I believe that we can solve this if we all work together. That means we must tell each other everything, no secrets."

Rialla stood up. "I am a Xan warrior and cannot betray my allegiance."

Oz stood in response and stared at her, speaking in a firm voice. "Your allegiance should be to the beings that you trust."

"And what about their allegiance to me?"

"Rialla, there can be no secrets between us. We need to be able to trust each other without doubts. Our lives may depend on it one day."

"Please, Vailen, do not ask me to betray my people. Do not make me choose."

"Rialla, if you know which side is right to align with in your heart, there is no choice."

Rialla lowered her head and stared at the table. Oz walked out of the room and left her standing there. Rialla let out a scream, which made Oz stop walking and turn her head. She didn't see Rialla leave the room, so she turned away and continued towards the control room.

Rialla sat in her chair at the table. She put her head in her hands. She sat for the longest time, letting her mind ponder all the questions that needed answers. The question that kept turning over in her mind over and over again was, why was Jessica murdered? Jessica was her friend. The only being that was ever her friend.

What do I know of friendship? Rialla thought. *There isn't a social system on Xanstar that allows friendships. Life is surrounded by duty to Xanstar. Nothing else matters. My only duty is to Xanstar; that's why I exist. That's why all Xans exist.*

Rialla sighed heavily. *Then why am I conflicted?*

Coming to Earth had opened her eyes to a different way of living.

There is more value placed on life here than on Xanstar, she thought. *Humans view life as a precious commodity. On Xanstar, lives belong to Xanstar. They are not yours to do with as you please.*

Relationships were nonexistent on Xanstar. The males and females of her home planet were equals. The Xans felt as humans did, but did not recognize those feelings. Xan's reproduction was not intimate, and Xan procreation was controlled by scientists of Xanstar to avoid intimacy and attention to feelings. The Xanoclax were brutal warriors who believed emotions were for the weak. Xan scientists genetically spliced similar qualities from male and female Xan warriors to increase the warrior population as needed. There was no physical contact between males and females other than combat training. No hugs, no kissing. No friends.

It is all so different here on Earth, she thought. *Bonding is more important than war. Family is a priority, but on Xanoclax, families do not exist. Jessica made an effort to share that with me. Jessica trusted me without knowing me. She didn't judge me; she accepted me for who I am.*

Rialla walked to the control room. Oz was staring at the floating screen, looking through lines of information. "What do you want to know, Vailen? I know what side I need to align with."

***

"Ms. Carter, would you like more time?" the chairman asked Maggie.

Maggie stared down at the files on her table and didn't respond. Bill leaned over and whispered, "Maggie, are you okay?"

Maggie looked over at Bill and blinked her eyes a few times. "What?"

"We're in the assembly hall. The chairman is asking if you need more time before they proceed."

Maggie smiled at Bill. "I'm okay, Bill."

The chairman said, "Ms. Carter, we are all aware of the tragic loss of your colleague and friend last week. We can reconvene at a later date if you need more time."

Maggie smiled at the chairman. "You are very considerate, sir. Thank you for your concern. But I think it's best if we continue."

"Very well," The chairman responded. He pounded his gavel and opened the meeting.

Congressman Johnson, who had been the most vocal with his concerns, began the questions.

"Ms. Carter, I am so sorry for your loss."

Maggie nodded. "Thank you."

"Ms. Carter, the debate continues regarding whether what you propose can be instituted constitutionally. We must protect all Americans' rights, no matter their beliefs."

Maggie looked at the panel for a minute and then addressed the representative from Alabama.

"I agree, sir. This country allows all men and women to have their own opinions and beliefs as they see fit. Our freedoms in this country have set the bar for so many others. Our constitution clearly states that all men are created equal, protecting the rights of all Americans."

Maggie looked down at Bill, and he smiled in support. She continued, "And yet, with such a magnanimous document as the Constitution, we still treat people of color as though they do not belong in this country. I am not suggesting we alienate every citizen's right to free speech. I propose that we identify racism in positions of authority that have the power to commit racist acts under the guise of the law. If we believe all men are created equal, then all men should be treated as equals under the law."

The congressman responded, "I believe we are doing our best to treat everyone equally."

Representative Frazier, who was visibly frustrated by Johnson's comment, spoke up. "There is no denying that there are good people within our police departments. But we cannot deny there are also bad people as well."

Johnson smiled. "Senator, there are good and bad people everywhere. Do you propose we create a new constitution for good people and expel the bad from our country?"

Frazier responded, "Sir, that is the most ludicrous comment I have ever heard. Do you not understand the point of this discussion? We are not discussing every citizen's right to freedom of speech. We are talking about government agencies that abuse their power and make decisions based on their personal beliefs, not the Constitution."

Maggie looked at the senators and said, "Can we all agree that there is a major problem in this country when it comes to racism? Can we stop an individual from being a racist? No, that would be impossible. However, we should explore the possibility of creating a department that can oversee racist behavior in positions of power. When an official crosses the line and harms another person based on the color of his skin, he violates that individual's constitutional rights. I don't understand what is so difficult about this premise. I don't understand how anyone can defend these racist acts."

Maggie had a few tears streaming down her cheeks. Bill reached over and asked if she was alright. She nodded.

Congressman Higgins spoke next. "Racism is a very emotional subject to discuss. For most of us, it can be frustrating to hear others speak about racism without personally experiencing it for themselves. With all due respect to Ms. Carter and members of the panel, I do not believe anyone is defending racist acts. I believe that we all want the same thing; I have to believe that. What is at issue here is not whether we are defending racist acts, but how we move forward under the law to create a department that protects all citizens' rights."

Johnson replied, "If we set out and establish the affliction as a marker for racism, then we will have a witch hunt on our hands. There is no established scientific proof that the afflicted are racist. They may have had racist thoughts that they never acted on."

Maggie calmed herself and responded, "Sir, I concur. I do not want a witch hunt with the sole purpose of exposing the afflicted. I suggest we use it as a guide to offer counseling and assistance. We would also establish a department whose sole purpose is to investigate racist acts without prejudice."

The chairman called for a recess and requested that the panel deliberate privately before returning to the next session. Maggie and Bill walked to the cafeteria to get a bite to eat.

The couple sat by themselves at a table. Maggie was staring down at her sandwich. Bill didn't say anything, waiting for Maggie to start the conversation. Maggie did, still staring at her sandwich. "You were right."

Bill stopped chewing and looked at Maggie. "About what?"

Maggie raised her head, "I should have stayed in Bends Creek and helped out there. I'm way out of my league here."

"No, you were right, Maggie. Whatever comes out of this, you must be pleased knowing you got them talking about it."

"Yeah, but is that enough?"

"It's a step in the right direction. This problem with our society didn't happen overnight. It had many decades to fester and get worse. We can't expect a quick fix. It will take persistence from good people like you to cause change. We have to be patient when there is no patience left to give. This fight will take time and be difficult, and I think it's worth it."

"And you, Bill." Maggie smiled.

"What?"

"It's going to take good people like you, too." Maggie reached across the table and squeezed Bill's hand.

The chairman's gavel pounded three times to start the session. He began, "It is the committee's consensus that a department that would single out afflicted individuals is unconstitutional. We have no scientific proof as of yet to substantiate that the affliction is solely associated with racist behavior."

Maggie lowered her head in defeat. Bill reached under the table and held her hand.

The chairman continued, "However, the idea of establishing a department to investigate alleged racist acts against persons of authority has merit."

Maggie raised her head in surprise. Her knees began bouncing rapidly. Bill smiled and didn't attempt to slow them down.

"This new department would serve as a bridge to build trust between communities and law enforcement officials. Knowing there is an oversight committee whose sole purpose is to investigate acts of cruelty that originate from racism will help build confidence in our system of justice."

Johnson was upset with the announcement. "Mr. Chairman, how will we fund this new department? What other departments must we cut funds from to make this possible?"

"Reparations," Maggie responded.

The chairman looked confused. "Ms. Carter?"

"We all know there will never be a decision to order reparations to descendants of American slaves. I don't know if there is an acceptable price that could ever be adequate for the atrocities committed against my ancestors. But a positive gesture to show that this country recognizes some action is needed would go a long way in the healing process."

Johnson looked at Maggie. "Ms. Carter, you have introduced an entirely different subject."

Frazier replied, "It's all related. Ms. Carter correctly says that a reparations act will never be passed. We have some states that believe that because they didn't have slaves, they shouldn't be involved in the reparations discussion. Others believe the burden of reparations should fall more heavily on the South, where the majority of appalling acts occurred. This debate will go on forever, sir. And it shouldn't, but it will. So what Ms. Carter proposes is that this is a way for the United States to make amends with this horrible part of our history."

Maggie spoke again, "Mr. Chairman and distinguished panel, I believe this country is becoming more segregated. People of color believe nobody cares about racism except those who are being victimized by it. Up until a few weeks ago, I was an African American who believed that. It was brought to my attention by someone I care deeply about, who said that we can't shut out anyone because of skin color. He made me realize that white Americans want racism to end as well. All they need to know is that people of color want them to fight beside them against all racism and vice versa. One of the best ways to do that is by forming this new department. This department will consist of blacks, whites, Asians, and others working together to fight racism.

African Americans can't fight it alone. They shouldn't have to. Racism is everyone's fight."

The chairman paused a few moments after Maggie had finished speaking. "Ms. Carter, to start this department, we must wait for a new reparations bill to pass. Even with this newer approach, it could take a very long time."

"Mr. Chairman, I respect the process. I propose we put it to the American people for a vote."

"How?"

"We propose a bill to have white citizens donate $5 annually on their tax bill to fund this new department."

"By donating, you mean to pay."

"Yes."

The panel began talking amongst themselves. It was clear to Maggie that not everyone on the panel agreed with her proposal.

Bill spoke up, "Mr. Chairman, sir?"

The chairman pounded the gavel, and everyone fell silent. "Yes?"

Bill looked at Maggie and then focused on the panel. "I don't know if my ancestors were slave owners. I don't know if my ancestors committed any horrible acts against slaves. But I do know that this country is hurting right now. I know that people of color are hurting right now. I know white people are confused about how to help. If giving $5 a year to help fund this new department will ease tensions just a little, then I don't have a problem with that. If that small gesture can lead to better relations with my fellow Americans, then I don't have a problem with that. I believe many white Americans won't either."

The Chairman answered, "Thank you, Mr. Jackson. We now have all the necessary information to decide on the next steps. Ms.

Carter, I want to applaud your efforts in bringing this proposal to the attention of this panel. I am proud that you are a citizen of this great country. Your intentions are noble, caring, and just. We will deliberate and discuss all the possibilities of your proposal. We will talk soon. Again, thank you for your time. Adjourned."

One tap of the gavel rang through the room.

Representatives Crandall, Higgins, and Frazier met Maggie and Bill outside in the hallway. Crandall spoke first. "Ms. Carter, you did a great job."

Higgins shook their hands and said, "Absolutely. Maybe I can convince you to enter Mississippi politics?" They all laughed.

Maggie smiled, "Thank you. So what happens now?"

Frazier answered, "Now we wait. The process could take a long time, and we have many other items to resolve. Some congressmen will no doubt be counting on this to disappear and get lost in the pile of paperwork. But the three of us will be fighting to push it through. Also, you gained a few more supporters from this hearing, so our numbers are growing."

"This sounds promising."

Frazier smiled. "It seems frustrating, but this is how the system works. We may not always agree with it, but there isn't a better system in the world."

Maggie and Bill shook their hands again and said goodbye. Maggie took Bill's hand, and they walked to the building exit.

"Bill?" Maggie said, looking up at him while they walked.

"Yeah?"

"I love you."

***

Oz and Rialla stood over Pete, who was still sleeping on Rialla's bed.

"I think it's cute how his nose sometimes twitches while sleeping," Oz said.

Rialla giggled like a young schoolgirl. "Yes, it is quite amusing."

Without opening his eyes, Pete grumbled, "I can hear you."

Oz and Rialla laughed.

"I don't see what's so funny," Pete said.

Oz laughed, "Well, if you could see it from where we stand, you would."

Pete sat up. "Okay, playtime's over, children. What's going on?" Pete rubbed the back of his neck, stretching his head around.

"Rialla and I need to talk to you. Please come to the meeting room as soon as you can."

When Pete got to the meeting room, Oz and Rialla sat at the table. Oz had a floating screen hovering over the table. Pete sat down and asked Oz for a cup of tea. He began sipping the tea and said, "So, what do we need to talk about?"

Oz looked at Rialla, encouraging her to speak. "What is it, Rialla?" Pete asked.

Rialla looked at Oz. Oz gestured for her to talk.

"I want to try to help," Rialla said slowly.

Pete was confused. "Help with what?"

"Discovering what happened to Jessica."

"How?"

"I would like to join your team."

Pete almost spat out his tea. "What team?"

"You and Oz."

Pete looked at Oz. "I didn't realize we were recruiting."

Oz laughed, "Pete, Rialla wants to align with us."

Pete put his cup down and looked at Rialla. He noticed she was serious. "You realize what you are saying, Rialla?"

"Yes, I do."

Pete continued, "We need to know everything you know to combine all the pieces. Hopefully, we can figure this out together."

Rialla nodded. "Where do we begin?"

Pete asked Oz to record the conversation moving forward. "Rialla. We need to start with your mission. What were your orders?"

Rialla looked at Oz, then back at Pete. "My orders were to hunt and kill the Wen herald."

"Did they say why?"

"We only receive directives; no explanations are necessary."

"How about the invasion? Do you have any information on that?"

Rialla looked puzzled. "What invasion?"

"The Xanoclax invasion of Earth."

"I am not aware of such an invasion."

"What did you say?"

"I am not aware of an invasion of Earth."

Pete threw his chair back and stood up suddenly. He put both hands on the side of his head and rubbed his skull rapidly. He paced around the room slowly as Oz and Rialla watched him closely. They were afraid to speak, confused at Pete's actions.

Pete stopped at the end of the room and turned, then leaned back against the wall.

"Before I come to any conclusions, Rialla, would you know if there was a planned invasion?"

"On all large-scale invasions, Xanoclax warriors receive extensive training to adjust to the atmosphere and environment of the target planet."

"Would you consider invading Earth a large-scale invasion?"

"Yes, I would. Any mission that requires invading a planet is considered large-scale in nature."

Pete walked slowly towards the table. "So you are telling me that the Xans have no plans to invade Earth?"

"Not to my knowledge."

Pete walked to his seat and sat down. He slumped backward and stared up at the ceiling.

Oz looked at Rialla. "Rialla, do you understand what you just said?"

Rialla looked confused, "Did I not help? I answered truthfully."

"I know you did, but you just made us question everything. Why were we sent here? What purpose are we serving?"

Pete continued to stare at the ceiling. "Pawns," he said softly.

Rialla asked, "What is a pawn?"

"A piece on a chessboard."

Rialla was confused. "I don't understand."

"In chess, pawns are used as sacrificial pieces to enable a victory for the king. We are now trapped in a similar game that has defined us as pawns. Just like the pawns on a chessboard, we are strategically positioned within this game by an unknown chess master to enable his victory."

"How do we disrupt the game?" asked Oz.

"Carefully. Very carefully."

Rialla said, "Herald, I am not aware of an invasion of your planet. But I do remember something else."

Pete sat up. "What is it?"

"When stationed as a guard at one of our bases, I overheard a conversation between two commanders. They were talking about the Wen's new herald. The new herald experiment was a success, which concerned the commanders."

Oz looked at Pete. "The Xanoclax know about Krix'x's plan to create a herald army to protect our home planet."

"Protect them from what?" Rialla asked, surprised.

"Invasion from the Xans."

"Why would we invade Wen'q'rixsh?" Rialla asked.

"To steal our tech," Oz replied.

"We are not thieves, Vailen. We do not invade for material objects."

"But you tried in the past."

"When was this try?" Rialla asked defiantly.

"It was before my genesis. It's in our historical data."

"Why isn't this invasion in *our* historical data?"

"Because you failed."

"Nonsense. All battles, failures, and successes are recorded for future generations to learn from."

Pete looked at Oz. "Oz, pull up all the data you have on the Xanoclax."

"We don't have any."

Pete looked confused. "How is that even possible?"

Oz shrugged her shoulders. "I don't know. I wondered about that myself."

Pete sat silent. He wasn't sure how to proceed with this new information. He looked at Oz and Rialla, their faces anticipating his answer. It was all too perplexing.

Oz broke the silence. "Maybe we start at what we know and work backward?"

Pete nodded. He felt his world crumbling around him. Everyone Pete was with was now tangled up in a lie: Maggie, Bill, the White House, the whole planet, and Jessica. The murder of Jessica Morales was part of this alien deception. But how?

Pete snapped out of his momentary stupor. "Good idea. Let's put everything we know on the screen and figure out a connection."

"On it," Oz began typing.

Pete walked over to Rialla. "Are you alright?"

Rialla looked up at Pete and smiled, "Yes, I am. It will take some getting used to, though."

"What will?"

"Friendship. I have never known it. I'm afraid I don't know how to react to it."

"Rialla, just let it come to you. It took me a while to gain my feelings back. I'm not even sure I'm at 100% yet. But I know acts of kindness are much easier to respond to than acts of hate."

16 PICKING UP THE PIECES

Jessica smiled and hugged Pete tighter as they lay on her bed. Pete smelled the freshness of her hair and smiled. Jessica pulled away slowly and looked at Pete with her big, hazel eyes that melted into his. She looked concerned.

Pete asked, "What's the matter?"

She smiled. "I'm not sure you can answer this, but I'll ask anyway."

"Go ahead."

"Do you believe in God or religion?"

"I'm not sure. I can't remember if I did in the past. What about you?"

"I believe there's something bigger than us. I guess that was thanks to my Catholic upbringing. But I'm not religious anymore. I just lean a little to the spiritual side."

"So you don't believe in a particular religion?"

"No. I would rather be surprised than disappointed when it's all over."

"That's an interesting take."

"Interesting take?" Jessica laughed. "What, are you a philosopher now? Come on, let me hear your take. Come on. Come on!"

"Pete, come on, wake up. Come on!" Oz shook Pete.

Pete rolled over. "What is it?"

"Sorry to wake you from your catnap, but we're ready. Come on."

Pete rolled out of his bed and followed Oz to the control room. Rialla was staring at the screen. Oz sat down and began highlighting what she and Rialla had accomplished.

Oz began, "Here's what we know."

1. Krix'x trained Pete to be a herald

2. Krix'x assigned Oz to Pete

3. Krix'x assigned a mission to Pete

4. Pete made friends

5. The mission succeeded

6. Pete captured a Xan warrior

7. Rialla found blue eyes on the visual

8. Discovery that there isn't an invasion

"So, this is what we have. What's next?" Oz tapped her fingers on the table.

Rialla leaned forward, "We should fill in the blanks."

Oz shrugged. "What blanks?"

"Well, there are so many. Where do you want to start?"

"How about the first one?"

Rialla lifted her head and circled the number one.

Oz's eyes narrowed. "What's the blank?"

Rialla leaned back in her chair. "Why was he chosen? Why not someone else?" Rialla pointed at Pete.

Pete joined in, "That's good, Rialla. Oz, can you bring up all your data for my training? Maybe the answer is in there."

Oz slid over to a different keyboard and monitor. She stopped typing and stared at the monitor.

Pete walked up to Oz. "What's the matter?"

Oz kept staring at the monitor on the counter in front of her. "Pete, there's nothing there. It's vanished somehow."

Rialla spoke up, "How is that possible?"

Pete looked over at the list on the large screen. "Oz, any information in your database for items two and three?"

Oz typed frantically. But her worst fears materialized before her eyes: file: empty.

"Pete, there's nothing there."

"What about the visual records you showed me about my training?"

"Let me see." Oz went through her visual data files. "Pete, there's nothing here."

"Oz, who has access to these files?"

"Anyone on the Council."

Pete walked over to Oz and put his hand on her shoulder. He made sure to lower the tone of his voice. "Oz, why would anyone on the Council remove a data file?"

Oz didn't answer. She kept staring at the screen that said 'file empty.' She had never experienced this before. Erasing data files that were crucial to a mission was not logical.

"Oz, come on, think. Why would they remove data from an ongoing mission file?"

Oz turned around and looked at Pete. "I've never heard of this before, Pete. I can't explain it."

Rialla walked over to Oz and Pete. "This is not good. The beings who are leading you are deceiving you."

Pete turned to her. "Rialla, we realize that."

"These beings are dangerous to our survival."

"Rialla, enough," Pete said, raising his voice.

Rialla took a step back. "I did not mean to upset you."

Oz looked at Rialla. "I know. It's okay, Pete. It's okay."

"Oz, how can we get that data back?" asked Pete.

"I can't get it from here. I would have to go back to the lab on Wen'q'rixsh."

"Alright, let's figure this out another way then."

"No, Pete. I have to get those files. There's a lot more to this than you and me. Don't you see it? The Wen rely on information. Information feeds our logic-based system. The system that connects me to all the others on my planet is deteriorating right before me. Who knows what other valuable data is being kept from us?"

Pete looked concerned. "We can figure this out together."

Oz stood up. "Pete, I need to go back and retrieve that data. You need to help me."

"I can't."

"Can't, or won't?"

"Both."

Oz walked over to Rialla. "Rialla, if you want to join this team, help me."

"How can I help?"

Oz pointed at Pete. "Talk some sense into that human! I must return to my planet, but I can't do it without his help."

"Why do you need him to help? Why don't you just return?"

"Because I am his guide and programmed to do as he wishes. I can't leave him unless he orders me to."

Rialla walked over to Pete. "Why do you forbid the Vailen to return home?"

"I'm selfish. I don't want to lose my best friend. Oz has been a part of my entire existence. My life began in that alley in Bends Creek. Oz was there when I awoke. She was with me before that, during my training. I have never gone a day of my life without her."

Oz walked over to Pete and hugged him tightly. Pete was surprised. She looked up at him. "Jessica taught me that hugs are for people you care about."

Pete hugged Oz back. "She taught you well."

Rialla walked over to Oz and Pete and wrapped her arms around them. Everyone began laughing.

They separated, and Pete looked at Oz tenderly. "Oz, I can't exist without you. You have to promise you will return to me."

"Come on, man. I've got this."

"So, how do we do this?"

"I contact Krix'x and request to go back for immediate repairs. When he arrives, you convince him that I need to be repaired. He will take me back, and when I get the files, I'll have them return me to our ship."

Rialla spoke up, "Sounds like a good strategy."

"Except that it's dangerous as hell," Pete replied.

Rialla tilted her head. "What is hell?"

Pete nodded quickly at Rialla. "I'll tell you later."

Pete turned to Oz. "So what if they put you on the table and try to extract all your collected information? Won't they find out about our plan?"

"I will review my recordings and delete anything that will expose our plan."

"What if they decide to keep you and send another Vailen in your place?"

"You will tell them you won't accept another."

"What if—"

"Pete, stop," Oz interrupted. "I've got this. Don't worry."

"How will I know you're okay?"

"You won't until I return."

"Oz, I don't like this."

"I know, Pete. Neither do I. But our world is turning upside down right now. We have to take action."

"When will you leave?"

"Now."

"Now?"

"Yes, I have already contacted Krix'x. Rialla, please go to another room so he doesn't see you."

Rialla started walking away. She stopped, turned around, and looked at Oz. "Good luck with your mission, Vailen."

Oz smiled at Rialla. "Thanks. Do me a favor while I'm gone?"

"Yes."

"Take care of this human for me, please. He's in constant need of help."

"Yes, I will," Rialla smiled and walked away.

The screen was filled with static. Krix'x was arriving.

"Oz, I didn't get a chance to say goodbye."

Oz smiled. "Don't say goodbye, Pete. Say hasta luego."

Krix'x appeared on the screen. "Why have I been summoned?"

Pete looked at Oz and then at Krix'x. "My guide requires a few minor repairs."

"Vailen report."

"I am having trouble with my zenostat circuit. I have been reacting slowly to my herald's commands. I need a tune-up."

"Very well. J9-1-7, do you require a substitute guide?

"No, I will be stationary for the next few days. I'll be fine."

Krix'x looked at Oz. "Did you leave him a communicator?"

"Yes, he has it."

Krix'x summoned a blue liquid capsule from the screen large enough for Oz to enter. She looked at Pete, and before Pete could say a word, they disappeared into the screen.

Pete sat back and stared at the dark screen. He felt alone.

17 TRAINING DAY

It had been three days since Oz left. Pete was walking around the ship, going stir-crazy. He didn't know what to do with himself. He didn't want to watch visuals anymore. He preferred not to leave the ship for fear of missing a communication from Oz. Pete walked into Rialla's room. He had purposely avoided going into her room until now for reasons that were unclear to him.

Rialla was on her bed, watching a visual. She looked away from the screen and saw Pete.

"What's up?" Pete asked.

"Up?"

"How are you doing?"

"Fine," Rialla responded.

"That's it? Fine?" Pete was a little annoyed at Rialla's one-word answers.

"Did I answer incorrectly?" Rialla sat up with a concerned look on her face.

"No." Pete sounded frustrated. "You didn't answer incorrectly. I'm just trying to converse with you, and you always answer with only one word. It's a little frustrating."

Rialla got up out of bed. "I did not mean to frustrate you."

"I know. I'm not angry. I'm just bored."

"So am I," Rialla confessed.

Pete smiled. "Would you like to train?"

"Yes, please!"

Rialla followed Pete out of her room and into a large, empty room. Rialla was confused.

"How do we train in here?"

Pete smiled. "Hold on a minute. Oz set up a voice command circuit so I could ask for what I needed." He commanded aloud, "Deploy training room module."

Mats immediately appeared at the room's far end and unrolled across the floor. They stopped at Rialla's feet.

Pete looked at Rialla. "What would you like to train with?"

Rialla was excited. "I would like to train using a brathrit."

"Brathrit?"

"I saw a human fighting with one on a visual. It's a long stick."

Pete commanded, "Two bo staffs."

Two bo staffs appeared on the mat in the middle of the room. Rialla excitedly ran to the center of the room, picked up a bo, and began performing various intricate moves. Pete walked over to her, smiling. As Rialla went through her multiple exercises, Pete stood by and enjoyed the show. Rialla's moves were precise and fluid. She flew through the air with the grace of a gazelle, twirling her bo staff at will. She ran towards Pete, jumped, and landed before him. Her distance from Pete was perfect; her staff extended to the top of his head. She let it rest there without moving. She looked at him, breathing heavily and smiling.

"I am impressed," Pete applauded. He took off his coat and walked to the center of the room. He looked at the Xan.

"You need more comfortable clothes, Rialla." He commanded aloud again, "Female sweatpants and a tank top."

Rialla looked down at her sweatpants and shirt. "Thanks," she smiled.

Pete had sweatpants and a tank top on, and Rialla smiled when she noticed Pete's muscles. Pete used his foot to kick his staff up into the air. He caught it with his right hand and began twirling it around his body, switching hands at will.

Rialla smiled. "Not bad."

Pete circled to his left, and Rialla moved in the opposite direction. Pete smiled. "So, can you fight without your suit, Xan warrior?"

Rialla smiled back. "Only one way to find out, human." She lunged at Pete and was surprised he dodged her advance so quickly.

Pete was walking in his familiar semi-circle, smiling at Rialla. Rialla lunged again, only to achieve the same result. Pete was too quick. She had to try another approach.

Pete began taunting her. "Next time I strike, no more, Mr. Nice Guy."

He attacked Rialla head-on. His staff was moving from side to side incredibly fast. Rialla barely had time to parry his advance. Pete lunged past Rialla as she twisted 360 degrees in the air over his head. To her surprise, when she landed, Pete's staff balanced above her head. They both smiled and continued. Rialla used her staff to swat Pete's bo upward. Pete flipped backward, following the direction of his swatted bo, and landed in a ready stance. Rialla moved toward Pete quickly, with her staff twirling at incredible speed. Pete did not step back. He stood in place and blocked each blow. On the final block, he dodged and riposted, knocking Rialla to the mat.

Both combatants were sweating profusely. Pete walked over to Rialla and held out his hand. "What do you think? Have we had enough?"

Rialla smiled and reached for his hand. As Pete began lifting Rialla, she swatted at his feet with her staff, sending Pete to the mat on his back. She immediately jumped on top of his chest and placed her staff across his throat. She moved closer to Pete's face, their noses almost touching.

"Now we're done," she laughed and stood up. Pete laughed in return and took her hand. As she pulled him up, he swung his feet at her ankles and sent her onto her back. He jumped on top of her. He moved close to her face and stared at her momentarily.

Pete smiled. "I can do this all day. It's your call, warrior. Are we done?"

Rialla laughed, and Pete grinned. It was a nice laugh; it made him feel warm inside. He couldn't take his eyes off her beautiful, emerald-green eyes. Rialla stopped laughing, looking nervously at Pete. She softly asked, "Are you going to sit on me all night?"

Pete smiled and pulled her up. "Thank you," he said.

"For what?"

"For training with me. If I'm honest, thank you for spending time with me."

Rialla smirked. "Anytime you want your ass kicked, just let me know."

Every day, Pete felt like the odds of seeing Oz again worsened. He was thankful for the training sessions with Rialla, which helped lessen the stress. Several more days passed, and there was still no word from Oz. Pete continued to train every day with Rialla. Each day, they trained with a different weapon. On the fifth day, they trained without weapons. Pete kept sliding and ducking Rialla's attacks, and she became visibly frustrated.

"Do you want me to let you land a few punches, warrior?" Pete grinned.

Rialla let out a scream and advanced on Pete again. He continued to block her every advance. She stopped and bent over, placing both hands on her knees. Pete walked up to her.

"Are you alright?" He asked in a concerned voice.

He noticed she was breathing heavily. He walked over to her and placed his hand on her back. When he bent down towards her head, Rialla screamed and hit Pete with an uppercut to his chin. Pete flew back several feet and landed on his back. Rialla straightened up and laughed.

"Ha," she yelled, "I caught you with your guard down."

Pete sat up on the mat and rubbed his chin. "Good one, I'll let you have that. But I promise it won't happen again."

They ended their training session and headed to their rooms. Before they left the training room, Pete stopped. Rialla looked at him curiously.

"What is it?" Rialla asked,

"Rialla, can I talk to you for a minute? I need to ask you something that's bothering me."

Rialla looked puzzled. She was still breathing a little heavily from the sparring. "Ask me anything," she answered.

Pete looked at her momentarily and chose his words carefully, "Rialla, why are you here if there isn't a planned Xan invasion? Why is it so important to stop me if the Xans didn't know why the Wens were creating heralds?"

"I would like to not speak of my mission," she spoke softly, looking away from Pete.

"Rialla, you can trust me. I thought we were a team now."

Rialla turned back and looked at Pete's face. She saw honesty and trust in Pete's eyes. "I do trust you."

"Then why can't you talk about it?"

Rialla put her back against the wall and slowly slid to the floor. She brought her knees to her chest and rested her forehead on her knees.

"Are you okay?" Pete asked.

Rialla didn't look up. "No," she said into her knees.

Pete walked next to her and sat down on the floor. "What is it, Rialla? You can talk to me."

"I feel bad about what I've done," she answered. "I tried to kill you."

"That's all in the past. You're starting over with us now. There's nothing to feel bad about."

She lifted her head and looked at Pete. Then she lay her head back down, keeping her gaze on Pete. "The Xans will not stop until you are terminated."

Pete looked surprised. "I don't understand."

Rialla closed her eyes for a moment. She opened them and explained, "You are a herald of the Wen'q'rixshi, and Xan warriors have orders to eliminate Wen heralds."

"I get that," Pete said. "But why? Why kill the heralds? You don't know their purpose. I don't understand."

"We thought they were building an army to attack us, not to defend their planet from us."

Pete looked away from Rialla. He stared at his reflection in the metal ceiling, concentrating on the image looking down on him. Pete stared for the longest time without saying a word. He might have sat in the silence longer if Rialla hadn't broken it.

"Are you okay?"

Pete kept looking at the ceiling. He answered, "I don't know," without taking his eyes off his image.

"I didn't want to tell you, but you wanted to know."

Pete looked at Rialla. "I'm glad you did tell me, Rialla. I needed to know."

"The Xan cannot allow the Wen to build an army of heralds. The Wen will use that army to attack Xanstar."

"Why do you think they will use a herald army to attack your planet instead of defending their own?"

"The Wen want to destroy us. I know you have been working with them, and the Vailen is trustworthy, but they aren't what they appear to be."

Pete stood up. He walked away slowly and then walked back towards Rialla. "So what are you saying, Rialla? The Wen are the bad guys, and you're the good guys?"

"No, I am not saying anything about who is right or wrong. I am stating a fact. Why is there no record of our planet in your Vailen's files? Why did the Wen create the tale of the Xanoclax's impending invasion of your planet? We can ask so many questions under our current circumstances."

Pete sat back down next to Rialla. "I'm hoping Oz gets back with these answers."

Rialla agreed, "I hope so as well. I am aligned with you both now. I do not wish bad news on either of you. But we need the truth, for I fear we may be in greater peril than we can fathom."

"What makes you say that?"

"A Xanoclax warrior does not kill innocents. Even if it helps us to reach a specific goal, a Xan warrior cannot shed the blood of innocent beings, according to our logic belief. I can tell you, with the utmost certainty, that the Xans were not involved in Jessica's murder."

Pete stood back up. He took a few steps and put his hands to his head. Pete said under his breath, "Jessica is dead because of me."

"No, that is not true."

Pete yelled and looked up at his reflection in the ceiling. He yelled again, raised his hand towards the ceiling, and shot an energy pulse at his image. The pulse struck the ceiling and dissipated into the air.

Rialla's eyes widened. "How did you do that?"

Pete looked at his hand. "I don't know how it works. I think it, and it happens."

"But you do not have any equipment on your body. You don't have your guide present. How is this possible?"

"The Wen can't explain it either. They made me promise to come to their planet to train other heralds. I think they want me back in their lab so they can run tests on me."

Rialla stood up and looked at Pete, concerned, "You cannot let them control you. You cannot help them."

"I am not going to do anything right now. I have to figure all this mess out."

Rialla walked closer to Pete. "Listen closely."

Pete looked into Rialla's eyes. They were standing face to face.

Rialla continued, "When I do not return to my ship, the Xan will try again. The next time, they will send two warriors. And if they fail, three, and so on. Your demise has become a top priority for Xanoclax leadership."

***

After showering, Rialla dried herself with a towel and wrapped it around her body. She walked to her room and retrieved a clean pair of sweatpants and a T-shirt. She was beginning to like the way her body felt in human clothing. *Human attire,* she thought, *was practical and comfortable.* The cotton material was soft on her skin, unlike her bodysuit. Warriors on Xanstar were not allowed to remove their bodysuits. The bodysuit had hundreds of wires connected to the nervous system, and it was impractical to remove it every time a warrior took off his armor.

The bodysuit served two functions. The primary function was to connect the warrior's nervous system to his armor. This connection provided the warrior with control of his armor through his thoughts. The armor could create weapons and react spontaneously to enemies' advances. The other function of the bodysuit was to conceal gender. The bodysuit completely covered the warrior from head to foot. Bodysuits were a significant component of controlling sexual encounters among the warriors.

Rialla's life as a Xan warrior was lonely compared to what she was now exposed to. She brushed her hair for the first time while seated in front of a mirror. She liked that her hair was getting longer. Oz had left Rialla the brush and other human beauty tools before she left.

Rialla kept looking at her face in the mirror while brushing her hair. She was thinking about the strange feelings she felt when Pete sat on her at the end of their training session. She didn't understand why her body temperature had started to rise. The heat she felt wasn't the same as the heat her body generated from the training.

Rialla realized that she was in a state of retrospection. To undertake a self-examination was not an ability that a Xan warrior possessed. She continued staring at her image in the mirror. She performed each brushstroke instinctively. It was like she wasn't brushing her hair at all. Rialla's stare captivated her and lifted her from her body. This feeling of relaxation made her feel lighter than a feather. Her body was brushing her hair, but she was drifting away. She never blinked. The trance was beautiful. She didn't want it to end. But it did.

The intercom rang, and Pete's voice came through. "Rialla, are you there?"

Rialla stopped brushing her hair and looked at the brush.

"Rialla? Are you there?" Pete repeated through the intercom.

Rialla placed the brush on the counter and went to the intercom. She pressed the button and replied in a soft, quiet voice, "Yes, I am here."

Pete replied, "I'm sorry to disturb you. Were you sleeping?"

"No, just relaxing."

"Would you like to join me in the control room for dinner?"

"Yes, I would. I will be there shortly."

Rialla finished getting dressed and walked to the control room. Pete had a table with two chairs between the control panel and the back wall. There was a vase of flowers in the middle of the table, and Pete had a steak in front of each dinner place. There was also a carafe of wine with two glasses.

"What is all this for?" Rialla asked, surprised.

"I just thought we could try something different tonight. Is that alright?"

Rialla smiled. "Yes, of course." Rialla sat at one end of the table, and Pete poured her a glass of wine.

"I didn't know how you liked your steak cooked, so I ordered it medium."

"That's good." Rialla didn't want to tell Pete that she had eaten the raw meat of an animal she had killed during her Xan training. Medium would do.

The two of them began eating and didn't say a word until their meal was almost finished. There were the occasional glances and smiles from each of them, but they chose to remain silent and enjoy the meal.

Just before they finished, Pete held up his glass. "A toast," He smiled.

"Toast?"

"Yes, you raise your glass and salute each other."

Rialla held up her glass.

Pete continued with the toast. "Here's to newfound friends and trust."

Rialla smiled, and Pete touched her glass with his, creating a soft sound. Pete began drinking his wine, and she copied his gesture. They finished their meal, and Pete stood up. He coaxed Rialla to follow him to the control panel. Pete had the carafe in one hand

and the glass of wine in the other. Rialla followed, holding her glass.

Pete commanded, "Two recliners."

Two reclining chairs that looked like they were taken from someone's living room appeared.

Rialla laughed, "What is this?"

Pete urged Rialla to sit in one of the recliners. She was amazed at how comfortable it was. Pete rocked back and forth in his chair, and Rialla's eyes widened. She began rocking back and forth. She was going a little too fast, and Pete tried to warn her to slow down. But before he could speak, Rialla's recliner flew back, and she did a backward somersault off the back of the chair as it hit the floor.

Pete got up and ran to her aid. Rialla was kneeling with both hands on the floor, laughing hysterically.

"Can I do that again?" she laughed.

Pete was laughing with her. "That's not what this chair is made for. You need to sit in it and rock slowly to relax."

Rialla stood up, and after she lifted the chair upright, she sat back down and began rocking slowly and more gently. "Is this better?" She smiled at Pete.

Pete nodded and leaned over the arm of the chair to grab the reclining lever. He pulled it back, extending his chair. Rialla followed his movements and extended her own. She was feeling very comfortable. She looked for her wine glass, but it was nowhere in sight. Pete commanded another, and Rialla nodded her approval.

"I want you to see something," he said. He turned on the screen, revealing the area outside the ship. He dimmed the lights inside the control room. The sun was setting, and the sky was changing colors. Rialla gazed at the large screen, never taking her attention away. The sky was turning deep red and purple.

"It almost looks like a painting, doesn't it?" Pete fixed his gaze on the outside sky.

Rialla, not looking away from the screen, answered, "Yes, it does."

"I can remember sitting in the alley watching the sunset. It always made me feel like there was something in the universe that was bigger than all of us. I don't understand why more people don't take all this in every day. If everyone simplified their lives and didn't stress so much, we wouldn't have half the problems we face today," Pete said, still staring at the screen. He looked at Rialla, "Man, I'm sorry. I'm rambling."

Rialla looked over at Pete, "No, it's good. I like listening to you."

Pete looked over at her. The light from the sunset hit her face perfectly, and he began to get lost in her wide, green eyes. He just sat and stared at her.

Rialla responded to his stare with a coy smile. "Are you okay?"

Pete looked away from Rialla. He was a little embarrassed. "Sorry, I got lost in thought for a moment."

They both stared at the screen, enjoying the sunset. When the sun finally disappeared from view, the park lights came on. People were walking across the Lawn in all directions. Some people stopped and took pictures of the spaceship. Kids were running around, some chased by their parents.

Pete began to speak again, "Many humans are innocent with good hearts. People are working every day, trying to make a living. They don't know what's happening outside their distinct worlds."

"It's better that they don't know what is out there. Humans must concentrate on caring for each other and making their world better for all."

Pete responded, "I agree."

Then, they sat back in their recliners and watched the world go by.

18 HOMECOMING

Pete and Rialla were training when they heard the alarm sound. They both stopped and looked at each other. Pete asked Rialla to wait in her room while he went to check out the alarm. He ran to the control room, where static played on the screen. Pete went to the control panel and turned the alarm off.

The screen went black. It had been almost two weeks since Oz left, and Pete stood in excited anticipation. Krix'x made his familiar entrance and began speaking.

"J9-1-7, have you anything to report?"

Pete wanted to yell at Krix'x to shut up and send Oz through, but he knew if he did, it would alert Krix'x to Pete's newfound emotions. Now was not the time to lose control.

"I have no report to make. I have not encountered any Xans in the past two weeks."

"Very well," Krix'x answered.

Rialla was watching and listening, peering in from behind a wall around the corner from the control room. Her curiosity got the better of her, and she could not sit in her room waiting.

Krix'x began moving off the screen. Another blue trail, thicker and more comprehensive than the trail behind his head, began rolling off the screen next to his face. The light was brighter from the second blue path than the stream behind Krix'x. It continued past him and stopped, suspended above the floor next to Pete. The control room was bathed in bright blue light, which caused Pete to squint his eyes. As the light slowly dimmed, an oval-shaped metal pod materialized at Pete's feet and slowly opened.

Pete held back his excitement when Oz stepped out of the pod. He noticed something different about her. Her outer core was polished, bright as a freshly cut sapphire. There were no marks on her core from all the wear and tear of time and battle. She was pristine. She looked like a newborn, free of flaws.

Krix'x spoke, "Vailen, report."

Oz answered, "All systems are fully operational and awaiting my herald's orders."

Krix'x looked at Pete. "Yes, this is the same Vailen previously assigned to you. She has gone through some slight modifications and programming."

"Does she remember our past experiences together?" Pete asked Krix'x.

"All past sequences are recorded into her memory database for reference when needed." Krix'x looked at Pete and Oz. The blue stream of light that brought Oz across the screen slowly retracted. Krix'x spoke one last time.

"J9-1-7, it has come to our attention that the Xanoclax will send more warriors. You need to prepare yourself, along with your guide, for the next encounter."

"I will," Pete answered.

Krix'x slowly withdrew into the screen and disappeared. Pete stood there in front of the screen. He slowly turned towards Oz and waited for her to speak.

"Is there anything you require at this time, herald?" Oz asked Pete in a programmed voice.

"Oz, do you remember me?" Pete asked, concerned.

"I have all your files in my database," Oz spoke again, deadpan.

"Come on, Oz. Snap out of it and talk to me."

"Ah, yes, I see," Oz looked up at the ceiling. She was reviewing her files on Pete. "Yes, there it is."

Pete got excited, "What, Oz? What do you see?"

"In my files, it says you like scratching your ass."

Pete looked dumbfounded.

Oz looked at Pete and smiled. "Gotcha!"

Pete laughed and hugged Oz. "I knew it. I knew you wouldn't leave me."

Oz pulled away from Pete slowly. "Never, Pete, never."

Rialla walked in and smiled. "Welcome back, Vailen."

Oz turned from Pete. "Did you keep this guy straight while I was gone?"

"I had to kick his ass a few times, but overall it was okay."

Oz smiled at her. "Thanks, Rialla."

Rialla nodded. "You're welcome."

Pete wanted to get down to the details of Oz's trip. "Come on, then. Let's hear everything."

Oz went to the meeting room, and Rialla and Pete followed. Oz clapped twice, and the lights turned on.

I still get a kick out of that, she thought, smiling.

Pete and Rialla sat on one side of the table, watching Oz sit on the other. When she sat down, she looked at them.

"Our suspicions and fears have proven productive," she started. Oz looked down at the table in front of her. She waved her hand across the table, and a large book appeared, encased in a clear, impenetrable box. Oz placed her hands on the box and stared at it momentarily. She looked up at Pete with a concerned look on her face. She moved both hands around the encasement as she spoke.

"I took this from our Hall of Cantrillion, which houses all our great books of science and historical data. This book was not on display or made available for public reading. My search for answers based on theories—or hunches, as you would say here on Earth—led me to this book. I have yet to open it and read its contents. I don't know if I want to find the answers since my theories are quasi-scientific. I also obtained our mission data files. I copied them to a drive and will connect to our system later."

Oz paused, staring at the book for several moments before continuing. "I believe that if I open this book, everything about my life as I know it will change. It may be best to tell you about the events that occurred before I open this book." Oz stared down at it in silence.

Pete glanced at Rialla, who was already looking at him. He asked Oz softly, "What did you find, Oz?"

Oz looked up from the book and began recapping her journey. "It was a little slow going at first. When I arrived, Krix'x ordered me to the laboratory. There was a team of three Draiksx waiting for me there. A Draiksx is on a scientific level just below a Traa'zel. They are brilliant, but their role is to perform experiments and repairs. They immediately connected me to their computers and ran diagnostics. One of the scientists began a scan of the diagnostics and told the other two that the preliminary scan showed zero errors. The other two scientists looked at me, puzzled. I sat up and yelled at them to get their heads out of their asses and do their job."

"They were shocked at first. I don't believe the scientists have ever heard Earth cussing before. I don't know if they were stunned by the language or the volume of my command. The two standing by my table ran over to the scientist at the computer. I asked how long it would take, and they said they weren't sure. I raised my voice again and demanded a precise time. They immediately formed a circle, and all I heard was mumbling. One scientist turned to me and said a few days at the most. I got off the table and headed out of the laboratory."

***

The science community of Wen'q'rixshi consisted of a campus of connected buildings on an island in the middle of Wexis, the capital city. The tall, steel monoliths had mirrored surfaces and stood out from all other buildings on the planet. There were no windows or balconies visible on the exterior of the buildings. The five tallest buildings encircled the perimeter of the island. A giant blue megalith rested at the center of the expanse between the buildings.

The campus, surrounded by water, was comprised of hallways that ran above and below the water that surrounded the island. The hallways connecting below the surface linked various rooms with diversified purposes, all constructed under the surface. Some of these facilities were for the Council's use only. The Council and other scientists used the non-exclusive rooms for experimental functions.

Oz walked out of the laboratory and down the hall. She wasn't sure how much time she had to find answers. Like most public buildings on Wen'q'rixsh, the hallway she was walking in was wide, with metal walls. The walls had mirrored surfaces that rose straight up without interference from décor or alcoves. The tall ceilings and lack of furniture echoed her steps throughout the hallway. Every section she walked towards remained dark until she came within a few feet. Once there, the section would light up, and the section behind her became dark.

Oz was only concerned with the science campus and didn't need to worry about leaving the island. She fought off the desire to visit her family and approached her mission logically. There would have been no decision to make in the past, but her exposure to the neon gases in Earth's atmosphere had slightly changed her mental rationale. Since exposure to the neon gases, Oz questioned all decisions logically and considered her emotional responses. She had concluded that logic with a slight touch of emotion was acceptable.

As Oz walked down the hallway, she noticed the area a few sections ahead of her was lighting up. She decided to use her protean ability to shapeshift to hide by dissolving herself into the mirrored wall. Her section went dark, and she waited for whoever was walking towards her section to pass by. She waited without concern because she didn't fear being discovered by anyone coming her way. Oz simply wanted to avoid communicating with anyone while she was there. If they were Traa'zels, and they asked a question, she would not be able to lie. It was better to avoid detection and communication.

As she waited patiently, Oz heard several deep voices approaching. A strange feeling swept across her mind. Oz sensed a slight familiarity with one of the approaching Traa'zels. They weren't speaking loudly; it was just idle chatter. When the figures walked by her, the feeling of familiarity grew stronger. She watched the three figures pass slowly by her. Each figure wore an identical dark blue robe draped loosely over their bodies. Oz could not see their feet as they walked, and they appeared to float just above the floor. The robes hung below the length of their arms and obscured their hands, and the long hood attached to each robe fell over their heads and concealed their faces. At certain moments, the tilt of their heads and positioning allowed Oz to see their blue eyes. Their eyes were like tiny, bright lacerations cut into the dark abyss of their hoods. All three figures appeared to be similar in height as well.

The Traa'zel in the center of the three stopped unannounced. The two others took a few steps forward, then stopped, looking back at him. The center Traa'zel was staring at the mirrored wall that housed Oz. The Council member stared at the wall, studying its surface.

Does he see me? Oz thought.

The Traa'zel stood there, staring directly at Oz's eyes. It was as though the two were competing in a staring contest. The Traa'zel tilted his head slightly. Oz froze and refused to blink. The Council member took a few more steps towards Oz. He began to raise his hand when one of the other Council members called out. He turned quickly and walked to the other two Council members. The sudden turn of the robe caused a slight breeze across Oz's face. A faint aroma, barely detectable, accompanied the breeze.

That odor, she thought. *Where have I sensed that odor before?*

Without saying a word, the three continued their walk.

Once the section became dark again, Oz waited a few minutes before regenerating to her normal appearance and continuing to walk. She turned back briefly and noticed that all sections were dark behind her. She assumed the Council members had entered a room. She continued her walk to the Hall of Cantrillion.

19 CHANCE ENCOUNTER

Oz approached a section of the hallway that widened to the right. The circular tract of the hallway opened to a large door that rested within a large metal arch. The arch was the lone aesthetic detail on the science campus. Oz had never known why the Wen had placed a decorative span above the door to the Cantrillion. Curiosity was not logical, and the arch's construction was never discussed, not even in texts.

Oz advanced toward the door, and it opened seamlessly and without a sound. The main hall of the Cantrillion was circular and opened to the ceiling. The atmosphere reminded Oz of Earth's libraries. Unlike them, reference materials housed in the Cantrillion were filed digitally and not paper-constructed.

Oz walked towards a large, round table in the center of the room. The table was divided into segments, each with a flat screen on the surface. Oz went to one screen and powered it up. She proceeded to enter requests for information on Xanstar. Every query resulted in the same response, 'no data on file.' Oz felt her emotional side taking over, and she became flummoxed by the lack of available information. She attempted every possible combination of data entries for Xanstar with no results. She knew the Cantrillian was the only building on Wen'q'rixsh that housed historical data. It was her only resource.

Oz noticed an elderly Brangstrid as he slowly approached the table. He had a round face that matched his round body. He resembled an Earth character she read about in fantasy lore that humans would call a 'dwarf.' He wore black-framed glasses with thick lenses that made his eyes appear more prominent than their size. His aqua-blue robe hung open on his round body. The hood of the robe rested on his neck. She could tell he was an elder because his hair was a light aqua, almost white. Younger Brangstrids had dark-colored hair and were quick and agile. This older one walked slowly and precisely towards the table.

When the elder approached the table, a section automatically lowered and adjusted to his height. From Oz's point of view, the Brangstrid was wholly hidden from sight by her table. She shifted her height to see over the table and observe him. He proceeded to conduct his research. Oz observed him for several moments while he entered requests into the display. He was very busy typing entries and ignored her indiscreet stares. Oz shifted back to her previous height and thought about the Brangstrid.

The Wen sought Brangstrids for their knowledge of Wen'q'rixshi history. They were the first inhabitants of Wen'q'rixsh and were the first to record the events of the planet. It was difficult to gain an audience with a Brangstrid due to the high demand for their attention. The Brangstrids' minds were capable of seeing outside of logic. It wasn't until hundreds of years after the Brangstrid's first appearance on Wen'q'rixsh that logic became the planet's sole philosophy.

Brangstrids lived longer than all other beings on the planet, but their population was dwindling. It wasn't logical for them to procreate with the different species on Wen'q'rixsh. Even if they were allowed, Oz thought, a Brangstrid would have difficulty finding a mate outside his race.

"And why is that?" The older voice came from under Oz's table.

"What?" Oz asked.

"Why would it be so difficult for a Brangstrid to mate outside his race?"

Oz looked in the direction of the Brangstrid and talked at the top of the table. "I didn't mean to insult you. I– wait, how did you know I was thinking that?"

"Have you been away from this planet so long that you have forgotten? Brangstrids read minds, my dear Vailen. That's why we don't pay attention to nosy gawkers as we go about our business. If we did, our heads would explode from all the unnecessary gibberish."

"It was not my intention to disrespect you."

The Brangstrid walked around the table and stopped at her chair. The top of his head was even with the arm support of her chair. He smiled at her.

"I've been waiting for you, Vailen. I've been waiting for some time."

Oz looked down at the elder Brangstrid, and before she could respond, the Brangstrid spoke. "We need to go to one of the research rooms and talk. Immediately, if not sooner. Possibly sooner than that. However, I am not sure if that is possible. Come with me, Vailen."

Oz followed the Brangstrid to a soundproof research room. The room was empty except for a table and two chairs. The Brangstrid climbed onto the chair and motioned to Oz to take her seat. The two stared at each other for a moment without saying a word. The Brangstrid spoke first.

"There isn't much time, so listen closely. Several Brangstrids, including yours truly, have come to believe that an invasion of Wen'q'rixsh is imminent."

Oz sat up and was about to speak.

The Brangstrid cut in. "Wait, let me finish. Like I said, there isn't much time to talk. We believe that events are now in motion to eradicate the existence of our way of life as we know it."

Oz looked puzzled. "What? How?"

"Meet me here tomorrow, and I will present you with some evidence needing your immediate attention. I believe this is the evidence you came back from Earth to procure."

The Brangstrid climbed down from his chair and headed toward the door.

"Wait," Oz called out.

Before she could ask, he responded, "My name is Braylin."

"Braylin? You're Braylin?"

The Brangstrid turned to Oz and smiled. "The one and only."

"What's this all about? Why can't you tell me now?"

Braylin sighed and spoke softly and calmly. "We must proceed cautiously, for the trouble comes from the enemy within."

He turned away and walked through the door, leaving Oz at the table with a million unanswered questions running through her mind.

20 HISTORY REPEATS ITSELF

Oz was lying on the table in the laboratory, thinking of Braylin while the Draiksx ran more tests. She lay there, patiently contemplating Braylin's parting remark. *The trouble comes from the enemy within.* His voice kept repeating over and over in her head. *The trouble comes from the enemy within.* She was pondering what logical evidence Braylin could have to reveal who the 'enemy within' could be.

"We need to reboot your receptor logic," one Draiksx told her.

Without moving, Oz replied, "Reboot that area, and do not go outside that framework."

"Of course," the Draiksx nodded.

Oz continued to think of Braylin. She was having difficulty resolving her perplexity about their prior conversation.

How did Braylin know I would be at the Cantrillian? How did he know me? She was concentrating so hard on Braylin that she almost didn't hear the three Draiksx discussing the result of the reboot. They appeared to be stumped by it.

Oz sat up and unplugged herself from the table. She walked over to the three Draiksx.

"So, what's up?" she asked.

The three scientists looked at each other, then up at the ceiling. They looked puzzled, and one replied, "I don't think anything is up?"

Oz tilted her head sideways, "Seriously? Come on. It's just an expression. It doesn't mean to look up literally."

The three scientists looked at each other and nodded. They understood.

"So, tell me. What are you finding on the reboot?"

One Draiksx said, "It appears the reboot was not the solution. We need to conduct other tests."

Oz patted the closest scientist on the back. "Okay then, why don't we pick up with this tomorrow after you put your heads together and devise another solution?"

The Draiksx looked at Oz. "We can run another test now if you like."

"Nah, I'm good. Let's pick it up tomorrow. Get your people to call my people, and we'll do that lunch thing, okay? Buhbye." And with that, Oz walked out of the laboratory.

The three scientists watched Oz as she headed out the door. One scientist called out, "What are people?"

The other scientist asked, "What's a lunch thing?"

***

Oz waited in the research room where she had first talked to Braylin. The more time passed, the more questions popped into her head. She waited for at least two hours, sitting all by herself. While she waited, she opened the screen on her side of the table. She searched for Xan encounters. Every file that came up concerned a Xan warrior attacking another species. After the attack, the visual continued with the Xan stealing the victim's life force. All data on the Xans consisted of violent and aggressive acts towards others. Not one background or historical file was available for research.

"There isn't any data on the Xanoclax," Braylin said, walking into the room.

"What makes you an expert on this subject?" Oz answered almost sarcastically. She was a little irritated that he had taken so long to arrive.

"Ah, I see your exposure to the atmosphere of Earth has affected your logic circuitry."

"How did you know that? Brangstrids aren't scientists. And you do not have access to High Council experiments or missions."

Braylin was carrying a black sack strapped across his shoulder. He climbed up on the chair and turned to Oz. He was breathing heavily.

"This gets harder all the time," he said, referring to the effort to sit upon the chair. He smiled at Oz and stared at her for a few moments.

Oz started to wonder if Braylin had experienced a heart attack and was frozen in place when his voice startled her.

"Right then," Braylin snapped out of his daze. He pulled a few books from his sack and placed them on the table. The books were ancient, and the binding was damaged in several places. Braylin had short, fat fingers that gently opened the first book. Oz noticed the care and respect that the book received from Braylin. He was in awe of the book. He looked many years younger as he slowly turned the pages.

"Ah, let's see. I know it's here," Braylin commented as he turned the pages slowly. As he purposefully lifted one page with his right hand, he placed the page gently into his left hand. He lowered it like a sleeping baby into its cradle. Oz sat, watching the elder Brangstrid, wondering what it felt like to love something so much, to treat it with such care. She had thought she felt this love for Pete and Jessica, but she didn't have the facilities to express how she felt the way the Brangstrid was now doing.

"I was afraid to bookmark the page for fear of damaging it," he laughed. "Maybe I should have written the page numbers down, hehe. Too old for this, I guess. I'm simply too old."

"What is this book?" Oz asked.

"This, my dear Vailen, is the Brangstrid historical recordings of events. We have documented significant events on our planet since the beginning of our time. There exist three records of historical accounts."

"What is it you want to show me?"

"All our books were donated to the Cantrilliar many years ago. The Brangstrid made copies of two of the books. The third was in progress when they were donated. At the time of the donation, all parties involved decided that two proprietors of the historical documents were unnecessary. Brangstrids were replaced by the logic of digital record keeping."

"But you kept your copies?"

"Yes. In the event logic dictated changing the records of our historical past, we would have the truth."

"Why would it be logical to change historical records?"

"History repeats itself, my dear Vailen. Logic or no logic, history dictates that beings will stray from the fold. And when they stray, they manipulate people into believing what they would have them believe."

"But that is an illogical premise," Oz retaliated.

"Is it?" Braylin chuckled. "When we first realized who we were as the first of Wen'q'rixshi, we lived with logic and emotions. We eventually trained ourselves and the generations that came after us in logical reasoning. We, and I mean all who occupied this planet then, decided that emotions were illogical and had caused transgressions on other planets."

"You were not born on this planet? What was your reason for coming here? Were you fleeing an injustice from your home planet? Or were you explorers?"

"Marvelous, marvelous," Braylin said in an excited voice. "I haven't had a conversation with another being that was this much fun in ages."

"I'm glad you're enjoying yourself. With respect, I don't want to rain on your parade, but why me?"

"Oh my word, I haven't heard that expression in a millennium."

"How do you know the language of Earth?"

"We'll get to all that. Let's focus on the matter at hand, for we do not have much time. Ah, yes, here it is."

"What is it?"

"The record of our first visit from another alien race."

"What race? Who was the first to visit?"

Braylin looked up from the book and stared at Oz through his round, black-framed glasses. He smiled, never taking his eyes off Oz. "Our first visitors? The Xanoclax."

Oz stood up abruptly, and her chair fell back. "How can that be?"

"It's all right here, in the First of the Three," Braylin smiled.

"Why are you smiling? This cannot be possible!" Oz went on.

"Why can't it be possible? Because it is taught by the Council of Educators that the Xanoclax is a violent, barbaric race whose sole purpose is destroying other civilizations?"

"Yes! That is the logical explanation that we learn from the day we are born through our education years."

"What if I told you that was all fabricated?"

"To what logical end? How does fabricating a story concerning the Xans benefit the Wen?"

"Over the years, the Brangstrids were told by the High Council that logic dictates that an evil presence is required to verify a good presence. One cannot exist without the other. The Brangstrids agreed not to disclose the true history to allow the continuity of logic and peace to flourish. We saw no harm in this falsehood because we knew the Xans were light-years away from our planet and surely would not be visiting again."

"Why would they not visit?"

"The Xan that visited us were refugees from the great Xan War. Our technology was given to them to enable their fight for freedom from enslavement. The Xan thanked us and returned to their planet. They produced weapons using our tech and went on to win the war and their freedom."

"The Wen is responsible for Xan technology?"

"Yes. Ironic, I suppose. The very beings we are taught to distrust are those we supplied arms to."

"How do you know so much about what happened to the Xan after they left our planet?"

"I communicate with other beings throughout our galaxy. I am aware of many events in our universe."

"Braylin, that is very dangerous. If the High Council knew of this, you would be banished."

"Yes, I know, but–"

Before Braylin could finish, an alarm rang in Oz's communication unit. It was a call from the High Council.

"Braylin, leave!" Oz shouted.

"Right, same time tomorrow, then?"

"Yes," Oz replied as she stalled the communication. She immediately opened her screen and began typing. The communication came through her screen. It was Krix'x.

"Vailen, report," barked Krix'x. His eyes stared directly into hers from the screen.

"I am at the Cantrillian doing research," Oz replied.

Krix'x looked around the screen on which he was transmitted. He noticed Oz's queries about troubleshooting logic circuitry. He read a few of them and looked at Oz.

"What is the purpose of these queries?"

"I am trying to assist the Draiksx with my repairs."

"I did not realize they were having issues completing the necessary upgrades. Perhaps I will assist them with the diagnostics."

194

"That is not required. I believe the Draiksx have narrowed down the compromised element in my system to a few calibrations."

"Very well. Continue with your research if it is logically necessary. We will need you active and back on earth as soon as possible. I do not wish to have the herald left too long without guidance."

"I agree."

21 DELAYING THE INEVITABLE

Whenever the Draiksx figured out a solution to Oz's dilemma, Oz ensured something else would go wrong and need repair. She didn't know how much longer she could delay the scientists. She knew the next time Krix'x had to call in, he would not hesitate to get involved and find a solution. Oz was positive that the scientists would never conclude that her attitude was born from trace elements in the Earth's atmosphere. The neon gases never surfaced in any scans the scientists made, and Oz knew she could prolong her stay as long as Krix'x was not involved. Once he was, she would have to surrender to one of the solutions determined by the scientists. If she didn't, Krix'x would order a reboot of all systems, and Oz would lose her memory of Pete and her time on Earth.

"Look, Braylin, I don't have much time left. We have met here for almost a week, and I think the history lessons are over. My long stay is already looking suspicious to the Council. We need to focus on the here and now."

Braylin sighed and closed the book gently. He placed both books into his sack and looked at Oz.

"You are right, Vailen," he smiled softly. He looked down at the table and folded his hands upon it. He sat there, staring at his hands, rocking them slowly.

"I have enjoyed our meetings, Braylin. I wish I had time to listen to more, but I must find the answers to what is happening."

"What do you believe is happening?" Braylin asked, still staring down at his rocking hands.

"I believe someone is manipulating our actions on Earth. My herald explains that we are pawns being maneuvered on a chessboard."

"Why do you think that?"

"Because our mission is a lie. In our mission, the Traa'zels clearly state that the Xanoclax will attack Earth, and we have found out they are not. There appears to be an imposter masquerading as a Xan warrior carrying out horrendous acts to make it look like the Xan are responsible."

"To what end?"

"If I knew that, I would not have come back to find out," Oz raised her voice.

Oz noticed Braylin had stopped shaking his hands on the table. He looked up at Oz. In the short time that Oz had known Braylin, she had never seen him this serious. He stared at her over the top of his frames for a few moments.

"I have met you here every day this past week, exposing secret information to you to see if I could trust you."

"What? All this was a test?"

"In a manner of speaking, yes, it was. I had to know with confidence that you could keep information from the Council."

"Why was that so important to you?"

"Because I believe that there is a subversive on the Council."

"How is that possible?"

"That will be revealed once we figure out the nature of this perfidious Council member's cause."

"How do we do that?"

"I believe the answer is in the Book of the Three."

"I don't think history will help us out. We need knowledge of current events."

"The third book is digitally recording daily events. Decisions made by the Council relating to missions and experiments are all a matter of record. These records are considered a logical necessity to help evolve higher intelligence. If we do not repeat past mistakes, we can rapidly advance intelligence and technology."

"But how do we get this recording without drawing attention to ourselves?"

"When we turned over our books to the Cantrillian, we did so with one stipulation."

"What stipulation?"

"To keep with our tradition, a hard copy would be kept in real-time as the digital record is being recorded."

"How is that possible?"

"We demanded that the Council create the tech to facilitate our requirement. As actions and events are digitally recorded, a digital processing unit creates a hard copy. It's quite nice, actually. The digital processor uses a font that matches our old handwriting. And the paper is imported from the nearby forest-laden planet, Frandier."

"So we get the hard copy?"

"Yes. Brangstrids are in charge of making sure the process works properly. The agreement holds the Brangstrids responsible for maintaining the hard copy system and any necessary repairs."

"So you have access to it?"

"Yes."

"But if we take it, they will know it was you."

"That's why we won't take it."

"I don't understand."

"I have made an identical book copy, right down to the binding."

"So why didn't you just read it and record the important information?"

"I do not have time to sit in the processing room and review all the pages. That is a highly suspicious activity. And I could not take the copy out of the room because I would be the first suspect once the fraudulent copy was discovered. Besides, what would I do with the information? I am in no position to effect any change. This information needs to be in the hands of an individual who can follow it up and make it right."

"You don't know what we will find, do you?"

"No, not a clue. I believe this is the best starting point in solving this mystery."

"So we go to the processing room and swap copies?" Oz fidgeted in her seat.

"Yes, and you take it back to earth with you," Braylin replied with raised eyebrows.

"How did you know to meet me in the Cantrillian the first day we met?"

"I was at the Cantrillian daily for three months anticipating your arrival. I didn't know what you looked like, but I knew you were coming."

"How?"

"As I mentioned, I have many interesting points of contact around the universe."

Oz shook her head. "Okay. Let's leave that discussion for another day. When do we do this?"

"Now."

***

Oz followed behind Braylin. She noticed the Brangstrid was in no hurry to get to the room. She surmised that his relaxed gait was due to his inability to walk faster. He took them through a corridor that led to an elevator. Before the elevator door opened, Braylin asked Oz to shrink so he could place her in his pocket. The Brangstrids monitored this area of the Cantrillian, and Braylin did not want her to pop up on the visuals. Oz did as he asked, and Braylin gently put her in his pocket. He pressed the button for the 135th floor. Before he could move away from the floor selection panel and into the center of the elevator, the door opened.

Braylin walked to the fourth door on the left and entered the room. He slowly looked around as though he knew it was the last time he would visit. Oz, peaking over Braylin's pocket, noticed him hesitate upon stepping into the room. The processing equipment was sitting on its own on a metal desk, its spool on a more undersized metal stand to the right of the desk. There was a podium sitting approximately 5 feet away from the processing desk. Sitting on top of the podium was the open, heavy, leather-bound book, welcoming the insertion of new pages into its binding.

A clear glass encasement surrounded the book on the podium. A mechanical arm dropped from the top of the glass and moved across the blank page in the book. The processing spool edited the day's events and digitally transmitted them to the arm. The mech arm gently turned the page when it was full and continued transferring the data to the next. This process continued until the processing spool was empty.

Braylin went to the book on the podium and hesitated for a moment. He stared at the glass enclosure briefly while Oz peered over the top of his pocket. From below, it looked like Braylin was deep in contemplation, maybe considering a change of heart. The glass encasement began to ascend from the book. Oz realized why it was important for Braylin to attempt the swap now. Braylin needed the data transfer to pause for an extended period, which would cause the glass cover to rise so he could switch the books.

Braylin reached into his sack, which rested against the pocket holding Oz. He pulled out a book. Oz felt another book rest against his pocket after he pulled the first book out. Oz didn't understand why Braylin brought two books. Braylin quickly swapped the copy with the original and walked out the door.

While they were walking out of the processing room, Braylin spoke. "I need you to come out and place the book inside your suit. Once you do that, shrink again, and I will put you back into my pocket."

They were down the hall from the elevator. Braylin had stepped away from where he thought the point of visual monitoring occurred. She did as he asked, and Braylin headed to the elevator with Oz back in his pocket. As the elevator door opened, another Brangstrid was standing inside the elevator. He was many years younger than Braylin and had bright, aqua-colored hair. He looked surprised to see Braylin.

"Master Braylin? What are you doing here?" The Brangstrid asked as he walked out of the elevator.

"Master Dranflee, how are you this fine evening?" Braylin tried to play the visit off.

"Fine, sir, but it was my rotation tonight. Did you forget?"

"Yes, sir, I did. I went ahead and took care of the maintenance tonight. You can be sure of that. Come on, let's go home."

"I think I should at least sign in. I don't want anyone to think I skipped out."

"I will vouch for you. Come on. The elevator is here."

Dranflee looked back over his shoulder as they entered the elevator. Just before the door closed, Dranflee jumped out. "I gotta sign in and out, Master Braylin. I'll see you in a few minutes."

The elevator proceeded to the bottom floor as fast as it went up. Braylin felt sure they were at the bottom before Dranflee put the key in the computer room door. Braylin walked away from the elevator and out the door of the Cantrillian. He went to the closest wall and waited for the lights to darken.

Braylin licked his lips and spoke to Oz, "Come on. Get out, quickly."

"That was close," Oz replied.

"It's not over. I need you to shift, or melt, or whatever you call it now, into this wall with the book."

"Why?"

"Please just do it. Young Dranflee will see that the book is open and awaiting insertion. When he looks at the book to verify today's transfer, he'll notice something is wrong and call for help."

Oz looked at Braylin. "You expected this to happen; that's why you have a second book."

Braylin smiled, "The second book will buy you more time to return to Earth." Braylin held Oz by the hand and looked up at her. "You have to figure this out and make it right. I believe that if you don't, this planet will feel its repercussions for generations to come."

Oz smiled softly and squeezed Braylin's hand. She hugged him, to Braylin's surprise.

"Wow, they are teaching you a lot on that planet, aren't they?"

"Someone very special told me this is how you show someone you care about them. I care about you, Braylin, and I wish you well."

"Same here, Vailen. Now, ensure you make this all worth it. Get in that wall!"

Oz shifted into the wall and watched Braylin walk down the hallway. Several Brangstrids appeared from several directions and surrounded Braylin. After a few moments of conversing amongst themselves, Braylin pulled the second book out of his sack. Oz couldn't hear their exact words, but Braylin was the only Brangstrid in the group smiling. The group proceeded to the Cantrillian elevator, with Braylin in the center. Braylin looked at the wall as the group passed Oz's location and winked at her.

Oz still winked back, even though she knew Braylin couldn't see her. She felt a hollowness inside. She remembered feeling this way at Jessica's funeral.

Oz waited a few minutes for everyone to get into the elevator. She stared at the group, mainly at the center, as they walked away. She reemerged from the wall and returned to her laboratory bed. She wanted to get back to Earth and get started unraveling this mystery. She would set the Draiksx up to give her an entirely successful update. She would do whatever they needed to approve her return trip to Earth.

22 OUT OF THE FRYING PAN

Rialla looked at Oz, who was staring at the book before her. She was confused and started shaking her head. Her disbelief turned to anger, and she let out a horrible, frustrated scream. Oz and Pete were still staring at the book, ignoring her. Rialla's eyes began to fill with water. The three of them sat silently, staring at the book on the table. No one was in a hurry to look inside. No one was in a hurry to see what the pages revealed. They knew it would be difficult to understand and believe whatever the book divulged. Not one of the three moved.

Rialla was the first to break the silence. "This cannot be," she shouted before walking from the table. "Xan technology was developed from Wen technology? There has to be a mistake."

Oz, visibly upset, spoke softly, trying to calm Rialla. "Rialla, we have all been lied to. But now we can work together and expose these lies."

Rialla returned to her seat. "No matter the cost?" she asked Oz.

"Yes. No matter how the truth affects our beliefs, we must expose it. We live in a world of deceit, and now we must stop the lies."

Pete finally spoke. "Oz, that was an amazing story. Braylin was very special and heroic in sacrificing himself."

Oz looked at Pete in a soft, sad voice and said. "I feel the sadness again, Pete. The same horrible sensation I had at Jessica's funeral. I feel the sadness you spoke of with Jessica. It's a horrible feeling, Pete. I want it to stop. How do you make it stop?"

Pete looked at his friend and got up from his chair. He pulled Oz up from her chair without saying a word. He wrapped both arms around her and held her tight. Pete locked onto his dear friend as if he would never let her go. The two friends stood there in silence. Rialla's tears began to flow as she watched them.

"Make it stop, Pete, please make it stop," Oz yelled into Pete's chest.

Pete spoke over Oz's head as he looked at Rialla. "It takes time, Oz. On Earth, we say time heals all wounds. You have to give yourself time to heal. We all do."

Rialla nodded in Pete's direction as she wiped her tears. She stood up and walked over to the two of them, wrapping her arms around them.

Oz looked up at Pete. "Did Rialla just come over and hug us?"

Pete smiled. "Yes, she did."

Oz began laughing. "Crazy bitch."

Then, the three began laughing, still holding each other tightly.

23 FOLLOWING BREADCRUMBS

The next day, when Pete awoke and went to the dining room, Oz and Rialla were already sitting at the table, staring at the hefty leather tome resting in the middle. They were both sitting, holding their tea, and not moving. They looked like two statues anchored around a silver pond. Pete didn't want to alarm them, but he had to get a cup off the shelf and pour hot water into his tea. He moved gently across the floor with great stealth to accomplish his tasks. He took a bite of a Danish and tried to wipe the crumbs off the counter. He was proud of himself for not making a sound. He glanced over at the frozen statues and sighed in victorious relief. But before he could bask in his triumph of silence, someone spoke.

"We noticed you the whole time, Pete. We weren't sleeping," Oz called out, looking away from the table at Pete.

"Your movements were admirable, but you walked down the hallway, making loud stomping sounds, before you got to this room. Also, you make a strange noise when you move your lips to chew, " Rialla chimed in and sipped her tea, not looking at Pete.

Oz laughed. "She's right, you know, you do chew loudly. You sometimes look like a cow when you chew."

Oz and Rialla laughed.

Pete walked over to the table, looking defeated. "You know I was trying not to disturb you two. And this is how you show me appreciation for my effort?"

Oz stopped laughing and looked at Pete. "Thank you. Nice try. But you still chew funny."

And with that, Rialla and Oz started laughing again. Pete sat down at the table, holding his cup with both hands. "Okay. Playtime's over. What's the plan here?"

Oz sat up and leaned over the table, staring at the book. "Rialla can read the Wen language, so the two of us will start diving in as soon as we finish our tea."

Pete had a surprised look on his face. "Rialla, how do you know the Wen language?"

Rialla answered, "I don't know it. I have received and processed the basics of the language from the Vailen."

"Processed it?"

"Yes. Beings of higher intelligence can communicate in any language once they receive the basics of the dialect."

Pete shook his head in disbelief. "All you need is the basics, and you're off and running?"

"Yes, I need the basics, but I am not running anywhere."

Pete smiled and looked at the book for a moment. He stood there, staring at the book, not saying a word.

Oz noticed he had a confused look on his face. "What's bugging you, Pete?" Oz asked.

"I am a little confused about how this book will help us."

"We are hoping that some of the recorded Traa'zel sessions will explain why the purpose of our mission is so deceiving."

"I get that part. I don't understand the recording of everything, for posterity's sake. What makes you believe the Council wouldn't have erased the sections of the recordings they did not want anyone to know about?"

Oz looked at Pete and turned her head to one side. "Did you think that one up all by yourself? Huh? Did you, huh?"

Pete smiled, "Okay. I know what's next. Go ahead and explain why I'm an idiot."

Oz smiled, her head still turned to one side. "Well, Einstein, that's a great question. Except…" Oz stretched the word 'except' out slowly.

"Except what?" Pete smiled, anticipating what was coming next.

Oz turned her head to the other side and continued, "Except that we are talking about a highly intelligent society that relies on logic. And as long as you and I have been together, you still haven't understood that an entity that exists on logic cannot deceive or lie to others. There is no logical benefit."

"So you're saying they record everything because they have nothing to hide? But someone has something to hide. Someone has sidestepped the logical nature of your society and sent us on this bogus mission."

Oz sat up straight and said, "I am 100% positive that if the Traa'zels discussed our mission, it's in this book."

Rialla now had a confused look on her face. "How can you be so sure?" she asked.

Pete continued, "If they are orchestrating our mission, which we now know is a lie, we have to assume that they flushed logic right down the shitter. So if lying about our mission is illogical for the Council, what makes you so sure they recorded sessions as normal?"

Rialla looked at Pete and then at Oz. "What's a shitter?"

Oz ignored Rialla's question. "If I am right, which we both know I always am, the answers are in this book."

Pete shook his head in disbelief. "I hope you're right. It still doesn't make sense that they would record their conversations."

"Their recordings are under lock and key and unavailable for public access. The security of the recordings is well known. There is no reason for any Council member to fear the recording of daily meetings. These recordings are for analysis if an experiment or mission fails. Our mission hasn't failed in the Council's eyes."

"So you're telling me it is logical to assume that the culprits are hiding in plain sight and using logic against the Council?"

"I'm counting on the fact that the agreement between the Brangstrids and the Council goes so far back that most of the Council is unaware that it even exists. As far as these culprits understand, the Council is the only agency with access to these recordings."

"Okay. Happy hunting," Pete said as he walked out of the room.

Oz got up and left as well. Rialla was left at the table, staring at her cup of tea. "I don't understand…what's a shitter?" She shook her head, lifted her cup, and sipped her tea.

***

An hour later, Rialla walked into the meeting room wearing sweatpants and a t-shirt. She sat down at the table across from Oz, who was scanning the book with her hand.

"Are you copying pages for me to read?" Rialla asked as she sat down at the table.

"Yes, I am," Oz replied without looking up. "Please tell me you haven't been hanging around Pete and picking up his habits."

"What habits?" Rialla looked shocked.

"The flair for stating the obvious," Oz looked up and smiled.

Rialla smiled back. "I still need more time with the herald to pick up his flair for sarcasm as you have, I see."

They both laughed. Oz pressed a few controls on her suit, and a stack of papers materialized on the table in front of Rialla.

Rialla pulled the stack of papers closer. "Have you narrowed your search to a specific timeframe?"

Oz turned the pages to where she had determined her starting point. "If I go back into my files, I can find my first meeting with the Council about our mission. Our search should include recordings from 2 years before that date."

"Do I have one year of recordings in front of me?" Rialla asked, gawking at the large pile of papers.

"No," Oz said. "You have one month of recordings, starting with the beginning of Y1."

"Y1?"

"Yes, you have Y1, one year before my first meeting with the Council about our mission to Earth."

"Please give me some background information about these meetings and what I should look for."

"There is a mission committee that is created by the Traa'zels. Each committee comprises several Draiksx scientists, a Cantrillia particle repeater that records all experiment procedures at every phase, and a committee leader, usually a Traa'zel. A Vailen is assigned to the herald towards the end of the procedure when he is ready to merge with his assigned Vailen. Every Cantrillia particle repeater mission recording will start with a mission description that includes a discussion of the mission schedule report. Following this description, there will be updates, results of experiments and procedures, and other conversations explaining the details of the project."

"So, what do you want me to search for specifically?"

"You should be able to see a pattern evolve as you read. The Traa'zels are very strict when it comes to following procedures. You will notice the norm of their procedures and recognize any unusual entries as you proceed through the pages."

"So the Cantrillia particle repeater records all conversations that involve a specific experiment?"

"Yes. Depending on the complexity of the experiment, extra particle repeaters are assigned to ensure all conversations become a matter of record."

"These particle repeaters…are they concealed or patrolling the area?"

"Normally, they're concealed. It's easy to forget that they are even recording in the room. A particle repeater will roam around the lab only in highly complex experiments."

Rialla looked up from the pages and noticed Oz was already reviewing the recordings. She smiled at Oz. "Thank you, Vailen."

Oz looked up from her pile of papers, "What for?"

"For trusting me with these highly secure documents."

Oz smiled at Rialla. "Bitch, please," she said. Then she went back to reading.

Rialla paused for a moment, staring at Oz while she was reading. Never in a million years would she have become friends with a Vailen. There was no scenario in the universe in which this would make sense. *The only way this could have happened was the way that it did. Must be fate,* she thought, and she began reading.

Oz could ingest more information at a more rapid pace than Rialla. She looked up several times and noticed Rialla was struggling with translating. But for the most part, she was doing well. The room was quiet except for the sounds of page-turning. The slight crinkling noise from the corner of a page-turning over seemed a lot louder than usual due to the deadly silence of the room. The two unlikely friends read for hours, occasionally stopping to get a drink or run to the bathroom.

It was early evening when Pete walked into the room and asked how it was going.

Oz looked at Pete and answered, "Nothing out of the ordinary yet. The details of the conversations in this book make for long, laborious reading."

Pete looked over at Rialla and saw her head buried in the pages before her. "How's it going?" he smiled at her.

"Fine," she replied without looking away from her pages.

"Okay then, I'll leave you guys alone," Pete shrugged and left the room.

Before Pete made it to the door, Rialla spoke. "Wait," she shouted.

Pete stopped and walked back to the table. Oz looked up from her book at Rialla.

"What is it?" Oz asked.

"There is a discussion about Earth's atmosphere that I have trouble understanding."

"Do you need help with the translation?" Oz asked.

"No," Rialla replied, looking at Oz, "This discussion seems out of place. It reads as a separate conversation from the project linked to it. Maybe I am missing other pages?"

Oz walked around the table and sat next to Rialla. "Let me see what you're looking at."

Rialla slid the document to Oz. Pete came over and sat on the opposite side of the table, watching Oz read the excerpts. He didn't say a word as she read in silence. When she finished reading the page that confused Rialla, she didn't say a word but hunted through the pile of papers.

Pete was curious. "What is it, Oz? What are you looking for?"

Oz ignored Pete and kept looking. She appeared to be deep in thought, processing newly discovered data. Pete recognized the look on her face from previous incidents. He knew to leave her alone until she was ready. Both Pete and Rialla remained quiet and still while Oz continued her search. They needed to sit still for only ten minutes before Oz finally spoke.

"Rialla, I think you found something significant," Oz said, looking at Rialla. She held three papers in her hand and slid the pile of documents Rialla had been reading to the side with her other hand. Oz laid the three documents before her, slow and deliberate, and explained.

"Rialla found a conversation that a particle repeater recorded outside the lab, possibly in another room." Oz stood up straight and continued, "It is possible that this conversation was going on without the participants' knowledge that a recording was taking place."

Rialla was confused. "How is that possible? You said everyone was aware of the particle repeaters."

"Everyone is aware of them; that's why this conversation is happening outside the lab."

"How do you know that?"

"Because the lab bot didn't record this conversation. A different particle repeater did. Each particle repeater imprints a mark at the beginning of a recording that identifies which bot is recording. Look here, see this mark? It is different than this one."

Rialla and Pete took turns looking at what Oz pointed to on the paper. A symbol at the top of one page looked different from the symbol in the middle. The first symbol looked like two thin parallel lines about an eighth of an inch apart, with a thin line running perpendicular to the two lines. The second symbol had the same two parallel lines but an uncentered circle between them.

Pete spoke up. "I see the two symbols, but why is this important? What is this conversation about?"

Oz looked at Rialla and smiled. "Earth's atmospheric gases."

"Why would they be discussing atmospheric gases?" Pete asked.

"That question, my dear Sherlock, is why this is important," Oz answered.

"Can you read out what you and Rialla discovered? Maybe we can try to decipher its meaning."

Oz sat down, took the first page from her hand, and began reading.

> Voice one: "How will you obtain more atmospheric gases from Earth? We need more samples to conduct more tests."

Voice two: "I believe our completed testing results are conclusive. We do not need more testing. Our efforts should focus on the development of the serum. We need that Draiksx to complete the synthesis of the gases."

Voice one: "The Draiksx will continue his work. Do you require more of the synthetic?"

Voice two: "I have had enough. We must make haste while Krix'x is busy with the other Council members preparing the human for the Earth mission."

Voice one: "They will be busy transforming the human. If he is like the others, he'll not survive the transformation, and Krix'x will need to find another human and start over."

Voice two: "Yes, that will work nicely. Can you ensure that the human will expire during the transformation?"

Voice one: "Yes, I have done so in the past. This time will be no different."

Oz lowered the papers slowly and looked up at Pete. Pete was sitting, staring at his reflection on the metal tabletop.

"Pete, are you okay?" asked Oz softly.

Pete didn't answer.

Rialla saw the concerned look on Oz's face and then the faraway gaze on Pete's. She wanted to say something, but she knew Oz and Pete had a lot of history together. She didn't want to get involved in their conversation unless asked.

Oz asked Pete again, "Pete, are you okay?"

Pete stared at the table and answered without batting an eye. "They killed other humans who were to be heralds. They tried to sabotage my testing. It is illogical for highly intelligent beings who exist on logic to lie and deceive. Isn't that what you taught me?" Pete was now staring at Oz.

Oz countered, "Pete, I know this information is upsetting. But we must find more evidence to get all the facts."

"I know, Oz," Pete replied. "Are you sure you want to move forward with this? The more we find out, the deeper we fall into the abyss of the illogical."

"We'll keep searching for more pieces, and then we will complete the puzzle together."

"What could they want with gases from our atmosphere?" Pete asked incredulously.

"I am not sure."

"And why would they need to make a serum containing liquified gases? Is this some underground drug cartel on your planet?"

"Pete, I don't believe there's a drug business on my planet. It's not—"

"Not what? Logical?" Pete cut Oz off. "But abducting innocent human beings and experimenting on them is? On top of that, willfully killing people? That's logical?"

"No, it's not," Oz said softly.

"And even though they mentioned Krix'x by name, we can't be sure he's involved."

"I agree," nodded Oz.

The room fell deadly quiet. The three sat there for what seemed to Rialla like an hour.

It was difficult for Oz to ignore the troubled look on Pete's face. Hearing that the Council purposely killed other human beings during their transformation was bearing heavily on his mind. His silence was as thick as a blanket covering the cold space of the room. Oz knew it was best to give Pete time to contemplate this new evidence alone. Talking to him now could take the focus off her hunt for the truth. She tried to divert his attention to other matters.

"Maggie and Bill would like to visit. They want to update you on how Maggie's proposals are going."

Pete was still staring at the table, deep in thought. He looked up as soon as he heard Oz mention their names.

"Yeah, that would be good. It would be nice to have our friends visit," Pete said in a far-off voice, not looking at Oz. He got up from his chair and headed toward the door. He spoke while he walked, without looking back at the table, "Oz, I'm going to rest for a little while, try to clear my head. When you talk to Maggie and Bill, please don't mention anything about what we have learned about our mission."

Oz watched Pete exit the room. She looked at Rialla. "Okay, we now know what type of conversations to look for in the transcripts. Are you alright to continue?"

Rialla replied, "Absolutely, let's get some answers."

"The date of this excerpt is approximately six months before I enter into the program. I have looked at all the entries up to two years before my participation date. I did not come across any unusual entries. So, I think we've narrowed it down. If there's any other evidence to obtain, it must be in this window."

Rialla nodded, "I'll keep moving forward, and you investigate up to the conversation I found."

Oz agreed, "Yes, that should cover it nicely."

"Can you put the two particle repeater markings where we can see them? The marking for the bot outside the lab would be good to focus on."

"Good idea," Oz replied. She programmed the images of the bot markings to appear on a visual on the table next to Rialla.

"Thanks," Rialla responded and buried herself in the next pile of papers.

Rialla and Oz began reading their respective piles of paper with newfound vigor. And although neither would show it, they were excited. They were getting closer to an answer, and the thrill of finding the next piece of the puzzle was a great motivator.

It was after midnight when Pete walked by the meeting room. He stood in the doorway and watched Oz and Rialla go through the papers. They looked like they were pulling an all-nighter to study for an exam they took the next day. He watched as they read. *Jessica would have liked to see this,* he thought. He turned and lowered his head as he walked to his room. Even though his emotions were not at 100%, he still felt her presence. He still missed her.

24 THE LIGHTBULB COMES ON

After several hours of intense searching, Rialla and Oz stopped and took a break.

"What are we missing?" Rialla sounded frustrated.

"They must have figured out that it wasn't safe to talk near the lab. I feared this would happen; they went elsewhere to discuss their plan."

Rialla was sitting up, looking down at the table, passing her fingers through the papers. She noticed different bot markings than the two they had previously discovered.

"Can you run a data search through these papers for all the bot markings present?"

Oz looked puzzled. "Why?"

"Maybe we should focus on the bots, not the recordings right now."

"The bots?"

"Yes. If we know how many particle repeater bots are involved, then we can try to place their locations. We've been looking at lab conversations. We happened to come across a conversation that didn't belong there. We should be looking outside the lab."

"So we run a search for the bots and discard all the bots associated with recording at the lab?"

"Yes. I assume the lab isn't the only space involved in recording conversations for posterity's sake."

"It's worth a try. After all, they wouldn't talk in the lab anyway." Oz narrowed her eyes, "I don't know why I didn't see that."

"You are emotionally invested in this search, Vailen. It is clouding your judgment."

"I can't be emotionally invested in anything, Rialla. It's not logical."

"It may not be consistent with your being before you came to this planet, but now, exposure to this atmosphere seems probable."

Oz sat up at the table. A battle ensued within her. Would she have to question every decision she made? How would she know if any conclusion would be correct now that emotions are involved? Oz only knew how to deduce through logic, so her assessments were always accurate. She thought that exposure to the Earth's atmosphere was a good thing. It was introducing her to a new world of possibilities. Maybe she was wrong to think emotions were a gift. Maybe mixing emotions with logic obstructed conclusions.

Rialla watched Oz and gave her a few minutes to analyze whatever she was thinking. She noticed that Oz was very still, almost statuesque. She could barely see Oz's chest moving as she breathed. Rialla waited for a few minutes and then broke Oz's trance.

"Vailen, are you okay?" Rialla asked in a soft, caring voice.

Oz didn't stop staring straight ahead when she nodded.

"I didn't mean to upset you. I apologize."

Oz turned her head to look at Rialla. "You didn't upset me. I am trying to calculate the disparities in my conclusions and determine if my conclusions were corrupted by emotions."

"It's not bad if you are experiencing emotions, Vailen. Perhaps, in many cases, emotions can give you an edge just as easily as they can hinder judgments."

"I would like to delve deeper into the philosophy of your assessments, but we need to press on with our search." Her tone was without emotion, sounding programmed.

Rialla smiled. She knew Oz was having difficulty reasoning through the possibility of emotional capabilities. She knew her statement about Oz being emotionally invested was being analyzed by Oz, even though she wanted to stop discussing it.

Oz spoke up. "I've run a data check on the symbols through my system. There appear to be bots around several important buildings within the capital city. If we are looking for Council members, they must be conversing in one of the capital city buildings. Otherwise, their actions would confuse the other Council members."

"Why would the other Council members be confused?"

"Council members only communicate with each other within the capital city's scientific and political complexes. A conversation between two Council members outside these areas is not logical and could cause unwanted attention."

"Can we narrow it down at all?"

"Only by bot markings, as you suggested. Maybe if we can find another conversation about our mission or Earth's atmosphere, we can narrow it down to the building."

Rialla raised an eyebrow, "Perhaps the miscreants have a specific meeting place to discuss their plans."

"Yes. We may find it by searching all areas outside the lab. I have placed all recordings in order of bot markings."

"So, how do we start?"

"You start on that stack, and I'll start on mine right here."

Rialla noticed a new stack of papers appear on the table before her.

"I don't think I can ever get used to you doing that," she laughed.

"It drives Pete nuts, too," Oz responded.

They went back to reading and searching. Surprisingly, it didn't take Oz long to find a questionable conversation.

"I think I have something," she said.

"What is it?" Rialla responded. "Read it."

> Voice one: "It's ready for testing."
>
> Voice two: "Did you get all the samples you needed?"
>
> Voice one: "I have."
>
> Voice two: "Fine. And the Draiksx? Is he on board with our plan?"
>
> Voice one: "He is."

Rialla sat up, excited. "Oz, you found it!"

Oz was still looking down at the paper. "This could be it, Rialla."

"You have doubts?"

"We need to approach this logically, from all angles," Oz tried to be analytical.

"Okay, so we need to search this bot's records to see what building this is, correct?"

"Yes. I have begun the search through our database. I should have answers shortly."

Oz's short, mechanical replies told Rialla she was trying to show no emotion. Rialla wished she hadn't told Oz what she did about being emotionally invested. She hoped this phase Oz was experiencing would be short-lived. She didn't like Oz the robot. She wanted her friend back.

Pete walked into the room. "Hey guys, how's the search?"

Oz looked up. "I believe we have narrowed our search," Oz answered in a monotone voice.

Pete looked at Oz and then at Rialla. He noticed the robotic way Oz answered, like the first time she had ever spoken to Pete.

"Did I miss something?" Pete asked, confused.

Rialla looked at Pete. "Can I show you something?"

"Sure, what is it?"

"Follow me, please." Rialla walked by Pete and out of the room. Pete looked at Oz. She was still reading and not paying any attention to him. Pete went out of the room and ran into Rialla in the doorway of another room.

"What's going on? You guys fighting?"

Rialla coaxed Pete into the room and shut the door behind her.

Rialla bowed her head slightly. "Pete, I may have done something stupid."

"What did you do?"

"The Vailen missed a logical assumption, and I called her out on it."

"I don't understand."

"I told her she was invested emotionally in our search, which is why she missed an obvious conclusion."

"Emotionally invested?"

"Yes. If anyone would notice her change, it would be you."

"Well, I have noticed her changing, but she blames the changes on the neon gases in our atmosphere. I thought she had that under control."

"The Vailen has not deduced a logical conclusion from the evidence of her changes and the conversations we have been reading."

"And you have?"

"Yes."

"Why haven't you said anything?"

"If I say something, it will cause her to withdraw further from what she is becoming."

"And you like what she is becoming?"

Rialla lowered her head again. "Yes, I do. I know what I am saying is selfish, but she needs to figure this out for herself."

"I'm glad you care about Oz, Rialla. That's a good sign of friendship."

"I am confused as to how to proceed."

"I know her. I've got this."

Rialla looked confused. "What have you got?"

Pete smiled at Rialla. "This situation with Oz. I can fix it."

Rialla smiled and followed Pete into the meeting room to see Oz sitting before a stack of papers. Pete walked over and sat across from Oz. He pulled his chair up and knocked on the tabletop three times.

Oz looked up. "Yes, Pete?"

"How's it going? Are you getting close?"

Oz looked back down at her papers. "I believe so," she responded.

Rialla started reading her papers, acting like she was ignoring their conversation.

"Knock knock," Pete said.

Oz ignored him.

"Come on, Oz, lighten up. Knock knock," Pete said again.

Oz continued to ignore him.

"Fine. Rialla, knock knock."

Rialla looked confused. "I don't understand."

Pete turned to her, "I say knock, knock, and you say, 'Who's there?'"

"Okay," Rialla smiled, sitting up, excited to play.

Pete tried again, "Knock knock."

Rialla grinned. "Who's there?"

Pete answered, "Spell."

Rialla replied, "Who's there?"

Pete laughed, "No, now you say 'spell who?'"

Rialla said, "Okay, W-H-O."

Pete looked at Rialla with his mouth wide open.

"Is that not how you spell it? What did I do wrong?" Rialla batted her eyes.

Oz looked up at Rialla, "You killed his punchline."

Rialla shrugged, "Punchline?"

"Yes. It's a joke. It's a play on words, but if you don't follow the progression properly, it doesn't work."

Rialla looked over at Pete. "I'm sorry I killed your punchline."

"No big deal," Pete sighed. "I was trying to lighten it up a little in here, and I screwed that up, too. Oz used to go along with the jokes to make me feel good. But now she's all serious, all business."

Oz pointed her finger at Pete. "Pete, this is serious work we are doing."

"I know it is, and I commend you and Rialla for putting so much time and effort into this. But that's no reason to ignore your friends."

"How can I ignore you if I am working? If anything, you are interrupting my important work."

Pete raised his voice a little. "Are you calling me rude?"

Rialla was shocked. *I thought the Herald was going to fix this?* She thought. *He's not fixing it; he's making it worse.*

Oz raised her voice a little to match Pete's. "Yes, I am. Mr. Rude-ee. Mr. Pete Rude-ee"

Pete raised his hands and rolled his eyes. "You could have given me a few minutes to appease me. But no, I am Oz. Kindness does not compute."

Oz's eyes widened, "Quoting *Lost in Space?* You remember that? Of all the quotes I presented to you from your movies and TV shows, that's the one you remember?" Oz was fully engaged in their argument.

"You also taught me knock-knock jokes as well."

"That's because you were always depressed. I had to think of something to cheer you up."

"So now you won't let me return the favor?" Pete said softly. He smiled at Oz, looking directly into her eyes.

"Stop it," she said.

"Stop what?" he said, continuing to stare.

"Staring at me, stop it. You know that affects me."

Rialla couldn't believe what she was seeing or hearing. Pete was getting Oz to act emotionally. He used only a conversation to win her over.

"So, can we do a few jokes then? I promise to leave and not bother you until you call for me."

"Promise?"

"Yes."

"Okay." Oz pushed the papers away from her and sat up. "Knock knock."

Pete answered, "Who's there?"

"A herd."

"A herd who?"

"A herd you were home, so here I am!"

Rialla didn't understand the joke, but Pete and Oz clearly started to enjoy what was happening.

Pete smiled. "Okay, my turn. Knock knock."

"Who's there?"

"Arfur."

Oz tried to figure it out before answering. She didn't have a guess. "Arfur, who?"

"Arfur got."

Oz gasped, "No, you didn't?"

Pete looked at Oz, "Okay, how about this joke? How much does a pirate pay for corn?"

Oz moved up and down in her seat excitedly. "Wait, I know this."

Rialla started enjoying the show they were putting on. She could see Oz letting go. She was getting her friend back.

Oz yelled out, "A buccaneer."

Pete laughed. "Too easy."

Oz went next. "What did one Frenchman say to the other one?"

Pete scratched his head. Rialla didn't understand how this could be a joke.

Pete gave up. "Alright, what did one Frenchman say to the other one?"

Oz raised her hands to her side, palms up, "I don't know, I don't speak French."

Pete and Oz laughed and looked over at Rialla.

Rialla looked at the two of them, puzzled, as they smiled. "I don't understand why that is funny. Why did you pose the question if you don't understand French?"

Pete looked at Oz, "You have a lot of work to do with this one. Good luck with that."

Oz smiled at Rialla. "We'll get you over to the dark side, don't worry."

The confused look on Rialla's face remained. "Why the dark side?"

Oz shrugged her shoulders, "Okay, Ms. Buzzkill. I'll explain it all later. But we should get back to work."

"Ms. Buzzkill? Is that my new nickname?"

"No," Oz said quickly. "I'll explain that later as well."

Pete got up and headed out of the room. He winked at Rialla as he passed her. She didn't understand that gesture but thought it appropriate not to say anything about it. Rialla watched Pete walk out the door. She realized that the more time she spent with Pete, the more she enjoyed his company. She looked at Oz and noticed she was watching her watch, Pete.

Oz smiled. "We have a lot of girl talk to catch up on, I see. You have to fill me in later."

Rialla acted nervously. "I don't know what you are referring to." She fumbled a few papers and started to read to avoid further questions about watching Pete.

"Rialla?" Oz asked.

"Yes?" Rialla answered, not looking away from the paper in her hand.

"I know this language is not your own, but it may be easier to read if you turn the paper the right side up."

"I know. I was inspecting the page for other markings."

Oz smiled. "Cool."

Rialla righted the page and began reading. She raised her chin and said, "Yes, very cool."

25 GRAY AND BLUE

A few more days of all-nighters finally produced results. Oz and Rialla narrowed the conversation to the bot with a circle symbol inside a triangle. This bot was assigned to record conversations at the Khirox building in the science complex. It was used for education classes for all ages. The building's classes were divided by age, science branches, and advancement level. It was in this building and from this bot that Rialla and Oz uncovered the truth.

Oz gathered all the pertinent papers and stored them in a database. The program she initiated put all the conversations in order by date recorded. Oz used her tech to record the data files for verbal playback. She was incredibly proud of the program that converted written words to verbal playback because a Vailen had written it. It was one of the earlier technologies that helped the Vailen rise in the ranks of the science community. What was so unique about this program was its ability to assign a specific voice pattern to conversations to track specific speakers. Once a voice pattern was recorded, it was assigned a unique variable. This variable represented one speaker throughout the program. It made it easier to differentiate the participants. Once all the information was recorded and ready for playback, she called Pete to the meeting room.

Pete walked into the meeting room. Oz and Rialla were sitting on one side of the table. Pete smiled at them as Oz raised a screen above the table and moved the controls on the table in front of her. All three turned their chairs slightly to face the visual.

"So, what did you find?" Pete asked anxiously.

Oz explained, "Once we narrowed the conversations to the Khirox building, I set up a search protocol for all recorded conversations. The limits of the search started from the date I took the book and went back two years. This search resulted in thousands of recorded conversations. Rialla and I found a few conversations related to our search parameters."

Rialla took over. "Here's the best part: the particle repeaters analyze voice data as they record. Particle repeaters assign a mark or symbol to each recorded voice."

Pete chimed in, "Like the marking for the particle repeaters?"

Rialla smiled. "Exactly. Oz was able to run a search on these specific markings. We received many conversations related to your mission this way."

Oz moved her hand across the controls and turned on the visual. "We collected as much data as possible and have not heard any of it. I have collated all the conversations by date, and it is now ready for playback."

"Awesome," Pete said. "Let's see what you found."

Oz began the playback. Two cloaked figures appeared on the screen.

"We have a visual of the recordings as well?" Pete was getting excited.

Oz replied, "Not on all the conversations, but most have recorded visuals. The program that decodes the written transcripts also connects to our database. Once we selected the files we wanted to hear, the database attached the available visual recording to the specific timestamp."

The cloaked figures began their conversation. They looked at each other, with their faces concealed under the hoods.

> Voice one: "Did you retrieve all the various gases from Earth as needed?"

> Voice two: "Yes."

> Voice one: "How did the liquifying process go? Did the Draiksx get it to work?"

> Voice two: "Liquifying the gases is complete and successful."

> Voice one: "I want an injection. Did you bring me a syringe?"

> Voice two: "Here it is."

The second figure handed over a needle with a turquoise, liquid-filled vial to the other hooded figure. The anonymous figure's cloak sleeves were so wide that only the vial was visible.

The playback pauses.

Pete looked at Oz. "So they're liquifying gases from our atmosphere for injections?"

Oz looked at Pete. "This explains why they are acting in an illogical manner."

Pete looked confused. "What do you mean?"

Oz continued, "Rialla deduced it before I did." She smiled at Rialla. "But my friend allowed me to work through my issues to see it myself. Thank you, Rialla."

Rialla smiled and nodded.

Oz continued, "They are liquifying the gas and injecting it directly into their bloodstream. What took the neon gas months to achieve on my system is taking only minutes with this injection."

"Why? Why inject themselves with the gas?" Pete asked.

"It is logical, Pete. Logical, if you want to cause chaos within a logical society. You know what to expect if you base all actions and reactions on logic. An illogical mind can control a logical society because the outcomes are predictable."

Pete sat up. "So this person knows how everyone will react to every possible scenario because of logic. These Council members can dictate actions for them all to follow."

"Yes."

"But, I thought the neon gas causes parts of your system to deteriorate?"

"It does by itself. From this conversation, it seems that these Council members combined multiple gases. This means there are Council members in positions of power who no longer want to be logical."

"To what end?"

"I don't know." Oz continued the playback.

The date and time stamp materialized on the visual as the exact two figures appeared. It was three days after the previous conversation.

> Voice one: "Are we on schedule?"

> Voice two: "All is going as planned."

> Voice one: "Has anyone questioned your actions?"

> Voice two: "No, it is as you concluded it would be."

End of conversation.

A few hours passed as the three listened to the recordings. The information was all the same; no specifics were mentioned during the conversations. The recordings did not reveal the Council members' names or additional information to help narrow the search for who was behind the experiments. It felt repetitive now. It was as though the two hooded figures knew the bot was recording their conversation. They deliberately avoided any language that could have been incriminating if another Council member had reviewed the recording.

Pete looked frustrated at the progression of the conversations. "Man, they know. How could they not know? The Council members are highly intelligent and could record conversations in code for all we know."

Oz replied, "We have to keep listening. They may slip up. The bot may catch them in a room they feel is secluded from the tech. Besides, arrogance can come into play now that their emotions are evolving."

Pete was confused. "How so?"

"I believe the correct human term is 'cocky.' These two Council members could feel like they are untouchable and get cocky. They could eventually screw up."

"You can't scan all the files for a screwup?"

Oz sighed. "Really?"

Pete nodded. "I know. I was reaching."

The following conversation, recorded several weeks later, offered a little more.

Voice one: "Did you add the Draiksx' chemical mix to the Earth prototype?"

235

Voice two: "The Draiksx successfully added the mix."

Voice one: "How long will it take to change the effect of their enhancement?"

Voice two: "The mix will be dormant for four weeks once they launch their enhancement on the planet."

Voice one: "And then?"

Voice two: "Mass confusion, as we planned."

Pete stood up. "Oz, are they talking about the affliction?"

Oz nodded. "I have heard Krix'x call it the enhancement in the lab."

Pete raised his voice. "Four weeks are up; what could it be?"

"I don't know."

"We have to call Krix'x immediately and let him know. Maybe he can head this off."

"Pete, we can't call him right now."

"Why not?"

"Because he will want to deduce how we found this information."

"Who cares?"

"Pete, he will know about the book we stole. And about Rialla."

Pete looked at Rialla. "I will protect you."

Rialla spoke up defiantly. "I don't need your protection."

Pete looked at Oz. "What if this change to the affliction is so overwhelming that Krix'x can't reverse the effect?"

The concern on Pete's face began to worry Oz. "Pete, we can't chance it. There is a bigger monster we need to catch. If we involve Krix'x, we may lose our chance. This villain may go into hiding, or worse."

"What could be worse?"

Oz sensed Pete's vitals reacting negatively. She needed to calm him down. "He may move up his timetable. We will not be prepared to defend against his next action."

Pete threw his chair across the room. His frustration was building, and Oz noticed his skin glowing. Pete took a few steps back and stared down at his glowing hands. He knew Oz was right. She was the logical voice in his head, always. He closed his eyes and raised his hands to his chest, palms facing down. He took a deep breath and slowly pushed the air out of his mouth as he pushed his hands downward, away from his chest. His hands moved away from his body as if pushing an invisible, immovable object towards the ground. When the breath finished, Pete had calmed down.

Before they could continue the conversation, an alarm went off from the control room. The three ran out of the meeting room, and Oz turned on the wall visual above the control desk. People were outside the ship, screaming at each other and throwing rocks and bottles at the ship. The police were trying to hold off the crowds, but the crowd's numbers were growing incredibly fast. It was like a massive mushroom cloud in reverse, with the spaceship at the center.

"Oz, scan the media and see what this is all about," Pete barked.

"Already on it," Oz replied. She turned up the volume for all to hear.

A TV reporter was broadcasting directly from the Lawn.

"It appears the affliction has taken a turn for the worse. Those who were adjusting to the affliction that began four weeks ago are now dealing with it all over again. This time, the responses are more violent. Those who are afflicted are attacking the saucer. Police cannot hold them back. It looks like– yes, they did. They trampled the fence down and are now rushing the saucer."

Pete looked at Oz, who looked at Pete in turn and pressed a button on the panel. An invisible force field surrounded the ship. The people in the front of the rushing crowd bounced off the field into the people behind them. Once the crowd realized they could get no closer, they threw rocks and bottles at the ship. Even though the debris bounced off, they continued to hurl objects. Their voices were loud and angry.

Pete sat down at the control panel, staring at the visual. No one inside the ship said a word. They just watched as the military attempted to disperse the crowds of angry people. As the military fought off the crowds, Pete, Rialla, and Oz continued to listen to the reporter.

"This change came without warning, and everyone is scared and angry. What does it all mean? No one knows. Maybe this change is preparing us all for what comes next? I'm sending it back to the studio."

The studio announcer took over. "Thanks, Nancy. We are now going to the Capitol Building, where Simon Rodriguez is reporting live. Go ahead, Simon."

"Thanks, Shonda," Rodriguez began. "I'm live at the Capitol, where Congress has called an emergency meeting with the top scientists from around the world. No one knows why this is happening. It appears that the affliction has taken a new direction, Shonda. Those who were afflicted are now seeing others as gray-skinned individuals, causing them to become scared and violent. The change is unbelievable. It's like living through a horror movie. Everyone is frightened, and chaos abounds. This new development is way too creepy for me to continue. Sorry, Shonda, back to you."

Silence fell over the ship's speakers. Pete looked at Oz. Then Shonda spoke in a soft, light voice.

"I don't know what to say." It sounded like she was fumbling through some papers, and her chair squeaked across the floor. The airwaves went silent.

"Hello?" It was Nancy, reporting from the Lawn. "I'm going to keep reporting until I hear otherwise."

Pete looked over at Oz and said in a commanding voice, "Call Krix'x now."

***

The gray, as the media called it, arrived quickly and hit the city hard. The gray-skinned affliction was terrifying. Out on Constitution Avenue, cars crashed into each other, drivers' attention drawn from the road to watch gray-skinned people running on the sidewalks. Crowds were screaming and crying in the streets, many falling to their knees. On the Lawn, people were screaming in terror while running away from gray-skinned men and women who were sightseeing. A woman looked down at her young daughter, who was holding her hand, and screamed. Her child had gray skin and looked like a zombie. The young girl thought her mother was playing and began to laugh. Laughing made the child's gray face more terrifying, and the mother fainted.

People stormed out of restaurants, turning tables over and crashing through glass windows to get away from patrons with gray skin eating in the restaurant. People charged out of shops, destroying displays and windows in their wake. A man jumped from the second floor of the mall to escape the zombie hordes rambling toward him. Several people in a hotel elevator became terrified and neurotic, beating a man because he had gray skin. Several patrons sitting at a bar threw their glasses and bottles at the gray-skinned bartender before running out of the bar. The police received so many calls concerning violent attacks that they had to let the phones ring unanswered.

Chaos and panic overtook the city, and local police could not control the mass hysteria. The president ordered the military to secure the city. The military patrolled the streets in Humvees equipped with bullhorn speakers, encouraging citizens to remain calm and go home. Troops patrolled the streets and directed people out of the city. Several platoons of army soldiers ordered the crowd attacking the spaceship to disperse, and were met with great resistance. Individuals within the crowd became hysterical when gray-skinned soldiers advanced toward them. The soldiers looked like monsters wearing combat gear while wielding rifles.

To add to the chaos, the afflicted soldiers dropped their weapons. They ran away from the terrifying gray-skinned creatures in the crowd. The troops were outnumbered as the crowd grew larger. The military commander had to keep calling in for reinforcements as more and more soldiers deserted. Eventually, the military had to fire tear gas into the mass to force people away from the ship.

Less than a mile away, Congressman Johnson was being rushed to a hospital by ambulance. When the gray affliction struck, he and his wife were out eating dinner with colleagues at a local D.C. restaurant. The congressman excused himself and went to the restroom. When he had been in the restroom for an extended period, his wife was concerned and asked the waiter to check on him. The waiter walked into the bathroom to find the congressman on the floor, unconscious. Later, when Johnson awoke in his hospital bed, he explained to his wife what had happened.

"I was washing my hands when I looked up from the sink. I stared at the image in the mirror. At first, I thought I saw a dead man's face or even a ghost. Then I realized I was looking at myself in the mirror. It looked like I was dead. The gray skin, the gray, my God, the gray."

Johnson was given another sedative and fell asleep. His wife stayed by his side as the faint sounds of sirens and distant screams wailed outside their window throughout the night.

The non-afflicted people evacuated public areas immediately when they saw the mass hysteria spreading. It was difficult for the non-afflicted to fully understand what was happening. A family of five, two adults and three children, ran as fast as they could to their car, past different people who were screaming and acting hysterically. Some of the afflicted D.C. citizens stopped in front of the family and screamed, terrifying the three children. The afflicted screamers pointed their fingers as the family hurried past them.

The hordes of afflicted running through the streets and sidewalks trampled anyone who got in their way. Strangers bent down to help those violently crushed by the charging crowds found themselves victims as well. The media caught the terror on the faces of the victims and attackers. There was no time for television stations to announce a disclaimer that the sights and sounds may not be suitable for everyone. The horror developed live in front of the viewers' eyes. The action was nonstop. People were screaming as they walked around with bloody faces. Several shots of people holding up the injured and trying to walk away from the bedlam-filled television screens. Cameras focused on blood and terror. Clothes were torn and bloodied, and children ran with their parents, screaming and crying, all adding to the surreal wave of accelerated chaos.

The station switched to a different camera that was covering the pandemonium. Pete watched anxiously as the panic and terror broadcast across the ship's visual and audio. His blood began racing through his veins. Pete realized that the hollow feeling in his stomach represented fear. Although fear was a new emotion for him, he identified with it immediately. He didn't like it. It made him feel helpless. Pete lowered his head into his hands and rubbed his face as if trying to wake himself.

The visual suddenly became static, and the ship's audio turned off. Familiar blue light emerged from the center of the screen. Krix'x's face appeared, and he glanced around the room. Krix'x saw Pete and Oz sitting at the control panel. Rialla had left before his arrival.

"What is it? Why have I been summoned?" Krix'x bellowed.

Pete stood up and looked Krix'x in the eyes. "I need you to come to the ship ASAP."

"Impossible." Krix'x's voice sounded surprised.

"We believe you and the Council are in danger. You need to be here physically."

Krix'x looked around the room. He tried to assess the situation, but no conclusion came to mind.

When his eyes returned to Oz, he shouted, "Vailen, report."

"Krix'x, you need to trust us. Please wormstream here immediately. You are in danger."

The screen went blank, and Pete looked at Oz. She didn't say anything. The silence in the room was deafening as they waited.

Questions ran through Pete's head. *If Krix'x doesn't come, does that mean he is a part of all this? If he is a part of this, did we now alert him to move his plans up? Krix'x can't be a part of this,* he thought.

Pete started pacing around the room, something new for him. He slowly paced from one wall in the control room to the other. After his second round trip, he realized he was pacing and stopped in front of Oz. She was sitting calmly in her seat in front of the control desk. Pete touched her shoulder, and they exchanged a solemn glance.

The lights flickered within the control room. The visual came on, and a small blue opening began to form inside the screen. The opening was a tiny blue dot deep inside the visual. The space between the front of the visual and the dot seemed to go on forever. The dot moved slowly toward the front of the visual. As it came closer, it formed a time funnel, with each section getting slightly more prominent as it approached the screen. The tunnel's beginning, created by the time funnel, was barely visible, engulfed in stars. The stars were bright in the black sky of the universe. The tunnel became more apparent as it approached the visual. The process from a tiny blue dot to a fully established tunnel took approximately three minutes.

A figure was lingering in the distance. At first, Pete couldn't make out the figure. He wasn't sure what it was. A weapon could have fired a projectile through the tunnel for all he knew. But as the figure came closer, it became larger and more lifelike. The figure moved as if in no hurry to reach the ship. When it reached the end of the tunnel, it was clear that he was a Council member wearing a familiar hooded blue robe. The figure exited the tunnel through the visual and onto the spaceship floor. He removed his hood.

Pete called out, "Krix'x?"

"What is this all about?" Krix'x asked. His head was completely blue and bald. His features were different than when he was on the visual. Pete observed that he wasn't as scary-looking in person. He was taller and thinner than Pete. The robe made him look heavier than he was.

Pete walked up to Krix'x as the tunnel disappeared into the visual, the same way it appeared.

"The affliction has changed."

"What do you mean, changed?" Krix'x bellowed.

"Everyone who was afflicted now sees others as gray-skinned."

"Impossible," Krix'x replied.

Oz spoke up. "Krix'x, it's true. Listen." Oz played the reporter's audio track.

Krix'x raised an eyebrow. "This is not logical. We tested every possible outcome."

Pete looked at Krix'x. "The one outcome you did not test for was espionage."

"Impossible. That is not logical."

"I am not going to waste time discussing logic with you. Oz will play a recording, and you can make your own conclusions."

Oz played a few conversations, including the one about the enhancement. Krix'x took a few steps from the control panel and looked at Oz without expression. He slowly turned his head and body towards Pete, and his eyes reddened. He began to raise his hand. Time seemed to stand still over the next few moments as every gesture continued in slow motion. Pete watched Krix'x raise his hand slowly. A weapon appeared in his hand, and before Pete could react, Krix'x fell to the floor.

Rialla was standing in the doorway behind Oz. Rialla had shot Krix'x. Oz, behind Pete, didn't see Krix'x raise a gun toward Pete. She turned back at Rialla and screamed, "What did you do?"

Pete yelled at Oz, "She saved our lives!"

Pete rolled the unconscious Krix'x over and exposed the gun in his hand. Oz sat down, hard, into her chair. It squeaked loudly.

Oz looked confused at the cloaked body on the floor. "I don't understand."

Pete bent down and inspected the body. "I had Rialla waiting in the back with a stunner."

"How did you know this would happen?" Oz asked.

"I didn't. Believe it or not, it was a feeling."

Oz bent down next to the body. Pete moved away and let her scan the cloaked figure. Oz looked at her readings and sat back on the floor, confused at what she was reading.

"This isn't Krix'x," she said quietly. Oz didn't know what was happening to her. She felt dizzy and was unable to stand. Rialla moved quickly and helped her to a nearby chair.

Pete looked at Oz. "I know this isn't Krix'x. Whoever the two voices are, this is one of them."

"How do you know that?" Oz said softly, her body swaying slightly in her chair, her hands gripped tightly on the arms of the chair.

"Out of all the recordings you found, only two voices exist. The same two voices over and over again. You verified that with your research. So, as far as we know, no other Council members are involved. A logical conclusion would be that this is one of them. Also, knowing Krix'x would discuss what we were reporting with other members of the Council helped."

"How did that help?"

"Krix'x needed verification of our claim. The next logical step was to discuss it with the Council. By doing this, the perpetrators would offer to come in his stead to find out how much we knew to adjust their timeline."

Oz looked at Pete. "I'm proud of you." Oz smiled and fell from her chair.

26 FACE TO FACE

Oz awoke in Rialla's bed, groggy, and rubbed her elbow. She looked around the room and saw Pete sleeping in a chair in one corner. Rialla was sitting on the other side of the bed with her head hanging down. Oz watched both of them rest for a few minutes. *These characters are my family,* she thought. They care about my well-being. They would do whatever it takes to protect me. Oz had never had this feeling before. She liked it.

She quietly got up from the bed and walked to the cell holding the Council member. He was standing with his back to Oz, staring at the wall. He didn't move when she entered the room. Oz knew he had heard her come in.

Without looking at Oz and still staring at the wall, he said, "Vailen, you know, holding me here is not logical. You will have to answer to the Traa'zels for this." His voice was slow and calculating.

Oz didn't answer right away. Her world, as she knew it, was in turmoil. Once, logic ruled, and now chaos was taking over. Chaos was implausible in a logic-based society. And yet, here she was, face to face with chaos itself. This Council member, who refused to turn around and face her, had created chaos from logic. He now controlled the future of her world. Oz began to feel light-headed again. She quickly gathered herself and responded.

Oz pursed her lips in grieved contempt. "In a logical society, I would answer for my actions; that is quite correct. But I am not on Wen'q'rixsh, and neither are you. I answer to no one on this planet, especially a traitor."

The Council member slowly turned around and faced Oz. He cracked a small, devilish smile and slowly walked toward the glass that restricted his freedom.

"Ah, I see," he spoke slowly, looking closely at Oz. "You have been exposed to this atmosphere for many months now. How do you survive it?"

"I created software to repair the affected circuits as they become infected."

"Ha," He sneered. "An intelligent Vailen, how original."

"Well, let me see. I guess that makes you a dumbass, then. I'm the free one, and you're the prisoner."

The Council member stared at Oz. He didn't reply.

Oz rolled her eyes at the Traa'zel. "Dumbass? It means you're very stupid."

The Council member laughed, and Oz found that odd. Council members do not show emotion. They are brilliant, logical, and emotionless.

"You're injecting the earth's gases, aren't you?" Oz frowned at him.

The Traa'zel clasped his hands behind his back. "Well, well. You are on top of this, aren't you? How did you ever know to look at the recordings? Better yet, how did you find the ones you played for me?"

Oz knew she had to be careful. She couldn't go head-to-head with him. He was intellectually out of her league. She didn't want to give anything away. For all she knew, this was part of his plan. To get

captured, get all the information he could, and return to
Wen'q'rixsh. She had to be patient.

"Why don't you tell me what the hell you are doing? That only
seems fair. You're upending our world and changing our society
for some selfish gain. Why don't you brag about how life will be
better for everyone now that you will control their lives?"

"I control no one," the Council member responded.

"But you want to." Oz was quick to reply.

"You don't know anything, Vailen. You have found only an atom
of information, but think you found so much more."

"Well, my dear traitor, I found enough to get you here, didn't I?"
Oz sneered at him.

The Council member's eyes turned fire-red. Oz thought he would
shatter the glass with his eyes if he tried to. But she quickly realized
his eyes carried no real danger. She walked over to the control
panel on the side of the wall.

"What are you doing?" he asked in a slow, menacing tone.

"You're going to go to sleep now. And when you wake up, you
may have all your body parts. We'll see."

"You wouldn't dare."

"Why? Because it's not logical? Nighty night."

She released gas into the cell, and within seconds, the Council
member fell to the floor, unconscious.

When he awoke, he was at the table where she had placed Bronson
Pike. His body was held down with the same thick metal straps. He
twisted his head, left and right, struggling to free his arms and legs.
No matter how hard he tried, he couldn't move any part of his
body other than his head. Oz declined to strap down his head to

allow him to look around at his surroundings. She wanted him to see how hopeless his situation was.

"Now, my dear Council member, I will get some answers. Being exposed to this atmosphere has helped me gain a new perspective on life. I rarely analyze the logical way to proceed anymore. Now, it's all about the pain," she said, approaching his face.

His eyes grew bigger. He began to sweat; not knowing what would happen next struck fear into his heart. His speech started out strong. "Vailen, I will see you destroyed for this."

"You have to take the bad with the good, traitor. Now that you have feelings, you will be experiencing fear. Fear is amazing. It can be so exhilarating. I have found it adds suspense to so many different situations."

Oz laughed like a mad scientist to add to the Traa'zel's confusion. His head began moving frantically from side to side. She pulled open a small drawer from under the table. Her laugh became eerie as she held up a glove for the Council member to see. She pulled the glove over her hand, and when she had pushed her fingers firmly inside, she let the glove go, making a popping noise on her arm. She laughed louder at the sound.

"You know what's amazing about acquiring emotions?" Oz walked around the table, talking to the space before her. She moved her hands in an overly expressive manner as she spoke to the air. "Now that I can feel, you see, now that I am acquiring emotions and feelings, it feels better to torture than to carry on a discussion. I credit it to an 'adrenaline rush.' That human term describes this new feeling precisely."

She reached into a metal container with her gloved hand and pulled out a Larxsha.

The Council member remained silent. He was in shock. Never in his highly analytical mind would he have seen this coming. He frantically tried to recalculate his prior research concerning this visit. All probable scenarios were scrutinized for every possible variable with every possible outcome. Torture was not an expected outcome of his analysis. And a Larxsha? He would have never included the possibility that a Larxsha would be on the ship, let alone be used to torture him. No, he thought, a Larxsha was never considered in his analysis.

Oz laughed, knowing what was going through his mind. "You never considered being tortured, did you? I'm sure you never added a Larxsha to your assumption analytics. Now you're experiencing shock and surprise. Yet more feelings to add to your new emotional repertoire. Aren't you excited that you got what you wanted? You are experiencing the plethora of feelings you so desired with your new drug. Now that you have received this wonderful gift, it will be used against you, Council member."

Oz held the Larxsha in her gloved hand. "The Larxsha is my organon of choice." She laughed proudly.

The Council member's speech devolved into incoherent logorrhea that Oz couldn't understand.
"Slow down, sir. I must comprehend your words, or I may command my pet incorrectly."

"Vailen, please reconsider what you are doing," the Council member begged.

Oz looked at the Council member with anger in her eyes. "Did you reconsider destroying our way of life? Did you reconsider inflicting chaos on this planet? What can you tell me, Council member, that will cause me to reconsider?"

"What do you want to know? Ask anything," the Council member pleaded.

Oz looked at the being squirming on the table, representing everything she respected on her planet. The Wen'q'rixshi depended on the Council for their guidance and leadership. Traa'zels were to Wen as the mythological gods were to the Greeks. This man, before her, was not worth her people's respect. This man was a selfish coward, a traitor to his people.

Oz released the Larxsha from its container; the protective glove did not allow the Larxsha's needles to penetrate her skin. She brought it closer to the face of the Council member.

"Earlier, on this very table, I almost got to watch a human penis explode from the inside out. But you are a Council member. You deserve more respect than that."

"Thank you," whimpered the scared man.

"No, since you are such an intelligent being, we'll let the Larxsha eat out your brain."

The Council member screamed. He knew he had to talk fast and offer crucial information to stop the crazy Vailen from proceeding.

"We poisoned the enhancement," he screamed.

"Boring," Oz sang out her response as she stretched her hand toward his face.

"We made up the story about the Xanoclax invasion of Earth."

"Getting colder," Oz continued to sing.

"We started the rumor to gain access to Earth's atmosphere. We started it to keep the Council busy with their experiments, creating heralds. We knew it was logical to try to help a civilization improve itself. The Council would jump at the chance to thwart a Xanoclax invasion."

"You see, Council member," Oz touched her finger to her chin, "I need to go beyond what we all know. I need more."

Oz walked around the table. She walked, waving her hands while she spoke. The added fear that she might accidentally drop the Larxsha from her swinging hand increased the Council member's stress levels. Whenever Oz waved the hand holding the Larxsha over his face, the Traa'zel's eyes widened, and he screamed.

Oz continued her oratory, "I need a symphony of information. I need something from you that will rock my world. Knock me right out of my socks if I wore any."

"Okay, okay. We have allies in a tribe on Xanoclax."

"Ah, now it's getting warmer in here. Continue." Oz sang her response as she waved her hand by his cheek again.

"The tribes in the southern regions of Xanstar want to take over their planet. We are both working together to that end. We'll rule Wen'q'rixsh, and they Xanstar."

"So Earth is involved for the gases? Nothing else?"

"Yes."

"Why are the Xanoclax after my herald?"

"I don't know," screamed the Council member.

Oz stopped and slowly walked around to the top of the table. The Council member eyed her the whole time as she walked. He was breathing in quick, frightened gasps, and Oz wondered if he would faint. She placed her gloved hand, palm up, next to his cheek. He screamed an ear-piercing scream as the Larxsha moved slowly off her hand and onto his face. The Larxsha moved slowly, its first steps off her glove piercing the skin of his cheek. It remained motionless on the Council member's cheek, awaiting a command to proceed.

"The southern tribes of Xanstar lied about the herald to their commanders. The Xan placed a bounty on his head. The southern tribes wanted the Xan command to be occupied with the herald while they gained strength. They are expending many troops in this cause, and their attention is directed away from their home planet right now, allowing the southern tribes to invade and take control of the planet."

The Larxsha took another step, following Oz's commands. When it took a step, the leg it pulled out of his cheek tore the Traa'zel's flesh from the inside out. He let out another horrifying scream.

"How many Council members are involved in your plan?"

"Right now? About half."

"Is Krix'x involved?"

"No. Krix'x is easily manipulated to do our bidding."

"Is he still alive?"

"Yes. We will not need force to win over the Council. We will use all things logic."

Oz pulled her hand away, and the Larxsha's leg tore through his skin again. He screamed.

Oz came closer to the man sobbing on the table. "Your name, traitor. What is your name?"

"Burraksis," he screamed out.

"Burraksis, what is your leader's name?"

"I do not know. No one does."

"How is that possible? Is there no roll call or membership accountability?"

"No," Burraksis was sobbing heavily now.

"What's your plan, Burraksis? How will you proceed?"

"Your herald has set us back greatly. We are now in the process of having Krix'x repeat the experiment verbatim on another human."

"You made Krix'x believe the Wen needed a herald army to protect us from the Xanoclax. How long has this plan been in place?"

"Many years now. I can't remember when it started."

"Where are you on your schedule with your new herald?"

"We are getting close. I believe a month to finish."

Oz put the Larxsha back into its container. She pressed a button on the table, and Burraksis fell asleep. She wanted him to rest and heal. She needed him at full strength when she continued her interrogation the following day.

It was all making sense now. A Wen Council member tasted emotions from the Earth's atmosphere, and it all went to hell from there. Oz wanted to know who the leader was. Knowing the leader could help her focus on a resolution. She went to the control room, leaving the snoring Burraksis on the table.

27 DELVING DEEPER

Pete and Rialla were sitting in the control room, waiting for Oz.

"Did you get all that?" Oz asked them both.

Pete answered first. "Yes, we did. We saw this from the very beginning. You are quite the actress."

"Who was acting?" Oz replied.

Rialla was staring at the visual, not joining in the conversation. Oz looked at her.

"You okay, Rialla?"

She stared at the screen, watching all the people screaming and crying. She looked at Oz. "You care about your people and planet, don't you?"

"Yes, very much," Oz answered.

Rialla looked at Pete, "And this bothers you greatly, does it not?" She pointed at the chaos on the visual.

Pete looked at the visual. "Yes, it does."

Rialla stood up, "I, too, care about my people and planet. Knowing what I know, I must warn them."

Oz looked at her with caring eyes. "How will you do that, Rialla?"

"I need to go to them and report this to my command."

Pete knew she was right. He stood up. "Can you communicate this to them in another way?"

Rialla looked into Pete's eyes. "How?"

"I don't know. Maybe transmit a communication to one of your ships?"

"How will I know they can be trusted?"

Pete looked at Oz. "You got any ideas?"

Oz lowered her head. "No."

"Rialla, can we take a few days to think about this, please?" Pete asked softly.

"Will you not allow me to leave?"

"You are free to come and go as you please," Pete answered quickly.

"Then, I don't understand what the problem is." Rialla looked at Pete, confused.

"I am going to attend to Burraksis," Oz said and walked away.

Pete watched Oz leave, then looked at Rialla. "I don't want you to go, Rialla," Pete said gently.

"Don't you want me to help my people?" Rialla asked, shaking her head.

"Of course I do."

"Then what is it? Please explain."

"I don't want to lose you," Pete said under his breath.

"I will come back, I promise."

"I don't want you to leave even for a little while, Rialla," Pete responded.

Rialla shrugged, "I do not know what to say."

Pete looked at Rialla and wanted to say so many things to her. He wanted to tell her he had feelings for her, but didn't know how to say it. Pete didn't want to force her to say something she didn't feel. Pete now understood how hard it must have been for Jessica to deal with him. He was very confused. He didn't know what he wanted Rialla to say. It had to come from her without his coaxing her. Maybe, he thought, he wanted Rialla to tell him how she felt about him the way Jessica explained her feelings. But he knew Rialla wasn't Jessica.

"Never mind, you don't need to say anything," Pete said sadly. "I don't have the right to ask you to stay."

Pete walked by her and put his hand on her forearm, looking into her eyes. She gave him an innocent, beautiful smile. Her wide green eyes begged for an explanation, but he knew it would be better if she made up her mind without his interference.

He walked past her and headed toward his room. He thought of Jessica and how her loss left him with a void in his heart. He thought Rialla was beginning to fill it. He enjoyed her company, their sparring, and their conversations. She had all the qualities of a good friend. He wondered if there could ever be more.

Pete walked into his room and opened the dresser drawer. He pulled out the manila envelope Bill had given him as he was leaving Bends Creek. He remembered that Jessica was going to go over what they found, but they never got around to it. He opened the envelope, and there was an FBI form inside. *Bill must know someone in the Bureau,* Pete thought. He began to read the form slowly. Pete was hesitant to see what was on the form. Before waking up in the Bends Creek alley, he didn't know who he was. He was hoping he was a good person.

Bill would have told me if I wasn't, Pete smiled.

He felt his palms sweat as he looked down at the FBI form and read the fingerprint search results. Then he felt his heart beat faster as he continued reading. There it was, right on the paper in front of him. Pete's birth name, Jonathan Jordan Park. His last known address was in the small town of Pichville, Indiana.

Indiana? Pete thought. *I wonder if I have any relatives or friends there. Maybe I can get Oz to run a search with this information and point me in the right direction.*

Pete took the envelope to Oz as she was attending to Burraksis in his cell. Burraksis was still out cold. Oz placed a bandage on his cheek while he slept.

"Oz, got a minute?" Pete asked.

"Sure, what's up?"

"Can you get me all the details you can on this file?"

Oz looked at the file and, without opening it, handed it back to Pete.

Pete was confused. "What?"

"I already did."

"Why didn't you tell me?"

"I wanted you to ask the way you want Rialla to ask," Oz said without taking her eyes off Burraksis.

Pete stared at Oz as she bandaged Burraksis. He didn't know what he would do without her. She was always looking out for him. She wasn't just a guide to him, not just a friend; she was much more. She was his conscience.

He moved his lips into a small, appreciative smile. "I get it. Thanks."

"All the information I collected is in the bottom drawer of your dresser. You know, the one you never open."

Pete smiled and headed back to his room. When he got there, he was surprised to find Rialla sitting on his bed, a few tears running down her face.

"What's wrong?" Pete asked as he placed the manila envelope back in the top drawer.

"I am confused and sad," she said softly, looking down at her hands.

"Why?"

Rialla held her hands together tightly and moved her thumbs in and out. She looked at Pete. "I do not want to leave my friends."

Pete sat down next to Rialla. He reached his arms around her, and she lay her head on his chest. Pete felt Rialla's warmth, and it made him feel relaxed.

Pete spoke in a delicate tone. "Rialla, we can help if you let us."

"How?" She whimpered sadly.

"Your people are equally important to us as humans and the Wen. We will all work together to correct this situation."

"You sound so confident about that," she said, raising her head.

Pete wiped her tears away with his thumbs. He smiled and began to get lost in Rialla's big green eyes. He wanted to swim in their big, beautiful, green ocean. He floated away in them for a moment.

"Are you okay?" she asked quietly.

Pete smiled. "I am. Rialla, why don't we sit down later and discuss a plan of action? We're going to need one."

"Okay. Thank you for being my friend," she said, leaving his room.

Pete wanted to fix everything. He knew deep down inside he had to try. Oz needed his help, Rialla needed his help, and Earth needed his help. He looked down at the dresser. Jonathan Jordan Park would have to wait.

***

Pete entered the meeting room and saw Rialla and Oz silently sitting there. Both looked defeated and tired. It was time to formulate a plan of action. They had to act fast for so many reasons. The gray affliction was tearing Earth apart. The Xanoclax would continue hunting Pete and fall to the southern Xans' coup. And the Wen, the Wen society was about to come apart. To move quickly, Pete had to act with confidence.

Pete sat at the table and began, "We need to finish reviewing the recordings."

Oz and Rialla looked puzzled. "Why? Burraksis told us everything about their plan. I should be able to finish my interrogation later today to seek information on the blue-eyed Xan," replied Oz.

Pete looked at Oz with excitement. "Oz, there is still a lot we don't know. We need to know who their leader is. How do they contact the southern Xan Tribes? Who is their Xan contact? And probably information we don't even know to look for."

Rialla sat up with new energy. "You are right. We need this information to formulate a strategy."

Oz leaned forward and passed her hand over the table. The visual floated above the table. She started the files from the point where they had stopped watching. There were a lot more files to go through than Pete expected. They all listened closely, stopping whenever someone had a question or comment. The recordings repeated many of the same conversations several times across various tracks. Pete noticed the file size decreasing on the visual. There weren't many files left. Before Pete gave up, he heard something unexpected.

> Voice one: "Did you bring me all her information?"
>
> Voice two: "It is all in her file."

Voice one began looking through a datapad handed to him by voice two. Pete couldn't see his fingers swipe the datapad screen because the robe covered everything.

Pete asked Oz to pause the visual. "Can we zoom in on the datapad? Maybe we can see who they're talking about."

Oz enlarged the visual and zoomed in on the datapad. The visual was adjusted, and the zoomed-in image was as clear as the original.

Pete watched the visual. "Oz, play it now to see if we can see who is on the DP."

Oz continued the playback. It had run for approximately 20 seconds when Rialla gasped.

"No," she cried out.

Oz paused the visual and stared at the screen with her mouth open. Pete stood up and tried to get closer to the visual. On the datapad was a clear image of Jessica smiling. No one moved or said a word.

After a few moments that seemed like hours, Pete spoke up. "Continue the playback, Oz."

Oz looked slowly at Rialla and then at Pete. "Are you sure?"

Pete nodded without taking his eyes off the visual. Oz continued.

> Voice one: "Is all the females' information enclosed?"
>
> Voice two: "Yes."
>
> Voice one: "Then, I will proceed."
>
> Voice two: "How?"
>
> Voice one: "I will use the Xanoclax warrior armor as I did on the Gamma Rex moon."
>
> Voice two: "Should we send someone else?"
>
> Voice one: "No, I want to do this myself. I want to make sure we succeed. If we fail, it will create a major setback."

Oz paused the visual. Pete still stared at Jessica's image on the Council member's datapad. He wanted to reach up and touch her face. His hand moved slowly from under the table and floated like a feather in a calm meadow toward Jessica's image.

Oz spoke before Pete's hand reached the visual. "Pete, are you okay?"

Pete stopped reaching for the visual and looked at Oz, embarrassed. "I don't know what...I zoned out, I guess. Sorry."

Rialla looked at Pete. "You don't need to apologize."

Pete snapped out of it when Oz turned off the visual. He sat down and looked at Oz. "Where's the Gamma Rex moon located?"

Oz searched and displayed the Gamma Rex moon on the visual. She then searched her database for all files relating to it. Oz stood up quickly and flung her chair back. She stepped away from the table in shock. Pete walked over to her and sat her back down in her chair.

Pete quietly asked, "What did you find?"

She looked at Pete with a blank stare. She turned away from Pete and touched the table in several places. Then, while looking at Pete, Oz pressed enter on the touch screen.

Pete looked away from Oz and up at the visual. It was the visual of the blue-eyed Xan killing Cass. Pete looked down at Oz, noticing she wasn't watching the visual. She had seen it too many times. Pete pressed the escape button on the touch screen, and the visual went black.

Rialla watched her friends as they looked overwhelmed by what they had seen. Pete sat down next to Oz. Oz leaned across her chair, and Pete put his arm around her. Rialla watched as these two friends' bond grew more assertive. The pain of loss pulled them closer to each other. She knew this bonding would make them stronger and battle-ready.

Rialla spoke after a few minutes. "Why did they do this?"

Oz sat up. She looked at the visual. "They did it because they wanted the Wen to believe the Xanoclax were barbarians. They did this to get the Traa'zels to believe that the Xanoclax was a threat. They did this to prey on the logic of all the Wen. They killed my sister as part of their plan to take control of our way of life."

"And Jessica?" Pete asked sadly.

"Jessica was murdered to keep us busy while they maneuvered their plan. Our Jessica was merely an object used as a distraction," Oz replied angrily.

Pete's body felt limp. He tried to raise his arms, but they were so heavy. He tried to walk away from the table, but his legs felt like two cement poles buried in the ground. He moved slowly across the floor toward the door. Oz didn't call out to him, and Rialla was silent as he disappeared through the door.

Rialla looked at Oz angrily. "They must pay for this."

Oz looked up at Rialla from the table. A slow, crooked smile emerged from her face; she looked like Alex from the cover of A Clockwork Orange.

28 PIECES IN PLACE

Pete slept for two days without waking. He was mentally drained and physically exhausted. He awoke to loud, horrific screams coming from down the hall from his bedroom. He got up quickly and immediately became dizzy. He sat on the bed, swaying back and forth. He wanted to move towards the screams but felt stuck on the bed. He tried to get up again, but he was pulled back down. He remained there, confused, for a few more moments. The screaming had stopped, so he lay down and fell back asleep. After a few more hours had passed, he struggled out of bed.

Pete stood up and swayed from side to side. He waited a moment until he felt centered, and the wobbling stopped. He ambled to the control room and rubbed the back of his head. His head throbbed like a lead pipe had struck him.

I wonder if this is what a hangover feels like, he thought.

When he arrived in the control room, it was dark and empty. He decided to try to see if Oz was in the meeting room. He found the meeting room empty as well. He looked in several other rooms and finally gave up the search. He went into the dining room and made tea. He sat at the table in the dark, sipping the tea and wondering what had happened to his head. He occasionally rubbed his neck, trying desperately to massage the pain away. He had never experienced this type of pain before.

The lights came on as Oz and Rialla entered the dining room. Pete put his free hand over his eyes and yelled, "Please turn them off."

Oz turned the lights off and headed to the table where Pete was sitting. Rialla followed her and sat in a chair beside her.

Oz looked at Pete with a concerned expression. "What's wrong, Pete?"

Pete raised his head slowly from his gaze, which had been focused on his hot tea. He inhaled the aroma provided by the steam from the cup. The hot steam relaxed him a little.

Pete inhaled the steam again and answered Oz, "I don't know what's happening to me. I woke up, and my head has been killing me. It's like small bombs are going off in my head, and the explosions are trying to tear through my skull."

Oz walked over and sat by Pete so she could speak softly. "Pete, you had an incredible blow to your processing units and biosyntax circuits. I did a scan while you were sleeping and am researching the results now. So far, it looks like your emotions overloaded the security protocols. I don't know the extent of the damage yet."

Pete turned slowly toward Oz. "I need something for the pain. I can't think."

Oz held her hand over the table, palm down. Blue light emanated from her palm, and Pete had to turn away from the light because it hurt his head. He didn't see the needle with blue fluid materialize on the table from the light. When the light vanished, Oz picked up the syringe and looked at Pete.

"This will help."

"What is it?" Pete asked quietly.

"LSD."

Pete looked at Oz, surprised.

"JK, dog. Come on, take your shirt off, and let me stick you."

Pete struggled to take his shirt off as every slight movement made his head throb harder. Rialla walked over and helped Pete remove his shirt. Oz inserted the needle into the skin on Pete's right shoulder. The liquid felt cool as it entered his body.

"What is this?" Pete asked.

"An old remedy, Mamma Oz concocted for you," Oz smiled.

Pete tried to smile back, but that hurt, too. "How long?"

"It should take effect in a few minutes," Oz answered softly. Rialla placed a bandage across the needle prick on Pete's shoulder. Pete looked up at Rialla. "Thank you," he whispered.

Pete sipped his tea a few more times and started to feel lighter. His head stopped throbbing, and he could feel his energy slowly seep back through his body. He sipped some more tea and looked at Oz.

"Thank you," he said, smiling.

"Don't mention it," Oz smiled back. "Feeling better?"

Pete's eyes widened, "I am."

"Cool, now we can get to work." Oz turned on the lights. It took Pete's eyes a few seconds to adjust.

"What are you working on?" he asked Oz.

"We received some more information from Burraksis and added it to everything else we know at this point," Oz answered as she was working her fingers across the image of a keyboard on the table. The visual above the table displayed a spreadsheet that Oz had created.

"So what we have surmised from all the information is as follows," Oz continued. "We know there is an organization on Wen'q'rixsh that has collaborated with the southern tribes of Xanstar. They have struck a deal to allow each to rule over their respective planets."

Pete watched the screen and waited for Oz to continue her report.

"Krix'x and other Council members who are not involved believe they need a new herald army to protect the Wen from the Xans. The Xans believe the opposite: that the heralds will be used as weapons to attack Xanstar."

Pete nodded. "Yes, this is what we know."

Oz looked at Pete, "Yes, we know the why now. But we still don't know the who."

"Did you get any more from Burraksis?"

"We did after a little more coaxing. Burraksis revealed that there is one mastermind behind the Wen coup."

"Who is it?"

"No one knows. I believe Burraksis because I nearly killed him for the answers."

"That was the screaming I heard?"

Oz didn't look happy with her answer. "Yes, it was."

"What's bothering you?" Pete asked, concerned.

"Having to torture with these traces of gases inside me is very confusing. I know I have to do it. Getting the information we need is logical, but it feels awkward. I am not sure what the word for it is. Weird is a better choice, I think."

"Emotions span a wide array of feelings, Oz. When you think you have it figured out and under control, another new one pops up."

Oz looked at Pete. "Kind of sucks, you know?"

Pete smiled, "Yes, I know."

Pete looked at the screen and began talking, never looking away from it, "So, your guys," he said, pointing at Oz, "want to change your world from logical to semi-logical by exposing Earth's gases to the masses."

Pete waited for Oz to nod in agreement before continuing. "And your guys in the south," Pete pointed at Rialla, "have a civil war planned." He looked at Rialla, waiting for her nod.

"And my guys are caught in the crossfire. Everyone is caught in the crossfire, including people close to me. Does that about sum it up?"

Oz and Rialla looked at each other before both nodding to Pete.

Pete asked Oz to turn off the visual. He looked at his two friends. They sat, waiting for him to spew answers to unravel this mess.

"I have a plan," he smiled.

29 THE PLAN

Oz and Rialla looked on anxiously at Pete as he sat at the table across from them. "What is it?" Oz asked.

"We must work this through to draw out the coup's leader. Without confronting the leader, he will continue down this path until he succeeds. So we disrupt his plan and force him to expose his identity to us."

Rialla looked confused. "How can you do that if the leader is light-years away?"

"We force him to come to us."

Now Oz was confused. "How?"

"I told you that all our people are important. I promised Rialla I would help her. And Oz, you know I'll help you."

"And…" Oz said, slowly anticipating an answer that she wouldn't like.

"And we start with the Xanoclax."

"What does that mean?" Oz asked.

"We solve the Xanoclax issue first. Here's how I see it working out. If we can convince the Xans that I am not a threat and that they need to return to their planet to prevent civil war, everything else falls into place."

"What's everything else?" Oz was confused.

"If the Xanoclax leave Earth and call off this so-called invasion, Krix'x will release the antidote, and the Earth will return to normal. Without an invasion, without a Xan threat, the leader will be pressured to make another move. It will likely be something bold, and he must expose himself."

"So your plan hinges on the Xans leaving? Just like that? The Xans are going to say, Sorry, we misunderstood you. You're really a nice guy. We'll leave you alone now?" Oz squinted at Pete.

"It will take a little work, but that's the gist."

Oz stood up and looked around the room. She wanted to leave the room but didn't know why, so she sat back down. She looked at Pete and started to speak, but no words came out. Her jaw opened, but it froze. She turned to Rialla, who was smiling.

"You're okay with this plan?" Oz asked Rialla.

With an even bigger smile, Rialla looked at Pete and answered, "Yes, I am."

Oz looked at Pete and then at Rialla several times. She was at a loss for words. What she was hearing was illogical. The Xanoclax did not negotiate.

"You both are crazy to think you can convince the Xanoclax to leave. Rialla, you said it yourself, your people do not compromise. What makes you think they will accommodate us?"

"Because I will be by the herald's side when he talks to my commanders."

Oz stood up, kicking her chair back. "No. No. No. I will not help you with this suicide mission. There must be a better way."

Pete smiled at Oz and walked closer. "Oz, you asked me to trust you when you returned home. Now, I am asking you for the same trust."

Oz yelled, "This is not the same, Pete. I wasn't going on a suicide mission."

"How do you know, Oz? What if the leader found you out? He would have tortured you for answers and sent a new Vailen he trusted in your place."

Oz was shaking her head defiantly. She didn't want to hear anymore. She lifted her arms, waved her hands over her head, and stormed out of the room.

Rialla looked at Pete as he watched Oz leave. "Should we go speak to her?" Rialla asked.

"No," Pete answered softly. "Let's give her a little time to work through this."

"Should we discuss how we will proceed?" Rialla asked excitedly.

"Yes, we must discuss how we approach your commanders with this news."

***

Oz was in the control room, running through her database, looking for answers to questions she didn't ask. She was hoping something would pop up randomly, but no answers appeared. She closed her database and began to consider Pete's plan. He was headstrong and would go through with it unless she could devise a better action plan. If his plan was as hopeless as she believed, she had to devise a way to protect him and Rialla.

She left the control room and headed to the armory, first taking a quick inventory of what weapons they had at their disposal. Oz looked over the supplies and concluded that most of the tech in the room would be displaced by the Xan when Pete and Rialla stepped onto their ship.

They may be barbaric, but they aren't stupid, she thought.

Her challenge was to protect Pete and Rialla without the Xan realizing they were protected. Oz looked around the room at the pieces of armor and weapons classified as non-inventory. She walked to the back of the room and stopped before Rialla's armor. She lifted the Xan helmet, stared into its eyes briefly, and smiled.

Pete and Rialla were still in the meeting room, discussing how to meet with the Xan. Oz walked into the room and interrupted them. "Okay. If I agree to this, we have to be smart about it. You let me take action to present the best possible scenario for your way back. Agreed?"

Pete smiled. He felt better knowing Oz would be helping. "Agreed," he answered.

Rialla smiled. "Agreed."

Oz continued to speak as she walked out of the room. "I should have a few items ready in a few hours to introduce to you. I will expect your full attention then."

Pete yelled to Oz's back, "Thank you."

Oz waved without looking back as she disappeared from the room.

Rialla picked up her discussion with Pete from where they stopped. She shook her head slightly, "I don't know if it is wise to approach it this way."

"I can't think of a better way, Rialla," Pete answered.

"Allowing me to bring you to our ship as a captive is very dangerous."

"I know."

"You killed Xan warriors. There will be many seeking revenge. I may not be able to protect you."

I am not worried about your protection. I won't need it."

Rialla folded her arms. "Your confidence will be your undoing."

Pete reacted with a short smile, "Maybe. Let's hope it works one more time."

Rialla went over the protocol for bringing a prisoner to the ship. She felt the Xan commanders would go off procedure due to the value of her prisoner. She didn't see a problem getting herself and Pete onto the ship.

"Herald, I can get you aboard our ship, but cannot guarantee your safety. I cannot guarantee a meeting with the commanders. Once I turn you over to the guards, we will be separated, and you will be alone."

"That's all part of the plan, Rialla. We must follow through with your ship's prisoner protocols for this to be believable. We discussed other options and concluded there weren't any. If I call for a truce, they will attempt to kill me before I get to your ship. You know this is the only way."

Rialla looked down at the table. She knew he was right. Her heart was heavy, and she felt that these next few days of preparing for the meeting with the Xan commanders might be the last she would spend with Pete. She didn't notice Pete getting up and coming to her side of the table. She was deep in thought. It wasn't until he gently touched her shoulder that she realized he was close to her. She looked up at him and smiled. He smiled back.

They sat there for several moments, staring in silence at each other. Those moments felt like they would last forever, but Rialla knew they would soon end. She waited for Pete to break the silence, but he never spoke. Neither wanted the silence to break. Rialla wanted to sit there and enjoy his presence, and Pete felt the same.

It took a loud clap from Oz to startle them back into reality.

"Okay, I have a few things I need to show you for your suicide mission. But before we go back to the lab, let's set up a diagram of the ship on the visual."

Oz started the visual, and a blueprint of the Xan warship appeared.

Pete looked surprised. "Where did you get this?"

"Guilty," Rialla raised her hand.

Oz continued, "Rialla drew a ship layout, and I transposed it onto the visual. It's no big deal. It's a simple architectural transformation."

"If you know what you're doing, maybe," Pete answered.

"I can't handle it when you act like a suck-up, so please," Oz smiled at Pete.

"I want to go over the layout with you both so we're all on the same page. If I need to make any adjustments to your equipment based on our discussion, I can make them. So let's go over this blueprint with a fine-tooth comb and cement it into our heads."

For the next three hours, the three friends went over the blueprint of the Xanoclax ship. Every time they finished one scan of the blueprint, they took another look with different variables. Oz wanted to consider the repercussions of every possible situation. She wanted an answer for every outcome they considered. She knew there was no room for a mistake. They would cover as many details as possible, including misunderstanding a Xanoclax warrior's intention or not knowing how to interpret an answer or a question. Rialla went over every room of the ship. She took great care in explaining every guard's responsibility on the ship. Oz was surprised at how thorough Rialla was with the details.

Oz turned the visual off and looked at Pete. "So the plan is to get on the ship and have an audience with the commander?"

"Yes," Pete answered.

"But you will not meet him right away. You understand this?"

"Yes."

"So when Rialla turns you over to the guards, and they put you in a cell, what's to stop the Xanoclax ship from leaving orbit?"

Pete looked at Oz, "That's where you come in. Rialla will establish a direct link between the ship's network and our ship. You'll infiltrate their systems and monitor their sequences. If you discover the command to leave the Earth's orbit, you can cause some system errors to delay the actual take-off."

"You make it sound so easy, Pete. You realize that their tech is different from Wen tech, right?"

"But it is based on Wen tech. How much more different can it be?"

Oz shook her head, "Be careful, human. You're getting way too cocky."

"With a team like this, how can I not be cocky?" Pete shrugged.

30 NEW TOYS

Pete and Rialla walked into the lab and saw Rialla's armor on a mannequin. Rialla paused as she entered. She moved slowly toward the mannequin and touched the armor. She placed her head on the chest plate, closed her eyes, and said a Xan prayer. She lifted her head and let her hand fall across the armor as she turned to Pete.

"This sight makes me feel good and sad at the same time," she said, smiling at Pete.

Pete looked at her armor. "Well, it scares the crap out of me."

Rialla laughed with Pete as they waited for Oz.

Oz walked in, holding a datapad in her hands. "I'm glad you both think this is funny," she barked.

"Just trying to release the fear, that's all," Pete answered.

Oz walked behind the mannequin. She made some adjustments on her datapad and looked at Rialla.

"Let's start with you, princess," Oz commanded. "I made some adjustments to your tech that you will have to get used to, so let's put this bad boy on and get started."

Rialla was excited. Since her time on the ship, this was the first time she had seen her armor.

"Where's my canvas?" Rialla looked around for the tech garment that she wore under her armor.

Oz smiled. "You don't need it anymore. I incorporated all the connections directly into the armor. All the synapse–nerve connections will be direct."

Rialla looked amazed, like a child on Christmas morning, opening the exact present she wanted. She slowly slid her armor on her body. Rialla made it look like a religious ritual as she glided through the process of equipping herself. Pete watched as the Xan warrior gently placed each piece of armor on her body. Each movement had a purpose, and he thought Rialla looked beautiful as she went through every piece of armor. After she put on her boots, she looked at Pete and smiled. She turned away from Pete and put her gloves over her hands. She raised her helmet over her head and slowly guided it to the top of her neck. She turned around and pointed her hand toward Pete.

A sting of fear shot through Pete's heart for a brief second. He raised his hand, and Oz screamed.

"Pete! What the hell, man?"

Pete stared at Rialla. She wasn't there anymore. In her place was a cold Xan warrior with a mission to kill the herald, to kill him. The red eyes were brightly lit in its helmet, and it stared down at him. Pete couldn't take his eyes off the red slits. The staring match between them caused Pete's eyes to water; he never blinked. Visions of past combat with Xan warriors shot through his mind. He opened and closed his eyes several times, trying to dismiss the images.

"I got lost in the moment, sorry," Pete answered softly. Pete lowered his arm, and Rialla lowered hers.

Rialla then raised her arms slowly and removed her helmet. "Would it be better if I kept this off?" she asked.

Pete smiled, "No, I apologize. I know it's you. Keep it on, please."

Rialla smiled at Pete and placed the helmet back on her head. She slowly turned to Oz, who was working on her datapad.

Rialla said, "What now?" Her voice bellowed out in a raw, deep rasp.

Rialla's raspy voice continued the visions in Pete's mind of previous battles. He took several breaths and relaxed. He wanted to concentrate on Oz and her refinements to Rialla's armor. Pete made his way to a stool beside Oz to observe.

Oz began, "Okay, you should be able to hear me inside your helmet now."

"Yes, Oz, I can hear you," Rialla answered excitedly. Her voice came out of Oz's datapad, so it was her voice and not the warrior rasp.

"I need you to manipulate matter and create a gun."

Rialla held her hand up, and nothing happened. "I can't do it."

"Give me a moment. I need time to allow the new system to adjust to your DNA. Once it does, you should feel…"

Rialla cut Oz off with a quick scream, "Ow!"

Oz laughed, "Yeah, that's about right. A little shock?"

Rialla laughed in response. "Thanks for the warning."

Oz continued, "Now try it again, Rialla. It should work this time."

Rialla raised her arm, and a laser gun immediately appeared. Rialla laughed and screamed, "It worked!" Before Oz could answer, the gun blasted a hole through the lab's far wall.

It was Oz's turn to scream. "Rialla! Don't move! You need to get used to the new commands."

Rialla turned to Oz. "Sorry."

Oz went through several enhancements with Rialla. She explained that the new hardware was 100% more responsive than her old tech. Everything she was able to do in the past would happen quicker now. Rialla had to control her thoughts to use the new system to its full potential. She could no longer plan a sequence of actions. All actions were immediately done without hesitation. Oz told Rialla to keep the armor on and practice.

Oz walked over to Pete. "You okay?"

"Yeah, I'm good," Pete said, nodding slowly.

"It's freaky, isn't it? Seeing Rialla in her suit?"

Pete watched Rialla practicing. "Yes. I have to get used to this quickly. All the fights, nearly getting killed, and so many more images keep rushing through my head."

"It's Rialla inside that armor, Pete. It's our friend in there."

Pete smiled at Oz. "I know."

Rialla took her helmet off and walked over to Pete and Oz, grinning from ear to ear.

"What do you think?" Oz asked.

"It's incredible. You are amazing, Vailen." Rialla smiled.

"Yeah, I know," Oz laughed.

Pete looked at Rialla, "You okay with the enhancements?"

"Yes. Getting the sequences down will take a little time, but not long."

Oz looked at Pete. "I cannot set you up with any obvious weapons. They will not pass their scans. I have made a few of my own that won't show up on advanced scans, but don't try to go through airport security with them," Oz laughed.

Pete looked at Oz. "I appreciate what you're trying to do. But we are not going on the ship intending to fight or kill Xans."

In an aggravated tone, Oz replied, "No, I know that. But you may need to defend yourself."

Rialla said, "The Vailen is correct; you may need to defend yourself."

Pete stood up and began to speak, but he stopped himself and walked out of the room. Rialla watched him leave. Oz started to follow Pete. She glanced back briefly and told Rialla to keep practicing.

"I'll be right back," Oz said to Rialla, disappearing from the room.

Pete was sitting at the desk in the control room, watching Rialla practice with her new armor. He didn't look up as Oz entered the room. She sat down beside him and watched the visual.

Oz looked at Pete curiously. "What is this all about?"

"Did you set her coms up in her helmet so she can contact her ship?"

Oz was puzzled. "That's part of the plan, isn't it?"

"Yes, it is. Will we know if she contacts the ship before or after the plan calls for it?"

"What are you saying, Pete? Do you think Rialla will betray us?"

Pete turned and looked Oz straight in the eyes. "When she puts that armor on, she is not Rialla as we know her."

Oz shook her head. "No, you're wrong; she's still our Rialla, not the Xans'."

"I want you to monitor her coms. Am I clear?" Pete said seriously.

Oz stared back at Pete. "Crystal."

They both walked back to the lab and saw Rialla sitting down, breathing heavily. Oz noticed several more holes in the far wall. The holes were smaller, and they didn't go through the wall, which indicated Rialla was improving.

Rialla looked at Pete. "Is everything okay?"

Pete smiled, "Yes, all good. How's the practice coming?"

"I think I'm getting better with it. I'm working from my past instincts, which are hard to break."

Oz said, "While there's a break in the action, Pete, you should try on your new armor." Oz opened a closet door and wheeled out a mannequin wearing Pete's trenchcoat.

Pete laughed. "That's my coat. Where's my new armor?"

Oz grinned. "This is trenchcoat, part deux."

Pete put on his trench coat and walked to the center of the room. Something felt different about the coat; it was much lighter. He performed a kata with precision and speed.

"What did you do to my coat?" Pete asked Oz.

"I added a few toys to it. You will find that you can materialize weapons like Rialla now. Granted, they may not be as sophisticated as the weapons she can create, but this will do for now. I can improve upon it later, after the Xan mission. When you get back home," she avowed.

Pete swung his arms around and up and down. He still couldn't believe how freely his arms moved now.

"Go ahead and try it," Oz encouraged.

Pete raised his arm and pointed to the far wall. A machine gun appeared in his arm, went off, and disappeared.

Oz laughed. "Looks like you need practice, too."

Pete kept trying different weapons, pointing them at the far wall. Oz smiled as she watched Pete. She looked at Rialla and observed that she wasn't laughing or smiling. Rialla looked like she was studying Pete. Oz looked away from Rialla and back at Pete.

Pete's paranoia is making me see things that aren't there, she thought.

31 OLD FRIENDS NEW NEWS

Pete was excited when Maggie and Bill invited them to dinner. He wanted to let them in on all he and Oz discovered about their mission. He often debated telling them with Oz, who played the devil's advocate and disagreed. But, in the end, Pete won the debate. They decided to tell Maggie and Bill. Oz was the big winner; she had always wanted to tell them, but she knew it would be best if Pete thought it was his idea.

It was a beautiful evening as the five friends sat outside at a rooftop table overlooking the Potomac. Pete was so happy to see his friends. He missed talking to them. He missed their responses and concerns but loved seeing the world through Maggie and Bill's eyes. Through the eyes of two people, he trusted so well.

A slight breeze blew across their table as the waitress took their orders. Oz was dressed in a blue hoodie and wore a knit cap that was able to conceal the majority of her features. She sat on Pete's left, and Rialla sat on Pete's right. Rialla wasn't sure what to order, and Pete helped her. Oz was there for the company because she had yet to learn how to digest human food without the help of Wen chemicals. She brought a few chemicals in a vial in case a dish was too appealing to resist.

They all ordered drinks, and Bill held his drink in a toast. "To friends," he said.

Everyone repeated at the same time, "To friends," and tapped each other's glasses. Pete smiled and started the conversation.

"How's everything going with your proposals, Maggie?" Pete asked.

Maggie was excited to talk about it. "I think we got pretty far with the House," she said. "We're picking up more interest, and hopefully, we'll have some news soon."

"That's great," Pete said.

Bill looked at Pete. "What's going on with all the gray? Do you know why this happened?"

Maggie poked Bill. "Give the man a break. Let him enjoy his drinks before you attack him with all your questions."

Bill looked at Pete. "Sorry. I didn't mean to be rude, Pete."

"It's okay. We've wanted to talk to you about what's going on for a while now."

Oz spoke next. "We have a lot to fill you guys in on."

Bill looked at Maggie and then at Pete. "That doesn't sound good."

Pete put his drink down and watched Rialla order another glass of wine. He waited for the waitress to leave, then took a deep breath and let it out slowly.

Maggie was concerned now. "Everything okay, Pete?"

"No, Maggie. But I guess I should come out and start. A Wen Council member is responsible for the gray affliction. He sabotaged the chemical mixture that created the affliction, and this is the result."

Bill and Maggie looked shocked. "Pete, did you tell anyone about this?" Maggie asked.

"No, because there is more to the story than just the gray," Pete answered.

Oz looked at Pete, "You should start from the beginning."

Pete looked solemnly at Maggie and Bill. He wondered how he could tell them that the mission was a fluke. How would they respond? Would they still want to be friends? He didn't want them upset, but couldn't continue the lie.

"It has come to our attention that the warning of a Xan invasion was a lie," Pete said, waiting for a response before deciding if he should continue. But no response came. Only shocked looks with mouths agape.

"I didn't know. Oz didn't know. We wouldn't have known without Rialla's help." Pete looked over at Rialla on her third glass of wine. She smiled at Pete, blinked her eyes, and continued drinking. Oz looked around Pete at Rialla and wondered if the atmosphere had an increased effect on Rialla.

Pete continued to receive no response from Maggie or Bill. "There is a coup in the making on Oz's home planet. Several Council members discovered that the gases in the Earth's atmosphere affect their emotional capabilities. They are trying to create a world for themselves that is semi-logical."

Bill had heard enough to respond. "So you're saying the affliction was bogus? It didn't have to happen? Earth was a pawn in an alien soap opera?"

Pete put his drink down. "Pretty much, yeah."

Bill had no response to Pete's answer. Maggie sat and stared at Pete, not believing what she was hearing. Bill finally spoke. "So what happens now?"

Pete looked at Bill, "The Xans believe I am a threat due to the lies they have been told. I will attempt to talk to them and see if we can begin to turn this around."

Maggie looked frightened. "No, Pete, you can't do that."

Oz looked at Pete. "Listen to the voice of reason."

Maggie continued, "Pete, you don't know what they will do to you."

Pete smiled at Maggie. "I appreciate how much you care; that means a lot to me. But I have to fix this before it gets worse."

"Isn't there another way?" Maggie asked.

"No, we've looked at all our options. If we get the Xans to leave, the Wen will administer the antidote and fix the affliction."

"That's a pretty big assumption."

"I think you're right, saying we need to fix this situation, Pete," Bill said. "But if something happens to you, who will help the earth? Who can we trust?"

Pete lowered his head and stared at his glass. He looked up slowly and replied, "You all mean so much to me. I couldn't feel it at first, but now my feelings are getting stronger. My feelings scream at me, saying I must protect the people who are important to me. I have to try, Bill. My feelings leave me no choice."

Pete looked over at Rialla. She was sniffling. Pete noticed Rialla had four empty glasses sitting in front of her. Rialla looked at Pete sadly. "That was so beautiful."

Pete looked at Oz, and Oz said, "Yes, she's drunk. I knew the atmosphere would break her resistance eventually."

Pete looked at Rialla and laughed, "Are you having a good time?"

Rialla closed her eyes and opened them slowly. "I was enjoying myself and this company," she said, saluting Maggie and Bill with her raised fifth glass of wine. Bill smiled and saluted back. Rialla looked at Pete, finishing her response, "Until you started in with all your sappy verbahjah," mispronouncing verbiage while lifting her glass to salute Pete. Rialla smiled and took another drink of her wine.

Pete looked at Oz. "Verbahjah?"

Oz shrugged her shoulders. "She's wasted, Pete. Maybe we should take her home before she hurts someone."

Rialla ordered another drink, and the waitress looked beyond Rialla at Pete. Pete took his hand and waved across his throat, signaling the waitress to cut Rialla off.

Pete looked at Maggie and Bill. Maggie smiled. "Take her home, Pete. We have a lot to chew on besides dinner tonight. Can we finish tomorrow?"

Pete smiled appreciatively at Maggie. These were real friends. Maggie and Bill have repeatedly proven that friends stand by each other despite obstacles.

"I would like that very much, Maggie. I think it would be safer for us to meet on the ship tomorrow." Pete tilted his head in Rialla's direction.

Maggie and Bill smiled. Bill stood up and shook Pete's hand, "You need any help?"

"No, sheriff, I've got this. Thanks."

Pete held Rialla and Oz's hands, and they tightbeamed to the ship. The waitress came out with the food. She looked shocked at the empty seats.

Maggie laughed. "We'll need three to-go boxes."

When Pete, Oz, and Rialla returned to the ship, Pete had difficulty keeping Rialla from falling. She was swaying back and forth and side to side.

Pete looked at Oz. "I'll put her to bed. Goodnight."

Oz smiled and walked toward her room. "Goodnight."

Pete was surprised at how heavy Rialla was. "Rialla, did you put on weight or what?" Pete asked as he struggled down the hallway, guiding Rialla while she leaned heavily on his body.

Rialla spoke softly, "That is not a question to ask a lady, sir."

Pete laughed. "You've been watching too much TV."

Rialla laughed out loud as Pete sat her down on her bed. She looked up at him with her big, round, green eyes. He began to melt inside. She sat there, looking into his eyes.

"You do not trust me, herald," she whispered.

Pete was surprised. "Why do you say that?"

Rialla held up her index finger and waved it before Pete's face. She tried to answer, but her body swayed so much that she fell back onto the bed. She laughed.

"Harold, don't lie to me, Harold. I know you do not trust me. I could tell by the way you saw me in my armor." Her eyes were almost closed. Pete smiled at Rialla, calling him Harold. He thought about leaving her there, but she didn't look comfortable.

Pete picked Rialla's legs up and moved them onto the bed. He removed her pink sneakers and quietly placed them on the floor beside her bed. He contemplated removing her clothes so she would be comfortable. He decided it would be more polite to leave them on her. Pete removed Rialla's jacket and loosened the buttons on her shirt to allow her more comfort. He stopped and stared at her shirt as it separated slowly. He paused before pulling her open shirt together and unsnapping the button on her pants. Rialla squirmed a little and sighed gently.

Pete looked up from her waist to see Rialla smiling down at him. He couldn't help noticing how beautiful she looked, lying on the bed. The small nightlight's soft glow around her face added sensuality to the moment.

Rialla reached for Pete and, grabbing his shoulders, pulled him slowly on top of her. When they were face to face, noses barely touching, Pete could smell the wine on her breath.

She placed her arms around his upper body and pulled him closer. "I saw this on the visual," she said softly. She tilted her head slightly and pressed her lips to his. Pete felt a wave of warmth rush through his body. He pulled away slowly.

Rialla looked sad. "Did I not do it, right?"

Pete smiled and swam in her eyes. "It was perfect." He leaned forward and returned the kiss. After a few moments, Pete raised his head and smiled at Rialla, who could barely keep her eyes open.

"I think you should sleep now," Pete whispered.

Rialla smiled, turned over onto her side, and fell asleep. Pete stayed on her bed, watching her sleep. He liked what he was feeling. But he was still uncertain about where Rialla's loyalties lie. So much depended on his trusting her to do the right thing. But he couldn't help but wonder how she would react once she was among her warrior clan again. Would she still want to be friends with a human? Would she care about him then as she does right now?

***

Bill and Maggie were sitting in the meeting room with Pete and Oz when Rialla walked in. Pete smiled at her as she held one hand to her head. Rialla walked slowly and deliberately. Every step she took was taking as much effort as the last. She slowly sat down at the table with her head bent down. Her head felt heavy, and she didn't want to exert the effort to raise it.

Bill looked at her. "Good morning, Rialla."

Rialla didn't look up at Bill. She waved her hand in a hello gesture at him. Everyone laughed.

Rialla looked up suddenly. "Please, not so loud." She lowered her head again.

Oz walked over and injected Rialla with the blue liquid she used on Pete. Oz ran her hand over Rialla's head softly. Pete admired how Oz cared for her.

Oz looked at Bill and Maggie. "Let's give the meds a moment to kick in and see if the wine princess wants to join us, shall we?"

Everyone sat in silence, waiting for Rialla's response to the drug. Rialla slowly lifted her head and smiled at Oz. "You are amazing, Vailen."

Oz replied, "Yeah, I know. I'm awesome like that."

Bill was shocked. "That's it? One shot and no hangover? Oz, you need to market that. You'd be rich."

Maggie laughed at Bill. "Calm down there, Wall Street. Don't get any ideas."

Bill was serious. "Maggie, can you imagine what this would mean to our planet?"

Maggie replied, "Yes, I do. It means people would willingly drink in excess with no fear of the repercussions. We'd create an alcoholic society on a grand scale."

Bill sighed. "Go ahead, burst my dreams."

Everyone laughed.

Pete told Oz to turn on the visual and play the recordings. After they finished, Maggie looked at Bill and then at Pete.

"Jessica," Maggie said in a whisper.

Bill squeezed Maggie's hand as he saw a tear fall down her cheek.

Pete nodded slowly. "They didn't know her as we did. These monsters used her to buy themselves time for their plan to conquer their race, so we need to stop them. They have no conscience."

Maggie began to speak. "Pete, they must be stopped, but we can't lose anyone else."

"This is a war now. Bill knows more than anyone in this room what that means. People are going to get hurt. Some may die. But without sacrifices, we can't win. We can't stop these oppressors from establishing rule over the Wen. After they succeed, who's next? Earth?"

"I know, Pete. I get it. But you need to be cautious moving forward. You don't know who you can trust. You must be extra careful until you know what you're up against. We can't lose you, either."

Bill nodded in agreement. "Pete, I know there's nothing we can do to help, and, to be honest, that sucks. But we are here if you need anything; you know that, right?"

Pete looked at his two friends. "I'm glad I'm regaining my feelings. I understand what all this means and how important friendship is. I am fortunate to have you both as friends. Even though I know I can trust you, it's better to feel it as well."

"When are you going to tell the White House about this?" Bill asked.

Pete hesitated and responded thoughtfully. "I don't want to say anything until after we attempt to reason with the Xan. At this point, what good would it do? It may elevate the chaos and cause more people to get hurt."

Bill nodded in agreement. "If you succeed in eliminating the gray from the planet, then no one will be the wiser."

"Yes, that's what I am counting on, " Pete nodded.

Maggie regained her calm, "Why are you starting with the Xans? They seem to be victims in this charade as well."

"That's exactly why we need to approach them. The one thing that binds us is that we are victims of being used for others' gain. I am hoping that logic and reason will prevail."

"And if it doesn't?"

"I don't know," Pete wandered off. "I don't know."

32 THE MEETING

Pete decided to tightbeam to an abandoned warehouse similar to where he captured Pike. Tightbeaming from the ship directly to the Xan warship would give the Xans the specific coordinates of the ship's interior. He didn't want the public to see Rialla in her Xan armor taking him prisoner, either. The three friends stood in a circle and looked at each other.

Oz spoke first. "Pete, are you sure?"

Pete nodded, "Yes, this is the only way." He looked down at his handcuffed wrists.

Rialla looked at Pete, "Whatever the end brings, I want you to know it was an honor being by your side." She placed the helmet on her head and, in the Xan warrior's low rasp, asked, "Ready?"

Pete nodded. Rialla communicated with her ship, and within seconds, they were tightbeaming aboard the cloaked Xanoclax warship that was orbiting Earth.

Pete and Rialla found themselves standing in the tightbeam room of the ship. Pete saw three armored Xan warriors standing like statues awaiting their arrival. When Rialla saw them, she immediately kicked Pete in the back of his legs, knocking him to his knees.

"Take this human dog to his new home," Rialla rasped to the three guards. Two guards grabbed each arm and dragged Pete behind the third guard, walking in front of them. Pete looked around and saw armored Xanoclax warriors lining the sides of the hallway. The warriors began making sounds progressively louder as more warriors joined the revel. Some sounded like cheers. Other sounds were angry. Pete kept his eyes open, wishing Oz were here with him.

The walls of the ship were completely black, void of any decoration. All the walls appeared slippery smooth, as if made of ice, and were punctuated by massive metal bolts in no particular pattern. The metal doors were twice the height of a Xan warrior.

This ship must be massive, Pete thought.

The two guards dragged Pete into the center of a room and dropped him harshly before walking away. They stopped just outside an indent in the metal floor. Pete looked at the slit in the floor and noticed it formed an outline of a square approximately 8 feet square around him. Before he could observe anything else, a loud humming noise emanated from the indentation on the floor. One of the Xan guards approached Pete and stopped before the line on the floor. He touched his weapon through the invisible barrier above the line. Pete was shocked when the weapon disintegrated. The Guard turned around and went back to his post. Pete got the message loud and clear. He wasn't getting through this barrier without them turning it off.

Pete remained on his knees and sat back on his haunches. The metal floor was cold. He looked around and was surprised at how simple the room appeared. A thinly sliced opening connected the four metal walls roughly ten feet from the floor. A soft green light projected from inside the thin opening, the room's only light source. Pete looked up and noted that the ceiling was at least twenty feet high. The room was a simple square, approximately ten feet by ten feet.

Pete stood up and looked at the two guards. "I have to relieve myself," he exclaimed. "Where do I do that?"

One of the guards turned around and faced the wall, his back to Pete. Pete saw the guard raise his arm and touch the wall. He couldn't see what the guard was doing because the guard blocked his view. Pete heard a rush of air behind him and turned around. A small circle, one and a half feet in diameter, began opening in the floor. Pete looked back at the guard, who pointed down the hole in the metal floor. When Pete had finished, the hole slowly closed. The metal floor was seamless; there was no way of telling where the hole was when it closed.

Pete turned away from the closed hole and sat in a lotus position. The low hum of the invisible energy wall was surprisingly relaxing. Pete began to meditate to focus his mind on his immediate situation. He wanted to clear his head of all idle chatter and thoughts that didn't pertain to his current quandary.

Several days passed before Pete received food. A guard brought Pete a metal mug of water and a small piece of bread. His meditation kept the hunger pains away, but his body ravaged the bread like Earth's last piece. He was surprised at how similar their bread was to Earth's bread. After that encounter, Pete began receiving bread and water thrice daily. He felt like they were trying to fatten him up before slaughter. When he slept, he questioned whether he had made the right decision about visiting the Xans. He could hear Oz in his sleep, saying, 'I told you so' repeatedly.

Another few days passed before two guards walked through the energy wall to retrieve Pete. They walked him down several wide corridors. They stopped in front of a massive metal set of doors. The two sentries turned and opened the doors slowly. As they opened, revealing Pete and his two guards, loud cheering began. Pete found himself in the center of an arena surrounded by hundreds of Xan warriors. He knew of this place from the stories Rialla had told him. Prisoners entered this arena by force to entertain the Xans. It was just like the days of the gladiators, slaves killing each other to gain their freedom.

The arena was a large, circular room resembling the Roman Coliseum. As Pete walked to the center, his feet kicked up sand and dirt. A twelve-foot wall encircled the dirt floor of the arena. Above the metal wall were several rows of stadium seats. Pete lost count after seven because one of the guards shoved him from behind to move him along faster. A Xanoclax warrior occupied every seat in every row of the arena. All the warriors were screaming and shouting in their native Xanstar tongue. Pete didn't need to understand Xanoclax to know they weren't yelling greetings.

Rialla must not have convinced the commander of my sincerity, Pete thought. He knew if Rialla couldn't get him an audience with the commander, this was the only way to do it. Pete had to fight and possibly kill Xan warriors to meet the commander.

Barbaric but specific, clean, and neat, Pete thought.

If you won your battles, you have proven your worthiness for communication. If you died, then no one had to bother with you or what you had to say. Very clean and neat.

Pete looked around the arena and stopped when he approached a squared-off area at the center of one seating section. He assumed the commander was the one with the bright helmet. Rialla was sitting to his right. It wasn't easy to see her beautiful green eyes through her helmet.

Better I don't see her face, thought Pete. *It may distract me.*

The commander stood up and moved his hands up and down to quiet the crowd. The commander pointed to one guard standing against the arena wall and nodded. The guard walked to Pete and handed him a translator. Pete placed the device in his ear. The commander began to speak in his native tongue to the crowd of warriors.

"We have captured the Wen herald!" Cheers and roars filled the arena. The commander moved his hands to quiet the crowd again. "Like all prisoners, this herald will be afforded a trial by combat, as established by our ancestors through our logic belief. He has previously faced our brave warriors and defeated them. In their honor, the herald will face the Three." The crowd roared louder.

Pete turned to watch the metal doors open, revealing three huge Xan warriors. The three warriors strolled to the center of the arena. All three warriors were without their armor. Two had smooth skin like Rialla, while the third looked scaly. He opened his mouth to scream, revealing three rows of teeth.

This warrior is from the southern tribes; I'll need to watch him closely.

Each warrior had a weapon of choice in their hands. One Xan had a long, metal club with protruding spikes and pointed tips painted with the blood of its victims. On the other hand, there was a shield with a prominent symbol in the middle, symbolizing his home planet, Xanstar. The symbol rotated and flung small, sharply pointed spikes skyward as the crowd cheered. The other Xan warrior chose to wield a massive, two-handed ax. Its blade looked sharper than any metal Pete had ever seen. On top of the ax was a large metal-spiked ball resembling the top of a mace. The southern Xan was the scariest of the three. He had two swords, one in each hand, with hooked ends resembling fish hooks. If this Xan caught Pete with one of those hooks, it would easily tear him apart.

The three Xan warriors stared at Pete, anxiously awaiting orders to rip him to shreds. A loud sound, like an airhorn, blasted throughout the arena. The three Xan warriors knelt on one knee and faced the commander.

The commander recited a short Xan warrior prayer. "We are Xan. Our duty is to Xanstar. May the Logic Belief guide us and protect us in battle." The crowd of warriors stomped in unison, sounding out one overwhelming thud. The left foot fell, thud. Then, the right, thud. It sounded like one massive heartbeat echoing through the arena. The sound, thud-thud, thud-thud, rocked the arena. It was a terrifying sound that would have unnerved any non-Xan in the arena. But Pete's emotions hadn't returned fully yet, and he wasn't affected by the stomping in the least.

Pete watched the commander and Rialla, who was sitting next to him. She leaned over and said something to the commander. The commander raised his hands and silenced the crowd. He pointed to a guard, and the guard stood at attention. A moment passed as the commander communicated with the guard in his helmet. The guard nodded and ran to Pete. The guard took Pete's coat off and threw a double-edged brathrit, a bo staff, down at Pete's feet. The guard then proceeded to bring the coat to Rialla.

Pete looked shocked. Rialla asked the commander to remove his coat. Rialla knew Oz had lined his coat with weapons to aid his escape. Pete looked at Rialla, confusion running through his body. Rialla sat in her armor, stoically refusing to acknowledge Pete's puzzled stare. Pete's head was swirling. Was he alone now? Was this an act of betrayal, or was Rialla protecting him? Pete had to let this action wait for a response because he had to face the three terrors rushing at him.

The first to get to Pete was the southern Xan. He began swinging his swords in a rapid X-formation. Pete remained in his position, dodging each blade, waiting for an opening. He saw one; the Xan turned slightly to gain more power in his thrust, and Pete seized the opportunity. As the Xan turned when he lunged forward, Pete leapt above his lunge and flipped in midair, thrusting his brathrit into the Xan's right shoulder. Pete's blade cut through the Xan's skin and pierced a bone. Pete assumed it was the Xan's collarbone. Pete felt like he had severed the bone in two. The warrior fell to his knees, blood pouring from his wound.

Before Pete had a moment to let it all sink in, the other two warriors rushed from both sides. He saw the ax swing at waist level while the club swung high. They wanted to cut Pete in half. They would succeed if he jumped or ducked their blows. Pete waited and leaped forward in a somersault through the warriors' swinging weapons. The two warriors missed and collided with a horrible thud. One warrior landed on his back, and the other dropped to one knee.

Pete rushed the warrior as he tried to stand. He swayed a little, not fully recovered from the collision with his fellow warrior. He was, however, aware of Pete's attack, so he raised his shield and fired its metal projectiles. One of his small projectiles sliced the surface of Pete's right leg, but it failed to slow Pete. He rolled under the projectiles and ended up behind the groggy warrior. He sliced the back of both his knees, severing his tendons. The large warrior screamed in agony and fell to his knees, then onto the ground, face down. Green blood was spewing from the backs of his legs like a geyser.

Pete rubbed the wound on his leg. He realized the cut wasn't deep and continued with the battle. The ax-wielding Xan swung his ax as though it were a light sword. He switched hands occasionally as he pursued Pete. Pete was amazed at his strength and agility. As the Xan approached, Pete waited patiently. His statuesque stance astounded the commander and the crowd alike. He stood directly before the warrior, swinging his ax at Pete's head. Pete didn't move. Rialla sat up, looking on intently. The crowd became silent as the ax fell, so quiet that the sound the ax made through the air could be heard everywhere within the arena.

Pete sidestepped slightly to his right before the ax could reach its target. His movement was so fast that no one noticed it. The warrior's full blow met the ground with a resounding thud. Pete felt the ground below his feet vibrate. The warrior hit the ground so hard he separated both shoulders and lay on the ground, writhing in pain. Pete walked over to the warrior and looked at the commander. The crowd screamed death as Pete lifted the warrior's head by his hair and raised his bo. The crowd roared louder. He raised his bo and swung at the head in his hand. He hit the warrior on the temple with his fist, knocking him unconscious. Pete leapt into the air and landed on the warrior's shoulders, knocking the Xan's shoulders back into their sockets.

The crowd became so silent that Pete could hear his every step in the sand. Every seat in the coliseum listened to the shuffling of Pete's feet across the ground as he walked over to the other injured Xan warrior. He was still bleeding and passed out from the loss of blood. Pete tore off his shirt while watching the commander. He ripped his shirt into two halves and wrapped each leg in a tourniquet to slow the blood flow.

He walked over to the southern Xan, who was standing, readying himself for an attack. His right shoulder was slumping below his chest. He carried the other sword in his left hand and tried swinging it at Pete. Pete blocked each swing with ease. His brathrit was twirling in front of the Xan's face. The Xan was frustrated and made one last effort with a do-or-die lunge at Pete. Again, Pete sidestepped and watched the Xan run by and eventually fall to the ground. The Xan landed on his right shoulder, which caused more excruciating pain. He screamed a horrifying sound that filled the arena.

Pete hit the Xan and kicked his weapon away. He stood over him and yelled up at the commander. The arena went silent as all listened. His translator worked both ways, so they understood his every word.

"I am not a threat to you. You have been lied to by the southern tribes. As you sit here, the southern Xanoclax tribes combine forces to attack your capital city. I am a decoy that keeps your attention and forces you from your home planet. If you choose not to believe me, you will become enslaved once again: this time, by your own people."

The commander rose and spoke to Pete. "Why should we believe an Earthling about such matters?"

Pete pulled the southern Xan's head up and yelled at him, "Tell him!"

The Xan laughed through his pain. Pete reached down and applied pressure to his right shoulder and could see the bone separated through his wound. The Xan screamed louder. Pete stared at the Xan commander as he placed three fingers inside the southern Xan's wound and tugged on the cut bone. The Xan almost passed out from the pain.

"Stop," he screamed. The Xan yelled, "The human speaks the truth."

Pete removed his fingers from the wound and dropped the Xan, who screamed as he hit the ground. Pete walked toward the commander, staring at him as he tossed his staff to the ground. Suddenly, he heard a scream from behind him. The southern Xan was within striking distance of Pete. The warrior had his left hand raised with the sword in his hand. Pete didn't have time to defend the Xans' oncoming blow. Before the Xan's blade came down, his body was split in two, splashing trails of blood over Pete. The ax Xan's aim was true, and it saved Pete. The crowd screamed. This time, the screams sounded like cheers of approval. Pete turned from the crowd and looked at the ax Xan. They returned mutual nods of respect.

Guards entered the arena and took Pete before the commander at the ship's helm. Rialla stood off to the commander's right, and Xan guards encircled the room. Several Xan warriors were sitting at their respective control panels at the front of the room. Guards escorted Pete to the center of the room and left him alone. He looked around the room.

So many guards, he thought. *Not good.*

The commander stepped forward, away from his control podium, and looked at Pete. He turned to Rialla and punched her in the face, knocking her down to the floor. Pete moved toward her, but saw her shake her head slightly to hold him back. Pete remained in the center of the room. The commander reached for Rialla's hand and helped her to her feet. Then he ambled, with caution in every step, towards Pete. As he did so, the guards stomped their feet in unison. First, their left foot thud. Then their right foot thud. They continued until the commander reached Pete. Pete braced himself for a blow similar to the one the commander had delivered to Rialla. Instead, the commander reached out his hand. Pete grabbed the commander's forearm, and the commander did the same to Pete. They shook hands.

"We owe you a great debt, human." Pete was still wearing the Xan translator. "My people on Xanstar have verified your story. They report sighting the southern tribes preparing for war. I have alerted our command on our home planet, and they are preparing for the ensuing battle with the south. You have potentially saved hundreds of thousands of Xanoclax lives."

Pete nodded and bowed slightly. "Sir, if I may. It was the Xanoclax warrior Rialla who brought me here. She did so to protect her people. She deserves your recognition more than I."

The commander responded, "You would make a great Xan warrior. You are bold, strong, and unselfish. We have much to learn from you, Earthling."

Pete nodded as a guard brought him his coat. The Xan commander turned back to Rialla.

"You are to be rewarded for your bravery, Rialla of The Iron Realms. What is it you desire?"

Rialla walked toward Pete and stood by his side. "I desire to stay on Earth and help my friends finish their mission to right these wrongs."

The commander looked at Rialla for a moment, then at Pete. "Very well. By law, you cannot be denied this request. We will keep in close contact with you and await your progress."

Rialla and Pete turned and walked to the tightbeam room. They didn't speak while being escorted by armed guards through the ship's corridors. Pete stepped into the small, tightbeam area, and Rialla followed. As they energized, Rialla grabbed Pete's hand.

33 HOME IS WHERE THE VAILEN IS

Oz was anxiously awaiting her friends' arrival. She now knew how Pete must have felt waiting for her to return from Wen'q'rixsh. She had never experienced anxiety before, and at this moment, she missed that ability. She tried to keep herself busy by watching the visual, but she got bored quickly. She was about to leave the control room when the lights flickered. Pete and Rialla were back.

Oz screamed out, "Yes! You made it back!"

Rialla removed her helmet and smiled at Oz. "I missed you as well, Vailen."

Oz hugged Rialla's face, almost suffocating her. She let go, and they both laughed. She walked over to Pete and started pounding on his chest.

"Do you know how much you had me worried? Of course you don't, you bastard." She continued to pound his chest. The blows became lighter and lighter, and Oz lowered her head into Pete's chest. "Please don't ever do this to me again, please."

Pete looked down at Oz and smiled. "Never again. If we can't go together, we don't go."

"I'll mess you up if you break this promise." Oz hugged Pete tighter.

"I know, Oz. You can be very scary."

Rialla turned away and went to the armory to change, not saying a word to Pete. Oz caught Rialla's look and asked, "What did I miss, Pete?"

"I'm not sure, but Rialla had a chance to ask her commander for anything, and she chose us."

"You think she regrets her choice?"

"I don't know. I can't figure females out. It's not my strength."

Oz nodded. "It's not, you know. It's definitely not one of your strengths."

Pete laughed at Oz. "Good talk. I'm going to change. See you in a few minutes."

Oz returned to the meeting room and got some hot tea for her friends. She was happy; at least, that is what she told herself. Unlike Pete, Oz had no idea what feelings were. She had never had any feelings or emotions to lose, like Pete. This was uncharted territory for her, and these revelations made her understand the motivation behind the coup. The Wen zealots wanted experiences outside of logic. They viewed logic as a prison that kept them from seeing the outside world for what it truly was. If they could break away from a logic-only society, they could experience more of what the universe had to offer. Oz felt sympathetic to their plight for the first time since she had discovered the reasons behind the rebellion. Now that she was capable of experiencing feelings, she struggled with right and wrong.

Feelings suck, she thought as she poured the tea.

Rialla was the first to enter the meeting room. She sat down, looking distant, as she lifted her tea to her lips. She didn't say anything to Oz. She sat in rapt contemplation momentarily, staring straight ahead, and sipped her tea.

"What's going on, Rialla?" Oz asked quietly.

Rialla shook her head slowly.

"Do you want to talk about it?" Oz placed a hand on Rialla's shoulder as she placed her cup on the table. Rialla turned to Oz and hugged her tightly. Oz smiled and returned the hug.

After a few moments, Oz said, "Is this a contest to see who can put the other to sleep? If it is, your hugs are a lot tighter than mine. You win, I concede."

Rialla released her friend and laughed. "I missed you so much. I missed this ship, and I missed stupid hot dogs. I thought I would never see you or all this again."

Oz wiped the tears from Rialla's eyes. "I don't know what's worse; never having feelings or having them and being unable to use them."

"I think never having them is better. You don't realize what there is to miss."

Oz nodded. "Makes sense."

Rialla sniffed. "In my 30 Xanoclax annuals, I have never shed a tear. I didn't know what they were. Not once did I cry, even in battle when I was injured. I have whimpered like a child since I have been on this planet. I have become so weak. I am not a warrior."

Oz sat up and made Rialla look at her. "Crying is not a sign of weakness, Rialla. If anything, it's a sign of strength."

"How so?"

"When you express your feelings to those you care about, you show them how strongly you feel about them. Ever notice how a being that suppresses their feelings is so angry all the time?"

"Yes."

"That's not a sign of strength; that's weakness. When you suppress your feelings, you become weak and can't control all the resulting anger."

"Is it that simple?"

"Yes, it is," Oz smiled softly.

"Then why is it so hard to understand?"

"Because we have a false sense of strength. The universe isn't better because of the warriors, Rialla. It's better for the lovers. Lovers of people, lovers of life, and so on. Because the universe thrives on actions of love, not war. It is harder to love than it is to hate. That's the sad truth throughout the universe. It should be the opposite."

Rialla laughed. "This planet's atmosphere agrees with you. Thank you, oh wise Mamma Vailen."

"Yes, my sweet Xan warrior. Home is where the Vailen is."

They both laughed, and Oz presented two cups of tea on the table. They smiled and toasted to home.

Pete walked in and smiled. "This is a sound I missed."

Rialla looked at Pete, sipping her tea. "You did well, human. Very well indeed."

Pete smiled. "Thanks. I couldn't have done any of it without you guys."

Oz looked at Rialla. "You have the visual?"

"Right here," Rialla said as she tossed the drive to Oz.

"Sweet, let's have a looksy."

Oz inserted the drive, and the screen appeared above the table in the air. At the beginning of the recording, there were scrambled frames after Pete and Rialla were separated. It followed Rialla through the mission. Pete was missing most of it, but the battle and the end meeting with the commander were all there. There was also a point before the end of the meeting that the visual looked scrubbed. It was clear that something was recorded in this short time frame, but it was not clear.

Oz looked at Rialla, "What happened here?"

"I'm not sure, and this is the first time I have seen the recording. Maybe I came across an electromagnetic pulse, and it jammed my signal."

Oz nodded, "Yeah, probably." Oz turned to Pete. "Do you mind if I ask a question about the arena?"

"Sure," Pete answered.

"We discussed how the Xanoclax rule with strength. We know that dying in battle is a reward for them." Oz looked at Rialla for her approval. Rialla nodded.

Oz went on. "Knowing this, why didn't you kill the three warriors?"

"I had to show the Xanoclax that I was different. That mercy is not a show of weakness."

"They would have killed you, Pete. The battle could have turned out differently. What were you hoping to achieve from this?"

"Exactly what happened."

"What?"

"A Xan warrior killed another Xan warrior to protect me. I gained his respect and, in turn, the respect of all the warriors present. That is the first step in negotiating. Once you have your opponent's respect, he will listen."

"You could have used your ability to create energy and ended the whole thing quickly. That would have gotten attention and forced the Xanoclax to listen."

"No, Oz, that would only have caused more problems. I had to do it by Xanoclax logic belief. If I had used a weapon that gave me an advantage in the battle, I would never have gained their respect."

"I really don't know what's going on here," Oz said, confused.

Rialla looked at Oz. "What is it, Vailen?"

"Pete is becoming more logical, and I'm drifting towards the dark side. What is this world coming to?"

"Maybe it's coming to its senses?" Pete laughed.

"Maybe it's coming to dinner?" Oz responded.

Pete and Oz laughed and looked at Rialla, waiting for her to take a turn. Rialla looked puzzled. Oz gestured with her hand, asking Rialla to say something.

"Maybe it's coming to our ship?" Rialla responded.

Pete and Oz turned from Rialla at the same time and stared at each other. Rialla sat up, waiting for a response. Pete and Oz started laughing, and Rialla joined them.

When the laughter stopped, Oz looked at Rialla and asked, "So, what happens now?"

Rialla stopped laughing, wiping the tears from her eyes, and replied, "The Xan commander contacted his superiors. We made him a hero, by the way. And they ordered his fleet home to help crush the rebellion."

Oz looked at Pete. "They're leaving?" she asked excitedly.

Pete smiled. "Yes. We did it."

"Do we contact Krix'x now?"

"No, we go on with business as usual. Krix'x will see it, and he will contact us. When he does, we demand he fix the affliction."

"Then what?"

"We can't know until someone contacts us. There is a possibility that the leader will approach us first."

Oz thought for a moment. "Is that a good or bad thing?"

"You tell me, Oz. We've talked a lot about the repercussions of the leader's actions. In one scenario, the leader uses the serum to control your planet. In another scenario, the leader seems to want the opportunity to share this discovery with his people. Do you think he should be allowed to do that?"

Oz looked at Pete. "I have been thinking about this a lot. I believe that some Wen may want to try the drug and experience feelings. It may be because of what they read or curiosity. But I believe a Wen citizen should have the choice."

"Do you think this leader is doing it for the good of the people? To expose them to new experiences?"

"I won't know until I ask him," Oz tilted her head and pressed her lips together.

"Then you answered your question. It will be a good thing if the leader approaches us."

Oz nodded.

"I'm tired, and I'm going to bed. Let's discuss all this in the morning. Thanks for the tea." Pete walked by Rialla and put his hand on her shoulder. "Goodnight."

"Goodnight," she replied, reaching for his hand, but she was too slow.

Oz watched Pete walk out of the room. She looked at Rialla. "Is everything okay between you two?"

"I think so," Rialla replied.

***

"So your plan is working?" Maggie asked Pete as they left the restaurant.

"So far, it seems like it," Pete answered.

"I can't believe they actually left. Are you sure they're gone?"

"100% positive. Oz tracked them as they left the Earth's atmosphere. They have a rebellion to prevent. They'll be busy for a long time."

"Well, let's hope the rest of your plan will work. It would be great to have our lives back to normal. Everything is happening so quickly."

"What happens to your proposal when the affliction is gone?"

"Nothing negative that I can foresee. The affliction was a catalyst to get everyone talking. I think it worked, and now we will press forward with creating a new department to oversee racial injustice. It's very promising."

Pete smiled. "Well, let's hope the rest of your plan works. It would be great to see something positive come out of all this."

Maggie and Pete were walking on the Lawn after meeting for breakfast. The Lawn wasn't as crowded as it usually was on a Friday morning. The city felt deserted, almost like a ghost town. All the gray-afflicted stayed home, leaving only the police and small numbers of people on the streets.

Pete wore his Nat's cap and sunglasses, along with his coat. Maggie was in jeans, a t-shirt, and a denim jacket. Pete looked down and noticed her pink sneakers.

"Must be popular; Rialla loves her pair."

Maggie laughed, "You can blame Jessica for this." She twisted her right sneaker to her left, then back again. "Jessica went shopping and bought us all the same pair. It's kind of cute."

Pete agreed, "Yes, I used to like how the three of you all dressed up like sisters."

Maggie grabbed Pete's hand and held it while they walked. "I miss her, too, Pete."

"I know," Pete smiled nervously. "She was a great friend." Pete tried to change the subject, "So where's the big dog?"

Maggie smiled; she knew Pete was uncomfortable talking about Jessica. "Bill went back to Bends Creek. He's needed there right now more than he is here."

"You're okay with that?"

"Yeah, I am. It's difficult to leave your home and start over in a new place, especially a crazy place like D.C. He needs time to slowly wean away from Bends Creek. He can't be pulled out of it suddenly. I need to allow him that time."

"You are a very understanding person, Maggie. Bill is very lucky."

Maggie laughed. "Yes, he is." She continued, "What about you, Pete? Is there anything going on besides saving the universe?"

Pete shook his head. "No, same old, same old."

Maggie laughed. "Really? You're quoting Bill now?"

Pete smiled. "He kind of rubs off on you, you know?"

"Yeah, I know," Maggie replied. "Pete, how are you doing?" Maggie asked, concerned. "Are you feeling…okay?"

"It gets lonely sometimes, to be honest. I take a lot of walks, which helps." Pete looked at Maggie and smiled. "This helps," Pete said, holding their hands up.

Maggie looked at Pete with a serious look on her face. "Pete, any time you need this or someone to talk to, you know you can always call me, right?"

Pete began to feel a warmth creep up inside his chest. "I know, Maggie. That means a lot to me. More than you can imagine."

Maggie swung their hands. "Good. Now that we got that out of the way, what's the deal with you and Rialla?"

Pete looked surprised at Maggie's question. "What do you mean, me and Rialla?"

"Come on, Pete, I see how you look at her. And it's pretty obvious how she feels about you, too."

"Did she say anything to you? How would you know how she feels about me?"

Maggie laughed. "This is so cute. It's like being in high school again."

"I don't understand."

"When we were in school, we would ask our friends if they thought someone you liked liked you. We'd play that whole game where Mary and Carla told Randall you liked him, and Randall's friend Michael told Shawna he liked you."

"Sounds like a confusing game."

"I'm sure you played it. You probably don't remember. Even so, you're playing it now."

Pete laughed. "Yes, it sounds like that, doesn't it?"

"Pete, life is too short to play games. If you feel something for Rialla, you should tell her."

"I don't know," Pete lowered his head.

Maggie stopped and pulled Pete around to look him directly in the eyes. "Pete, it's okay to move on with Rialla. Jessica would have wanted that for you."

"It's not that easy, Maggie."

"I know." Maggie pulled Pete in close and hugged him. "You're not replacing Jessica with Rialla. Jessica will always have a place in your heart. Rialla is a good person, and she cares for you. You can't go wrong with that."

Pete nodded as they began walking again.

"Plus," Maggie continued, "that killer body of hers doesn't hurt either."

Pete looked at Maggie. "You think so? I never noticed."

"Yeah, right. If you ain't seeing that sh:t, then you are very blind, sir."

34 THE VISIT

It had been 72 hours since the Xanoclax fleet left the Earth's atmosphere. Oz was monitoring all the communications equipment for a signal from the Council. She met Rialla and Pete in the meeting room. They were sitting at opposite ends of the table. Each had a cup of tea and a datapad in front of them. Rialla watched an Earth movie, and Pete played a video game. She stood in the room, staring at the two of them. Neither Pete nor Rialla looked up from their datapads while Oz stood there.

"Aren't you worried that no one is coming?" Oz yelled at Pete.

Pete was startled by her shout and dropped his datapad on the table. "Man, I almost beat the next level. Oz, why are you yelling?"

"I'm worried that it's been three days since the Xans left, and we have yet to hear from anyone on Wen'q'rixsh."

Pete picked up his datapad and started playing his game. "Relax, if we don't hear anything…"

The communications alarm interrupted Pete as it went off. All three ran to the control room, and Oz opened the visual and waited for the signal. The visual was solid black. They waited patiently for the static to appear as it usually did before Krix'x contacted them, but the screen remained black. Oz scrambled her fingers across the communications panel, desperately trying to open a signal path for Krix'x's translation.

Pete looked at Oz as she pressed multiple combinations on her keypad. "What's wrong?"

Oz replied, never looking away from the keypad, "I'm not sure. It is acting like the signal is being intercepted and jammed."

Rialla looked surprised. "Jammed? How?"

"I don't know," Oz said frantically. The alarm was still beeping loudly.

Pete walked over to the visual, staring at the screen. Something wasn't right; this had never happened before. He looked down at Oz. "Stop."

Oz kept working on the keyboard, not realizing Pete was talking to her.

"Oz, stop," Pete repeated.

Oz looked up, her fingers hovering over the keyboard. "Why, what is it?"

"Don't ask any questions, Oz. I need you to move away from the control table now," Pete yelled.

Pete grabbed Oz by her closest arm and pulled her away from the control desk. He turned, pulling Oz, and yelled for Rialla to run out of the control room with them. Rialla reached the door first, and Pete shoved Oz through the door as the equipment under the control desk exploded. The pressure from the blast blew out the inside walls of the control room. The energy discharge surged through the door and flung Pete and Oz into the air. Pete was airborne until he collided with a metal wall just below the ceiling in the corridor. The explosion sent Oz careening across the floor until she slammed into a metal wall.

The inside of the ship went dark. The smoke from the burning cables and several open fires was thick. It slowly blew into the outer room, completely consuming Pete, Rialla, and Oz. Several moments passed before Oz stood in the smoke. She felt like she was waking up from a bad dream as her body swayed back and forth. She found it difficult to orient herself due to the blow from the explosion and the thick smoke. She tried to stand still and fight the vertigo. She heard the hissing sound of pressure escaping compressed canisters. Oz looked around and tried to navigate her location, but the smoke was too thick. Her head hurt, and she lifted her hands and rubbed her head once her body stopped swaying.

Was I knocked unconscious? she asked herself. *If so, how long was I out?*

She estimated that the blast had hurled her about twenty feet. Oz knew Pete took the biggest hit, and she frantically called out to him.

"Pete, Pete! Are you okay? Where are you?" Oz tried to see through the smoke but couldn't.

Oz needed to clear the smoke and find the others. She called out an order to the computer system, "System, initiate protocol 4-3-7 in the main control room." Oz waited, but she heard no response. "System, do you hear me?" Again, she stood there in the smoke and waited. And again, there was no response from the ship's computer system.

She was about to call out to Rialla when she saw a pulsing blue light coming from inside the control room, illuminating the haze. From where she was standing, the blue light was pulsing approximately thirty feet in front of her from the control room on the right. Sparks fell from the ceiling as the smoke turned blue every two seconds. She stood frozen, staring at the pulsating blue light engulfed by the smoke.

While she stared at the blue light, almost hypnotized by its steady, rhythmic, two-second beat, the smoke around her body began to move slowly toward the control room. Then it accelerated, like playing a visual in reverse. Oz looked around the floor and the walls, watching the smoke gain velocity toward the control room.

Maybe the computer system is working now, she thought.

The hissing noise from the canisters died down. Escaping compressed air from cut refrigerant lines burst in loud pops every few seconds. The computer equipment not destroyed by the blast made continuous pinging noises, as if a wrong command had been entered into the system from a keypad. Electrical buzzing noises from severed wires filled the room, like mosquitoes swarming the microphone of a public address system. An occasional zapping noise from cut wires touching each other echoed in the background, creating a technical ambient soundtrack. Small patches of fire spread out along the floor. Oz couldn't help but think that the crackling fire from burning wires smelled like one of Pete's cooking mistakes.

Before Oz could figure out what to do next, a female voice cried, "Oskalan? Oskalan, come out, come out wherever you are."

Oz couldn't move. Her feet felt cemented to the floor as she tried to lift her leg to take a step. She began to breathe heavily. She checked her systems to see what was causing the breathing abnormality, but all systems checked normal.

It has to be the atmosphere causing me to feel anticipation or fear.

She didn't move, waiting to see if the voice called out again. She didn't have to wait long.

"Come on, Oskalan, come here. I want to speak to you." The voice beckoned from the control room. "I know you're there. I sense your movement and presence."

A sudden electrical shock ran from Oz's head and coursed throughout her body. She recognized the voice coming from the control room. It was a voice from home that she hadn't heard for a long time. Her eyes widened as she lifted her left palm, and a blue light energized her hand. She could now see what lay on the floor as she slowly approached the voice. Oz stopped suddenly. The debris from the explosion impeded her path. She moved around the chunks of metal and pipe, moving several pieces as she walked. As she moved, she kept her eyes on the pulsing blue light from the control room. She kicked several small pieces from blown-up computers and other tech hardware out of her way as she tried to clear a path to the control center. Her feet crunched as she carefully walked over small pieces of the computer relay system and the visual playback system equipment. The blast blew back a significant piece of the control center wall. It embedded it into another wall in the hallway. As a result, Oz had to walk around the wall to get into the control room. The pulsating blue light was brighter now without the obstruction of the smoke.

Oz came to the edge of the embedded wall. She placed her right hand on it and hesitated before looking around the corner into the blown-apart control room. For the first time, she was convinced that she felt fear. The anxiety began in the hollow of her stomach and slowly crawled to her heart. Her heart rate rose rapidly, and she started to breathe fast, shallow breaths.

The voice cooed, "Oskalan, let me see you."

Oz didn't want to move. She didn't want to know who was around the corner. Oz touched the wall with half her face while the other half peeked around the corner. She stepped out from behind the wall when she saw a tall figure. Standing before her was a Council member draped in a blue robe, the large hood covering his face. Oz stepped cautiously toward the figure. The pulsating blue light filled the room, and Oz could feel it pulse in time with her heartbeat. The bright, blue light took on a life of its own. It began pulsating so quickly that it acted like a strobe light, causing their shadows to bounce in rhythm on the remaining wall of the control center. She waited for a response from every step she took. When she took a step, and there wasn't a response, she took another. When Oz was close enough to touch the figure, she heard the voice again.

"Oskalan, don't be afraid," The robed figure said calmly, taking a few steps away from Oz's hand. Then, the figure raised a hand slightly; the alarm went silent, and the blue light became constant.

The figure bowed, raised her hands, and slowly removed the hood. Oz watched the hood slide off the figure's head. The removal of the hood seemed to take forever. Her heartbeat increased, and for the first time, she understood the phrase 'passing out from panic.'

"I have missed you, sister."

Oz took a few steps back in shock as the figure raised her blue Vailen head. Her arm was still in front of her, dangling in the air, reaching for the hood. Her fingers were trembling.

"Cass? How is this possible? You're dead," Oz's quivering lips whispered.

Cass stood there, smiled, and looked at Oz with loving eyes. "I needed everyone to believe I was dead, sister. I am sorry that I deceived you, but it was necessary."

Oz took a step forward. She became angry, the surprise and shock of seeing her dead sister alive quickly wearing off.

"Necessary? Necessary to cause me so much pain over a lie? I have grieved every day for you. I have felt so much…"

"Sorrow?" Cass cut Oz off.

"Yes, sorrow," Oz snapped back.

"How is it possible to feel sorrow, sister? You are a logic-based being. Sorrow is illogical."

Oz pressed her lips together tightly, then opened them and shouted, "You know how I feel pain now. That's why you're creating all this chaos! I'm not stupid, Cass."

"I know that, Oskalan. I would never say you were," Cass smiled, acting coy.

"Why are you doing this, Cass? Why are you deceiving our people and me?"

Oz kept staring at Cass. She had changed; Cass wasn't timid anymore. She moved and spoke with a confidence she never possessed back home. Cass was the one who waited for Oz to answer questions from the Council when they were in school. Cass never volunteered for projects unless Oz would be there to help. Oz always helped Cass complete assignments, but mostly convinced her she was as intelligent as all the other Vailens. The first time they were separated was when Cass received her orders to guide a herald from the Quantos System. Oz remembered how they had spent the night before discussing her assignment. Cass was unsure she was the logical choice for the assignment, and Oz spent the night convincing her she was. The next day, each embarked on their separate assignments; that was the last time Oz had seen Cass until now.

Cass looked over at Oz and smiled. "This planet's atmosphere has exposed me to a new vision, Oskalan. I can see how robotic our lives are. I can see everything so differently now. The colors are brighter and have a deeper meaning." Cass looked at her fingernails fondly. "Words have new meanings, like learning a different language. My life is now full of purpose and adventure."

"You call killing innocent people an adventure? What happened to you, Cass?" Oz had difficulty believing this was the same Cass she had bonded with over many years.

"I am evolving, Oskalan, just as you are. And I want our people to know how having emotions can open up a new universe. I want our people to see and feel what we see and feel."

"Why can't you let the Wen choose for themselves?"

"How can they choose if they do not know what the choice encompasses? They need to experience it first and then decide," Cass said matter-of-factly.

"Cass, the gases are like a drug. It isn't natural. You're suggesting that our people become addicted to and dependent on a drug. If you get our people hooked on this drug you have created, then you can't call any decision free will."

"What is the problem with taking a drug that opens you to a whole new world, Oskalan?"

"It's not a natural progression, Cass; it's forced on them. If our people were meant to have emotions, we would have them. We would have evolved into that. You don't know how the long-term ramifications of being exposed will unfold."

Cass started to become annoyed. "We must expose our people to these gases to allow them to choose, Oskalan. No one will stop that from happening, and I would prefer you to join me on this journey. I don't want us to be enemies, Oskalan. I love you."

Oz lowered her head; looking at her sister was getting more difficult, "And I love you, sister. But what you are doing is wrong. It feels like you're attempting to become a ruler of our people. You want to make choices for them. You want to control them."

"And what if I do?"

"Then we cannot be sisters, Cass," Oz said quietly.

Cass looked surprised. "How can you say that? We have always been sisters. You would abandon me like that?"

Oz still had her head lowered. It was hard to look into Cass's eyes. She knew if she looked into her sister's eyes, she would become emotionally weaker. She wasn't strong enough right now to win this argument.

"Cass, I will always love my sister. But the sister I love would not do the things you are doing."

Cass was becoming visibly angrier. She glared at Oz with steel eyes. "Oskalan, you and your herald have put my plans behind schedule, possibly by a year or two. I cannot tolerate distractions anymore from either of you."

Oz raised her head in defiance. "And what does that mean, sister?" Oz responded, deliberately putting extra emphasis on the last word.

Cass came closer to Oz. "It means that if you continue to impede the progress of my plan, I will take action to eliminate you both."

Pete walked in after listening to much of the conversation. When he walked up to Oz, Cass took a few steps back from them. Pete stood by Oz's side, looked at Cass, smiled, and then looked back at Oz. "This is Cass?" He asked Oz.

"In the flesh," Oz answered Pete, feeling a little more secure now that he was by her side.

"Wow," Pete said, acting surprised. "We all thought you were dead."

Cass was not impressed by Pete's sarcasm. She didn't respond, keeping her eyes on Oz.

"How in the world did you pull that off? Actors? Oz, do you have actors on Wen? No, wait, acting would be illogical. Let me guess, Cass, don't tell me." Pete was holding up his hand, signaling for Cass not to speak. He placed his other hand on his chin and nodded several times, pretending to think. He jumped up excitedly and threw his hands in the air.

"I got it," Pete cried, waving his hands back and forth. "It was you in the Xan suit. You killed one of your own, Vailen, to make it believable. Am I right?"

Cass still looked at Oz, doing her best not to hear Pete, but he was too loud. She noticed the sad look on Oz's face as she waited for her to answer. Small, blue droplets slid down Oz's face from her eyes. Cass was not yet used to these reactions from the new drug. The sorrow in her sister's eyes was becoming unbearable.

Cass answered, never removing her gaze from Oz. "Yes, it was me, human."

Oz fell to her knees and sat back on her haunches. She lowered her head and shook it slowly back and forth. She couldn't believe what she was hearing. Cass was her sister; they had been together since she could remember walking. Cass was in the majority of her Wen memories. Now, the sister she grew up with had become something beyond her comprehension. Cass had turned into something evil.

Pete wanted to comfort Oz, but he pressed Cass for more answers. "Where is Krix'x?"

"He's getting ready to journey here. I believe he scheduled his visit for tomorrow. I wanted to talk to my sister before he arrived," Cass said in a low, sad whisper as she watched Oz on the floor.

"Does he know about your plan?"

"No," Cass answered bluntly.

"Aren't you afraid we'll tell him?"

Cass looked up and glared at Pete with glowing red eyes. "What you tell Krix'x is of no concern to me. Anything you tell him, he will deem illogical. It will take him more time to figure it out than it will for me to complete my schedule."

"What about Earth? Are you going to release an antidote for the affliction?"

"That's under Krix'x' control, not mine," Cass answered, her eyes dimming to their normal brightness. Cass yawned and turned her back to Pete. She was tired of all Pete's questions.

"Am I boring you?" Pete raised his voice.

"You are," Cass answered simply, walking away from Pete and Oz, looking over the devastation in front of her. "I came to say my peace to my sister, and I have. Now I will go." She kicked a few pieces of the debris to the side as she turned and faced Pete. She

325

tilted her head with a tight, insincere smile and said, "I have work to do."

"You know I will fight and stop you," Pete threatened. He was more confident knowing Cass wouldn't be involved with curing the affliction.

"I know you will try, herald. That is why we are creating our own herald. I think you will be amazed at how ours turns out." Cass laughed as if there were an inside joke.

Cass waved her hand, and Burraksis appeared next to her. He smiled at her as Cass tightbeamed him away.

Oz stood up and pleaded, "Cass, please reconsider what you're doing."

Cass walked over to Oz. She hugged her sister and kissed her on the cheek. "If it weren't for the drug, I would have never known what this felt like," she whispered to Oz. "Think about all the feelings we can now express to each other, Oskalan."

Oz looked at her sister's blue eyes. Cass's eyes pooled with blue water, waiting to flood her cheeks. Oz hugged Cass for the first time, and maybe, Oz thought, the last time.

Oz pulled back from her sister and nodded. Cass nodded back and vanished, never looking Pete's way.

Pete walked over to where Cass stood, "How did she do that? She didn't use our screen to translate through."

Oz looked at Pete sadly and said softly, "She must have a ship cloaked in orbit."

Pete walked over and held Oz in his arms. They both stood there silently for several minutes, standing amongst the rubble. The crackling of touching wires sounded off every few seconds.

Oz raised her head. "Rialla."

Pete smiled. "She's fine. A few cuts. She's mending right now."

Pete looked at the damaged screen. Oz turned her head across his chest and looked at it as well. She scanned the room, never taking her head off Pete's chest.

"Pete?" Oz muttered.

Pete answered, still holding her, "Yeah?"

"I may need to borrow your credit card."

They both laughed.

35 ALIEN ASSISTANCE

Oz and Rialla spent the rest of the night and the next day cleaning the destroyed rooms of the ship. Oz was concerned that she wouldn't have access to the Wen database until they finished repairing all the ship's critical systems and components. Most of the ship's tech was most vulnerable within the control room. The defenselessness of the spot was why Cass chose to enter there: so that she could destroy it. Oz always knew how intelligent Cass was, but now that she had turned into something evil, Cass's intelligence level scared Oz.

Oz could assess the damage once the debris was clear, and they took an inventory of damaged components. She got one of the satellite computers to work, but the main servers were still heavily damaged. Cass's entry into the control room sent energy across all the communications ports and terminals, rendering them useless. Oz observed that the servers took the brunt of the energy surge, and the central processing units had fried and melted away into indescribable globules of starcasium metal. Without Krix'x's help, she feared that the ship would remain in its current state, stranded on Earth.

Her primary concern was creating an entry point for Krix'x's arrival. Communication with Wen'q'rixsh was impossible. Oz began to feel anxiety creeping in on her. Her anger grew as she blamed her exposure to the Earth's gases for her miscalculations and inability to solve their dilemma. Every miscalculation put a weight on the time scale, and Oz feared that the scale would become too heavy to lift. She needed technical expertise, and she needed it now. Every moment bought Cass more time to complete her plan unimpeded by Council interruption.

Oz screamed and sat back on the floor against one of the repaired walls. She put her head on her knees and wrapped her arms around her legs. Rialla rushed in from the discard room, where they were incinerating the debris that was not repairable. She came in through the new entrance to the control room and saw Oz on the floor.

"Are you okay?" Rialla asked.

Oz didn't answer right away. Rialla walked closer to her.

Oz looked up. "I can't do this, Rialla."

Rialla looked confused. "Do what, Vailen?"

"I can't fix this ship. I don't have the proper tools, the parts, or the time I need. And my home planet doesn't have that much time. I can't do this." Oz sounded lost and helpless.

Rialla sat down next to Oz. "Well then, let's give up, move into Georgetown, and get jobs. I heard Chinatown is cool."

"Rialla, this isn't funny," Oz replied, her voice muffled by her knees.

"I'm serious. If you are giving up, we must make the best of our situation."

Oz looked up and smiled at Rialla. "You are getting good at this, aren't you?"

Rialla smiled, "Yeah, me likey."

Oz laughed, "You can't steal my line, you know."

They looked at the control desk, loose wires, and unconnected equipment. Rialla and Oz stood there for a few minutes before heading to the dining room to take a break. Rialla poured the tea. She brought Oz a cup as she sat down across from her at the table.

"Talk to me. What's going on?" Rialla asked Oz.

Oz lowered her tea slowly to the table and looked at Rialla. "When I didn't have these feelings, every task I attempted moved forward smoothly and according to logical predictions. These feelings are acting like a weight that slows me down mentally. I take a step forward, but I end up many steps back. I can't determine how to compromise between logical reasoning and these emotions. The emotions are more of a hindrance and nuisance right now."

Rialla spoke in a soft, concerned voice. "You need to ask for help, Vailen. Repairing this ship within a limited timeframe is a huge burden for any being to bear."

Oz looked at Rialla. "I get that, but Pete's in the White House trying to calm everyone down. His hands are tied. And I don't know how much more you can do to help. You're already overburdened yourself."

"Maybe you should let me judge how burdened I am? Tell me what you're most concerned about, and maybe we can figure it out together."

Oz smiled. "Thank you, but I am unsure what you can do."

"Maybe nothing, but maybe discussing it with me will allow you to relax and develop other options."

"Okay, I'll try," Oz nodded. She took a long sip of tea and placed the cup on the table with both hands. Oz sighed deeply, leaving her hands on the cup. She looked over at Rialla, who patiently waited for her to continue.

Oz went on, "I am having difficulty managing all the technical repairs." She hesitated.

Rialla leaned forward. "And?"

"The time constraints I have placed on completing the repairs complicate my progress. I am finding it difficult to concentrate on the repairs due to the uncontrollable pressure on my brain."

Rialla looked concerned. "You are experiencing anxiety and stress, Vailen. You have to control your feelings."

"I don't know how Rialla. I'm so confused." Oz lowered her head.

Rialla came around the table and sat by Oz. She gently placed her hand on her shoulder. "Let's prioritize the problems. What is the most pressing problem causing you the most concern?"

Oz lifted her head slowly and looked at Rialla. "I have to try to repair our communications portal to have Krix'x arrive with help. If he can get Wen scientists and engineers here, the repairs will take hours instead of days. Every minute we lose enables Cass to move forward with her plan to contaminate my world."

"Can Krix'x get here by other means than your communications geo-slipstream?"

Oz nodded, "He can bring the equipment and help we need by ship through the wormhole dimension doors. But we can't transmit a help signal, so we're stuck."

Rialla smiled. "What if I have a way to get our help transmission to Krix'x?"

Oz looked at Rialla, shrugged her shoulders, and said sarcastically, "Yeah, right, and I have some land in China for sale."

Rialla looked confused, "Why?"

Oz smiled, "It's a joke humans use when they don't believe what someone is telling them."

Rialla wrinkled her nose. "Why don't you believe me? I have never lied to you."

Oz said softly, "I'm sorry, it was an inappropriate comment. Please, go on."

"I can get a message to my people, and they can deliver it for us."

Oz looked surprised. "What makes you think they will help us?"

"We have gained their respect, and that is a powerful weapon to have on our side."

"But how will you contact them? They left our space several days ago. They could have traveled through the necessary wormhole to be on Xanstar by now."
Rialla stood up and began walking out of the room. "Pour us some more tea, and I'll be right back."

Oz watched Rialla leave. As she poured the tea, thoughts raced through her head. No matter how hard she tried to figure out what Rialla would show her, she came up blank.

Rialla walked back into the room, wearing a big smile on her face. Oz couldn't help but return the smile and said, "Why are you so happy?"

"I found this," Rialla held up a device the size of a smartphone.

Oz's eyes widened. "You have a qurray transmitter?"

Rialla couldn't stop smiling. "I have a psiwarp transmitter," she corrected Oz as she held the device up.

Oz looked confused. "That looks exactly like a Wen qurray transmitter. It transmits pulses through a galaxy system wormhole to other systems in the universe."

Rialla placed the device on the table. "Do you remember the Brangstrid's story about the early Wen helping the Xanoclax?"

"Yes, the early Wen helped the Xanoclax by providing weapons and technology. They used it to help win their freedom."

Rialla said, "Yes, Vailen. The Wen and Xanoclax worked together. That explains how we developed our psiwarp transmitter. We worked together once, and there is no reason we cannot do the same now."

Oz sat down, still staring at the transmitter. "Rialla, what will you tell your people?"

Rialla sat down next to Oz. "We need to discuss that and develop a convincing dialogue to plead our case."

"We need Pete to get back here. He'll know what to say and how to ask them for help."

Rialla nodded, "I agree, but can you contact him?"

"Yes. I fixed our communicators first. I didn't want him to leave unless we could contact each other."

"Let's get him here then," Rialla agreed.

***

Pete entered the ship's meeting room with a concerned look. He had spent the whole day reassuring the president that the gray affliction would be alleviated as soon as he contacted the Wen. Many world leaders who participated via secured visuals kept the frantic questioning going for hours.

"Why can't you contact them right now?" A few leaders yelled out.

"Why did this happen?"

"Is it reversible?" And so on.

Pete did his best to remain calm during the meeting, but answering the same questions repeatedly raised his frustration. Pete was worn down mentally and found himself raising his hands and screaming out loud.

"Stop," he commanded.

The visuals became silent, and the president looked at Pete with a surprised look.

Pete said, "I know you are scared and want the affliction to end. So do I. Right now, we are trying to communicate with the Wen. Please understand that they are light-years away from our planet. It's not like we can dial them or text them on our cellphones. Give us a little more time, and we will have answers for you."

The room and the visuals were silent briefly, but the volume of the yelling and questions grew louder. It was as though someone had turned down the volume on a TV set and slowly turned it up again. That's when Pete received a signal from Oz to return. Without saying goodbye, Pete tightbeamed to the ship.

Oz watched Pete walk into the meeting room. "How did it go?" She already knew the answer by the look on Pete's tired face.

"It's crazy," Pete answered. "All the leaders were panicking and wouldn't listen to anything I was trying to tell them. It's like they wanted to keep asking the same questions until they heard what they wanted to hear."

Rialla looked confused. "What did they want to hear?"

"I don't think they knew what they wanted to hear. These leaders wanted me to snap my fingers and make it all disappear. They were unrealistic and unreasonable."

Oz said, "They're scared, Pete. They see you as the person who brought this hardship upon them and want you to fix it. Logically, it makes sense, but emotionally, it's too demanding on their psyches to handle."

Pete took off his coat and hung it around his seat. He sat down and sighed, "Yeah, well, under different circumstances, this would make for a great thesis project for a behavioral science major. But now, we must solve this quickly before the planet tears itself apart."

Oz looked at Rialla and then at Pete. "We need to contact Krix'x and get help to repair the ship," Oz said. "We can't contact him because our transmission systems are damaged. I can't repair them without his help, and I can't contact him to ask him for the help I need."

Pete lowered his head into his hands. "Do we have any options? Or are we dead in the water waiting for Cass to complete her scheduled takeover?"

Rialla said, "I can contact my people and ask for help."

Pete raised his head with a surprised look on his face. "Would they do that?"

"I can ask," Rialla said, shrugging her shoulders.

"What do you need from me?"

"We need to decide how to ask."

Pete looked confused. "I don't understand. Don't you know how?"

Rialla nodded. "Technically, yes, but you have gained their respect as a true warrior. You have been elevated in their eyes and accepted by the Xans. It is you who should make the call. They will not understand why a Xan warrior is asking for help. It is not something we do."

Pete smiled at Rialla. "So it's below you to ask for help, but appropriate for me?"

Rialla looked confused. "I do not know what you mean by 'below me'."

"It's a saying on this planet that suggests one person is better than the other."

"I don't feel that way."

"I know, it was sarcasm at its worst. My bad. You'll understand sarcasm better over time by hanging out with me," Pete laughed. "Tell me how to proceed."

Rialla showed the transmitting device to Pete. She explained that she would contact the closest Xan vessel to Earth's galaxy. Once she made contact, she would hand over the transmitter to Pete. Rialla pulled out a translator device for Pete to use.

"How long do you think this will take?" Pete asked while he snugged the translator in his ear.

"Depends on where the closest vessel is on the wormhole charts."

"I don't understand."

Rialla explained, "Xan and Wen technology is far superior to your planet, yes?"

Pete nodded.

Rialla continued, "Your civilization has not even scratched the surface of the potentiality of wormholes. Right now, Earth's scientists have trouble locating them, and with their primitive tech equipment, will continue to flounder. They have succeeded in discovering black holes, but at the rate these scientists are going, it will be a millennium before they make any real, usable progress."

Pete shrugged. "Okay, I get it. We're way behind. How do you make it work?"

"Our technology allows us to utilize wormholes as shortcuts from different points in the universe. We have diagrammed specific points on our celestial maps that allow us to travel anywhere we desire."

Oz looked at Rialla. "Another gift from the Wen, no doubt."

"It was all part of the original aid from your people, Vailen," Rialla said.

Pete was shaking his head. "I'm not a physicist, but how can you survive the radiation and the possibility of the wormhole collapsing?"

Rialla looked surprised. "Wow, you have been doing your homework."

"I've been reading up on this stuff, trying to understand how you're all space jumping," Pete said.

"He was reading some of our data files with our transcriber software," Oz said.

"We have equipped our ships with anti-grav thruster energy. Our complicated engine drives can boost a ship with incalculable speed to burst through a wormhole."

"So fast that you don't feel you are in it?"

"Precisely," smiled Rialla.

"How do you get communication signals across them?"

"We broadcast on a frequency that encompasses several complicated bandwidths. I'll skip their description to save time. But these frequencies bounce through the wormhole to the next point. The trick is to follow the celestial wormhole chart to see how a wormhole aligns with the point you want to broadcast to."

"Have you figured that part out already for our purposes?"

"Yes, the Vailen and I worked on the coordinates while waiting for you to arrive."

Pete looked at Oz. "And the time? Do we have a limited gap to broadcast in?"

Oz smiled at Pete. "You get it now, don't you? Now you understand why I only received updates from Krix'x and the Council at specific times."

"Yeah, I understand how it works," Pete said. "When is our next available broadcast time?"

"Ten minutes," Rialla said. "We need to get started."

36 MESSAGE IN A BOTTLE

Rialla began signaling the Xanoclax space fleet. She wasn't sure which ship she would hail since she didn't have the Xanoclax fleet schedules. She tried hailing a ship several times. After about her fifth try, her face started to show concern.

Pete looked anxious in response. "What's wrong?"

Rialla shook her head. "I'm not sure. It never takes this long to make contact."

Oz asked Rialla to hand her the transmitter. She took it out of the room for a few moments and returned. Oz handed the unit back to Rialla.

"Try now," Oz said.

Rialla tried again, and this time, a voice answered. Rialla looked shocked. "What did you do?" she asked Oz.

Oz smiled, blew on her fingers, and wiped them on her chest.

Rialla smiled at Oz and continued with her transmission to the Xan ship. Rialla spoke in her native Xanstar tongue. The translators in Oz and Pete's ears worked perfectly.

"This is warrior X32, Rialla of The Iron Realms of Xanstar. Who am I speaking with?"

"This is Commander Zaex Alcorda of the Xanoclax spaceship Xubbass-Q. Why have you contacted us?"

Rialla handed Pete the com. Pete looked at Rialla, and she nodded, indicating that he should start talking.

"Commander Zaex Alcorda, this is the Wen herald J9-1-7." Pete stopped and stared down at the transmitter. There was a moment of silence from the transmitter. Pete looked at Rialla, and she held up a finger as if to say, give it another minute.

The commander's voice finally came across the com unit, "Yes, Wen herald, what is the reason for your transmission?"

"Sir," Pete began, "with all due respect, I need your assistance."

Again, there was a long pause. "In what way could I assist you?" The commander asked, confused.

"Sir, the conspirators who helped the southern tribes plan the coup against your government have attacked us and destroyed our technical capabilities." Pete paused. When there was no reply, he continued. "I need you to contact my commander and relay a message for me."

"What makes you think your commander will listen to me? Who's to say I'm not setting him up for a trap?"

"Sir, our only hope is to stop the conspirators from continuing with their plan to overthrow Wen'q'rixsh. If they succeed, they may assist the southern tribes in your civil war."

The silence was longer than the previous other pauses combined. Pete wasn't sure if they were discussing options or had disconnected from non-interest. After several minutes, the commander replied.

"What is the message and the exact coordinates of your commander?"

Pete repeated the coordinates for Krix'x that Oz had written down for him. These coordinates belonged to Krix'x alone and were not shared. Then Pete began his message to be delivered to Krix'x.

"Krix'x, this is Herald J9-1-7 reporting. Other Council members attacked our ship. Our ship and tech are severely damaged. The damages are beyond our repair capabilities. We need you to send help immediately so we can help stop the fall of Wen'q'rixsh."

The commander came back, "Is that all?"

"No, add this to the end of the message," Pete spoke one more line and thanked the commander for his time and assistance. He was careful not to use the word 'help.'

The commander signed off, and the three stared at each other for several moments without saying a word. Then Pete asked Rialla, "How long do you think it will take for the commander to relay our message?"

"Minutes," Rialla replied. "What I don't know is how long it will take Krix'x to believe it and respond."

Pete nodded. It was up to Krix'x now. Several reactions were possible for Krix'x. Krix'x could ignore the message as a hoax, which was the most logical scenario. He could listen to the message and decide to discuss its contents with the Council. If he told the Council, the rogue members would most likely incarcerate Krix'x, and no help would come. Or, Krix'x could respond by sending the help they needed. The last reaction was what Pete wanted, but it wasn't very likely.

Pete looked at Rialla and then at Oz. "How long will it take for a ship to get here once they get our message?"

Oz answered, "Less than an hour, Earth time."

Pete got up and headed to his room. "I'm going to take a nap. I want to be wide awake when they get here," he said without looking back.

"He is confident that this message will work," Rialla stated.

"Yes, he is. But then again, he has to be," Oz replied.

They both nodded slightly.

***

Pete awoke a few hours later. He heard loud noises outside his room as he lay in bed. Pete could hear several unfamiliar voices over the clamor of construction. He sat up slowly and walked toward the control room. Several Wen technicians walked by him in a hurry. He noticed they were blue-skinned and bald like Oz. Pete smiled. Help had arrived.

Pete found Oz working on the main servers with several other Vailen. "Is Krix'x here too?"

"No, he is scheduled to arrive shortly. We are trying to get ready for his arrival. He told everyone to have visuals ready for his arrival in a few hours. That was an hour ago."

"Will you be ready?"

"Not sure, we're doing our best," Oz answered, never taking her eyes off the server.

"How many people are here to help?"

"Krix'x sent four Vailens, a Draiksx, and two Throes."

"Throes?"

"They are available for manual labor and construction tasks. They are great builders. They see repairs and projects without the use of building details."

"You mean blueprints?"

"Yes, they see the building or repair without any guides."

"That's impressive," Pete said. "Anything I can do to help?"

Oz stopped and looked away from the server. "You can go back to bed."

Pete raised his hands in a defensive posture. "I got it. I'll stop bugging you and stay out of your way."

Pete walked out of the control room. He passed a tall, muscular bronze Wen. *Must be a Throe*, he thought.

Pete walked by a tech room and noticed Rialla working on a few computers and other devices Pete didn't recognize. Another Vailen was working at the table next to her. There was a big metal box on the floor that Pete assumed housed repair parts. She looked busy, so he stayed out of the room to avoid disturbing her.

Pete returned to his room and pulled the manila envelope out of his drawer. He then moved to the bottom drawer, where Oz put the file containing all the information she had gathered on Pete's true identity. Pete sat on his bed with both files on his lap. The file Bill gave him was on top of the file Oz created in response to Bill's discovery. He sat there momentarily, took a deep breath, and placed Bill's file on the bed. Pete opened Oz's file and slowly read the pages.

The first page was a verification of the information Bill gave to Pete. Pete felt the hair on his arms start to tingle. He was getting nervous or excited, and he wasn't sure which. He turned over the next page, and it was a photograph of a woman. The woman in the picture looked to be in her forties. She was a brunette and had a warm, friendly smile. At the bottom of the image, there was some handwriting. It looked like Oz's chicken scratch, which made Pete smile. Oz had written, 'Pete's mom.'

Pete stared at the picture. He tried to conjure up a memory of the woman with a friendly smile in the image. Pete kept staring at it, but nothing came to mind. He had no recall of this woman. When he looked at her picture, he wanted to feel something, but nothing came. He sat on the bed for the longest time, holding the photograph and staring into his mother's beautiful hazel eyes. He wanted to go to her. He wanted to know everything about his past.

He slowly placed the photo back down and turned over the next one. This photograph was of a little boy dressed in a baseball uniform. He was posing for the camera while holding a baseball bat over his shoulder in a ready-to-swing position. Pete looked down at Oz's writing. It said, 'Pete, age twelve.' Again, Pete stared at the photograph, hoping to revive his memory, but nothing. The young Pete in the picture looked happy. Pete smiled and turned over the next photo to see a picture of twelve-year-old Pete and a dog. The dog was sitting next to Pete, who was on one knee. The dog had his tongue hanging out of one side of his mouth.

Pete placed the photograph of his mother on his dresser, leaning it against the mirror. He returned the two files to the bottom drawer and sat on the bed. Pete wondered if it would be wise to visit his mother while all this chaos was happening. He wondered if she was afflicted. He wasn't sure why he thought that. Pete looked at his mother's picture and himself in the mirror. He toggled back and forth several times between the picture and the mirror, trying to see similarities. After his third look between the two, something happened. For a moment, he saw himself as that little boy, hugging his mother after what looked like a baseball game. The image stayed with him for a few moments. Pete smiled and walked out of the room to the control room to await Krix'x's arrival.

37 THE GANG'S ALL HERE

As Pete walked toward the control room, the alarm sounded. Lights flashed intermittently, and the siren sounded in the ship's speakers. While he hurried to the control room, he smiled, knowing that some of the ship's systems were working. The damaged wall of the control room was gone, giving the control room a more open aesthetic. Pete saw a large metal archway installed in the place of the old entrance door from the hallway. The arch led into the new open control room.

The visual was larger now due to the missing wall. The Wen lifted the veil of disguise, and the control room appeared overwhelmed with tech. Pete couldn't help being impressed by what he saw. The metal that replaced the damaged floor was shinier than the previous floor. The inside walls of the control room's metal walls were also shiny and smooth. The metal control console expanded across the room in a U-shape and had several chairs at various stations around the desk. One Vailen was working on the right side of the desk, programming controls and computers. In the middle of the control desk, just below the newly extended visual, another Vailen was working under the counter. All personnel were hard at work and ignored the alarm.

Oz walked up to Pete, smiling. "What do you think, boss?"

Pete looked like a child visiting a toy store for the first time. "I don't know what to say."

Oz laughed, "Well, there's a first time for everything."

"The alarm?"

"We're testing the system, that's all."

Pete just stared into the new control room. "Cool," was all he could say.

Rialla approached the archway and smiled. "Now, *this* looks like a real command center."

Pete and Oz smiled. Rialla asked Pete and Oz if they could all talk in another room, away from all the commotion. Pete and Oz followed Rialla into the meeting room.

"What's up?" Pete asked.

"I wanted to know what I am to expect now that Krix'x is coming. Will I be hiding in another room again?"

Pete looked at Rialla. "No more hiding. We're a team. Right now, we must focus on fixing the crisis, not politics."

"Agreed," said Oz.

Rialla smiled. "Thank you."

Pete looked at Rialla, "No, Rialla, we need to thank you. Without you, none of this would be possible."

"Agreed," Oz said again.

Pete looked at Oz. "Now what?"

"I'm worried about exposing these Wen to this atmosphere for too long."

"When will Krix'x be here?" Pete asked.

"He's waiting for our signal."

"Well, the sooner, the better, don't you think?" Pete asked.

Oz went to the control room and ordered one of the Vailen to hail Krix'x. The large screen went from black to gray static to completely blue. Pete watched as the time funnel appeared inside the screen just as it did when Burraksis arrived. He leaned over to Rialla and told her to stand outside the control center.

"You know the drill," Pete said to her.

"I thought you said I didn't have to hide?" Rialla asked, confused.

"You don't. I mean, you do, but just until we know that this is Krix'x."

"Got it."

"Rialla, make sure it isn't Krix'x before you fire. If you shoot him accidentally, we'll never convince him you are on our side."

"Okay," Rialla said and left the room.

The tiny figure began walking through the funnel. It was getting more prominent as it moved closer. Pete looked at Oz and whispered, "One day, you must explain how this works."

Oz whispered back, "Your mind would explode if I tried."

They both smiled and watched the Council member step through the screen. The Council member walked with confidence and authority. Pete was sure this was indeed Krix'x. Krix'x lowered his head slowly and raised his hands to remove his hood. The stern, emotionless face caused Pete to stare. Krix'x's face demanded respect and accountability.

He has the face of a leader, Pete thought.

Krix'x moved slowly and purposefully, inspecting the new command center. He looked over every component critically. He pointed to some lights on the panel and commanded a Vailen to repair them. He slowly turned away from the command console and walked toward Pete and Oz. He was half a foot taller than Pete, which made him approximately seven feet tall. Krix'x was a tall, dark, intimidating figure who looked like he glided across the floor.

Pete smiled at Krix'x. "I see you got my message."

Krix'x did not return the smile. "I do not know how you were able to get a Xanoclax commander to do your bidding, herald. It is puzzling to me."

"We should go to the meeting room. We have a lot to fill you in on."

Pete led the way, and Krix'x followed. Oz walked behind Krix'x. She was still intimidated by him. Now that she was feeling fear, she wondered if fear was controlling her at this moment. She was hoping it was respect for his authority that she was feeling.

All three sat in the meeting room, and Oz turned on the visual. She played the records, the scene where a Xan warrior killed Cass, and the video about Jessica. The documents regarding the tainting of the Wen Herald program seemed to interest Krix'x the most. He had Oz replay that specific recording several times.

Oz turned the visual off and brought up the lights. Krix'x sat remarkably still and quiet in his chair. Even while sitting, Krix'x was an imposing and intimidating figure. The stern expression on his face didn't change. He showed no emotion while watching the visual, and no emotion now as he spoke.

"This information suggests many things, herald," responded Krix'x calmly.

Pete looked at Krix'x. "Yes, it does. My planet, Xanstar, and Wen'q'rixsh are all affected by these Wen deviants."

"Explain."

"For one thing, there is no Xanoclax threat to Earth or your planet. This rumor was a tool the Wen Council traitors used to keep attention off their plan to control your planet."

"Impossible," Krix'x reacted. "All the information we have received on the Xanoclax impending invasion was verified many times over."

"It was verified by the people planning the coup, Krix'x. By the Wen Council members who are involved."

"This is not logical."

"How do you explain the Xanoclax commander's transmission, then? If there was an impending invasion, why would they help us?"

Krix'x paused and raised his arms, placing his elbows on the table. He put both hands in a prayer position, bouncing his index fingers off each other several times. Krix'x was visibly contemplating Pete's comment.

Oz sat in awe of Pete as he confronted Krix'x. She didn't understand how Pete could communicate so easily with a Council member.

Krix'x stopped tapping his fingers. "Where is your Xan comrade now?"

Pete admired the level of logic that Krix'x employed to determine the actual situation.

Rialla stepped through the meeting room door and said, "I am here."

Krix'x didn't turn around. He waited for Rialla to take a seat at the table. His frozen look never changed.

"You are the one who contacted your people to help us?"

"I am."

"Why?"

"Because we are all deceived by the same beings intent on destroying our worlds as we know them."

Krix'x looked away from Rialla to Pete. He then slowly turned back to Rialla. "There is no Xanoclax invasion scheduled for this planet?"

"No."

"There is no scheduled invasion of Wen'q'rixsh?"

"No."

Krix'x looked away from Rialla and turned his gaze to Oz. "Vailen, what do you report?"

Oz answered, "Krix'x, the Vailen Cass is now leading some Council members in an attempted coup of our planet."

"How will this coup be accomplished?"

"They have discovered that the atmosphere of this planet affects the Wen biologically. Exposure to great lengths of the gases of this atmosphere triggers emotional responses."

Krix'x, for the first time, moved in his seat. He sat up and leaned forward towards Oz. "Continue."

"They plan on injecting our people with a liquid form of the gases they created. Once they inject the majority of our people, they will become dependent upon this new drug. This dependency will allow

Cass and the other traitorous Council members to control the planet."

Krix'x turned to Pete. "Herald, we must immediately return to Wen'q'rixsh and avert this possible disaster."

Pete responded quickly, "Wait a minute. We need to solve our issue here on Earth first. These people have suffered enough."

"It is logical to proceed to Wen'q'rixsh immediately. There lies the greater danger. These Earthlings are not at risk."

Pete stood up, walked to the head of the table, and looked directly into Krix'x's eyes. The tension in the room increased rapidly, and Oz pushed herself back from the table. Rialla, seeing Oz's reaction, mimicked her.

Pete broke the silence, "I will not leave this planet unless it is free from the affliction."

Krix'x stood up calmly. "Then we will leave without you."

"Why won't you lift the affliction from my planet?"

"It would take time, and we do not have time."

Pete looked at Krix'x. It was his turn to analyze the situation and devise a logical solution for Krix'x. Pete began crunching different scenarios in his head. *What makes sense?* he thought. *What am I missing?* He looked up at Krix'x, who was still standing there with his stern face, staring at Pete.

He's waiting for me to say something. He's expecting me to respond, but how? What is it he needs to hear? Pete looked away for a second and then responded.

"If you remove the affliction, I give you my word that I will travel to your planet and help combat this coup."

Oz and Rialla looked shocked. They glanced at each other and then turned their attention to Pete. He looked defeated, his head slightly lowered.

Krix'x nodded slightly to Pete, and without saying a word, he turned and walked out of the meeting room. Pete sat down hard on his chair, causing the legs to scrape the floor. Oz and Rialla looked at Pete and waited for him to say something. Neither of them wanted to be the first to break the silence.

"It's what he wanted," Pete finally said softly.

Rialla moved closer to Pete. "What?"

"He wanted assurances that I would go to fight his battle. Now that I have figured out who I am, I have to leave? Damnit, this is not fair."

Oz now moved closer, "No, it's not, Pete. But you know what I always say?"

Pete looked at her and smiled, "No, Oz, what do you always say?"

"When life deals you lemons, make iced tea."

Pete laughed and hugged Oz.

Rialla watched, puzzled, "I thought it was lemonade?"

They laughed harder.

38 AND SO IT WAS

Pete, Rialla, and Oz walked to the command center. There was a chair in the center of the room with a prominent figure sitting in it. Krix'x swiveled the chair around and looked at Pete.

"We will be leaving in four Earth hours," Krix'x commanded.

Pete walked up to the chair. "And the affliction?"

"The antidote takes approximately 72 Earth hours to complete its cycle."

"Then we leave in 72 hours to verify."

Krix'x swiveled his command chair back around, away from Pete. He stared at the visual of the humans protesting outside the ship. Without turning back to Pete, he said calmly, " No, we will leave when we complete repairs in 4 hours."

Pete approached the command chair and swiveled Krix'x back to face him. Everyone in the command center stopped what they were doing and watched Pete. Pete looked around the room. He didn't feel any threats developing, so he looked back at Krix'x.

"I will not leave until I can verify that my people are safe and free from this bullshit. You started this mess, and I want it finished. I want to be able to see it finished."

"You will, J9-1-7. You will."

"How, from space?"

"No. From here, on Earth."

Pete looked confused. Then he realized. "You already set the antidote into the atmosphere before you came here, didn't you?"

"Yes. 70 hours ago, to be precise."

Pete pointed a finger at Krix'x, "You are a prick, you know that?"

Krix'x reacted without emotion. "No, I didn't know that."

Oz walked up to Pete. "Pete, you have two hours before it ends. You should go see the president and contact the world leaders."

Pete turned to Krix'x. "We will finish this conversation later."

***

Pete was in the White House, watching the President and her advisors call as many world leaders as possible. They set up the visuals in the East Room and called the media to participate. Everything was in place with about fifteen minutes left to the end of the affliction. Pete stood at the podium and faced the visuals, the people gathered in the room, and the media. The President sat to Pete's left.

Pete said, "We have all experienced some pretty amazing things these past few months. It has been difficult for everyone, and we have all suffered. The affliction, the gray, is coming to an end shortly. There will be no residual effects once the affliction ends. Soon, it will be business as usual on planet Earth."

The media's broadcast cameras that were present zoomed in closer to Pete on the podium. Pete's final speech was broadcast across the world. Networks interrupted all scheduled programming. Pete's speech was broadcast in Times Square, causing New Yorkers to pause and listen. Wherever there was a television on planet Earth, Pete's face was on it, and the world listened.

"I am now speaking directly to the citizens of my home country, the United States of America."

Pete paused for a few seconds and continued, "Our anger and the hate that results from our prejudices toward each other have been exposed to us all over the past few months. The affliction has taken our faults and amplified them beyond measure. We have all come face-to-face with these faults and witnessed the confusion and paranoia that hate and prejudgment convey.

I am speaking to all Americans, no matter what your background. Whether you are white, black, Asian, Hispanic, Jewish, Catholic, Baptist, Muslim, French, Irish, Italian, and on and on and on. I could take an hour reciting every category of American classification and still not name them all. How does no one in this country see a problem with this?

America is a great country; we call it a melting pot. The idea is that America melts all backgrounds together, and we live as one free society. Somehow, we have lost our way and allowed hate groups' popularity to repudiate this greatest of all principles. We are continually segregating our interests and competing for attention. The use of social media to champion causes of hate and anger has quickened the pace of this country's self-destruction. The social media in this country is wrongly titled. We should call it what it is: the segregation media.

If you hate me because of how I look, that's on you. I am not going to retaliate or argue with you. I refuse to hate you in return. If you hate me because of the way I choose to practice my religion, the same response from me. I refuse to get angry or hate you; how you feel is on you, not me. I will not validate your anger and hateful beliefs by publicizing them. Instead, I will publicize all the good and empathetic people. I will champion positive social interaction with all Americans. I encourage all of you to do the same."

The senators, congressmen, and congresswomen sitting in the East Room listened, stood, and applauded. The President stood up. Pete smiled and motioned with his hands for everyone to sit back down.

"Every one of us can make a difference by treating others the way we want them to treat us. Don't waste this event by dismissing it entirely. Remember what we all have been through during this horrible time. Always remember what it felt like when others viewed you as non-empathetic. Never forget the horror you felt the first time the affliction struck.

Make this world better for each other and the generations to come. Does it matter what color our skin is? Does it matter how we believe or don't believe in God? What good do anger and hate bring? It should not be easier to hate someone than to love someone. It should not be easier to argue than to try to understand."

Pete continued, "We are fortunate to live in a world where the good still outweighs the bad. Let's not turn it the other way around. Empathizing is not difficult at all. It is not difficult to be nice to each other. It is not difficult to understand each other. We make it difficult for no sound reason. We have a chance to take this hard lesson we have learned and make our world better. Don't blow this opportunity."

Pete looked at the President and smiled, then turned back to the camera with a serious look.

"Remember, they are always watching." Pete raised his hands together in the form of prayer. The tops of his index fingers touched the tip of his nose. He closed his eyes and vanished.

The gray affliction ended as quickly as it began. People were crying in the streets. So many were hugging each other and laughing. Pete, Oz, Rialla, and Krix'x watched the reactions on the ship's visual.

Oz looked at Pete. "How long do you think it will last?"

"I don't know, Oz. This planet had the shit scared out of it. We'll see."

"It is logical to assume that illogical beings will devolve back to what makes them comfortable. This sense of euphoria will not last long," Krix'x commented.

Pete stared at Krix'x. "It would be nice if you remained silent on this."

Oz stared with wide eyes at Krix'x and back at Pete. She was waiting for a battle to ensue.

"Pete," Oz whispered. "Why don't you take time and tell your friends goodbye?"

Krix'x turned to Pete and then back at Oz. Oz looked at Krix'x and continued, "Their addresses are in your dresser. I can set the coordinates if you like?"

Pete looked away from Krix'x and smiled at Oz. "That would be good."

Pete walked to his bedroom, grabbed the picture of his mother, and put it in his coat.

39 A FINAL FAREWELL

Oz told Pete that Bill and Maggie were home in Bends Creek because they had decided to take a break from the big city for a while. That's how Pete ended up on their front porch ringing their doorbell.

Maggie opened the door. "Pete," she screamed and lunged forward to hug him.

"Hi, Maggie," Pete said softly.

Maggie smiled and urged Pete to come inside her house. Pete walked in and saw Bill sitting on the sofa. Bill stood up and walked over to Pete.

"Hey, man. It's over, huh?"

Pete smiled and shook Bill's hand, "Yeah, finally, we're all done with this mess."

Pete sat down on the chair across from the sofa. Bill sat opposite Pete on the couch. Maggie came in from the kitchen with some tea.

"Thanks, Maggie," Pete said as he took Maggie's cup of tea.

Maggie sat beside Bill. "So what brings you back to your roots?"

Pete smiled. "This does feel like home, you know?"

Bill tilted his head a little. "What's up?"

"Can't get anything by my buddy, the sheriff, can I?" Pete said nervously.

Maggie looked concerned. "Pete, are you okay?"

Pete placed his cup on the coffee table in front of him. "No, not really. I have to go on a long trip pretty soon. And you know how bad I am with goodbyes, right?"

Maggie and Bill sat silently, waiting for Pete to fill them in. "I have to go to Wen'q'rixsh to help Krix'x and Oz."

Billed yelled, "Holy shit, man. That's like a zillion miles away." Pete looked at his friends with a sad face. "Yeah, it's pretty far."

Maggie asked, "How long will you be gone, Pete?"

"I'm not sure. I just wanted to make sure I said goodbye to you guys. You mean the world to me. You are the best people I know. I wanted you to know that."

Pete stood up. Maggie and Bill stood, too, staring at Pete. "Can't you stay for a little while longer?" Bill asked.

"I wish I could, but Krix'x has me on a tight schedule."

Maggie began to cry, "Damnit, we're always saying goodbye to each other. You need to hurry and take care of all this bullshit and come back. You need to settle down and enjoy your life, Pete."

Pete didn't wait for Maggie to come to him. He walked over to her and embraced her tightly. He then let her go and hugged Bill. Maggie was surprised when Bill hugged Pete back; it made her tears flow even harder. Pete turned slowly, realizing this may be the last time he saw his two friends.

"I'll never forget what you both have done for me. You have shown me the true meaning of friendship. I will always love you both for that."

Before Bill or Maggie could reply, Pete vanished. Maggie turned to Bill and squeezed him tightly. Bill held her and said, "Damn, I hate it when he does that."

Maggie laughed into Bill's chest, still crying.

***

Pete found himself on another porch, this time in Pichville, Indiana. He didn't know how to proceed or speak with his mother.

Hi, Mom, it's me, Jonathan. Nice seeing you. I have to go light-years away now. Good talk, He thought sarcastically to himself.

He looked into the house through the porch window. He saw her sitting in a chair, watching television. He was about to knock when he saw a young boy run over to her and jump on her lap. *He looked four years old, maybe five,* Pete thought. He watched her hold her son and play with him. They laughed together the whole time Pete observed them. His eyes began to water slightly. He wanted to be that little boy again and feel the warmth of his mother's embrace.

Pete decided to leave. He didn't want to disrupt his mother's new family by popping into their lives. She looked so happy with her son. And yet, Pete wanted that happiness back for himself, and he wanted to be that little boy. But Pete wasn't sure whether he would do more harm than good if he knocked on the door. Logically, Pete told himself to knock on the door and deal with whatever resulted. Emotionally, he said it didn't feel right to knock. Not now, maybe another time. Pete turned away from the window and walked away.

Before Pete could tightbeam back to the ship, he heard a woman's voice come from behind him.

"Hello? Who's out here?" she called out. She couldn't see Pete in the dark.

Pete didn't answer. She called again, "Please, tell me who's there."

Pete turned and continued to walk away from his mother.

"Johnny? Is that you? Johnny, are you here?"

Pete wanted to run to his mother and hold her. The tears began rolling down his cheeks, "I have ruined so many lives. I won't ruin yours, Mom," Pete whispered to himself.

He looked one last time at his mother and vanished.

Pete's mother walked off the porch and away from the porchlight to where she thought she saw someone. She began walking through the dark, stopping after each step. She heard a sound like paper crackling under her right foot. Pete's mother reached down and picked up the piece of paper. She looked around one final time and saw no one was there. She walked back to the porch, and once standing in the light, she looked at the paper in her hand. The object in her hand wasn't a piece of paper. It was a photograph. Pete's mother brought her hand to her mouth to quell her gasp.

It was a picture of her twelve-year-old son, Jonathan, in his baseball uniform.

40 THE HERALD OF MY EYE

Pete tightbeamed back to the ship. He walked by Oz and Rialla without saying a word. He entered his room and placed his mother's picture on the dresser. Pete removed his coat, threw it onto the chair next to the dresser, and lay on the bed. He buried his face into his pillows. The pain was excruciating. He knew Oz wouldn't have a secret potion for this type of aching. This emotional pain hurt more than the hangover he had experienced the other day.

Oz and Rialla came into his room and quietly sat on either side of him. Oz spoke first. "What's up, man? Have a bad night?"

Pete turned around and faced Oz. "Yeah, it pretty much sucks."

Oz looked at Pete. "Krix'x is still sitting in your chair."

"How much time before we leave?" Pete asked.

Rialla answered, "We have at least 2 hours left."

Pete looked at Oz. "Shall we?"

Oz perked up. "Hells, yes."

Rialla smiled. "What am I missing?"

Oz answered, "A lot of fun if you don't hurry and get dressed. We are going to party like it's 1999."

"I don't understand," Rialla said.

Oz yelled at her, "Just go, get dressed!"

Pete laughed as he watched Rialla run out of the room. He looked at Oz. "At least I still have you."

Oz smiled back. "You know it."

The ship's alarm went off before Pete could get out of bed. Pete looked at Oz. "Is this another test?"

"It shouldn't be unless Krix'x ordered it."

They both ran to the command center. Krix'x was still seated in the command chair.

Pete yelled out to him, "Is this a test?"

Krix'x replied calmly, "No."

Pete looked at Oz, "What's coming in?"

Oz screamed over the loud alarm, "Not sure. There's nothing on the visuals."

Pete ordered the Vailen closest to him to help Oz identify the source of the alarm. He moved swiftly across the control console to see what he could see. Most of the switches were in Wen. He looked at the other Vailen standing beside him, staring at the visual. An image popped into his head from the tech files Oz gave him to scan for educational purposes.

"Can you set up an astral power block just outside the transmission point coming into our visual?"

"If we set up an astral block when it explodes, it may suck everyone through the energy void it creates."

"Just set it up; we may not have to detonate it. I want it there in the event it's needed."

The Vailen nodded and looked back at Krix'x for approval. Krix'x nodded, and the Vailen began working on Pete's request. When she finished, she showed Pete the switch on the panel that would detonate the block.

The alarm went silent, and a figure began walking toward the command center from inside the visual. The time funnel was extended fully and awaited its passenger to finish his journey. Everyone in the command center remained silent and still. Pete was staring at the visual, watching the figure come closer. It was a Council member; the blue robe and hood were easily identifiable.

The Council member slowly exited the time funnel onto the command center floor. He took a few steps toward Krix'x and slowly removed the hood from his face.

Oz yelled out, "Cass, what are you doing here?"

Krix'x stood up from his seat and spoke. "Vailen, report."

Cass let out an evil-sounding laugh and walked up to Krix'x. She levitated to look Krix'x in the eyes when she spoke.

"My dear Krix'x," Cass began nonchalantly. "It is so good to see you here on Earth. How are you enjoying your visit? Taking in the sights at all?"

Krix'x stared at Cass. "What is the meaning of this outburst and disrespect?"

"I wanted to introduce you to our new herald. I wanted to be here to see the look on your faces when he arrives."

"What new herald? How is this possible?"

"Krix'x, you are so bound to logic that you are blind to reality. Knowing how a logical being will react under different circumstances is a great advantage. Everything I have done, I have done right before your very eyes. And with your approval, I may add."

"Impossible," Krix'x responded.

"You really need to get out more, Krixxy," Cass laughed out loud.

Pete walked up to Cass, "You need to leave now."

"I don't think so. It would be impolite to leave before the guest of honor arrives, don't you think?"

Smoke began to pour out of the time funnel through the visual. It quickly filled the command center. The smoke caused the temperature to rise in the command room, and Pete began sweating. It was too difficult to see anyone in the room.

Pete couldn't attack or defend with all the smoke in the room. He yelled out, "Oz, do something!"

Oz replied, "I'm on it." Oz called out a command to the ship to suck all the smoke out of the command center. When most of the smoke had disappeared, Pete looked for Cass. There was still some smoke pouring out of the time funnel. It wasn't as thick as before, and he could make her out in front of the visual, standing in the ship in front of another figure still inside the time funnel. The smoke returned to the visual, Cass, and the other figure.

Cass yelled, "Ladies and gentlemen, meet your new competition."

Pete wiped the sweat from his eyes and looked at the figure inside the visual. He wiped his eyes again and yelled out. "How? How is this possible?"

Oz was trance-like, staring at the figure inside the visual. She couldn't move, and she couldn't say a word. She was in shock. Even Krix'x appeared to be stunned.

Pete dragged his feet slowly towards the figure and dropped to his knees. "No," he cried out. "Please, God, no!"

The figure smiled down at Pete and, in a happy female voice, said, "Hola, Pete! Miss me?"

To be continued...

ABOUT THE AUTHOR

MJ Petrin was born in Biddeford, Maine, and spent his early years in the coastal town of Camp Ellis, where small-town life set the stage for big imagination. At ten, he traded quiet shores for the buzzing streets of Miami, Florida, where wandering downtown became its own kind of education—one filled with colorful characters and life lessons you won't find in any classroom.

Music was his first love, and in his twenties, MJ hit the road with his brother in a rock band, playing clubs across the country and collecting stories along the way. The amps are turned down these days, but that energy shows up in his writing.

Now living just outside Baltimore, Maryland, MJ prefers a quieter pace, steering clear of social media drama and political shouting matches. Instead, he channels his creativity into writing science fiction and adventure stories, often weaving in threads from his experiences and today's world to keep his stories relevant, meaningful, and unpredictable.